Also by Stephen Swartz

Year of the Tiger

A Novel

Stephen Swartz

Year of the Tiger

Stephen Swartz

MYRDDIN PUBLISHING GROUP

UNITED STATES · UNITED KINGDOM · AUSTRALIA

ISBN-13: 978-1-68063-021-3

ISBN-10: 1-68063-021-0

www.myrddinpublishing.com

Cover Design by Iris Schaeffer

Tiger! Tiger! burning bright
In the forests of the night,
What immortal hand or eye
Could frame thy fearful symmetry?

William Blake

{ 1986 }

THE HUNTERS AND THE HUNTED

"There are only two kinds of people in the world," says the brash fellow on the right, his square chin raised too proudly.

"Two kinds of beasts, also, what say?" the other fellow retorts.

"True—the hunter and the hunted."

"To the hunters!" cheers the one on the left. He lifts his empty hand, fingers curled around an invisible goblet.

Ripples of heat cut the landscape into flickering shelves of fact and fantasy, the air waxing and waning, each current with its own ceaseless rhythms. Blowing dust obscures their journey. Over the rumble of the engine, the jostling of the jeep hitting bumps and ditches, Rupert, the older *sahib*, tells his story:

"Grandfather was a man among men. I dare say, right there with Corbett, and Patterson in Africa. Yet our grandfather failed to write about *his* adventures. No, sir! Content to go about his hunting with quiet efficiency and only tell tales to relations. It's a fact, surely: game warden in the United Provinces the same time as Corbett.

"One incident he made a great deal about in later years: marauding tiger back in, what? nineteen-twenty-one thereabout. Cat terrorized thousands in two mountain districts—annual pilgrims by the hundreds, mind you. The Man-Eater of Rudraprayag! Heard it? Survived years of poison, traps, armies of hunters. Bloody cat claimed a hundred humans. Cunning so magnificent villagers called him *shaitan*—devil! You could never appreciate its evil soul without spending weeks of the bloody steaming, humid days and bone-chilling nights hunting the beast."

Words became muted as the hunting party headed deep into the wooded valley where locals have known tigers to roam.

Introduced to the guide, their *shikari*, only the night before at base camp, the brash one with the fabulous imagination was Rupert; his younger brother, Reggie. The professional hunter from Kolkata agreed to this unauthorized excursion because the pay was right. Yet he never promised to laugh at their jokes, or cheer their false bravura.

Scoring the grassy landscape with their tires, the two open-topped Land Rovers rumbled ahead, choking beige clouds billowing behind them like parachutes.

The *shikari* curses under his breath, brushing dust from his face, as Rupert continues, shouting over the jeep's engine, disrupted by the jolts of the vehicle.

"Grandfather and another officer went after the reward. They knew the cat hunted in a mountain territory separated by a narrow raging stream. In that district there was only one bridge spanning the gorge, a long suspension bridge. You know: wooden planks sewn together with ropes, wide enough for one adult to cross, swinging freely when the night winds pick up.

"When news reached them that a kill was made on the north side of the river, they hurried to their ambush site at the bridge. Mind you, the tiger always went to the opposite side of the river after his kills—this single bridge had to be the way! Through the dark hours, they hide in the tree branches at each end of the bridge.

"Hours went by, eyes straining to keep the bridge in sight with the thundering roar of the rushing stream below. Finally Grandfather caught sight of the cat, blue in the moonlight, standing midway along the bridge. The beast padded across the ragged planks, confident and nimble, a fine supper in its belly! Grandfather raised the twin-barreled shotgun to his shoulder, aiming, wondering why his partner—perched in a tree by the end of the bridge the bloody beast was approaching—hadn't fired a shot. If he was going to get a good shot, he'd have to get it off while the beast was on the bridge.

"He aligns the sights, prods the branches to move for a clear shot.

His finger's on the trigger, starting to squeeze it as the cat's chest falls into the sights. The beast pauses, looks back.

"Then his partner drops from the tree behind the cat. He flings his single-barreled shotgun to his shoulder and fires. But he rushes it: the shot strikes the cat's rear paw. The cat turns around, starts toward him! No time to reload, so he pulls out his service revolver, cranks six shots before the tiger's claws are slapping him down on his back—puncture marks in his throat.

"Grandfather drops from his tree, rushes onto the swaying bridge, somehow keeping his balance despite holding the shotgun and ignoring the rope railings.

"The tiger looks at this other man, eyes glowing in the night, blood-stained paws pressed over the quivering body of his partner—who's bloody-well shocked stiff. His larynx's torn open, can't even scream!

"Grandfather fires a shot at the cat but the swaying of the bridge throws his shot off. The tiger rises from his partner and in a flash it charges him—as he scrambles to reload, the bridge swaying. A handful of shells fall through his shaking fingers down through the planks into the stream below. But he still manages to shove one into the breech.

"He swings the barrel center as the tiger bounds toward him, its powerful shoulders and hindlegs propelling his body straight at him. Grandfather jerks the trigger—the blast splatters the left shoulder of the beast and the tiger is halted. However, the kick of the shotgun throws Grandfather back against the ropes—his feet grappling for balance on the thin planks. He grabs at the rope, slips—his shotgun drops down into the swirling rapids. He tries to hold the rope but his full weight's pulling him down!

"The bloody tiger recovers from the blast, pads over the bridge. He said the cat just paused a few breaths where he grasped the ropes, swaying against the bridge, unable to pull himself up. The cat gives him a clever Dick grin, eyes burning in the night!

"Grandfather saw the blood from the wound as it padded off, hoped the wound would bleed the cat out after a few days. But he was wrong. The beast killed more before that Corbett fellow was called in—and after more victims, and weeks of stalking and setting ambushes, he finally managed to do in that *shaitan* tiger.

"So Grandfather spent the night hanging from the rope stretched across that gorge—the river raging below, chilling night air above, sweat oozing from his nerve-rattled body. By morning, locals happened onto the bridge and found him—and a piece of the cat's toe, clipped off by his partner's shot!"

The *shikari* chuckles—as the jeep hits a rock, flinging them off their seats. He takes delight in Rupert's animated speech. But the driver and *shikari* cannot help but be amused by these aristocratic playboys who fancy themselves hunters.

"His partner nearly bled to death. But he survived, discharged from the Army, never to utter a word the rest of his life. Had no bloody throat! Yet Grandfather lived to hunt again, yes, and eventually to father two sons."

"And one of them was our father," chimed Reggie, the younger brother, grinning with pride.

"So why you hunt tiger?" asks the *shikari*.

"Grandfather was killed by a tiger."

"Eventually," adds the younger man.

The *shikari*, nodding, doesn't see any point in asking for details.

"Another story, eh?" Rupert chuckles. "Back in camp, I'll tell it."

The *shikari* knows his job is not to keep a client's bold talk going.

"This is the year of the tiger," Rupert continues, with a teasing leer at his brother. "In the oriental calendar. Every twelve years. This is the year for tigers. Nineteen-eighty-six! This is our year."

Sporting fine red jackets, the two young *sahib*s resemble the British soldiers who once ruled the Indian subcontinent. They explained before how the uniforms give them strength. The simply-clothed Bengali men in the lorry following them find it strange that these white hunters would wear the heavy jackets in the intensive heat of Orissa.

"You see, good fellow," Rupert goes on, "since Grandfather's day, our family has hunted tiger every twelfth year. Father bagged his cats in sixty-two and seventy-four. Now it's our turn to do the family honor here in eighty-six. In ninety-eight, our sons will join us."

"However," Reggie cuts in, "we aim to do Father one better. We'll go into the fray in the style of the Moghuls. We shall kill our tiger with bow and arrow, with spear and lance, not with some high-powered rifle. Then we shall eat its heart with our bare hands—to show our mettle, as our father's sons, our grandfather's grandsons."

"Chips off the old block!" Reggie laughs.

Not all of the words does the *shikari* understand. They have said this is their first hunt. He will lead them to a tiger, help them kill it, collect his money and feed his family. What they do with the beast does not concern him.

Boiling dust clouds mark their passage as they race to the naked hillock that rises as sentinel over the valley. It stands crowned with a single gnarled acacia tree. A tiger was seen there in the past week.

She springs from the amber grass, an orange flame, her second leap bringing her forepaws across the rump of the *sambar* doe. The startled deer whirls on its hindlegs and spins away as the tigress rights herself and doubles back, cutting through the tall stalks. Two leaps and her claws rake the hindquarters, forcing her down into the grass. Her claws pin the doe against the earth as she places her long fangs around the sambar's narrow, panting throat. One quick bite and the sambar lies motionless.

The herd gathers in the cloud's shadow, alarmed at the attack. The young doe was weak, lagging behind the herd as though ill. They remain alert until their leader decides the danger has passed and they resume grazing.

The tigress raises her head, whiskers quivering with the exercise, and roars her success. Her tail curls above the grassy sea, flicking as she maneuvers the deer, carrying it in her jaws.

"There!" the driver trumpets at the streak of orange in the grass, turning the jeep toward it.

"*Sahib*! We have tiger in sight," the *shikari* confirms.

The male tiger lounging on the hill sees them approach. Beneath the gnarled old tree, he springs to his feet.

The creature standing tall in the rolling boxes struggles to grasp the thick vine which bends over the top of the box, pointing a foreleg ahead at the tigress dragging her kill into the forest.

"Look!" the *shikari* cries.

Rupert and Reggie stare at the orange blur.

"*Sahib*, that one look female."

Rupert leans forward, bracing himself against the jeep's roll bar, shouting at the *shikari*: "That's good! I fancy nailing a lassie."

The tigress secures the doe in her jaws, lifts it off the ground. She turns to regard the approaching dust storm, led by two rolling boxes. They descend on her. She starts to run with the doe, sees the shadow of the vehicles closing and drops the carcass, racing out of the grass ahead of the hunters.

Seconds after she has escaped, the boxes halt side by side before the abandoned sambar, billows of dust riding with them and mixing with the dust kicked up by their tires. They relocate their prey as the sambar herd scatters away from the treeline.

She is a flame in the yellow grass, racing into the forest, out of sight.

The hunters jump from the jeep as the pack of beaters stumble out of the lorry.

"After her!" Rupert shouts, pointing.

The *shikari* calls instructions to his men in Hindi and they charge into the forest. Beside the second vehicle, bows and arrows are held at the ready and the lances are unstrapped. His assistant checks his rifle, loads it. The *shikari* automatically reaches for his pistol, safe in its holster. The men split up, two remaining with the vehicles, the others running after the two eager young fools, their guide rushing after them.

From his hilltop vantage, the male tiger sees what has transpired. He pads to the front of his fortress for a better look. He sees most of the man-creatures following his mate into the cover of the forest.

They pull sticks and branches from the second rolling box. Others carry the sticks that throw fire. He has seen those weapons previously, knows their terrible power. He knows what it means, what *they* mean. He sees what they bring with them, following the lead of two such men as he has never before seen. They have red fur on their bodies, black on their hindquarters and they seem to bear evil.

He bounds from the hill, racing for the forest.

She knows the twisting paths of the jungle like her own mind, rushing through thick vegetation, sometimes where no path exists. The men are in close pursuit, the Bengali men with their spears. She tries to trick them, running up one trail, doubling back and running down a different trail. She darts through undergrowth, leaps over fallen logs, dodges vines, sidesteps erupted tree roots.

Branches of monkeys scream, marking her escape. She dares not roar at them, hurrying through the forest as the men approach. They are faster and smarter than she had considered. Their voices are loud and close.

Padding quickly down a sloping trail which leads to a ragged gorge, she halts in mid-stride, spinning on her pads, spotting a hiding place.

She will lay up under the rock ledge which shields a small clearing on the opposite side of the thicket. She backtracks several steps, marking the trail, hoping they will proceed down it and not stop. Then she leaps through the bushes and turns around in her hiding space, compacting herself as much as she can. She lies quiet, calming her breath.

The men arrive panting, spears poised.

She watches them through the leafy mosaic.

Their leader, armed with a shotgun, stops them as he inspects the trail. Something is not right here, he decides.

She sees his confusion, feels the searching of his mind. She will be found and so she prepares herself, cringing against the stone wall at her rear, coiling her hindquarters, ready to launch through the bushes.

One of the men hears her shuffling, turns toward the bushes—

She leaps!

The bushes explode and men fall away, so startled they cannot hold their spears ready. One man is on the ground, unhurt, bowled over by her lunge. She bounds away, down the trail, toward the gorge. The men collect their wits and hurry after her, spears pointed.

The male tiger pounds past the vehicles, snarling at the stunned attendants. He breaks into the forest, following the red-furred hunters who follow the Bengali men. He must go slow, maneuvering through the winding trail, listening for her location.

She crashes down the winding trail, twigs snapping and branches raking her coat, blind in her frantic attempt to evade them. They are close. She can feel their tiny feet patting the earth.

Tearing into a clearing, she scatters three peafowl. It does not look familiar. She must have made a wrong turn but there is no time to retrace her steps. Ahead is a giant jungle tree, its massive erupted roots forming two sides of its own gorge.

As the men break into the clearing, she leaps toward the roots of the tree, whirling around and setting herself between them, barring her teeth and claws to them. The men hold their distance, impressed by her vicious display.

Their leader, the big, muscular Sikh, parts the men and stands before them shouting directions. They form a semi-circle around her, spears pointing at her. She swats her paw at them as they jab at her. She snarls at them, slapping the spearpoints. Her forepaw is spotted with blood from the cuts of their blades.

Suddenly, one fearless man dashes to the center of the circle, his spear poised, and lunges forward with a lethal thrust. She dodges the lunge and her claws shoot forward, throwing him to the ground. Long flaps of skin hang from his chest, torn from his collarbone down to his belly. He lies in shock as the young, red-uniformed hunters arrive with the *shikari*.

Immediately assessing the situation, the *shikari* orders his assistant to keep his rifle aligned on the tigress. He turns to his clients.

"We must kill this tiger before we lose another man. We must shoot the rifle. Now, good *sahib*. Sorry, but you may fire the shot."

Before either Rupert or Reggie can answer, the Bengali men launch their spears at the beast that killed their companion, stabbing at her flanks and her slapping forepaws.

Again she lashes out at one of the men.

He falls away holding his throat, severed veins waving through his clenched fingers, blood spraying.

The men jump back, holding their circle of spear points.

"Now! You must decide! What will you do?" the *shikari* demands.

They hesitate, never before seeing a man killed by a wild animal. Their eyes bulge in astonishment at the sight of so much blood. They realize they have only one rifle among them.

"*Sahib*, decide!"

Rupert breaks from his trance, signals the two archers forward. They notch arrows and join the circle of spears, letting several arrows fly against the frantically pawing tiger. They are to disable her, not kill her. That honor goes to their employers.

The *shikari* directs the spearmen to poke with spears until the tiger falls back under the onslaught. She growls fiercely, but this time the men stay out of reach of her claws.

With the tigress held back against the roots of the tree, the hunters in red step forward, one with the fire stick, the other with a smooth, polished cricket bat. She is too wounded, too exhausted to fight. She can only let loose a roar as one holds up the rifle.

"Remember what you said, ol' fellow," Reggie calls to his brother, "no guns for this beast."

Rupert is suddenly hesitant. "Yes, certainly."

"Let's get on with it, Rupert."

"Right-oh!"

14

He steps forward, raising the butt of the rifle and brings it down hard and quick, striking the female tiger in her ribs. A crack echoes in the clearing. Again he swings the weapon downward, breaking her body. The other hunter joins in, flinging his cricket bat against her soft belly. Her roar sinks to a fatigued growl as she claws meekly at her tormenters, unable to move from between the roots of the tree. Soon she lies still, breathing shallowly as they continue their attack.

"For Father! For Grandfather!"

Finally, they stand back, out of breath.

"Right," grunts Rupert, breathing hard, his brilliant red uniform soaked with sweat. "That ought to do."

He turns to his brother, rubbing his sore arms.

Reggie pauses, feeling the smooth wood of the cricket bat in his hands, blood stains along it. "That will do."

"Let's go home," Rupert calls to the *shikari*.

"But—but, *sahib*, what of the hide?"

He throws a glance at the beaten, bloody body of the tigress.

"It's too torn to be of any value." He grins at his brother. "And we've no place to hang it, do we?"

He hands the rifle, its butt stained with blood, back to the *shikari*'s assistant, straightens his stiff collar and starts down the trail.

The others follow him only with their eyes, startled by his behavior.

Rupert pauses down the trail when no one follows. After a moment, the others are convinced of their employer's insanity. They gather their weapons, a few men facing the dying tigress with their spears held high against any rush.

A rustle of leaves. A great weight moving quickly through the forest. The men halt, listening, feeling the earth rumble, their faces reflecting slow realization and rushing terror.

The male tiger bursts into the clearing, roaring an earth-shaking noise which crumples the hearts of the Bengali men. They scramble in every direction.

The *shikari* grabs the rifle from his assistant, aiming as the tiger leaps onto the back of the tall Sikh in charge of the beaters, wrestling him to the ground and removing his neck with a single bite. The others are thrown back around the perimeter, fearful for their lives.

The archers notch arrows, fling them wildly at the tiger, missing in their panic. He leaps toward his mate, kicking one man away, tearing off the face of another spearman.

He slashes his way through the fleeing men until he is able to get between them and his wounded mate. The remaining men hold him back with their spears. Others escape down the trail, two scale trees.

The *shikari* holds his rifle against his shoulder, his trigger finger shaking, eye focused across the sights.

When his assistant has regained his breath from the tangled fight, seeing the tiger's attention consumed by his mate's injured state, he grabs his shoulder where he caught a claw while offering a painful grimace for Rupert and Reggie.

The *shikari* eases the tension on the rifle's trigger as he, too, sees the devotion of one tiger for the other, a strange, tender moment oblivious to the hunters. The two men descend from their trees, hurry away.

It is a touching scene. The *shikari* remarks he has never seen or heard of tigers behaving as this pair does. He is puzzled. Perhaps he will talk with the man from the wildlife preserve about it—but, of course, he won't mention this hunt.

"You lucky this day, good *sahib*. We have two tigers! You pay twice to us, yes?"

Rupert, mind numb from the bloodshed witnessed, cannot reply.

"Our license only allows one," Reggie blurts out.

"What license?" the *shikari* asks. "You go to Government House for this hunt? But we make deal with you, *sahib*! No license."

"Let's get out from here!" Rupert grumbles, grabbing the rifle from the *shikari* and stalking off.

The Bengali men do not hesitate following at a quick pace, carrying the mangled bodies of their comrades.

1

OPEN YOUR EYES. Golden, gleaming in the night, marking your soul.
Your breath is hot, dry, your moans are silent.
Light from a quarter moon prints its reflection on those yellow eyes.
You blink and stare long into the night—

THE EYES.
Always the eyes: searing into his consciousness. The eyes that mark him, that brand his dreams—shining fiercely in the night, taunting him, flickering with hate, like captured demons fighting to be free.

Always those amber orbs—calling him—piercing him—boiling his blood—sucking the life from him—

Run your tongue over your teeth, a drop of blood from the corner of
*   your mouth falls to earth, creates a scarlet puddle in the dust.*
See it in the darkness?
You see blood in places no other creature can.
Your mind races with frantic energy, plotting—

He usually awoke when the hateful eyes became too bright, too intense. Then he would scream. He would reach out, punching—or throw his arms around himself, protecting. Then they would come for him, comfort him—

Sounds of agony, of weakness, of death come on waves of hot, heavy air, striking your ears with pain. You snap shut your eyes.

Again, raspy like a shock of dry savanna grass tightly clasped, as strained as the dusty air is to rise above the dry, caked ground, cold and hollow—
Feel it in your heart?

He follows the golden eyes, beacons in the sacred night, showing the way...leading him on....

The earth erupts in puffs as you pace—an anguished moaning dying away with every step.
Still you pursue it? Have you abandoned it?
Now you return—yet cannot forgive yourself?
You must end it—soon.
You will end it: only then will there be peace for her.
A breeze sways the trees of the small wood and a bird cries out—
To your fortress, to your heaven you have come, bearing the burden that will torment you the rest of your days.
Rising starkly against the wide plain—the hill, crowned with the gnarled ancient tree, broken and scarred, branches swept low by its weight.
The moon hides in shame. Shadows of the night lengthen, spreading over the entire knoll, darkening as you mount the hill with your burden—
The strength of the earth pulls against you, muscles stretch taunt, but at last the earth yields.
Watch with unflinching eyes: the blood that seeps, cuts lay open to flies, deep bruises, the slanted gouges—
Her eyes never blink, never stare, only plead. In those angry eyes, do you see your past and present together? See the pain inside her?
You must end it.
She knows it must end soon, the marks of death on her body, crumpled bones inside torn flesh, reservoir of blood seeping out.
Rise to your paws—slowly, with determination.
Hover over her, feel her life flowing away—but she lingers.

Touch your lips to hers, brush your nose to hers, nuzzle cheeks.
You whimper, part from her, and she can only utter a low whine—
It is then, only at that moment, that you notice the impending sunrise,
*   sliding so languidly across the engulfing horizon like thick, seeping*
*   blood.*
Moving away like a fading whisper, the great expanse of the plain—
Let your cry be loud and long, exploding over the landscape, awakening
*   animals of the day and frightening those of the night.*
Let your roar echo in your mind—and before the echo can fade, return to
*   her side.*
Breathing a low sigh, you inhale sharply and raise your dusty foot—regard
*   its message, the tool of your act, for a silent heartbeat—*
before bringing it down hard against her neck. There is a snap which rings
*   out across the dawn.*
It is done.
Now mount the largest root of this ancient tree. Roar into the dawn!
Shake the fatigue from your striped coat, flick your tail.
Let loose another roar for the mate whose misery you have ended, and as
*   warning for the red-clothed hunters who killed her.*

Karl Edwards shot straight up in bed and froze, drowning in icy sweat, shaking from the imaginary chill that slapped him cruelly to consciousness. Chest heaving rapidly, his lungs could not suck in air fast enough—just like the first time he had the dream. Staring ahead into the darkness, wiping streams from his face, he waited for his breathing to return to normal.

Against his will, he grasped at that first dream, that first night, only a few weeks earlier but now seeming so long ago.

Waking suddenly, he had glanced over at his wife, Leona, soundly asleep beside him, facing away—

He sighed, felt his distress beginning to overwhelm him again, and lay back on the moist sheet. He could not forget her. He wondered what she might be doing now, in her new life, with her new lover.

Karl fumbled with the buckle on the strap, released it, and slowly swung his feet to the floor, feeling ordinary and average in every way. He sat on the edge of the bed, head in hands, and for the hundredth time tried to figure out what had gone wrong.

After awaking from the nightmare, he went out on their apartment balcony. He heard Leona call him from the bedroom. She had sounded worried in her sleepy voice.

"What's the matter, dear? You have another bad dream, sweetie?"

Frowning, he realized now that her affair with the neighbor had been going on even then.

"It wasn't a dream," he had whispered.

"Oh, Karl...."

They were following the script. Now it was his turn to respond: "It was real."

He knew what she was thinking: He's gone crazy. He dreams of tigers every night. If he would only see a psychiatrist, she constantly prodded him, he would be all right. He should have seen it coming. Then he could have prevented it. Maybe. He was still sane enough to understand how he must have appeared to her.

"Just another bad dream," Leona's sing-songy voice drifted back to him. "They all seem real."

"Bullshit," he muttered, stepping away.

She followed him.

"Come back to bed, darling," she cooed. "We can make love. That'll make you forget your nightmare."

"Dammit, I gotta tell somebody," he barked.

"Then tell it to a shrink."

"I don't know what the fuck's going on in my head!"

He was growing desperate. So he would proceed to describe for her the horrible details of his dreams: the hunt, and the murder of his mate by a pair of hunters wearing red jackets—

He'd have to pause then, overcome with nausea.

Each night the dream came to him, burning off more of his sanity, tearing away his peace. What was going on in his head? Or, what was going on in another world, in the jungles and plains of India, in the heart of the beast?

Laying back, he fastened the strap across his waist so they would not suspect that he'd been up during the night, then closed his eyes and sighed. He had to finish the dream, he knew, even if he didn't want to. That was required for his cure. Maybe just once he could sleep through the night without repeating the horror.

You work through the night—

The ground, cracked by the blazing sun, does not yield easily. Yet the pit slowly grows deeper, wider. Muscles cry out for rest but you ignore them.

Soon dawn cracks a watery orange crescent at the end of the world. It is finished. But do not yet rest. Be gentle with her. Tug at your mate's lifeless body, to the edge of the pit. Ease her body down into the dirt-lined hole—nuzzle her cheek—

Roar again if it eases your pain. Let the other creatures scatter across the plain.

Then begin the task of replacing the dirt.

The sun rises, burns. Do not cease your work. You cannot. There is time for rest only when this task is completed. Pat down the earth, melding it into a smooth mound, as the blazing bronze disk overhead strikes down through the bare branches of the gnarled old tree—

You fall, struggle to rise. With your remaining strength, pull yourself into the shadow of the largest root, and wait for evening.

You breathe with pain, regarding your work: the dark mound which covers your mate. She is there, asleep—forever.

Glazed are your eyes, remembering days past. Recall them all, and plan for tomorrow. You always have been able to plan.

Remember?

You are special—not like others of your kind. Now use this special gift to aid in hunting your mate's murderers.

Do not let them rest.

2

KANSAS CITY, MISSOURI

By 7:35, ALTHEA MCCARTNEY was easing her red Mustang onto the interstate, breaking into the swelling rush hour traffic as she gave her auburn hair a flip. Drivers flipped fingers as she checked her make-up in the rearview mirror. Then she wiggled and squirmed against the seat, her starched white uniform stiff on her back. She hoped she could get away with wearing a pantsuit today; all her dresses were still in the laundry basket, unwashed during her long holiday.

A truck driver, then a businessman in a BMW, cursed her as she swerved across three lanes to make the exit onto Blue River Parkway.

Ignoring them—as she did all people who threatened her peace—she tried hard to sustain a decent smile. For once it did not come naturally. Even though it was a bright, fresh morning, the air moist with a hint of the summer's approaching warmth. Even though it was her first day back from her first annual vacation. Even though her horoscope said she would meet a new friend today. It just had to be a good day.

She switched on the radio, heard her favorite news-talk station, then switched to the public radio station on FM for New Age music. She settled back, soothed by the electric harp, a few Balinese bells, and a bamboo flute thrown in for good measure. It was the soundtrack of her lifestyle: she had decorated her studio in Raytown in oriental style, one entire wall a portrait of Mount Fuji rising over the Izu Peninsula and

Sagami Bay on a fine summer morning.

The car slowed as she turned up the long drive, passing through the iron gates of the Eastwood Institute. Winding through the landscaped lawn, she rolled to a halt in her usual parking spot beside the hickory tree. She gazed out over the manicured grounds and Penn Valley Park on the next hill where the stately tower of the Liberty Memorial rose, keeping watch over the wide downtown skyline.

She rubbed her eyes, felt tears start to well up but sniffled them away. Time to go back to work. It was time to begin her life, her reality, once more, she told herself. Fantasies were for fools. Now it was also time to face her supervisor, Mrs. Wolfe.

After a moment to straighten her cap, looking in the mirror, she stepped out of her car.

The man in the crisp white shirt and black trousers of an orderly smiled at his favorite nurse, opening the door. Welcoming her back from vacation, he asked with a wink how her honeymoon trip to the Ozarks had gone. Althea, in her typical, unassuming manner, stated she had learned to water ski—but her husband was more interested in the Royals games, disgusted with off-season trades which had given away the heart of last year's World Series team.

"Sorry to hear that," the orderly offered, meaning her honeymoon, as he locked the heavy wooden doors behind them. Then he thought about the team: "They'll be contenders again this season, awright."

He hooked the key ring on his belt.

"Oh, by the way, got a wild one on your wing, Miss McCartney. From the police. He's 'Attempted Murder' and 'Attempted Suicide'. Won't let nobody near him."

Althea tried hard to smile, fearing the lies about her honeymoon would be written all over her face.

Mull this kill—chew on the meaty hindquarters—resting at the edge of
    the glade near the village. Grab a chunk of the bloody flesh.
Raise your head and gaze out through the undergrowth. Below, the man-
    creatures move about their small nests, ignorant of your presence.
You wait, hope to spot the red-furred ones among them. The crude,
    rasping sounds of their laughter still burn your ears.
Dropping the half-chewed meat, grief sweeps over you.

*Remember the day you met, the one who became your mate, your beloved
    Brighteyes—*

*The jungle trail was lush with summer foliage, thick with ferns and
    bushes, vines and stately sal trees. The air hung heavy between the
    plants.*

*You ran past the brook, bounding over smooth stones, padding over leaf-
    strewn paths, limber body stretching and flexing beautifully as you
    swept through the world.*

Alive!

*You entered the clearing, dimly lit from the dense leafy netting, and she
    was there. Sunlight flickered through breeze-shifting branches,
    spotting her tawny coat with sprays of golden light.*

You regarded her, eyes falling into line with hers.

*She did not drop her gaze, but dipped her head—a greeting. There was no
    threat between you and her. It was your season.*

*She flicked her tail. Your scent had marked the largest tree in the
    clearing. It caught her attention and drew her there.*

*She was hungry, in heat, lashing her ringed tail nervously. She eyed the
    magnificent male before her—it was your territory she entered: you
    were lean, lithe, and powerful. Smelling the scent for weeks now, she
    was never able to find you.*

Until now.

*You snarled and turned away, moving back in the direction you came.
    She followed as you moved through the winding trail, down a slope to
    a cool, dark pool hidden among a pair of opposing cliffs and a gentle,
    grassy bank.*

There, glancing over your shoulders at her, she dropped in the grass.

*As you approached, she stretched fully on her belly, facing you. And your
    head rose regally, watching her. Eyes connected. She was no ordinary
    cat. You were special, too, she purred.*

*You snoozed in your own spaces, feeling comfortable with each other's
    presence, until the cool of the evening arrived.*

*With a yawn, you sprang up and stretched. She awakened at the sound.
    Again eyes touched, and minds reached for each other. Bodies drew
    close. She dropped to the ground, posed on her four paws, white-furred*

belly to the earth, her head lowered.
And you rushed to her—brushed her whiskers. She purred. You offered a
rumble deep in your throat—knowing you had found your life's mate.
With a grunt, you moved behind her, quickly straddled her.
Her tail flicked against your muzzle as you bit at her neck, growling. She
turned her head, curling back her lips, roaring at you.
Return the roar!
You shook violently against the cool earth. Dismounting, you dropped
back and flopped down. She rolled onto her back in the dewy grass,
purring. In the widening moonlight, you gazed at each other, feeling
a mutual warmth. You mated again during the night, and in the
morning. The days were filled with the roars and grunts of sex, and
all who heard left you and her in peace.
Remember how you wondered then if the sensations were real?
If they came not from within you but from a place you could not
imagine? From the one you called your twin?
You lie now across the sun-warmed rock, a tasteless meal left unfinished.
All life is tasteless now.
Scan the village, watching, waiting.
Life has no joy, no meaning now. That is what you hate most of all: they
have taken that strange joy from your world.

Strapped into his bed Karl lay motionless, unconscious, arms folded, hands over his chest, corpse-like.

Pale morning light streamed through the sterile white curtains drawn across the window next to his bed. He was the only occupant in this semi-private room, but the other bed was made up in anticipation of his cellmate. The subdued sounds of Muzak and the bustle of the morning nurses filtered in through the closed door.

Eventually his door swung open and a pretty, young nurse entered carrying a tray. As she shifted it to one hand, her auburn ponytail sweeping off her shoulder, she closed the door with her other hand. The cup of pills slid to the rim against her bosom. Standing beside the sleeping patient's bed, she noticed the brown leather restraining strap across his waist. Some patients slept fitfully and often fell out of bed. She brushed her hair back, regarding this new patient's tormented face, the tense muscles, the twisted sheets.

Balancing the tray in one hand, she reached for his shoulder with her other, hesitating. Fresh from a long briefing about her new patient, she had been told about all the trouble the staff had had with him over the past month while she was away.

She reached for his shoulder and timidly shook him.

He stirred but did not awaken.

"Wake up, Mister Edwards," Nurse McCartney spoke softly, gently shaking his shoulder again.

He remained still.

"Please wake up, Mister Edwards."

Mrs. Wolfe burst into the room.

"What are you doing, Nurse McCartney?" the beefy old nurse boomed. "I thought I told you to give him these pills."

"He won't wake up," she replied.

"Of course not. You have to shake him"—she dropped her heavy, callused hand to Karl's shoulder—"like *this*."

The older nurse gave the man a violent shaking until he startled awake—in time to experience her slap to his face.

He was groggy, but conscious.

"Mister Edwards, are you awake?" she howled.

He nodded his dizzy head, looking absently around the room, trying to focus. His eyes fell on the cute, slender nurse standing at the foot of the bed.

"We have some medicine for you, Mister Edwards. Are you awake enough to take it?"

He did not immediately respond. Appearing groggy, she gave him another slap across his cheek.

"Stop that," he snapped.

"We have some pills for you to take, Mister Edwards." Mrs. Wolfe glanced at the tray held by Althea. "You forgot his glass of water, Nurse McCartney."

She set down the tray and hurried out, Karl's gaze following her.

"No, I don't want it," he said.

"It's for your own good. Your doctor prescribed this for you and I intend you to take it. Now, won't you take these nice little pills?"

He shook his head.

Nurse McCartney returned bearing a small plastic cup of water. She set it on the tray but Mrs. Wolfe frowned at her until she picked it up and handed it to the patient.

"Here's your water," Mrs. Wolfe said, glaring at Nurse McCartney holding the glass out for him. "Now be a good boy and take your pills."

"Get outta here!" Karl shouted. He slapped the cup of water at Mrs. Wolfe, who jumped back, bumping the tray and spilling the paper cup of pills on the floor.

"Well, then, Mister Edwards," she growled, brushing her wet uniform, "if you won't take the pills, then I'll have to give it to you in a needle."

She turned to Nurse McCartney. "Watch him."

Mrs. Wolfe stormed out of the room.

Karl mumbled something, laying back.

"What did you say?" asked Althea.

Karl's attention shifted to the young nurse.

"I said that bastard's gonna pay. And that stupid bitch, too!"

"Who? Missus Wolfe?" she asked, puzzled.

The Wolf burst through the door with two muscular orderlies in tow, casually pushing Althea out of the way.

"Turn him over!"

Mrs. Wolfe had the needle armed and ready.

The orderlies ripped back the blanket and sheet and lifted Karl by his arms, flipping him onto his stomach, regardless of his abdominal stitches. The bandage tore loose. One orderly jerked down his pajama pants to bare the patient's posterior.

Karl continued to struggle but the target was open. The old nurse swabbed some alcohol over his buttock and slammed the needle in.

After the shot, the orderlies returned him to his back, pulled up the sheets and fixed the strap in place once more.

"I don't want to sleep," he cried out.

The orderlies exited.

Mrs. Wolfe smiled proudly. "Good night."

"But it's morning, goddammit!"

"Come, Nurse McCartney."

As the Wolf pulled her briskly from the room, Althea threw a sympathetic glance back at Karl.

3

EARLY JUNE: THE ORISSA HILL COUNTRY, EASTERN INDIA

*AWAKEN. LONG SHADOWS of low hanging clouds block the sunlight.
Golden eyes scan the landscape, nostrils draw in a cacophony of
scents.*

*With a dull throb in his belly, he rolls to his feet atop the uneven stone
slabs at the base of the scrubby hillside, feeling the sizzling heat
against the pads of his feet. Like other creatures, he waits, watching
the sky.*

*Black, like soot from a distant volcano, folded in jagged shelves. Together
they lay as a crumpled blanket, smothering the scorched earth and
blotting out the arcane sun. The prelude to an annual festival in which
all creatures, all vegetation, even men bow humbly in thanksgiving.*

*He smells moisture in the clouds and welcomes it. He climbs higher on
the hillside where he can oversee the shadowy plain he has crossed.*

*The hills have finally found him, holding him in their loving forests,
cradling him in their maternal valleys. He will never again face the
burning agony of the plain—*

*The sky rumbles, shakes the earth. He waits, tongue flicking moisture
from the air. He surveys the string of hills below the slow-boiling
clouds. Streaks of crisp, wild light dance between the clouds and the*

treetops as the storm clouds roll toward him.
A rumble of thunder crescendos overhead, crackles, explodes.
He waits. Below his rock-crowned oasis, a small herd of chital stand in
formation on the plain, facing the approaching storm. The quickening
wind drops their scent to him but he is not ready to hunt.
The claps of thunder shake the chital from their steadfast stance and
wracks his head as it rides rough overhead.
He pads down the hillside to escape the storm as the clouds open wide
and torrents of water fall as though plunging through ruptured dikes.
In the thick curtains of rain, he sees the deer darting away, seeking refuge
from the storm. The air is cool. Birds are grounded.
His coat is matted with life-giving moisture, easing his thirsty flesh. The
rain roars down like a mighty waterfall, deafening the sizzle of
lightning and eruptions of thunder.
His paws strike the hard, pebble-strewn plain as he pads across it,
charging away from the monsoon.

Karl's eyes popped open, frightened, hearing the splatter of rain on his window.

He sensed the door of his room opening, but that was not what had awakened him. Feeling strangely refreshed, his muscles seemed strong and taut. He sat up in one swift motion, his eyes staring ahead at the bare plaster wall, His ears picked up the sounds of Nurse McCartney carrying a tray across the room. He was becoming good at seeing without his eyes.

"Wake up, Mister Edwards," she sang, her back to him, not noticing he was already sitting up.

He tugged at the sleepwalking straps.

"Did you sleep well?" she asked.

Karl let out a loud sigh, stretching his arms over his head as she unbuckled the strap.

"I feel great." He pinched his shoulders together, stretching.

"Well rested?" She smiled at him, tending to the tray. "You should be. You've been asleep almost twelve hours. How can anybody sleep so long?"

He chuckled, scratched his week-old beard.

"It's easy for me. The only way to pass the time in a place like this, huh? When I'm awake, I have to deal with reality and the ol' doc says I just can't do that. Not yet, anyway. So, I don't. I just sleep through life."

Her smile always seemed genuine. "But you miss so much that way."

"Are you kidding? I'm not missing a damn thing *here* when I sleep. I mean, except your pretty face smiling at me every morning. I like *that*."

She blushed and he was impressed by her rosy cheeks.

"You're the only good thing about this place, you know? I wouldn't miss one of your five-minute sponge baths for anything in the world."

She pouted. "I have to give you another bath this morning."

"I don't mind." He chuckled. "Perfect ending to a perfect night of perfect dreams."

She nodded politely. She had been informed about her patient's dreams, about his make-believe tigers, how he'd tried to kill his wife and then tried to commit suicide by cutting his belly open. It was hard not to think about all that when she was with him. He seemed like a nice man, except when he would use swear words. When he did, she was reminded of her father, who cussed a lot during her childhood, especially when he got drunk and beat her mother.

She prepared the sponge, the soap, and the basin of water, moving them on the rolling table to the edge of the bed. Karl had already pulled off his state hospital pajama top. Lurching up, he slipped down his pajama pants and sat with the sheet pulled over his lap.

"Am I ever going to be get a real bath?"

"Of course you will." She filled the sponge from the basin. "As soon as your stitches heal completely, you'll be able to have a real bath. But you'll have to wait in line. We've only got two tubs."

"You mean when these stitches heal, I gotta bathe myself?"

She blushed again. His only entertainment during his waking hours was to flirt with the nurses, knowing how they were disgusted by him. But Nurse McCartney was different.

"So what nice dreams did you have during your twelve-hour nap?"

She beginning the sponge bath.

"Changing the subject?" He gazed at her face as she moved the sponge over his chest. "I dreamed I killed my wife's lover."

Keeping a steady expression, she continued with the sponge, working it around his stitches. She'd heard other patients' declarations which were just as strange.

"Well, you asked," he said with a loud exhale.

"Yes, I guess I did."

She moved around the bed to wash his back. Most of her patients were women or elderly men. They were no threat to her. Her experience was limited, but she was a professional. Karl was different than the others.

Pressing the sponge to his shoulder blade, a stream of warm water ran down the length of his back.

"Ah, that feels so good," he sighed, laying his head against her arm. "I think you like your job."

She did not respond but her cheeks blushed anew.

"What's your name, Nurse McCartney? I mean, you've been giving me these intimate little baths for a couple weeks and we're not even on a first name basis yet. I feel like I'm just a plaything to you, just a toy to be used and then discarded." He laughed but it sounded artificial.

She stopped her bathing.

"Sorry, ma'am." He looked away. "I didn't mean to embarrass you—really. It's—I mean, I'm—aaaa...."

"It's okay, Mister Edwards."

She sensed he was about to cry, probably thinking about his wife's affair, and she was strangely sympathetic.

"Call me Karl, awright?"

She smiled, reaching for the towel to dry him.

"Okay, but only in private. We're supposed to use last names with patients." She briskly toweled his back and he moaned with pleasure. "I have to be careful or Missus Wolfe will *kill* me—I mean, uh, she'll get me in trouble."

"Yeah, I've seen her. A real bitch."

She blushed again and he noticed.

"Yeah, a real...."

"Go ahead. Say it."

"All right, she's a real...*bitch*."

"See? The world didn't end just because you said a bad word. Sometimes those are the only words that fit. You got no choice but to use them. How else are people gonna know you're really angry unless you cuss?"

Althea leaned back against the unoccupied bed there, gazing over at Mr. Edwards. She sighed, was about to speak—

"You should be finished washing Mister Edwards by now, Nurse McCartney."

It was the gravelly voice of Mrs. Wolfe, calling from the hallway.

Karl noticed Althea's frightened twitch.

"Don't worry," he told her, voice hushed. "You're doing fine, Althea. Just need a little more confidence."

She hurriedly gathered her supplies.

"Thanks, Mister Edwards."

"Karl—remember?"

She nodded her head, turning with the tray in her hands.

"Nurse McCartney!" the Wolf howled.

"I gotta go...Karl."

"I like you."

It was so sudden it sounded like a thunderclap in a clear sky. He didn't know why he said it, but he did like her. Then he remembered what he'd been told once when he was young: you can't tell if a waitress or a nurse really likes you because being friendly is part of their job. Still, Althea was his only reason to wake up in the morning.

"I—like you—too," she responded with hesitation.

He could not tell if she was just being polite, or if she was sincere.

"When will you come back, Althea?"

"I—I don't know—"

A bellow interrupted: "You have other patients, Nurse McCartney!"

"I'll try to—"

The Wolf burst into the room, shooting a hateful glare at Karl. She shifted her gleaming dagger gaze to Althea.

"I was trying to give 'em a little more personal touch, Missus Wolfe."

The head nurse's eyebrows merged across the top of her nose. Her eyes burned like bonfires. She took Althea firmly by the arm, escorting her from the room.

"See you later, Mister Edwards," Althea called back before the door swung shut.

He moves away from the village, through the thick forest to the west, skirting the herds of Man as best he can without detection. The village holds no red-furred men that he can see with his keen eyes during several days watching them.

Passing through a sparse area of woodland, following the nullah—the winding stream with sandbars and deeply cut shores—

He comes upon a group of five man-cubs playing in the brush. They bounce a spherical object between them, kicking it with their hindpaws. They make unusual sounds, like the red-furred men did: a rolling, hearty barking sound.

However, from the young man-creatures, it takes on an air of joy. Coming from the red-furred men, arrogance and fear were what he heard. He has no feelings for these cubs, but how can they be the same kind as those of red fur?

They run down the trail, his gaze following them from behind the mosaic of leaves. He sees they are joyful, as he once was. Will these young creatures one day grow to become the red-furred adults?

His belly wretches with the thought. He is only hunting those who butchered his beloved mate. Only them, only the red-furred men, wherever they may hide.

He breaks from the brush, pads down the trail after the man-cubs.

Soon he has lost the sound of the cubs' chatter. The trail takes a sharp turn as it parallels the nullah. Below the slope, where the stream cuts away the soil, he finds them.

Two are in the stream, splashing in the cooling waters. The other three are on a strip of sand, pulling off their white fur, revealing their brown bodies. He knows it is a habit of men, changing their fur.

He moves down the trail.

"Shaitan!" one of the man-cubs shrieks from the swirling waters.

The others turn to look as his ragged, white-furred ruff disappears from the bare slope where he watched them. More desperate, frantic words follow. They scramble to dress and run away to their nest.

4

LATE JUNE: THE EASTWOOD INSTITUTE

KARL SHIFTED IN THE CHAIR, refusing the traditional couch.

"I'm so glad to see you beginning to open up," the silky voice of his psychiatrist, Dr. Lyons, broke the long silence.

He was a small man with spectacles and goatee, hiding in a narrow-lapelled charcoal suit with a purple paisley tie.

"Yeah, so what?" Karl sneered.

The doctor's office, at the end of the east wing, was a room of rich earthy tone designed to calm the patient. Karl never ceased to relax when he sat back in the soft upholstery. His body would relax, but his mind was ever vigilant. He refused to let his cure come easy.

In his time at the Institute, he had been visiting his psychiatrist three times a week. He said nothing the first week, then only one or two word answers the next week—despite having a reputation for endless vocalization with the nurses. These complete, brief sentences, seemed like a major break-through.

During Wednesday's session, Karl suddenly decided to talk. It was mostly at Althea's suggestion. Like the many reporters who had wanted to hear his story, he feared the doctor would twist his words. Karl didn't want to deal with that frustration again. But Althea had convinced him it really would help to talk about his problems with someone—even a psychiatrist.

"I'd be happy to talk to you," she said one evening well past the end of her shift, "but I'm no psychologist, so I don't know how helpful I could be. But I'm happy to listen."

He nodded, smiling only for her. Her voice, soft and sweet like a flowery fragrance wafting on the breeze, drew the tension from him. At the same time his guts tightened.

"If you'll go and talk to Doctor Lyons, I'll bring you a surprise," she coaxed him. "I promise."

His will melted.

After that session, she had indeed surprised him: after the others had gone, she returned with a sack of real food—hamburgers, fries, and chocolate milkshakes for both of them. And tucked under her arm was a bamboo flute. They ate happily, laughed with a bubbly, carefree energy. Finished eating, she played her flute and the delightful notes made him believe that the world had not passed him by after all. There was still hope. The music brought out a child-like innocence in him.

Before she left for the night, he kissed her hand in mock chivalry—at that moment wanting to kiss more—and bowed low to thank her for the special attention. She promised to teach him all the strange things she believed in, like reincarnation, Zen, and the New Age. He told her he looked forward to it, and he really did.

"What's been happening since our last session, Mister Edwards?" The doctor sat back in his leather chair in front of his mahogany desk, notebook and pen poised. "I thought we did so well. Have you changed your mind about talking to me? I hope not. I was just beginning to enjoy your story."

"I told you, dammit, a million times: It's no goddamn story."

"Of course not." The doctor took a breath. "I really want to know what you're thinking, what's on your mind. Just talk to me, anything at all. Is that all right?"

"Just talk to me, anything at all," Karl mocked.

"Yes. Go ahead."

"Yes, go ahead," he mocked again, making a face.

Dr. Lyons chuckled.

"You think I did that for your amusement? I did it for mine."

"Of course."

"So what do you want me to say this time? Got any more of those confessions for me to sign?"

Dr. Lyons sat up, ready to take notes.

"No confessions to sign. Why don't you start by telling me how you feel about your wife's affair."

"Oh, so you're going to start with the tough questions, huh? Let me think...."

He was ready for that question, as much as he had been for his first session with the doctor.

"I feel...uh...." He thought of the best wording, not wanting to be misquoted, "that I'm not feeling what I should feel."

"That's a very good answer, Mister Edwards."

"Damn straight."

"Tell me more."

Karl sighed, then waxed profound.

"I feel...as though I should feel more anger. Maybe I didn't really love her. I mean, we talked about divorce a few times before. But we always made up at night. Then one morning my life was turned upside-down...and you know the rest."

Dr. Lyons did not look up during his pause.

"No more nightmares?"

"Boy, doc, you sure know how to bring a conversation around, don't you? No, my 'nightmares', as you call them, are about *tigers*, not my wife."

"You're still having them?"

"You think my nightmares are because of problems with my wife?"

"Not necessarily. Haven't they stopped since you've been here?"

"Hell, no." He glanced to each side, looking for spies. "I just don't go telling everybody about them. That's what got me sent here in the first place—or have you forgot? I thought it didn't matter. I thought a guy could say whatever he wanted without people pointing at him, saying he's gone loco."

Karl laid his head back. "It's a disappointing world."

"Is it?"

"I'm raving now, aren't I, doc?"

"No, go right ahead."

"Can't write fast enough? Maybe I should talk slower."

He paused for the doctor's reply but got only the sound of pen on paper.

"Careful, doc. You're gonna get writer's cramp."

"Did it ever occur to you," Dr. Lyons interrupted, looking up from his note pad, "that your wife might have been a nymphomaniac? Did you ever consider that possibility? Do you understand that word?"

"You mean she wanted to screw every man she saw?"

"Well, yes—that's one definition."

"She was a virgin when I met her, and didn't date other guys after that. We got married then, right out of high school. And we—"

The idea of his wife making love to another man made him sick and he reached for the cup of water on the table beside the chair.

"Better?" Dr. Lyons asked.

"It will never be better."

"And why do you think that?"

Karl replaced the glass on the table.

"Because I'm locked up in this fine institution for who knows how long—and if I ever do get outta here, I got nothing waiting for me. No parents, no kids, no wife, no job, no pride, no self-respect. Nothing. And who knows what that bitch is doing with all my stuff? They're probably screwing in my bed. If I walked outta here today, I don't even have a goddamn set of clothes to put on. You know, she even told me once before she's not gonna file for divorce until after I'm released. Now ain't that the shits? She's gonna milk my unemployment checks as long as she can. Hell, I might as well be fucking institutionalized for the rest of my life—if the state's so damn willing to send me to a place like this, then...hell, let'em pay my room and board for the rest of my life!"

"Calm down, Mister Edwards."

His head began to hurt.

"Headache, Mister Edwards?"

He rubbed his temples, squinting his eyes.

"Good guess. It must be about time for my session to end, right? I always get headaches when it's time to go."

Dr. Lyons turned to the clock on the wall. "But it is time. Sorry, Mister Edwards, but we'll have to leave it there for today. Remember where we were and we'll pick up there next time."

Sleeping stories, dreams are: vague, dancing images, muffled, breathless words, twisted and gnarled like a coiling vine wrapped around the trunk of a saja tree, gradually choking its host. The meanings are always unclear, undefined, insensible, cold.

Do they predict future events? Or does the dreamer act to make the dreams true?

You do not control your destiny. Your dreams cause your actions, cause the results of action.

You brood, feel the burden of his dark dreams and of the power they hold over you, as you sit on a ledge protected from the sight of men by ample forest cover, sunning, drying your musty coat, stretching your tired muscles.

You have come far during past days, across fields broken by the horns and antlers of Man, spotted with the seedlings of nameless vegetation; across dirt roads peopled with carts, bicycles, and walking Men; through forested hills, skirting calm-surfaced, lily-flecked lakes; deep into the unknown world, to a place never dreamed.

You have seen this place in a dream, greatly puzzling and strangely compelling. You recognize it and that disturbs you. Can it be that you recognize the village because it is the place of the red-furred men? Are you making your own history, or falling down the path your dream has laid before you?

Shrink from the thought, return to oblivion as you sun yourself.

Your mind aches; you have never thought so intensely. Your power of reason has increased since that terrible day when your mate died, but you have not the intelligence yet to understand how that might be, or how best to use this gift.

If nature, through whim or design, has given you the capacity to use this mind as does a man, then you will turn that gift into a weapon.

You will forge your man-like brain into the razor claws and rapier fangs that will strike down the red-furred creatures.

5

"YOU SEE, KARL," SAID ALTHEA, continuing to wax evangelically sitting on the next bed, feet swinging casually to her fervent words, "one of the things that's different in Buddhism than in any other religion is the selflessness, and the denied *atman*. It goes back to what I said last week. The idea of *karma* in Buddhism—which, of course, came after the practices of Hinduism—is very different from the ideas written in the *Upanishads*. It's all related to how we see the soul, or the *atman*. When we meditate, we try to reach our inner-self, our soul, trying to obtain that knowledge which can only be found there—and which is based on the countless life experiences our souls have accumulated. That's why meditation helps us live our lives better in the present."

Karl tried to be polite. He loved listening to her sweet voice and he enjoyed the bright glow as she preached, but his blue-collar background left him far behind the New Age. Factory workers did not meditate.

"Then what about all this reincarnation stuff I keep on hearing about?" he asked. "TV gurus. Is that like what you're talking about?"

"Well, you see," she said, her voice a curtain of cheer, "if good acts produce a subsequent good existence, and evil acts cause bad ones, and *then* if everything returns to nothing after death anyway, what is the transmigrating substance? If we're assuming there is no self, then what's the basis for the birth and death cycle?"

"I don't know. What?"

Her cheeks glowed when she was filled with the spirit.

"Exactly! So, for about three hundred years back then, everyone was arguing about these inconsistencies. All the religious schools thought about it day and night, but nobody came up with any good answers. Then, finally, there came to be a brand-new school called the Mahayana school and they taught a new concept called 'perfuming'. Their idea was, like, everything we do, good and bad, sticks to us like perfume. It even permeates us like perfume stinks up our clothes. And the whole effect—that is, us, our perfume, and the way in which it permeates us— all that combines to give each person their unique character, just like their own special fragrance. So everybody has their own particular balance of good and evil, because each of us is different."

"You must be overloaded on the good side," he muttered, offering a smile, unable to resist.

She blushed, caught her breath.

"Meditating is like talking to your big brother, and he's inside of you, someone wiser than you who can advise you. Or, it's like being able to go back in time to one of your ancestors and ask them for advice, but the ancestor is really *yourself* back in a previous life."

"Yeah, I get it. Sorta like, 'Those who cannot remember history are condemned to repeat it.' Heard that in a movie."

"That's right. Since we have in us all the experiences of countless lives, it's only a matter of reaching deep down inside ourselves to find that past life. It's our own history, and if we can learn it, then maybe we'll learn *from it* and not, as you said, be condemned to repeat our mistakes. And we'll get better and better until one day we'll be able to enter Nirvana and never experience pain and suffering ever again."

She held a triumphant pose, her gaze fixed firmly but serenely on something very distant.

"No more pain and suffering, huh?" He frowned.

She lost her smile. "Well, yes. I guess so. That's how it's supposed to work."

"So you're saying—what you mean to say is if I do this meditation stuff, and say all those voodoo words, then I can sorta direct-dial my past lives?"

"Well, it takes lots of practice."

"Have you ever reached any of your past lives?"

"Almost. But I'm still a beginner."

He shook his head. "Blind leading the blind."

Althea pursed her lips. "No, my eyes are open, opening wider and wider to the universe every day, Karl."

"How long does it take?"

"Sometimes it takes a whole lifetime."

He frowned. "I don't have that much time. How am I supposed to get answers to my life and solve my problems now—before I go to my next life?"

"I don't know, Karl. I'm just a beginner."

"But this interests me." He stared at the far wall, past her, over her shoulder. "Hear me out. You gave me an idea."

"What's that?"

"This past life shit, you really believe it?"

"Yes."

"And this soul stuff?"

"Uh-huh."

"Then let me ask you something. If these souls go from body to body in all these different lives, like you say, and they go into good bodies when they're good and into bad bodies—I mean, like shrinks turning into dung beetles or, uh, lawyers becoming some parasitic tapeworms, ya know, living in people's bowels—when they're bad, and all this shit goes on for thousands of years, then when does it all end?"

"It ends—"

"Yeah, I know you said when we reach the highest level of perfection or total fuckin' goodness—but *then* what?"

"Well, it's—"

"It's still not an answer to life, or what life is. It still seems more likely to me that we all just showed up here like pimples on the earth's butt and making a mess of things ever since. And someday we all get *zapped*. Know what I mean?"

Althea laughed and, although it sounded pleasant to him, he felt bad that she found humor in his seriousness.

"Think again—carefully," he whispered intensely. "If humans and animals are the same, if they're all on the same path—humans representing the results of the lives lived well, animals being the lives that were messed up—then it would be true that the animals of the world, every one of them, also have souls, regardless of the goodness or badness of them. Am I correct?"

She heard his words, but the fierceness of his manner stunned her and she could not immediately answer.

"You mean, you wanna know if animals have souls?"

He nodded.

"That's easy, Karl. Of course they do. That's why Buddhists are vegetarian. They don't eat meat because that's what animals are."

He nodded again.

"Do *tigers* have souls?"

The question caught her off-guard. She thought first that she had let her guard down again, dangerous with some patients, even though Mr. Edwards was not as vicious as others on her wing. But she could not forget her detailed briefing on Mr. Edwards. His obsession with tigers.

"Oh, I probably should be going now," she said, pushing off the unoccupied bed. "See you tomorrow, okay?"

She turned and stepped toward the door. Just when she thought she was getting to know him, he would say something which would jolt her back to reality: he was a mental patient and she was only his nurse. Not his therapist—or his guru.

What an odd question, she thought.

Then she glanced back before the door swung shut.

"Of course they do."

The sun sits fat and lazy on the edge of the world, a tiger-orange which runs watery through the clouds. The sky, once a ceramic azure covering the earth like an overturned bowl, fades into a cottony amber blanket, touched with crimson stripes and lavender shadows.
As the hills grow dark, the forests graying with the dusk, some animals flee, others awaken.
You awaken.
The dimmer light is easier on your eyes. They flare into a florescent gold, searching the dusty landscape, studying the approaching evening. Only your eyes move.
The dying firelight on the horizon outlines the twisted, gnarled branches of the sandalwood and acacia on the hills. Flocks of birds alight on the boughs for the night, weighing them down, dissolving into silhouettes, crying out to the moon. Russet grasses rattle with a new breeze, the first of the evening. They crinkle as they bend, lending a

steady percussion to the night's tuning.

Below the blood-red line melting along the horizon, shapes scatter across the rolling plain before your watchful eyes.

You have become a good hunter in adulthood.

Now you wait.

You do not hunger. You do not want for sleep. You wait because that is what you wish to do at this moment. You know you have this freedom, now that the commonness of your life has been shattered. You have only one purpose in your life tonight, and the past night, and the next night, and the next—to eternity.

Having no mate, no cubs, no fellow beasts of any kin, you welcome this final challenge.

You bathe in its horrid implications, feel the warmth of killing, the cool satisfaction of revenge. You have the tools. You have the will.

Now you have motivation.

You stir—a mere heartbeat out of place which causes the flesh to pulse irregularly, and a bird darts from the brush, screaming into the night its warning of your presence.

You offer a muffled growl, loud enough to shake the earth a mile away. Other frightened beasts and birds flee.

Standing, you feel the ache in your loins. It has been long enough for your muscles to recover from their unnatural burden, from their unsightly, gruesome task. You do not wish to dwell on it, shake it off. But your loins continue to ache. You recognize the ache, not of stress and activity, but of desire.

Between your eyes, in the center of your mind, your mate stands unscathed. She poses, her coat fresh from the pool, her eyes bright, yellow as the autumn moon. Her shoulders are strong, powerful, sensuous and graceful as she approaches. Her tail flicks the air as she pads silently to you. She pauses, turning her whiskered face back over her shoulder, inviting you, calling you with those luminous golden orbs and moist, pink tongue sliding out of her mouth between her fangs—

She was the one who named you. Recall how she watched you take down the sambar buck, the largest of the herd, drag it across the marsh into the thicket.

As you dropped it at her feet, she could not avoid noticing your forepaw. The pad of your right foot was different, smaller than the left forepaw, and she growled her amusement at your deformity.

Two snips and a husky coo. That was your name: Roundpaw.

It did not hinder your hunting, but it caught her attention, perhaps more than your masculine striding or the savage throat take-down you used on large game.

But not her—she was a silly creature, too full of youth and playfulness to be concerned about her next meal. She knew you would always provide. She knew you must separate during the year, each to go your own way, to meet again during the next heat, somewhere in the jungle.

You would find her, she knew, she would find you. And he knew her call anywhere he heard it, across the plains, through the forests, anywhere—

When you called her, it was a bark and two coos: Brighteyes.

It suited her, with her large, round, amber disks which seemed always to accentuate the sunlight or your own reflection, even during the monsoon seasons when little sunlight shone.

Also in the night.

So many images and actions that were hers, that would be hers no longer. Such a steely, beautiful creature she was: tawny-coated like the most brilliant dawn you could imagine, powerful and strong as the great earth itself, fleet-footed and quick as the searing flashes of light in the night sky during a rainstorm, steadfast and wise as the old, gnarled tree which crowned that ancient hillock where she is buried.

A clap of thunder splits your mind—not from the sky but from within you.

Them. The men.

Humans in red fur, with branches that fling other branches, sticks that pierced your mate's flesh, other sticks that spewed fire like the sun.

They came in square rocks rolling on round stones, slithering across the land like snakes, regardless of the gouges they left behind in the proud earth.

And who were they? Beasts of two legs.

They cannot run as fast as you, nor climb trees like you, nor carry a full

46

adult sambar in their jaws for miles through the forest—

Why did they flee their nests and venture into your territory, cross your land, harass creatures, and murder your mate?

The nights are never cool enough for you, more when you fill with hate. The brief, pleasant memories of Brighteyes are not so strong they can hold out the anger that burns within you.

Now you do not want to keep it out.

You have rested with your mate's image between your eyes.

It is time to continue on your trek.

You spring from the thicket, not surprising any other creature, each aware of you, the wayward tiger.

You hold the image of the red-furred men in your mind, seared into your brain. When you find them, you will know them. They are the ones you will destroy.

You bound away from the thicket, padding across the dark plain, birds crying out their warnings, a deer springing away.

You do not care.

You want to tell them, but you do not know how. Not even the strange language inside your head would be effective. You are not hunting them. Now you cannot move anywhere in the open without drawing the attention of every being in sight, sound, or scent of you—

And you have no desire to hunt any of them.

You are only hunting men now.

6

SECOND WEEK OF JULY: KANHA WILDLIFE PRESERVE

DESPITE THE OPPRESSIVE HEAT of mid-day, his attention is drawn to movement in the sea of elephant grass below his rocky outpost. The flickering stalks of golden grass, bent with the breeze, rustle like waves of an ocean, reflecting the brilliant sunlight into his sleepy eyes.

Scanning the marshland, he sees the young *gaur*—the Indian buffalo—a small calf he could take for dinner if it were alone. But its mother grazes nearby, unconcerned for his presence on the hillside, upon the rocks, beneath the sweeping *saja* branches, deep in the shadows. His eyes fall upon an upright, two-legged creature: one of the native men that inhabit the land, covered by the patch of white fur around his body, his limbs naked; he carries a long staff in his forepaw as he steps carefully through the hip-high grasses.

Roundpaw's eyes move to the monstrous hulk of the bull gaur, its fierce horns glowing in the sunlight. Its massive head bends low, grazing, its high, arched back and mighty shoulders gleam in the heat. He will not try to take such a beast. The bull knows this, too, although he has yet to detect the tiger's scent.

Closer, between the gaur family and his hill, a second brown man stands in the tall grass. Roundpaw stares at the two men, wondering why they would be near the gaurs. But his eyes are suddenly stabbed by a burst of red amid the amber grass. It is a man. Not a native, he stands red-furred and white-faced. *There*! Among the grass: behind the other men, in a grazing stance, holding that which Roundpaw recognizes as the fire stick which spits stones of death.

He raises his ruffled head to better see them.

Although he cannot recall the details of the man-creatures who murdered his mate, the red fur of their chest, forelegs, and shoulders, and their pale, naked faces, and their horrible fire sticks ring clear in his mind. Can this be one of them?

Before, in that hot afternoon so long ago, he did not have time to think, to reason, to decide what his actions would be. He simply acted to save his mate, resulting in the mutilation of several man-creatures. He has spent the past weeks filled with hatred and filling himself with the desire for death. He is stupefied by the situation which lies before him. He has seen his enemy, after many days of searching, and the decision has arrived.

He feels a heavy, paralyzing air fall over him. He cannot move. He cannot act. Something has halted his actions, his thoughts, frozen his will. It is not *right*, he knows.

He must forget his inbred fear of the musky creature. He must do what he has vowed. It is what he has dedicated the brief portion that remains of his life, for he knows that with the killing of Man, his own life will soon end. That is the law of the land, although many of his kind, and many other creatures, have fallen at the hand of the upright beast without ever having struck first against them. Nature is just, he knows. Only the presence of Man disturbs that balance. Only the removal of Man will restore it. And if not each and every man-creature is to be blamed, then surely those which bear the red fur must be the spoilers of the land, and therefore must be removed. This fact, as well as the precious life of his mate, impel him to spring to his feet. He stretches on the granite slab as spots of sunlight dabble his tawny coat.

It is time to act.

Tucking his ears back, he yawns, grimacing to expose those sensors in his mouth which absorb the scent of Man. His nerves begin to rattle with fury. The red-furred men have returned—one of them—and the time is right for destruction. He bares his claws, sharpens them against the trunk of the *saja* tree rising beside the small cliff. He flexes his leg muscles, feeling the energy in them.

He bounds down from the rocks, his blood hot, his mind aflame with hatred.

The hunter wears a red plaid hunting vest, its pockets filled with everything from chewing gum and a small Hindi phrase book, to extra .457 bullets for large game. His shirt is khaki, sleeves rolled up to his elbows, dark sweat stains under his arms and down the center of his back. He wipes his brow with his free hand as he drops to one knee in the grass, the stalks around him rising to his shoulders in his kneeling position.

One of his native guides has signaled for him to halt as the distance is now correct for shooting the giant trophy. They wait ahead of him, ready to distract the gaur should it decide to charge.

At that moment, the bull snorts and the three men freeze, waiting for the fidgety bovine's next move. The bull only sneezed, dust from the grass, and not a charge.

The hunter, an American from Cleveland, an investment banker by trade with a lust for big game hunting, has his license for the gaur in his hip pocket. He has paid well his two guides, and has chosen the gaur to add to his vast collection of trophies, a tradition he maintains from his father. It is the only similarity with the British hunters who hunted many leagues away and were led by men from a different village. The villagers are quite happy to rid themselves of the ugly bovine who competes with their livestock for grazing.

He raises his rifle, a little heavier than what he is used to handling. He checks the sights, tests the balance in his hands and against his shoulder, re-aligns his knee and legs to find a steadier position from which to shoot. Finally, he pulls back the bolt and slides the long, fat bullet into the chamber, slamming it home as he has done so often. His nerves are on edge, blood hot with passion. He does not feel the cruel, blistering sun, or notice the line of dark thunderheads approaching from the southwest. He flips off the safety and pulls the rifle back into his shoulder.

The nearest guide—standing to the right—steps quickly back toward him, motioning for him to wait. Puzzled, he lowers the rifle, struggling to make out the guide's Hindi-plagued English. When he comes to within twenty meters, they have the communication straight. The other guide holds his ground, eyes sitting on the slightest twitch of the gaur's bulk. He knows that if his tremendous set of horns does not spear him in a charge, the thundering hooves and locomotive power would easily trample him underfoot.

Roundpaw crouches low in the grass, stripes blending perfectly with the stalks. He pauses, muscles taut, nerves acute, his concentration steady. He pads forward slowly, carefully placing each paw where it will not snap a twig or flick a blade of grass to alert his victim. His belly brushes the cool, moist earth, head lowered. He slides through the grass with stealth, so smoothly, without a single unnecessary movement.

The red-furred man has left a trail of parted grass behind him as he moved forward, making the task of stalking him easier. Roundpaw's nose catches the acrid scent of the beast. He almost sneezes from the odor.

The hunter carefully replaces the butt of his rifle into his shoulder. His hands steady the wooden stock, his index finger falling alongside the trigger. His cheek rests casually against the stock and his eyes fall into alignment with the sights. Squaring his shoulders, he adjusts his breathing as he maintains the strained kneeling position.

The bull gaur senses a disturbance and raises his monstrous head, horns swaying, chomping a mouthful of reeds and grass. He regards the three men, unconcerned. His eyes cannot focus on them when they are not in motion, not realizing how innocent he appears when set within the cross hairs of a rifle scope.

Roundpaw can barely stand the stench of the man-beast as he slinks his way through the bent-grass trail of the hunter—thirty meters—fifteen—

He pauses mid-way in the path, deciding. His hindlegs fold beneath his hips, his forelegs feeling for a tight grip which will add to the power of his launch. His shoulders tense with anticipation. It has to be right, he tells himself, allowing himself one brief moment of thought. He sees the red fur covering his torso, the tan hair on his hindlegs, the pale, naked face, and the fire stick. He sees the weapon raised, directed at another creature, and whether it be himself, another tiger, or another four-legged beast, he seethes with hatred.

His tongue slides to his left canine tooth, rubbing it.

The hunter's finger slides up, settling in the curve of the trigger.

The gaur, dumb-faced, stares at its killer, innocently and naïvely chewing its meal.

Roundpaw's ears twitch.

A bird cries out from somewhere, and one of the native men barks to the hunter. He is waved off by the red-furred one, who chooses not to heed the warning.

Roundpaw cannot wait any longer. His body is coiled so tightly that he will explode if he does not launch himself. His hindlegs shiver with the strain, his whiskers bristle, his eyes burn.

He bursts from his crouch—orange lightning rippling through the grass, two leaps bringing him across the back of the red-furred Man. As he is struck from behind, the hunter's aim is thrown to the right and the gaur-directed bullet hits the guide, who drops like a bag of millet to the earth, his face hamburgered and his hands grasping what remains of his skull. The hunter cannot fend off the attack, he knows in the first second of battle, but he feels an obligation to try. He cannot simply lie there and allow the beast to have its way.

The hunter reaches for his knife, pinned beneath him somewhere, hooked to his belt. With his other hand he tries to protect his throat. He cannot feel his shirt and chest muscles being stripped away. He does not feel the pain he always thought he would. He sees the hot, violet liquid spraying over him and he knows it is his. Somehow, it does not frighten him; there is no time for fear. Didn't he once tell his buddies at the gentleman's club, even jokingly, that he desired as a method of death to be ripped apart by a crazed lion? Close enough.

The tiger poses fearlessly over the red-furred man's disintegrating form. Claws are whirling, never-ceasing shredding machines, shaving layer after layer of flesh from the chest of the man-creature, digging deeper for the heart of the beast. Warm blood spurts into his face, wets his eyes, mats his fur. His long fangs grasp the throat of the wriggling, screaming creature. He feels the fangs pierce the windpipe, feels them meet inside, one from the left and one from the right. He jerks his muzzle violently—once—and the tube is ripped free of the creature's neck, open-ended tubes spilling their verbal contents into the gulf. The screams cease as the creature discovers its vocal cords hang from the dripping yaw of his attacker.

Thew man-creature becomes discouraged, and his flailing arm lessens its frantic motion. He feels the blazing Indian sun warm his heart, open to the hot breeze. His breastbone shatters with a crunch of the cat's sharp teeth. Suddenly, his heart beats wildly as he realizes he is not going to survive. He panics, tries to scream. Then his heart slows abruptly, and stops.

The hunter decides the time has come for him to close his eyes and dream of home—the little woman and their four kids, the mortgage and the car payment, the noisy teenagers next door, the sexy new secretary at work. He feels the tiger's bitter breath burning his face. He feels his body relax—he has never felt so relaxed, so calm, so utterly at peace. He is filled with an overwhelming sense of oneness with nature, as though he, like the birds, the beasts, the flowers, the trees, the cool earth below, and the endless sky above, were all part of a greater, universal whole. The feeling is exhilarating, and he casts his useless body away like a ship setting sail for an exotic port. The hunter's spirit hovers a few moments over the crazed beast, the blood-stained grasses and his torn remains, pondering why he waited so long for this inevitable, glorious finale, before flying free of all the pain and suffering of the world he has known.

Karl awoke screaming, arms flailing, and it took four orderlies to restrain him. Through his frantic vision, he saw Nurse Wolfe preparing a needle. He cried out that he was all right, but she rammed it into his exposed hip just the same.

"That's not the way it's supposed to be," he declared, struggling to sit up. No-one there understood what he meant; it was well known in Eastwood that he was insane. "Dammit, it shouldn't be that way! You should've stopped before it's too late!"

Wolfe waited as his muscles began to come unstrung against his commands. He flopped awkwardly in his bed, seeing her jotting notes in his official case record.

"Don't write anything!" he shouted. At least he thought he was shouting. The tranquilizer reduced his shouts to mere mumbling.

He knew what he meant. It was nothing that concerned her or any of the Eastwood staff. He was screaming at the tiger in his dreams, beseeching him to retreat from the destruction that was now too late to undo. His world was unraveling around him, breaking apart between his mind's eye and taut reality.

It seemed a long time as he lay in bed, willing himself to remain awake and alert, staring at the ceiling. He did not know if the trauma had lessened or if he had just gotten used to it. He kept trying to sit up. As he lay back after the second try, he felt as though he could get up from bed if he had to. He preferred to rest, analyzing the dream he experienced, waiting for morning.

Between the dull throbbing in his chest and the steady ache in his head, his vivid consciousness began to waver. He slipped back and forth from the soothing pastel walls of his room to a steamy, vegetated world of jungle bird calls and incessant thumping of native drums. Sweating profusely, he listened to the drums, then the birds, then the rustling of the leaves around him. A breeze wafted over him, humid and heavy, pressing him deeper into his mattress. The drums faded away, then the birds.

In the hours that followed the attack, dozens of villagers armed with their picks, spades, and an occasional illegal ancient and dangerous rifle followed the surviving guide to the place where the bloodstain reclined seductively in the grass. Not much remained after the vultures had their fill.

The frightened guide, his voice quivering, his gestures wild, told of the harrowing encounter. He told how the tiger had pounced from behind the kneeling *sahib*. He told how the hunter had barely defended himself, how he seemed to surrender to the murderer. He told how the beast quickly ripped open his chest and abdomen, biting out his throat but leaving the outwardly flung arms and legs untouched.

Now those limbs, and a clean spine and ribs, were all that remained of the Cleveland banker. Having paid ten-thousand dollars for the guides and the license, the villagers offered prayers for him, willing his transmigration into the body of a sacred cow.

From his ledge, Roundpaw sees the gathering of Man and curses them.
He does not feel proud, nor does he have any sense of heroism—even
  though he knows he has rid the land of one more animal-killing man-
  creature. He has avenged his mate's death by half.
Now, where is the other red-furred man?
He hates the taste of man—acrid, walking death, a disgusting dinner. He
  rinsed his mouth, washed his parched throat after the attack,
  smoothed his battle-ruffled coat. He abhorred the red splotches on
  his fur which he could not wash away. He did not eat the man; he
  could not bear the taste.

Lying in the shade, he hears the chattering of birds and the barking of the man herd below. He will depart at dusk, continue onward in his search. Meanwhile, he will rest, trying to squeeze the afternoon images from his consciousness.

Now he is marked for execution.

The fat sun melts in the crux of two distant hills, like an overripe orange. But the heat does not subside with the arrival of dusk. Through the steaming afternoon he has waited, musing at the brown men's frantic barking at the site of the kill. Now, they are gone.

He must seek a place to rest for a few days, where he may wait out the man-creatures' hunt, as certain as the annual monsoon rain. Save for the hills which cradle the dying sun, all is flat. No place for a rogue tiger to hide.

Slowly, he rises to his feet, tail twitching.

The birds in the treetops burst into song, warning every creature in the area, reporting his every movement. He raises his huge head and growls at them. It is a vain attempt for the birds know they are safe from him, and they sing on. No longer handsome in his fresh battle blood, he no longer concerns himself with his image. What is important for him is to be able to fight, to kill the murderers of his mate.

With a coarse snarl, he pads wearily away from the stand of trees, out to the shoulder-high grass, parting it with his mighty chest.

He points himself toward the fireball in the hills, forever following the light which marks the home of the red-furred men.

7

KARL COULD BARELY PRY HIS FEET LOOSE from where they were locked, hooked inside the bend of his knees. Agony, then the warm rush of circulation, pricking his skin like a thousand needles. He groaned.

"Don't be so dramatic. It's not that bad," said Althea. "I've been doing it for years."

"For years, yeah." He grimaced. "How can I meditate in such a painful position?"

She ignored him.

"The future is not all there is. The reason people are always talking about the future is because they don't have it in their grasp. It's like a fear of the unknown. They try to get to know the future by talking about it or by planning it. Planning ahead is their only way of controlling the future, or trying to. It never works. Those of us who strive to become enlightened know the future isn't important—and by letting go of it we actually gain possession of it."

"You're confusing me again."

She looked at her watch. "Oh!"

"Is it...?"

"Yes, I'm afraid so." She shook her hair off her shoulders. "I've got to be going. Don't wanna be late for my aerobics class."

"How can you go to some class and jump around to goofy music like that?"

Althea leaped up like a grasshopper, leaving her dancing on her toes.

"Come on, up with you," she sang, not caring if she was heard. It was after hours and she was off duty.

When she sprang up from the floor, he could not help but notice her bare, skinny legs as they darted past his face. Devoid of the usual sterile-white stockings, they now glistened with perspiration. When Althea bent over to pick up her athletic bag, stretching her legs, he had the urge to reach out and touch them.

"Well," she huffed, letting out a big breath, tying her blue sweater around her slender waist, "it's time, I guess."

"Yes," he sighed, lowering his head.

He still sat on the floor when she patted his head.

"I'll leave you with this one thought, O Student of Enlightenment." She grinned, gazing down at him. "'In what's seen, there must be only the seen; In what is heard, there must be just the heard; In whatever is sensed, there must be only the sensed; In whatever is thought, there must be only the thought.'"

He shook his head, maintaining a grin. "Okay.... What's that?"

"An old Buddhist *sutra*. A saying. It means you should concentrate on what things really are, not on what you perceive them to be."

"Yeah, okay. I think I got it."

"Remember..." she began.

"...the thought's everything," he finished.

"Just like Freud once said: Sometimes a cigar is just a cigar."

He chuckled. "It is."

With only a heartbeat's pause, catching him unprepared, she bent over and kissed the top of his head.

LATE JULY: THE DECCAN, CENTRAL INDIA

The tepid air grows dank about him, shadows covering him.
The resounding drip of a stream echoes through the lush vegetation,
settling in the clearing formed by a widening of the footpath. Seeing
the cool, clear pool, hidden among the shadows like a dying cloud, he
pads around the bend in the trail. A series of basins, each larger than
those above, seven in all, mount the terraced side of the hillside. As

he studies them, water collects in each and overflows one drip at a
time down into the next basin.

A reflection of light from somewhere paints the quiet surfaces of the pools,
striping them in long, shimmering silver lines. And the water drips,
drips, drips, each hollow ring filling the forest silence.

Roundpaw pauses, flicks his tail and sniffing the stench of decay. Man
has been long away from this place, and yet, still does the darkened
jungle path feel the touch of Man.

Grimacing, he yawns, twitches his ears.

In the days and nights he has traveled from the marsh of the red-furred
man's kill, driven by the angry, fearful herds of brown-skinned men
with sticks, he has climbed from the dry scrub forests, finding his way
deep into the wet, thick woodland, the ancestral hills, where water is
born.

All creatures, even the Man beast, were also born here. It is the womb of
the continent. Here he is safe from the warriors. Here he can find the
peace he seeks, where he can rest, where he can brood on murders
past, where he can plan murders of the future.

He has returned to the ancient hills to meditate on his life and his
impending death. Such is the will of his primeval heart, the heart of a
beast, not a man-creature.

The mark of death is about him now. He has killed Man; the other
creatures of the forest see the brilliant mark upon him. They know the
man-creatures will soon follow.

He is hemmed by the humid, emerald mossy blankets on the walls to
either side of the path. The trail is dirt, strewn with red, crisp leaves
and soggy, black ones. Overhead there is no sky, forbidden by the
intertwining branches, a canopy of lush green.

Regarding the cliff's ascending pools and descending waterfalls, he listens.
The cool, rhythmic dripping is hypnotic, soothing his weary soul.

He pads to the lowest pool, carefully bounding over a low, enclosing wall
of set stones made by Man. Inside the yard, the grass is thick and
wet, soft and sweet smelling. The pools beckon him.

Ascending the slope, they call him. He gazes upward, golden eyes
following the watercourse in reverse until his weary eyes meet the

brilliance at the summit of the seven cataracts. That is where the sun has settled, there to reside and light this sacred park, this holy shrine, built in the depths of the jungle where no man beast may spoil it.

He laps at the pool, refreshing himself, then naps at its base.

The sun is low when he awakens and there is only darkness beneath the forest's horizon. In the fading glow of sunset, he sees the trees as black, silhouetted temples. Among them, overhead, high above his pool at the top of the cliff, he notices the dark, outlined shape of strange, haunting design.

He gazes up, and pulls himself up the steep slope beside the terraced pools, two steps for each level, until he reaches the top.

Before him, the crumbling towers of an ancient Hindu temple rise above the swirl of evening-blackened underbrush, previously hidden among the afternoon's greenery. They sprout like thick-trunked trees from the spacious yard, surrounded by the lush, carpeting grass, enclosed further by a low stone wall.

In this oasis birds cry and monkeys chatter, as though they were the only remaining worshippers, oblivious of his death mark in the sunset-sprinkled blackness.

The temple stands as three conical towers joined by canopies and walkways. They are each made of cut stones and chips of clay tiles winding upward to the top of each tower. The surfaces are sheets of decaying paint, peeling away at random, leaving pieces sticking out, but they are in fact intricately carved designs of great detail hung with patches of kinky moss. Piles of small, broken stones and tiles dot the yard where the temple decays, long down the road to negligent destruction. More decorative than functional, the supporting columns are chiseled into stacks of separate shelves, each carrying minute carvings of ancient Man. All the miniature figurines depict in the endless collection of statuettes an infinite variety of human mating positions: females wearing tall, spiral headdresses adorning their heads.

Roundpaw cannot see them clearly except where the moonlight reflects off the figures, highlighted in the evening darkness. He longs to know why Man behaves in such a manner; to make sport of nature and *natural acts is somehow blasphemous.*

The center tower, the largest of the three, gourd shaped with a narrow stem rising to the sky and a wide base bulging from the earth, spirals upward on twisting tiles and stones, the entrance away from him. Broken tiles have left a jagged opening in the wall, like the sharp teeth of a monster's mouth. A narrow staircase winds around the tower, up to a second floor where another doorway beckons in the moonlight.

Pushing his head inside the opening, he sniffs for food. Satisfied there might be something inside, he bounds through the hole, landing on a floor of smooth plastered tiles. The room is dark though moonlight leaks through tiny spaces between the loose stones. In the weak light, he sees another staircase winding around the inner wall up to the second floor. He pads to the first step, sniffs, takes another step.

On the upper floor, he moves into the wide moonbeams which fall languidly through the spaces. The beams compliment the marks of blood on him that refuse to come clean.

Stepping aside, he watches the final crimson glow of the sunset-streaked sky, reminding him that as long as the sun burns in the sky, he has a vow to fulfill.

There is still one red-furred man-creature walking the land in arrogant upright style. He must find him.

The cool breeze, the chatter of monkeys, the cry of birds, the distant drip-drip-drip of the pools, the musty stench of jungle, combine to dull his mind in the same way that Man is made sad by the beauty of his world.

Such beauty overwhelms the senses. It causes a dulling of the mind, a peaceful immobilization of thoughts. It is its own reward. Whatever the eyes, ears, nose, and tongue digest of the world's beauty, the consciousness routinely mixes with practiced emotions and forms a melancholy gruel. Beauty always causes sadness. Perhaps not initially, but always finally. It is the fear that beauty will last and someday man or beast, mere mortal creatures, will no longer be able to experience it that is distressing. Perhaps, he wonders, that is why Man is so quick to destroy the beauty around him, for in that way, he knows it will not outlast him.

He seethes with jealousy, flooded with the cold, peaceful, dull, painful
  ache of fate. He is in anguish watching the mystical, reverent sunset
  closing before him. That which is beautiful will endure, that which is
  not shall die away.
Feeling ugly, and with the crisp claws of death clenching his heart,
  wringing his mind,
Roundpaw drops to the floor of the room, lays his weary head upon his
  forepaws and slips into a deep sleep.

Dr. Lyons regarded his patient across the carpet.

"Wake up, Mister Edwards."

Karl stirred, opened his eyes.

"You dozed off," said the doctor. "Just long enough to miss most of what I was telling you about my conclusions thus far."

Karl yawned, sat up. "Sorry, doc." He yawned again, pulling himself awake. "I had the weirdest dream. Well, I guess it wasn't so weird—not for me, anyway."

"Did you dream of tigers?"

"No, I didn't dream of tigers, doc." His voice twisted into the whine he used whenever people didn't believe him. "I dreamed of *one* tiger. Only one. One goddamn tiger. But I don't dream *of* tigers; I simply dream. If tigers walk into it, it's hardly my fault."

The doctor turned to a fresh page on his notepad. "Tell me what you dreamed."

Karl breathed deeply. "He was in the jungle, and he found this, aaa—I guess you'd call it a temple of some kind. Real old, crumbling, broken down. But it had these carvings on the walls. They were carvings of people. Naked people. And they were in hundreds of positions."

"Positions...?"

"Yeah, like for screwing. I guess they were, like, ya know, showing all the different ways people can have sex. It was kind of creepy, tell you the truth. All these naked women. And they had these tremendous breasts. Big, round, like melons—not real at all. And their hips were so perfectly round—like they were statues of some kinda fantasy women, ya know?"

"Were you aroused?"

"Aroused? You mean, turned on by these statues? Hah. Don't be weird, doc. But some of the women *were* awfully nice looking, even for statues."

Dr. Lyons studied his patient.

"Have you been thinking more about your tigers?"

"I keep telling you, there's only one. And why do you keep calling him mine?"

"Isn't he yours?"

"He's not mine. Tigers don't belong to nobody. They're as free as the wind. They go where they want and do as they please."

"I see." He paused to write notes. Not looking up, he said: "Tell me more about these tigers of yours."

"You know, doc, I've been trying to figure out how we can be in each other's dreams. I've been thinking a lot about it in the time I've been here—which is plenty—and I've come to the conclusion that—are you ready, doc? Okay, I believe there's some sort of a cosmic connection between me and this one tiger. Yeah, I only see him when I'm asleep, and I guess he probably sees me in his dreams, too, who knows? I sure can't imagine what he'd think of what he saw in my world—or if he'd even understand any of it. You know?"

Karl glanced at the doctor for a sign of approval.

"Aren't you even a little bit surprised, doc?"

"What do you mean by surprised?"

"I mean, I've just told you a pretty goddamn weird thing, and you act as though I'm telling you the recipe for boiled water. Aren't you shocked? Doesn't it make you think I'm even crazier than before?"

"Not at all." More writing. "Whatever you say is fine."

Karl slapped the arm rests. "I don't get it, doc. I'm in here because you think I'm crazy. The court thinks I am. But I can't say crazy things here and have people believe I'm crazy?"

"Calm down, Mister Edwards." He continued writing.

"Does this make sense? I don't think it does, but it's the only thing I can think of. Anyway, you're the shrink. You're the one that's suppose to figure out all this shit and cure me."

"That's how it's supposed to work, yes. However, I find you to be a most extraordinary case. In fact, your case may prompt a good journal article."

"Journal article?" Karl squinted at the doctor.

"Yes. Your case is remarkable. I should write it up for publication."

Karl grinned. "Really? You gonna give me credit?"

The doctor chuckled, nodding. "Certainly."

Relaxed, Karl felt better than expected. "Okay. But don't use my real name."

"Now, again, how long have you been dreaming of these tigers?"

Karl's sigh of frustration exploded.

"I don't choose to dream about him. It just fuckin' happens. You know dreams aren't voluntary. I can't just pick what I dream about."

"Did you dream of these animals as a child?"

"I don't remember—no, I didn't."

"Did you go to the zoo often?"

Karl watched his psychiatrist, who seemed to read the questions off a list from his notebook.

"No more than any other kid."

"When did you begin having these hallucinations?"

"I began having these hallucinations, as you say, when my mate was murdered."

"Your mate?"

"Wife."

Karl sat on the edge of the chair. He felt a vision enter his head, born of answering the doctor's stupid questions. The idea forming in his mind seemed important, so he tried to concentrate on it, even as the drugs he had been given began inducing a headache. He put up with the pain and focused.

"I guess the strong emotional upheaval in his mind—the murder of his mate by those damn hunters—that incident broke through the flimsy curtain between our minds."

His eyes were glassy, his gaze extending beyond the doctor's desk, out the window to a distant land where he could see the reality of his sanity. His body froze, slipping into a relaxed state of alertness, like the meditation Althea had told him about and tried to teach him. It seemed natural to him now, though, and he focused more intensely on his new idea, molding it, manipulating it into words that could be spoken from senses he could only feel.

"Mister Edwards...?"

He realized he was standing, filled with the sensation that he was deep inside his body looking out through his eyes like they were the windows of a house.

"I've seen everything he's seen.... And he must've seen and felt everything I've seen and felt. Don't you see? It has to be so. He must feel what I feel—like I feel what he feels. And see what I see.... It has to be. It's the only explanation that fits—the only one. And it does fit, doc. Listen to me. How can I convince you? It fits. Why can't you see that?"

"Sit down, Mister Edwards."

The cloud disintegrated around him and he saw the office in its true perspective, heard his voice echo around him as though someone else was speaking. He realized he had been raving, but he did not remember what he had said. He was embarrassed at his outburst.

Karl stopped, his face flush with excitement.

Dr. Lyons sat back, watching him.

"Well," the doctor said after a long silence, "that is certainly an interesting point of view. Perhaps we can talk more about this idea next time—when you're feeling better."

"I'm feeling fine, dammit! Why do you always assume I'm one way when I'm the opposite? Why do you always twist around what I say to fit your own interpretations?"

Dr. Lyons reached for the intercom on the corner of the desk.

"I'll call an orderly to help you back to your room. You can rest there. You've had a distressing morning."

"How the hell would you know? You aren't me. I'm the only one who knows how I feel!"

The door opened.

"Here's the orderlies now," the doctor announced, turning to them. "Take him to his room. I'll call his nurse."

The two orderlies moved to either side of Karl, taking him gently by his arms.

They passed the nurse's station where Karl grimaced at Althea. She offered a sympathetic pout, a gesture which did not go unnoticed by her supervisor.

"And another thing. You're spending too much time with Mister Edwards." Mrs. Wolfe's jagged mouth scrunched forward. "Patients aren't supposed to like it here. Your cheerfulness is ruining the proper atmosphere. If patients don't like being at Eastwood, they'll be more cooperative and willing to work hard and be cured so they can leave."

"But shouldn't we be more compassionate?"

"Sometimes I think you confuse *com*passionate with passionate,

Nurse McCartney. I've heard about some of your escapades from the night nurses. Perhaps we should move you to a different wing, where you can concentrate on your work."

"Please don't do that, Missus Wolfe." She choked up. "I can concentrate here. Really, I can."

Mrs. Wolfe frowned.

"I don't think you have the maturity—and experience—to handle your duties on my wing, Nurse McCartney. The patients we have here are not the gentle ones. We've got murderers, rapists. They can be troublesome, and I think a more experienced nurse would be able to handle them better." She paused for emphasis. "Mister Edwards is a dangerous patient. He's a suicide case—and attempted murder, too. You know that."

"He's not dangerous," Althea spoke up, remembering the confidence he had shown in her. "He didn't kill his wife. And his wound was an accident, not suicide."

Mrs. Wolfe crossed her arms.

"Nurse McCartney, are you trying to diagnose patients now? You don't even have the facts of his case straight. You're not a doctor, you're a nurse—and not a very good one at that!"

8

FIRST SUNDAY IN AUGUST: ACROSS THE STATE LINE IN KANSAS CITY, KANSAS

WHEN BLOND-HAIRED, blue-eyed Rebecca Hopkins opened her apartment door, she couldn't believe her eyes. There he was: the handsome figure of her wayward boyfriend, standing humbly in the hallway. She wanted to scream. If she did, however, it would only drive him away again and she wanted him so badly she just grinned.

"Hello," the tanned Ron Priestley said with his usual cute smirk.

She pulled her pink bath robe tighter, and caught her wet hair up in a towel.

"Just like that?" Becky snapped. "You think you can come waltzing back so easy?" She expected more from him, like an apology, but she held back. "You got some nerve."

"Ah, Becky—"

"Where the hell've you been? I haven't heard from you since—since goddamn April. Shit, Ronnie! Are we through or aren't we? At least I thought that's what you said last time I kicked you out of my life."

She stepped away from the door, retreating into her apartment with the door open and he followed, assuming an invitation to enter.

"But you keep coming the fuck back!"

"I am truly sorry," he intoned as though reading from a cue card.

Closing the door behind him, Ron gazed at her wet, dripping, terrycloth draped body, a little thicker than before. She returned to the bathroom. Memories of their year living together in that cheap flat off Mission Road and Rainbow Boulevard came to him. When they were good, they were very good; when they weren't, they were with someone else. That's how fools in love fall.

She dropped the robe, ignoring his eyes, and stepped into the steamy shower, water already running.

"I'm not asking you to take me back," he told her through the plastic curtain.

"Goddammit!" she screamed. "What the hell's going on, Ronnie? You're acting so goddamn weird, you must be on drugs. You been screwin' some other bitch?"

He ignored her angry remarks, looking away, seeing himself in the foggy mirror, a vague form he was tempted to draw a face on. That only made the guilt worse.

"Tell me," she roared, turning off the shower. She grabbed her towel, began drying herself. "What the hell's gotten into you?"

With the towel wrapped around her slick body, she stepped out of the shower and stood thumping her foot on the bath mat.

It was time to give up his masquerade.

"I was...with someone," he muttered.

"What'd you say?" She tried to find his face as he kept turned away. "I don't believe what I just heard, dammit. Who was it this time? That horny pig in Radiology? The bitch in, what was it?—doesn't matter. Don't you know those women at the K.U. Med Center are the absolute raunchiest—"

He spun around and landed a hard slap on her cheek, knocking her back a few steps. She grabbed the shower curtain with one hand to steady herself, holding her face with the other hand. It was a game they first played when they moved in together during medical school.

"Sorry. That was an accident," he muttered.

"This was no fuckin' accident, asshole!"

Becky caught her breath, holding her cheek. His words filled her with anger and her hands went up to strike him. The towel slid down her body and dropped to the floor as she pounded his chest.

"Stop that," he spoke barely above a whisper.

He took her wrists in his hands, held her away.

"What do you mean by that?" she cried. "Affairs are *not* accidents."

He pushed her away.

"It's like I said. I had a...a fling. Nothing serious. It's done now."

"When? Why? How?"

"She was just someone I met, and...uh—she's nobody. Forget it. But she did make me realize how much I missed you."

"What kind of bullshit is that? You missed me? That's a laugh! What kind of deviant sex did she refuse to do with you that'd make you come crawling back to me?" She picked up the towel, wrapped it around herself again.

"Come on, I'm serious." He had his hands out, begging.

"Who was she?"

"Some girl."

"Some girl. Don't hand me that! What's her name?"

"Missus Edwards."

She stood stiffly, her eyes widened at the sound of that name.

"*Missus*? She's married?"

"That's why I broke it off," he said but a twitch in his voice let her know he was lying.

"You don't even know her name?"

"The wife of my neighbor." He hung his head like a naughty little boy. "She lived across from me. You know, that crappy apartment by Rosedale Park. Behind the barbecue place? You know how she was always teasing me. I told you. You remember, don't you? I had to move out of there quick."

"Had to?"

He stepped toward Becky.

"Oh, I missed you so much, babe, and she was just...there."

She held her hands up. "What, that old married cow?"

He jerked himself away from her.

"How could you? That blonde bubblehead? She's at least ten years older than you."

"She's only five years older," he muttered, turning to the bedroom like it was his place. "This looks nice."

"Come back here," Becky called sweetly, following. She saw how upset he was, decided to take it easy on him. He was a good actor, but maybe he was being sincere this time. "So how did it happen? What were you doing with this Missus Edwards bitch?"

He grabbed her by the arms, tried to push her backwards out of the room but she held her ground.

"Dammit, don't shut me out, Ronnie. You came here to see me today. You must want me. Come on—tell me."

Acting or real? He seemed to be crying.

"Leave me alone."

"Don't, Ronnie. I care about you. I wanna know what happened. How come you had to move, like you said? Tell me. I wanna help. Are you in some kind of trouble?"

It wouldn't be the first time. The antics he pulled in med school. He almost didn't finish. Then his mother getting breast cancer. And his father in that car wreck. It was amazing he was as sane as he appeared.

"Baby...," she cooed, reaching for him.

His muscles felt weak as he threw himself on the bed, rolling onto his back. She sat down beside him, caressed his chest. The rich scent of his cologne was intoxicating.

"How can you leave me out of something like that?" she asked. "You should've come to me, baby. You did the right thing. Don't you believe I want you in my life? We can start over again—really."

He wanted to scream his reply at her, but he didn't want to show his teary face. But she just kept talking.

"Is that why you came back? You didn't come here cuz you love me, did you? You just wanna fuck, don't you? I know what you like. Uh-huh. Your wild party with the old cow crashed big-time, so you came home again, my dear Doctor Priestley—back where you think you can get some decent hard-core sexual favors. Am I right?"

He rolled himself to the side of the bed, swung himself upright, feet on the floor, and grabbed her around the waist. They tumbled to the floor, she on top of him, the towel loose again. He pressed her flushed cheeks tightly between his hand as his mouth swallowed her thin lips. She pushed hard against him.

"I need your father's rifle," he spoke as they parted. "Do you think you can get it?"

"Anything for my lover," she moaned, not really hearing him or caring what he asked for. His skilled fingers kneaded her butt like bread dough, his nails scoring her flesh.

Her hands dug between their bodies, unfastening his pants, ignoring the crumpled medical report that fell from his hip pocket.

"Fuck me—like you fucked—Missus Edwards!"

He released her, pushed her roughly away.

"You're just like *her*! You're all the same, all fuckin' sluts and whores."

Becky sat up. "You're wrong, Ronnie. I want you for who you are: the best fucking Ob/Gyn in Wyandotte County. Johnson County, too! Screw those fuckin' Yuppie doctors. I don't care how many women you have, Ronnie. Do what you want. But keep screwing me good like you always do."

Raising his hand to slap her, his eyes met hers. He curled his fingers tight, making a fist, then punched the carpet. She put her hand on his shoulder.

"Are you gonna help me or not?" he demanded.

"What do you want me to do?"

"Murder."

"What...? *Murder*? What do you mean?"

He couldn't look at her, stared off at the window.

"You want to kill somebody?" she asked, voice hushed. "Who is it?"

He seemed to blow smoke rings at the window, flexing his lips for a minute. "Her old man. He's the only witness. The only one who can identify me. And he *would*, too. How pissed he was when he caught me with his wife! He'd kill me if he had the chance."

"Oh, baby...."

"But it's *me* who has the chance."

"You serious?"

He reached for her and they leaned in, hugged.

"It's him or me."

"I know, I know."

He sat back on his feet, then stood, pulling her up with him. He scooped her up in his arms and flung her onto the bed. Then, seeing his positive HIV results from the public health clinic open on the carpet, he kicked it under the bed and dove on top of her.

Karl felt Althea's presence in the room but did not flinch from his meditation pose. Perhaps he'd finally found that level of calm where he was super-relaxed and super-alert simultaneously, where he could see with his mind, hear with his heart, and be at peace with the universe. If he didn't have a cramp in his leg, he probably would've also jumped for joy at his revelation.

"Are you okay, Karl?" she asked, halting, seeing his consternation with his leg.

"Yes, fine," he grunted after a moment of silence. He reached for his calf. "I think I've finally achieved this *satori* experience you told me about."

Her smile leaned to the right. She chuckled. "Are you sure?"

"Yes," he said in an even tone. "'*Satori* is like...'like the brightest idea you can have, but without the idea.' You told me that. Let me see. '*Satori* is not a product of the intellect. Rather, it involves the wisdom of our whole body and mind as one.' Is that right? Did I say it right? That wisdom is always there and in *satori*, whatever illusions have been covering that wisdom from our direct view, they suddenly fall away."

Her mouth dropped open in awe of her student.

"You told me." Karl didn't move a muscle. "Also you said—or maybe it was some Zen philosopher—'If you look within yourself and find your true face, then the secret is in you.'"

"I never told you that."

"Then maybe I read it in one of your Zen books. You said the moment of *satori* comes to people only after years of work but in a sudden or abrupt way, while engaged in meditation or some routine daily task, and it's triggered by some vivid sight or sound."

"Yes...?"

"It's come to me...during meditation...and it was triggered by the sound of your first step into my room."

He sighed, a long, deep ventilation, his chest heaving as though it had held in his breath for hours.

"Althea, I have the answer."

"To what?"

She helped him up, onto the bed.

"To my question."

"Which question was that, Karl?"

He could only smile, feeling the great burden raised from his back.

"The ol' doc has pointed me in the right direction and I found my own answers, just like the Zen student with the old master. Oh, he doesn't know it. But whatever he did do—I mean, whatever line of reasoning he's taken with me, whatever path of analysis he's used on me—I tripped over the answer I've been seeking."

"And what's that? Wait—first, what's the question?"

"Exactly." He grinned. "First the answer, then the question."

The door opened the instant Karl began to speak. Another nurse peeked inside.

"The Wolf's coming. If she catches you here again...."

Althea sprang for the door.

"Gotta go, Karl. I'll be back, though, to hear about it. Promise."

He didn't hear her last words, enveloped in the amazement of his discovery. Bathed in the sensation, he smiled like he had never smiled before. Just as the Zen philosopher Hui-neng had said, he had looked within himself and he had found his true face. He knew that the secret to his existence lay within him. It was like the famous Arc of the Covenant, he suddenly noticed. Containing the wisdom of the ages, it was forbidden to those who guarded it. Now he'd found the key to his own Arc—rather, he'd learned where the key could be found, and it certainly wasn't inside the walls of the Eastwood Institute for the criminally insane.

Ah, Althea, he sighed. She was a dear girl, but whether or not she had any feelings for him, and whether or not he in his heart actually cared for her, the first order of business was to get out of Eastwood. That was paramount. If she was hurt, emotionally or otherwise, then so be it. No, he couldn't be so callous in his actions. She didn't deserve to be treated that way. She could lose her job. But she was his only way out. He had to find a way to gain his freedom without hurting her.

Raindrops from the dawn-streaked leaves, and he sniffs the fresh, musty scent of morning. Flicking his tail, Roundpaw feels the heaviness of the air, as though the dawn rain could soon fall again. The sky is hazy except for a tear on the horizon where sunlight bathes the distant hills.

He pads down the staircase encircling the tower of the ancient temple, splashing in the puddles formed in depressions on each step. To the front of the temple he goes. There, stretching beyond the flat, stone floor once used for the rituals of Man, the grass is thick, rain-soaked. Low walls of cut stones enclose the yard. Portions have fallen away, piles of crumbled rocks. He rears back and places his forepaws on the top of the wall, seeing the dirt road running parallel, extending into the forest mist in each direction.

A creak echoes through the moss-covered trees, his ears perk.

He waits, listening and sniffling. The nerves in his body tighten. He is ready for action. The call is familiar. The odor is familiar. Man, the putrid beast, is approaching.

Staring down the road from behind the wall, he sees a tall box rolling on two huge wooden disks pulled by two oxen. And there is the man, walking alongside them, flicking his stick at their legs.

How Man loves his sticks!

Roundpaw drops his striped body behind the wall, tucking his tail out of sight. He is not afraid of the man-creature, but he knows if he is seen, it will bark its fear. Other men will come and chase him with their fire sticks. He could easily strike down the man and avoid the whole episode, but that is not necessary. This creature wears the typical white fur and walks on spindly, brown hindlegs.

He is not a hunter.

The swarthy, barefoot woodsman leads his two oxen down the road. They strain beneath their yoke as they pull the heavy cart piled high with teak logs. The two wooden wheels stand as high as the man himself, creaking and swaying with each turn, slipping through the mud of the road. He slaps his long cane pole at the nearest ox.

Passing the entrance to the temple yard where two stone dogs wait, eyeing each other across the gap, they continue on their way, the man, the oxen, and the cart, the striped face unnoticed.

Turning back into the yard, his eyes catch an orange flicker in the shadows of the temple. Yes! An animal.

He steps closer, squinting, trying to pierce the blackness of the temple's entrance. Then, as if an illusion materializing, a furry bundle of tiger cub leaps through the doorway, hopping repeatedly as it chases a darting butterfly.

Roundpaw freezes at the sight of the tiger cub playing in the yard.

Where is the mother?

The cub's attention is easily diverted by the mouse scurrying through the grass. He pounces, misses. The mouse hurries away. The cub pounces again, chasing its toy.

Suddenly, around the back side of the temple, a second cub springs from the shadows. The first cub leaps onto the second, wrestling, snarling, yelping at each other.

Roundpaw is silent, watching. Cubs so young cannot be far from their mother. He sniffs the air. His ears cut through the hush of the forest. He must be careful. He does not wish to fight a tigress distraught over the safety of her cubs.

Enough, he decides. He has searched the area with his eyes, ears, and nose. The cubs can only be trouble for him here at his resting place.

He lets out a roar, enough to be heard only in the yard. The cubs freeze, tripping over themselves as they turn to face him, their eyes wide open, their whiskers shaking.

Expanding his chest and ruffling his white throat fur in mock challenge, he roars. He does not have to snarl a second time before his challenge is met by an adult tigress, bolting through the temple doorway into the yard.

She quickly checks her cubs and spins to face Roundpaw, her teeth barred, returning her own snarl.

He remains silent, maintaining his stance, his eyes squinting fiercely.

She gathers her cubs, nudging them back toward the temple's entrance. Once they are safe inside, she returns to the yard, her attention fully directed at the intruder. She regards him, judges his power, ferocity, and cunning.

He stands stiffly at attention. She is the first female he has encountered since the death of his mate. She and her cubs remind him of his own offspring, now grown.

She snarls. A quieter, softer snarl now, devoid of threatening tone.

Inside, he begins to feel ill as his memories torment him. His muscles twitch, nerves shake. His throat tightens, he cannot utter a sound. She flicks her tail, offers a purr.

"Karl?" Althea gently whispered. She stood beside his bed, dressed in jeans and a light pullover, shaking his shoulder. "Wake up, Karl."

His eyes popped open, feeling the rush of emergency, ready to kill.

"What time is it?"

"It's about two."

"In the morning?"

Althea nodded, shrugged her shoulders, offering an embarrassed grin. "Sorry."

"What's the matter?" he asked with a yawn.

"That bitch is gonna move me to a different wing. Starting Monday."

He yawned again. "Why?"

"She says I can't handle my patients. Says I'm too young and too immature to take care of all the dangerous patients we have here. Dangerous patients...like you."

"Like me? I'm not dangerous."

She sat on the edge of his bed.

"That's what I told her. But she thinks I'm being a smart-ass. She made me cry. That on top of everything else. I'm *so* angry at her."

A moment of silence fell between them and she stared sternly as doubt began to register on her face.

"What's the matter?" he asked, seeing her expression.

She smiled politely. "Karl, you didn't really...you know...."

"No, no, no," he replied, shaking his head.

"I knew you didn't. You wouldn't hurt anybody. I know you pretty well now. I can see your inner self. Your inner beauty, your inner peace, your...."

He placed his hands on her shoulders to shut her up. Enough hocus-pocus, he thought. She leaned toward him, propping herself up with one arm, her heart beating faster as she regarded him.

"No matter what they say." He spoke slowly, as if every word was too important to risk mispronunciation. "You can be sure I'm not crazy. I acted crazy, but it was in a moment of extreme stress. I don't know what you've been told about me, but I'll tell you myself. I never killed anybody in my life, although there's sure a few I'd like to. I was just having a lot of nightmares is all—hell!"

He looked away to gain a moment to calm his aroused nerves. When he returned his gaze to her, she still smiled peacefully.

"Okay, what happened was my wife was screwing with the neighbor, and he got her to think I should be put away. Just because I was having some bad dreams. He told her I was going crazy. That's all there is."

He saw her staring at his stomach, the sheet fallen aside to reveal the scar.

"My belly wound was not a suicide attempt. It was that bastard pulling a knife on me—like it was me doing something wrong trying to defend my wife. Hell, how'd I know they were...together? I thought he was trying to rape her. Turns out it was by mutual consent and all that shit. In my own damn apartment. And he pulls a knife on me! Maybe he didn't know who I was. I mean, who the hell else would have a key to the apartment? Except him, I guess. But then he tells the police I went wild and tried to stab them both. That's what happened."

"I'm sorry, Karl."

"He's some kinda doctor so they believed him. Instant paranoid-schizophrenic diagnosis. And my darling wife of six years lied like she'd been doing it all her life. Took his side. Said I threatened her. She was scared of me."

Althea was holding her breath, feeling the warmth of his hands on her shoulders, hearing the huskiness of his whispered words.

"I believe you, Karl."

At that moment she fell against him, like she had lost her strength, and hugged him. The movement surprised him but he did nothing to discourage her. His arms fell around her slender torso, holding back the urge to pull her tighter.

"I'm sorry," she whispered. "I didn't mean to."

"That's okay," he whispered, knowing in his heart that she was exactly where he wanted her.

Looking over her shoulder into the darkness of the room, he stared at something that did not exist. His eyes saw beyond the walls of the room, to an uncertain future, and fragments of his dreams returned to puzzle him. Her heart beat against his chest.

"I knew you couldn't've done anything," she mumbled, caressing his chest.

He could feel her lithe figure against him and her soft brown hair, tied in a ponytail, tickled his neck.

"I'm glad you're here...anyway," he heard someone whisper in a voice that sounded like his.

77

She raised her head, gazed into his eyes. She felt his breath. Tilting her head, her lips pressed against his. He seemed to jump at first but their mouths settled into a warm, tight, comfortable seal.

It was only a moment. Parting, her lips hovered over his. Her face was different somehow. His heart was pulsing like the rolling thunder of an approaching storm, drowning out whatever she was saying. He decided it must not be important and pulled her into another kiss.

He remembered what the touch of another person was like: the warm, physical sensation of it, the emotional jumbling that raged, the very thought of *touch*—so long denied—

"You know," he began, parting from the kiss and speaking in a rush, "I think I've come to a realization."

Her dreamy eyes fluttered. "Realization?"

"I've realized that I have to get out of this crazy house before I go crazy. It's that simple. I was sane when I got here, but the longer I stay —and the more I try to convince the damn shrink I'm okay—the harder it seems for me to get out."

She did not reply, resting her head on his chest, warm and safe in his embrace, climbing up and lying beside him on the bed.

"They'll never believe I'm sane. I guess their idea of a sane man is an ignorant zombie who sees pink elephants in their black ink blots."

She gave him a hug. "I know, I know."

"It's harder to get out of a mental institution than from a prison. In a prison you know how much time you have and when you serve it, you get to leave. But not here."

He noticed he had been stroking her hair.

"What would you do if—I mean when—you leave?" she asked him, barely a purr.

"I dunno. I've got nothing to go back to. I'd have to do something new. Go somewhere new."

"What if you escaped? ...But they'd only find you and bring you back. Or put you in some worse place—some place where I couldn't see you."

"Not where I'm going."

She lifted herself to meet his eyes. "Where would you go, Karl?"

"I don't know. Somewhere far away, where they could never find me. Maybe deep in a jungle. It'd be so far away...."

He sat up suddenly, knocking her aside. A thought had struck him and he had to be perfectly upright to receive the incoming message. Beside him, Althea righted herself. She kicked off her shoes and drew up her legs.

"But...I'll never be able to escape unless you help me, Althea."

The words echoed in the room, sounding much louder than they actually were. She shushed him, looked around as if searching for spies.

"You're the only one I can trust now."

She sat up beside him, her hand on his belly. "Do you know what would happen to me if I did help you?" She stared intensely at him.

He returned her serious stare and it cut into her. She looked away. They both knew the answer. He shook her shoulders, calling her back, and their eyes met again.

"Dear Althea. I can imagine what would happen to you. So come with me."

"But where? Where can we go? You have nothing—nothing at all. You just said so."

"I have a future. And I have you. Don't I?"

He smiled sincerely.

Her moist eyes rained, her heart rippling. Embracing him as tightly as she could, she kissed him hard, her body burning with desire.

"I—I can't just leave. No matter how much I—I—I love you, Karl."

He wrapped his arms around her as they lay back on the bed. She slipped into the crook of his arm, her head on his shoulder, hand once again on his chest.

"I need you, Althea. I need your help."

He heard soft sobs and gave her a gentle hug.

"Are you with me?"

"I want to help you, but—it's such a *crazy* idea."

"Please, Althea." His hands slid under her blouse. "Please don't say 'crazy.'"

She rolled her blouse up and unhooked her bra.

"I won't, Karl. I swear. I'll never ever say 'crazy' again."

9

ALTHEA FELT SO COMFORTABLE where she lay that she didn't want to awaken. Cradled in secure warmth, she was in her mother's arms. But it was Karl's arms that held her, the sheets wrinkled between them.

She noticed the room growing lighter and her eyes popped open. She was in Karl's room, not her apartment. Cursing, she pulled her hand free and stared at her watch. Her shift was beginning.

Karl stirred as she climbed out of his sleepy embrace. He smiled at her touch. Slipping into her jeans and blouse that had been kicked beneath the bed, she tried to recall what had happened, but it was all a jumble. She hurriedly brushed her hair, rubbed her eyes, kissed him goodbye.

Outside, she could hear nurses talking at their station, preparing for the day. There was no way she could make her shift; her nurse uniform was at home. If she could just slip out without being caught, she would call in sick.

She never meant to stay all night. Thinking of Karl and how Mrs. Wolfe was going to send her away, she had to see him, no matter what time it was. Only a few minutes, then she would go home. What a liar! If she expected to stay the night, she would have brought her uniform. It was all a joke, she cried, trapped.

She listened at the door. When it seemed quiet, she opened it and stepped into the empty corridor. She was lucky. Spying on the nurse station around the corner, two co-workers stood behind the desk with their backs to her. She sprang from her hiding place, slipping across the intersection just as Mrs. Wolfe arrived.

Panting, Althea stood flat against the wall, out of sight.

"Nurse McCartney?"

The words cut her in half.

"Nurse McCartney," Mrs. Wolfe called from the nurses' station. "What *are* you doing?"

Althea stepped into the light, feeling very naked in her jeans and blouse. The nurses were astonished.

She stood paralyzed.

"Why aren't you in uniform?" asked Mrs. Wolfe.

Shrugging her shoulders was her only answer. She felt weak, dizzy. "I don't know."

The meat oozes with blood—fresh blood, from the torn flesh of a recently killed chital doe. He had pounced on the straying animal from the top of the terraced pools, pinning the deer against the rim of the lowest basin as it had lapped at the water.

A quick chomp to the throat—

He munches ravenously, having eaten little in the past several days.

Whenever he gazes across the steaming body, the tigress is watching, waiting at the end of the yard. Her cubs sit to each side of her, their sorrowful eyes showing their hunger. They yelp at their mother but she remains silent.

This new tigress is simply a mother with cubs to feed.

He was the one who caught and killed the chital. It is his right to dine first. If any meat remains for the tigress, it will be because his stomach is full and he cannot eat another bite. He tears off a long strip of flesh from the succulent thigh. The deer is so small that there is not enough for two adults to eat their fill, less a meal for cubs.

They begin to whine and the tigress lowers her head to nuzzle them.

He hears her belly rumble—

He feels the fullness of his belly and he stands, moves slowly away from the chital carcass. He pauses long enough at the edge of the yard to see them go to the deer and eat.

Through the main entrance of the temple he goes, mounts the steps to rest on the cool stone of the upper floor, listening to the tigress and cubs outside.

There, images from his past swirl beneath his eyelids and he welcomes them—for they are full of joy.

When Karl awoke, he still felt her presence, smelled her scent on the sheet. He sat up, scared of his thoughts and of himself. The day formed around him, his mind forcing out the clutter which had accumulated during the night. Daylight brought reality.

But his daylight hours were really the nighttime of his alter ego, the tiger. It was a subtle transformation. Like the infamous character of horror movies, the Wolf Man, he changed into the Tiger Man. A shiver ran down his spine. When he slept, the tiger was active. When he was awake, the tiger slept. It was beginning to make sense to him. He had figured it out all by himself.

Maybe that's what I really am, he thought with fear. Tiger Man. He liked the name. Perhaps, that was what he was: a mutant who nightly transformed into a tiger and stalked the earth. He liked the idea.

Chuckles flowed from him like a babbling brook after he told his psychiatrist.

"Is that so?" Dr. Lyons commented when Karl finally paused from his lengthy elaboration.

"That's all you have to say, doc?"

"You had a nice dream about a nurse, accompanied by a nocturnal emission. That is quite normal."

"It was more than a dream."

"I assure you, Mister Edwards, nurses aren't permitted to sleep with patients. She didn't spend the night with you." Dr. Lyons checked that Karl understood. "No matter how much you may have wished for it."

Althea adjusted the collar of the white uniform for the dozenth time, a spare borrowed from Nurse Mendez. The white stockings were from Nurse Jackson. White shoes from Nurse Smithers, who was heading home from the night shift.

"Nurse McCartney!"

The gravelly voice bounded down the hallway as the Wolf strolled down the corridor as though taking in the morning air, satisfied that all the daisies and jonquils were standing at attention.

"Yes, Missus Wolfe?" Althea mumbled.

Passing before the station, the Wolf wore a grin wider than her sagging jowls.

"How are you feeling now, Nurse McCartney? You don't look like you're feeling very well. Getting enough sleep this week? You look tired. You must be working much too hard, Nurse McCartney. Oh, yes, I know it's your duty—as you say—to make all of our patients feel comfortable, but must you stay all night? No wonder you don't get enough sleep."

"Missus Wolfe, I can explain—"

"Well, that's fine. It so happens I've arranged for you to do just that. You can explain everything—like how you ever got to be a nurse in the first place. You can explain it all to Doctor Baldwin."

"But why?" Althea exclaimed.

"Why?" The Wolf feigned laughter. "You don't know? I'm sure you can figure it out, *Nurse* McCartney. Hah, hah—I'm sorry. It's just that the word 'nurse' with your name attached makes me laugh." She broke into a forced laughter. "I think I'll call you *Miss* McCartney from now on."

Althea sniffled. "What did you tell Doctor Baldwin?"

"I told him exactly the facts—no more, no less—as observed by myself and others on the staff. It may come as a surprise to you, but your professionalism is, I'm sorry to say, *Miss* McCartney, sorely lacking."

That was what she expected to hear but the actual words hurt much worse, and her hastily planned rebuttal had flittered away.

"I've arranged for you to see Doctor Baldwin," the Wolf continued, intensifying her voice, "so you can plead your case to him. He already has my report. Too bad it's not up to me, or you'd be out months ago. I know I shouldn't have been so kind, but—well, I suppose I do have a soft spot somewhere."

"In your head," Althea mumbled.

"That's it!" the Wolf exploded, then caught herself, not wanting to lose control in front of others. She flicked on a big smile. "No need to trade insults. By the way, I forgot to tell you yesterday, but your meeting is—I'm *really* sorry—but you now have only five minutes to pull yourself together. You don't have much time, so wipe away those sad, little tears."

The last incantation was successful. The floodgates opened, spilling streams down Althea's cheeks.

Mrs. Wolfe grinned. "Here, have a tissue."

The night is moonless, filled with the noisy silences of chirps, cackles, squeals, buzzing, and humming of the forest creatures. An occasional growl also breaks the quiet. It is a peaceful night, embraced by the summer's humid heat. The temple is still, the grass in its yard wet and cool.

Roundpaw pads along the familiar trail, a weary pace. As he approaches the yard, the tigress is waiting for him, alone.

She offers him a small chevrotain killed earlier. His belly aches of hunger but he ignores its haunting call. Instead, he drops to the ground before her, his eyes burning with hate, lit with internal fire. She is startled.

He lowers his death gaze. In the jungle darkness he has seen his future as surely as if it were shown to him in the blinding afternoon sun. There is but one path for him. His only choice is to go down that path, or not go on it at all. Yet, if he goes, there is only the one path available.

The tigress snarls politely, flicks her tail over her back.

The days at the end of the dry season, he tells her through his snarls and barks, churls and purrs, were the last he was at peace. He died long ago, when he stared defiantly into the crosshairs of the red-furred men's fire stick. The upright beast did not spew hot stones at him, but his spirit died on that day.

Behind him he felt, heard the agony of his dying mate, destroyed by the red-furred men. They did not eat her to survive, nor did they steal her coat as do the poachers. No, they just killed her, with no thought—

For their amusement. For their entertainment.

The tigress narrows her eyes.

He has pursued the red-furred creatures through the monsoons, across great blistering plains, through forest-covered hills, skirting man nests and crossing man paths. His is a journey that will end in death. The terminus of his trek, his life, the petty life of the red-furred one, and of the legend itself—will all be at once, on a special, distant day. Then, all will be branded into the landscape, seared into the airways above, sung by the birds, chattered by the monkeys, roared by the cats.

He is the martyr. He is the chosen one—chosen by Man. He is their savior. This realization has come to him during his midnight stroll, but he has pondered the idea since his arrival at the temple. It has been a time when his mind has begun to increase in acuity, assimilating more easily with the human mind lurking deep within.

The tigress rises, checking on her two sleeping cubs, but Roundpaw calls her back with a snort. He growls angrily and she returns to the soft, moist grass. The tigress regards him, licking her canines.

He has found and killed one of the red-furred creatures.

In the fashion of men, he has killed. Without provocation, without need, without warning, without enjoyment.

But it is done. Great herds of men have followed him, desiring to kill him in return. They have forced him to hide in this deepest and darkest part of the forest.

When he senses they have forgotten him, he will once again spray his scent, sharpen his claws, focus his golden eyes on the blood-red sun, and hurry away. Always in the direction of the setting sun, always along his path—the endless, interminable path. The path of destruction.

Roundpaw sniffs the chevrotain, tugs at its fur with his incisors.

Its odor is delicious, still warm in the humid night air. As he eats, the cubs awaken and cry out for their mother.

He chews quickly, crushing bones too small to separate from the flesh, and wonders why he has told this strange tigress of his mate's murder.

Does he want her to accompany him?

No, he reminds himself, tigers do not accompany tigers—that is a man-creature's habit. Curse them! Now they pry into his brain.

One day, he will meet them and they will know him. He will know them, too, and he will pause only long enough for them to realize who he is. He is the avenging devil—the shaitan—from the Bengal plains come to kill them.

Then he will.

The door burst open, startling the secretaries in the outer office.

"Please don't patronize me, Doctor Baldwin," Althea shouted as she stormed out of the director's office. "At *least* don't do that! I don't need your stupid letter of recommendation. I won't let you trade me like—like some baseball player. If I'm not good enough, then just fire me. That's all you have to do."

Dr. Baldwin offered a tired sigh. "Miss McCartney, I don't *want* to fire you."

"Is it too hard for you? Is that it? Then let me help you out, doc. I quit. There—that relieves you of responsibility."

"Miss McCartney, I'm sure you don't mean that. Think of your career. You don't want to throw it away like that. You have a quiet and gentle nature. There's a place for that. Please give Children's Mercy Hospital a try. I've already arranged for you to interview there. We'll consider bringing you back later. Maybe you'll prefer it there. Who knows?"

She halted, turned to him, painting a devilish grimace on her face. "You may consider this my two-week notice."

"Listen here," he barked, "I'm *trying* to be nice. I don't have to arrange another job for you. I don't have to give a recommendation. But if you want to be stupid and ungrateful, go right ahead. We don't need you here."

He threw the door shut behind her.

As she walked determinedly down the hall, her mask melted. Tears coursed down her face even as she tried to sniffle them back, wiped them away, heading for her station to gather her belongings and change back to her civilian clothes. She would have to suffer the smirking face of the Wolf, but she was ready.

With long, confident strides, she approached the desk, her aura spilling ahead of her. Mrs. Wolfe looked up as Althea bore down like a torpedo. She came to an abrupt halt and despite a flushed, tear-streaked face, she held her head high and stared down at Mrs. Wolfe, whose satisfied grin vanished.

Althea spoke directly to her ugly face: "Bitch."

"What was that?" the Wolfe growled, shocked.

"I said B-I-T-C-H: bitch."
"Let me tell you one thing—"
"Save your breath."
Before the Wolf could reply, Althea had stalked away.

Roundpaw hears the sounds, perks his white-tufted ears—

CLICK CLICK

In the silence of the afternoon forest, all fauna watch the intruders. His ears capture the dry snap of twigs beneath their paws, the slap of leathery bushes swinging against their loins, loud jingling of metal disks in the folds of their smooth, forest-hued fur. Mostly, it is their peculiar odor which calls his nerves to alertness. The acrid, musky scent can only be that of Man, no matter which flower essences he bathes in to hide from the creatures of the forest.

There are two upright beasts, one with short head fur of brown, the other with longer, straw-yellow fur cascading down its back. Both have hindlegs naked below the knees, and smooth, olive green fur above where dark semicircles form beneath their forelegs, marking their musk glands. They are adults, though the tan fur on the short-haired one's face makes identification difficult.

They carry small black boxes dangling on flat vines around their necks as they walk. With measured steps, they halt along the trail, raising the boxes to their faces with their forepaws. Always the click click. Perhaps they are eating. The beasts point off the trail in both directions, apparently at various species of birds, purring in a casual manner.

They are not hunters; they carry no sticks.

Roundpaw listens to them as they approach the ancient Hindu temple. Hiding in the brush opposite it, he watches the man-creatures, looking for any aggression. Behind him, the slope falls sharply into another ravine, clogged with brush.

They will soon see the temple and, as such creatures invariably do, they will follow their curiosity and explore it. The jumbled ravine behind him is his only route of escape.

Roundpaw sniffs the air for the tigress and her cubs. He grimaces,
widening his grin, exposing his mouth to the scents on the breeze.
They are hiding behind the temple, the same thick brush he traversed
coming up the slope alongside the terraced pools.
That is their escape route, if the man-creatures should stay at the temple.
The cubs are with her. Should the tigress be forced to defend her cubs
against the human beasts, he realizes, the encounter would certainly
bring another herd of hunting men into the forest to pursue them and
kill them. It is better they pass without incident.

CLICK CLICK

Roundpaw wants to be certain of the silence of the cubs.
The male beast purrs to the female, followed by directing her vision to an
overhanging branch of a nearby saja tree.
Her head wavers and she bares her teeth. They step to the base of the
gray-barked tree, pushing down protecting bushes. A mongoose darts
away between their hindpaws and the female grins. The male swings
his black box over his shoulder and extends his forelegs overhead,
reaching for the lowest branch.
With a small leap, he catches hold of the branch, tries to pull himself up
and onto it. Finally he succeeds and rests atop the sturdy branch, his
hindlegs dangling over either side, in the manner the leopard hangs its
prey.
Roundpaw watches them, deciding whether to offer a roar of warning.
Usually the sound of his voice alone would send the man-creatures
fleeing. This time, though, he does not wish for any human to know
he is present in the forest.
A macaque high on the branch of another tree begins to chatter,
identifying the large beast mounting the neighboring tree.
The male poised on the saja branch points at the monkey, raises his black
box to his face, showing it to the forest.

CLICK CLICK

Roundpaw decides they can spot the temple from their vantage point.
He hears the rattle of bushes pushed down, a great weight moving
through the wood. His nerves switch. He sniffs the breeze. It is the

tigress, moving steadily but not stealthily toward the human beasts.

Then he sees what has happened, sorting the images through the tight-knit brush separating him from the trail. One of the cubs has wandered away from the temple yard, found the trail to the man-creatures.

The female man barks—

"Oh, look, George. Isn't he so darling?"

"Quick, climb up here!"

"What's the matter? It's just a little cub."

"Get up here," the male growls. "His mother's got to be close by. Here, take my hand. Quickly!"

He leans down, lowering his foreleg to her.

She takes his paw and braces her hindlegs against the trunk of the tree, struggling to scale it.

The great chattering of the monkey troop, scattered over several trees.

The bushes fall away and the tigress emerges.

With a glance to either direction, she cannot find her wayward cub. Instead, she finds the dangling leg of the female man as she tries to pull herself up onto the branch. Man has always been the criminal in the forest. No judge is needed.

The tigress lunges at the drooping hindleg, her claws sinking deep into the human's calf. With a sharp tug, she wrests her from the male's grip.

"Christ!" she roars. Off balance, the male tumbles from his perch and crashes to the ground beside her as the tigress drags her from the brush onto the dirt trail.

The female human scrambles to her feet, tries to run, with her left leg in shreds she cannot move far, overtaken by the tigress, nips at the wounded hindleg.

After several paces, the tigress secures a tight grip on the hindleg and wrenches the limb off the ground, raising her large, striped head, and drags the roaring, clawing female man down the trail.

In desperation, she grabs at anything—a fallen vine, a tree stump, a rock, anything—to delay the tigress carrying her away.

The tigress bites harder, giving the bloody limb a hard jerk which strips

flesh from bone, separating the screaming man-creature from the
dripping mouth of the tigress.

Spread out in the trail's dirt, the upright beast roars.

The male human scrambles to his feet, holding his injured foreleg. His
box lies in the dirt where he landed beside it. He calls after his mate,
then stumbles out of the brush onto the trail.

He finds a tree branch the length of himself and the thickness of his wrist.

"My God, George! Help me!"

She has left a scratch down the center of the trail, parting the dried
leaves, painting them with the red of her hindleg. Far down the trail
now, they approach Roundpaw's hiding place.

The male human hobbles hurriedly to where the female lies, dragging his
stick with him, limping on an injured foot, roaring for his mate.

Roundpaw feels for him what he has heard named in his dreams as
sympathy. Although he has sworn anonymity, perhaps it is time to
act. These man-creatures were not hunting.

The male human raises the stick, wielding it like the native men
creatures, holding it in his forepaws before him.

Roundpaw springs from his thicket, padding onto the trail. He sees the
male human scurrying before him. He sees the tigress far ahead of the
man-creature, licking at the bleeding body of the downed female
human as she attempts to crawl away.

He sees the prone female, arms flailing wildly, beating at the face of the
tigress. He sees the cub playing unconcerned alongside the trail
where her brother has joined her to chase a butterfly.

The roars of the female man rip through his ears, reminding him of the
agony of his mate while she was tortured by the red-furred man-
creatures.

Roundpaw bounds down the trail, rushing past the male human, thrown
to the dirt by the sweep of his passing. Racing along the path, he
reaches the tigress and her victim.

"My God—no! Please, God, no!" the Man roars from behind, the sight of
two tigers hovering over his wounded mate shattering his heart.

Roundpaw roars at the tigress. His rough growls alarm her. This is not
the way tigers behave, she snarls. Yet she obeys and leaves the

bleeding female man. She offers the chunk of flesh torn from the hindleg, but he refuses it. The taste of man is too bitter.

Seeing she has been freed, the female man crawls away on her belly with what strength remains, rolling off the trail into a thicket. Her hindleg continues to pour forth her essence, staining her fading world a dark crimson.

Roundpaw nips at the whiskers of the tigress, urging her to return with him, telling her of her cub's safety.

With an angry sneer, she complies, turning with him toward the temple.

They pass the male human, armed with the stick, eyes white, his scent marking his fear.

10

SITTING CROSS-LEGGED ON THE FLOOR, her torn purple leotards stretched tightly over her knees, Althea held her bamboo flute up to her lips and blew long melancholy tones. The song was hers and reflected her heart, filled with decaying notes in the minor keys. The notes filled the room the same way the scent of formaldehyde permeated a morgue.

Now the bland afternoon had become the violet haze of her dreams.

She spun on the floor, fixing her eyes on the red LED numbers on her clock. Seven p.m. exactly, and the noise outside was deafening when the cicada suddenly ceased their din. She felt an ominous tugging at her heart as dark thoughts grew in her mind. She cursed through the angry notes of her flute: She was an only-child and an orphan, single and alone, out of a job, out of luck. She felt more alone in the world than she had ever felt before. If she were to disappear overnight, no one would notice. That thought hurt most of all.

She lowered the flute to her lap, choked up.

That was the reason she had to do it. There were times in a person's life, she told herself, when risks were not only approved but required. And it was not only to get back at Eastwood, she tried to convince herself. It was not to get even with the Wolf, either. There was more to it. A lot more. To prove she existed, she had to shake up her life. Every thought forced her to stare straight into the blinding fire of Fate. She had no choice but to follow the light. It was the path. It was the way.

She grabbed her journal and scrawled the poem that had rushed into her head. About the Light, the Path, the Way. It was also a poem about Sorrow. Only sorrow was real, she decided. All other emotions were only degrees of sorrow: happiness merely its mildest form. Whenever she might think beautiful thoughts, the hideous shadow of sorrow always colored her perception. Beauty never lasted, and that was why she would show her poem only to Karl, if she ever had the chance—before its beauty died. He would understand.

She stood and stripped off her moist leotards, done with yoga for the day, tossing them to her overflowing laundry basket. She felt the gloom start to lift from her body and mind.

Freshly showered, she returned to her futon where she stretched out and meditated. Later, her alarm clock broke the silence. She switched it off, knowing the moment had come. She dressed quickly, grabbed the grocery sack beside the door and left for Eastwood.

Two black-clothed figures ducked and darted among the branches and shadows, pursued by the glowing moon. Reaching the safety of the grove overlooking the Eastwood Institute, they pulled off their ski masks. Dropping to the ground, their knees bent, feet planted firmly against the earth, they readied themselves. Becky removed the binoculars from her knapsack. Ron unzipped the soft-leather rifle case.

A dog began barking from the used car lot next door to them and they froze momentarily in the shadows.

Ron tore open the box of bullets.

"Careful," his accomplice whispered.

Shells spilled through his fingers, hit the ground.

"Quiet."

Becky stood, stepping down the slope to the edge of the shadows. She put the binoculars to her eyes, scanning the rows of windows along the wing of the hospital. She didn't know which window belonged to her lover's demented adversary. She searched for a window from which any of Eastwood's guests might happen to gaze out.

"Ready," Ron called in a hushed voice.

He turned on his heels in the squatting position and Becky's eyes met his as the dog, satisfied, fell silent. She went to his side, leaned down and pressed her lips to his head. Wrapping her arm around him, he stood.

"Tonight is our night," he whispered, holding her in a one-armed hug, grasping the rifle with his other hand. "Tonight, we shall rid the world of another lecherous criminal. Once his twisted lies are told, they will certainly put me in prison. That would end my medical career and my service to mankind. I know you understand, Rebecca—that's why you're here. We must remove him, the only witness to what happened. And in this sacred sacrifice, we will consummate our new life together."

"You're so fucking romantic, Ronnie," she cooed.

He pressed roughly against her, pinched her face in his free hand and kissed her hard on the lips.

"I love you," she muttered through the kiss.

"I'm glad." He took a glance at the moonlit walls of the building. "I never want you to leave me."

A grin played on his face, striped by shadows, his eyes glowing with a blinding, internal fire which Becky had never seen before. The time was near; his aura was chilling rapidly.

"He always stares out the window before he turns the lights out. Or *they* turn them out, whatever."

Handing the rifle to her, he moved to the spot he had chosen, lowering himself into the depression shielded by the bushes. He extended his legs, knees bent, planting his heels. Like he had practiced out at Lake Jacomo. Once comfortable, he signaled for the instrument of sacrifice.

Becky lowered the rifle into his waiting arms.

His hands cradled the stock gently, settling it into position. He pressed the rifle butt to his shoulder, braced his elbows on the meaty portions of his thighs. Satisfied, he scanned his target over the top of the barrel, then slid his cheek against the stock, his eye falling into alignment with the scope. The crosshairs dissected the window, almost matching the metal bars.

The curtains danced with the tepid breeze. Every few sways they would be sucked through the open window, waving at the warm night. Beyond them, he swore he could see movement in the room, but with the curtains in motion, he wasn't certain. It did not matter; he knew his target's habits. Any minute now.

Ron rolled his hand around the stock, dropped his finger to the trigger.

Closing the door behind her, Althea saw the moonlight streaming through the curtains, felt the tepid breeze.

She noticed she was shaking as she extended her hand.

"Karl...?"

Her voice sounded so loud she cringed.

"Karl, wake up."

He stirred, tugging at the sheet. She shook his shoulder harder and he rolled onto his back with a loud sigh.

Bending over him, she planted her lips on his. His eyes opened suddenly and she jumped back. For a few seconds he thought he had died and gone to heaven. In the misty haze of the curtain-dimmed moonlight, Althea appeared as either a ghost or an angel in her white nurse uniform. From her white shoes, up her white legs and her white dress, to her pale face and nurse cap, she was a vision of Nirvana. The flapping curtains added to the illusion, attaching angelic wings to her pristine figure.

"Althea...?"

She tried to speak, lost her voice, and simply nodded.

"What's the matter?" he whispered.

She held her head high, swallowed hard, trying to form the words. But she couldn't, no matter how hard she tried. The paper sack she carried crinkled in her hands.

"What's that?" Karl asked, pointing.

She glanced at it, remembering. "Here—take it."

"What is it?"

"Take them. You'll need them."

He sat up, took the sack from her. He stared inside. "Clothes?"

She pursed her lips, narrowed her eyes.

"What's going on?" he demanded.

She frowned. "You can't escape in hospital pajamas, can you?"

"We're...escaping? *Tonight*?"

She looked quickly back at the door. "We have to hurry, Karl."

"Damn, I was starting to make some real progress."

Althea waited by the door, surveilling the corridor.

"Sorry about the fit," she said when Karl appeared, dressed in the plaid golf slacks and polo shirt, one size too small. "They belonged to my dead fiancé. He got shot at his bachelor party."

"Not by you, I hope," said Karl.

"No, the other woman."

She took his hand, leading him down the corridor.

Ron saw a flash of light in the room centered in the scope. He hesitated, raised his cheek from the stock.

"Check the window again," he instructed Becky.

"What's wrong?"

"I think he got up and left. I saw the door open. Probably went to the john."

Becky knelt beside him, monitoring the window with her binoculars.

"Dammit, what's taking him so long?"

"Shush!"

"What time is it, anyway?"

Becky lowered the binoculars, glanced at her watch. "Ten minutes later than the last time you asked."

He fell back from his seat, earth moist against his black T-shirt.

"He must've come back into the room," Ron suggested, sitting up once more. "Just a flash of light when he left, so maybe he returned when you blinked."

"I did not blink," Becky insisted.

"He has to be back in the room by now," he mumbled. "When is he going to stand by the window to reflect on the misery he's brought to the world?"

She checked the windows again. "You sure?"

"It's been long enough."

Becky stared at the dark window as Ron raised the rifle and lay it into his left hand, curling his right hand around the stock. Lowering his eye to the scope, he aligned the crosshairs.

"Yes...yes...he's there," he remarked, squinting one eye. "I can see something there."

"It looks the same to me," Becky said, lowering the binoculars.

"No, he's there."

"Then it's finally time, my dear."

"Yes," he spoke softly.

His concentration was at its most acute, steady to the point of shaking. He took a deep breath, held it, released half of it, and let his finger pull back the trigger.

Hand in hand Karl and Althea hurried through the double doors, into the humid night. Their shoes clattered across the asphalt pavement as they reached her red Mustang. Althea quickly unlocked the doors.

"Give me the keys," he insisted.

"Why?"

"Just give'em to me."

"But—"

"Come on," he demanded, and grabbed her wrist. The keys dropped out of her hand. He bent down and scooped them up, turning to the driver's side.

"Karl, what are you doing?"

He climbed into the driver's seat, motioning for her to get in the passenger seat.

"Dammit, Karl, it's my car."

He turned the ignition and the engine purred. She jumped in.

"Answer me," she exclaimed.

He shifted into reverse, and spun the car around in the parking lot, heading it down the long Eastwood driveway to the street.

"I'm sorry, Althea," he said as he maneuvered the car.

"What...?" She couldn't speak, shocked by her plan backfiring. Her throat clenched, tears welling up in the corners of her eyes.

"Stop that," he snapped, easing the car down the drive, slowing as it neared the exit. "There's no need to cry. You did good."

As he paused to check the traffic, from out of nowhere there came an explosion. It sounded like a tire popping, but in the milliseconds that followed, he realized what it was: a shot from a gun. It echoed across the grounds of the Eastwood Institute, followed almost simultaneously by the frenzy of shattering glass.

He glanced at Althea, then threw his head forward against the steering wheel.

"Karl!" screamed Althea, leaning over, checking.

He grabbed her shirt collar, jerked her head below the dashboard. Twisting his head where he lay, he glared out her window up the hillside to the moonlit wing where the window of his room was shattered by rifle shots. In the other windows of the wing, lights were flicking on like a telephone switchboard. He could not tell clearly from which direction the shots were coming, but it was over in a few heartbeats.

"You saved my life." He watched the building, dotted with lights.

"What'd you say?"

She didn't know what was happening but she was frightened. Her hand searched for his leg, clenching his knee as she tucked her head against his thigh, not daring to look up.

"Keep your head down. We're getting out of here!"

She turned, rolling her back against the seat.

He hit the gas and the car lurched into the street.

"What's going on?" she asked again.

"Not now. I don't have time to explain."

He hadn't gone a couple blocks when his headlights splashed across two running figures clothed in black. His instinct was to hit the brakes, but he let the car coast until he was close enough to see who they were.

Althea raised her head cautiously. She glanced out the front window and saw only the road ahead of them.

"Is it okay now?" She swung herself up.

"I don't know."

He squinted his eyes, focusing on the figures.

They paused in the road, like burglars caught in the act, frozen in the spotlight. Their eyes seemed to glow in the dark like cats. Dressed in black with ski masks concealing their identity, Karl was more curious than cautious. One of them carried a long, leather bag the size and shape of a rifle. The other dragged a small knapsack. He saw tufts of blonde hair protruding from the back of the ski mask and noticed the figure had feminine curves as she hopped over the guardrail on the opposite side of the road and headed into the brush.

The other figure was rigid by the side of the road, staring back.

Transfixed by his curiosity, not realizing the car was still in motion, Karl broke from his trance and slammed on the brake.

The car screeched against the pavement, weaving, as the tires grabbed the asphalt. The headlight beams danced across the road, crisscrossing the fleeing figures. Finally, they came to a halt almost sideways in the street, the engine stalled, lights pointing off the road in the same direction the first figure had fled.

Karl lifted his head through the open window to get a better look.

"What the hell're you doing standing in the middle of the road? And wearing black so nobody can see you, huh?"

Through the narrow slits of his mask, Ron's eyes bulged as though they had seen too much and could not contain it all. Was the light playing tricks?

Becky called from half-way up the slope, but he ignored her.

He ripped off his ski mask to have a clearer look.

Karl's eyes widened as he bumped his head against the window.

"What the hell...?"

Ron could not believe what he saw and uttered a curse.

Karl recognized the face staring back at him. Even in the darkness, he knew it was that bastard he had fought in his apartment, who had stabbed him, who had raped his wife. He would never forget that face.

What the hell was he doing here? He couldn't figure out why, but who else would be firing into his hospital room in the middle of the night? The same bastard that put him there. And if this was the same bastard, then was the blonde woman accompanying him...his wife?

"Leona?" he called out. The woman didn't answer.

His attention returned to the bastard. For several heartbeats they regarded each other, marking in their minds every wrinkle and pore, studying each other like lovers or painters, eyes locked in a visual wrestling match.

In a flash the doctor had the leather case off his shoulder, zipper torn open, reaching for the rifle inside.

Karl grabbed at the key in the ignition, not taking his eyes off his opponent.

"He's got a gun!" Althea cried.

"Yeah, I know."

Ron had the rifle in his hands, dropping the case, fumbling in his pocket for a cartridge.

"Let's get out of here!" screamed Althea.

Karl turned the key and slammed on the gas pedal. The engine choked, then rumbled to life.

Ron stood beside the guardrail. He steadied his aim as Becky came back to the roadside.

Karl jerked the gear shift into reverse and hit the gas. The car lurched, shot straight back a hundred yards before it cut a wide arc and the rear bumper smashed against the guardrail there.

He glanced back over his shoulder out the rear window.

"Let's get out of here," Althea shouted.

Karl revved the engine, tried to pull the stick out of reverse and put it in first.

Ron shoved the cartridge into the chamber, fifty yards up the street, raising the butt to his shoulder. He stared down the length of the barrel.

"He's gonna shoot!"

Karl didn't need Althea's warning. He took the stick and rammed it into fourth gear, held the clutch down and gunned the engine. His other hand slipped the steering wheel into a new alignment which would propel the car straight into the bastard. The engine roared, the tires spun and smoked.

He popped the clutch and the Mustang shot ahead, narrowing the short distance instantly. Althea threw her arms against the dashboard and screamed.

Ron held the rifle still, careful of his breathing, aiming over the top of the scope as he squeezed the trigger.

The first shot flew over the roof of the car, scratching off a strip of vinyl. The second pierced the windshield in the uppermost corner of the driver's side, barely missing its target. If he'd had time for a third shot, it likely would have hit the mark. Instead, the shooter had to dive over the guardrail as the chrome bumper hit, scraping a ten foot line down the side where he had been standing.

Ron jumped up, immediately reloading as the Mustang continued on, veering away and roaring down the street. He set the sights between the two red tail lights as they raced away. He squeezed the trigger. His breathing was heavy and his aim was off.

Again he loaded, but by the time he could raise the barrel and lock the sights on the red lights, they had faded. Left standing in the middle of the road, surrounded by the din of crickets, his heart pounded in his chest, his head swimming.

Becky went to him but was afraid to touch him. She pulled off her mask and ran her fingers through her hair.

"Was that...?"

Ron nodded solemnly.

11

TASHI VILLAGE, MADHYA PRADESH, CENTRAL INDIA

THE POTTED PALM WAVED in the rare August breeze, stirring the heavy air over the veranda.

Doctor Hansen, British expatriate and village physician, stepped through the doors of his bungalow to greet his old friend and nemesis, Ian McDonnell. They shook hands, clapped shoulders as the houseboy brought iced tea.

The doctor told at length about the two photographers, and the injuries they suffered from their unexpected encounter with a tiger.

"Nae tigers in these parts," Ian grumbled.

"Seems one has moved in," said the doctor.

Ian tugged at his gray handlebar mustache, released a long sigh, listening to Dr. Hansen's explanation. He crossed his khaki-clad legs, shook some red dust from his old army boots. With a high, bald forehead and brilliant white hair where there was any, he felt the heat of the afternoon sun after removing his pith helmet.

"They was lookin fer it, if yew ask me, nosin round th' woods th' way all them damn photeegraphers do. I says they got wha' they was due. Damn tourists. Wi' their damn camera, an' their damn carefree attitude, waltzin' Matilda doon a wooded lane, eh? Aye, they got wha' was comin' to 'em, they did."

The doctor could not hold back a grin.

"Agreed. We've no tigers in our forest," said Hansen, pointing across the lawn to the edge of the woods.

"'Lessen yew count tha' ol' tigress been layin up a-there since last May. She probably th' one tha' got 'em," Ian responded.

"Oh, that one's harmless enough. She's old—but in good health."

"Tha'll do it. Them man-eaters we've dealt with in th' past was old—if they weren't injured besides. Maybe we'd better give a good look up there."

Hansen smiled, handing an assortment of legal papers to the old soldier with the offering of an equally ancient fountain pen.

"Then you can go ahead and sign these forms."

"Ain't a-signin' no damn forms jus' cuz some damn tourists get bit by tha' ol' tigress. T'ain't my doin'. I'll take a look, but I ainna signin' one damn thing."

The doctor sat up, frustrated. "There you go again. Dammit, Ian. You have to sign these forms. It's the law. Every tiger attack or killing's got to be reported and as you're the only bloody hunter we've got—no matter how damn stubborn you are—you have to sign them so I can send them off. Now sign the bloody forms."

Ian tugged again at his mustache, a warning tightness in his gut. Taking the forms in his hand, he held them at arm's length, squinting his eyes.

"They dinna make nae sense, anyways."

"Your spectacles, Ian. Put on your spectacles. Christ, if I'd been a tiger, you'd be dead or dying now. I've been looking after you ever since I came here."

"And 'tis 'preciated," Ian nodded, carefully unfolding the bifocals retrieved from his shirt pocket. "And 'tis nae only tha', me bonny lad. Yew an' me bein' th' only whites in th' village, we've got tae be friends. 'Course, we'd be natural enemies if we bein' back home, me on me beautiful Loch Abey, you 'way in yer dirty, rat infested London—"

"Easy, Ian, easy," the doctor cautioned.

"Nae like th' old days, eh?" He began reading over the forms. "Then we had kings an' viceroys tae take huntin. Them's th' good days, eh, doc? Nae now, when we've got them prissy tourists, them bloody picture-takers. Lord, yew canna walk on a photeegraph, nae wear one, fer Christ's sake. Wha's th' point tae it, I ask yew?"

"Sign the bottom line while you can still see it. Then get your gun."

The watery blue ink blotted the page but Ian blew a whiskey-tainted breath to dry it. He sat back with a loud, tired sigh, tossing the pen atop the papers.

"There. I hopes yew be satisfied now."

"Not quite, Ian. You've still got to go up to the ruins, check that old tigress."

"Canna yew jus' turn in th' papers like I did't? We both know we ainna got nae tiger up here. Damn tourists probably saw a panther er some wild dog."

Hansen scooted his chair closer, glancing around the veranda to make sure his assistants were out of earshot.

"Actually, the girl looks quite bad."

"Eh, really. How so?"

"I've pieced her leg together as best I could, but.... It'll probably heal, unless it turns septic. In that event, I'd have to take it off. But even at the best, she'll be a cripple. There's no muscle left on her leg below the knee, and too much damage the remainder. She'll be dragging it around wherever she goes. That I'd swear to."

"Indeed," Ian contemplated, uncrossing his legs.

"And there's another matter, also."

"Eh? An' wha's tha'?"

"The teeth marks.... Definitely a tiger. If that's your tigress, Ian, then she put some deep marks along the girl's shinbone. I've seen tiger bites before, but these frightened me. Could be our gal's not as agèd as we give her credit. The man said they saw a cub just before the attack."

"Our lassie?" Ian shook his head. "Why, tha' sly gal."

"'Twould seem so. But that's no reason to hunt her down. I would call it self-defense, if I were asked."

Ian smirked. "Yew mean tae tell me, she got cubs now? Tha' lassie!"

Hansen signaled to the boy, hiding in the shadows of the eaves, to refill their iced tea.

"Perhaps you should take someone with you. Or a few men, in fact. I dare say, if she's likely to be spooked, wouldn't want anything to happen to you. You're an old man now, Ian, and you're not as limber as you were when you were chasing after tigers with Colonel Corbett."

"Aye, them's th' fairest days I e'er had."

"Yes, indeed."

They both paused, pleasant thoughts in their heads, sipping the freshly poured tea.

"There is one more item, though it's probably only the man's outrageous ramblings. He swears he saw *two* tigers. Two *adult* tigers, that is. Seems rare this time of year."

"Aye."

"Could be the poor cub's father."

"Tha's certainly an earful!"

"Thought I'd mention it. In case you need the information."

Ian laughed, slapped his hand on the table. "Two adults, yew say?"

"Yes, two. But then, the man was raving."

"Aye, raving. Double-vision, eh! And yew must take me fer a fool tae go after *two* adults—lordie!"

"Nothing to worry about. Take some men with you, if you wish."

"Think yew kin get me tha' broon farmer fella tha' hunted wi' me last time we went tae tha' temple? When we was clearin' oot the wild dogs? Wha's his name? Jon, I'm thinkin 'twas. He's a good aide. Aye, need *someone* tae carry me gun these days. I'm gettin tae be old now, like yew said."

The doctor stood, set down his drink, and extended his hand to his friend, who shook it.

"I'll hold back the report until you've had a chance to see how our gal is getting on. And you take no chances up there, do you hear me? I don't want to have to piece *you* back together again."

Ian waved him off.

"Don' yew worry, doc. Tha' ol' lassie an' me's great friends. Why, if I be a tiger meself, we'd surely be mates!"

The red tail lights of Althea's Mustang split the graying countryside.

"What happened back there?" she asked, breaking the silence. She had dared not utter a single word since the rearview mirror was shattered. It had taken most of that time for her breathing and heartbeat to return to normal.

"You saw what happened." Karl's mind needed to focus elsewhere, not answering silly questions. He was working on his timetable.

"Are you an agent or something?" She stared at him. "I mean like the CIA, or the FBI—or IRS—maybe it's the AMA...?"

He let loose a chuckle.

"I'm just an ordinary citizen, Althea. And that other ordinary citizen back there was trying to kill me. The same one fucking my wife. The same one who helped her put me in Eastwood. Now he's trying to kill me. I don't know why, but a rough guess is he's afraid the shrinks will believe what I say after a while. At least, *he* thinks they will. The shrinks at Eastwood think I'm paranoid. I prefer to call it cautious. Now that you've seen him in action, what do *you* think?"

Behind them the sun was painting the dawn sky.

"Where are you taking me?" she asked, just above a whisper, her voice not hiding her fear very well.

"I'm not taking you anywhere. I'm going where *I* need to go. You're just along for the ride."

"Karl...?" she spoke meekly.

"What?"

"Are you kidnapping me?"

"What...? Of course, not."

"Then why are you treating me like this? I thought you were one of the good guys. We were friends at Eastwood—weren't we? Did I do something wrong? Say something bad? Please tell me 'cause I have to know. I thought I was helping you by getting you out of there. You seemed sane to me. Now, I don't know. Maybe you're crazy, maybe you are a criminal. I just don't trust you anymore."

He downshifted and rolled to a halt on the gravel shoulder of the road, the fields of corn tall on either side, catching the sunrise.

"Althea...."

She waited.

"Althea, I like you. Yes, we were friends at Eastwood. We're *still* friends, but I have things to do, and I have to do them as soon as possible—things I knew I would need to do just as soon as I got out. I didn't *plan* on escaping last night—and not with your help. Sure, no doubt I'd still be there, probably for a long time, without your help. So thanks for that. Believe me, I do *most graciously and humbly* thank you for that, but when I saw the opportunity, I knew it was time to do what I had to do. It's Fate—like you taught me—*karma*, you called it."

Althea crossed her arms. "I didn't teach you *that*."

"Sorry, but I guess I used you. I pretended to like all the meditation crap and Buddhist shit to make you happy because—hell, I don't know— maybe I thought I could get you to help me. Certainly weren't anybody else gonna help me. But I didn't expect you to come to me in the middle of the night and say 'let's go.' I was thinking more along the line of sneaking my personal effects to me, and maybe some clothes, is all, but…. Damn, now you got yourself in trouble. That's beyond anything *I've* done."

Her eyes were open wide and misty.

"Bullshit!" she exploded.

"What?"

"That's bullshit. You weren't playing. I could tell. You're not the first man—"

"The second?"

"You were really falling for me."

"Yeah?"

"Yesterday, Missus Wolfe sent me to Baldwin's office, hoping I'd be fired. They wanted to quietly send me away to another hospital. Where I could handle the pressure, they said. Instead, I quit. I didn't want to work at any other hospital unless I was hired by *them*. So I quit. I got pride. I'll find another job tomorrow—or the next day. I can do it; I'm a good nurse. Damn good…except for one fault."

Karl smiled sarcastically. "And what's that?"

"You should know."

He lay his head back against the headrest with a sigh. The sky was light now. In the buttery dawn he could see her face clearly.

"It's been a long night and I'm really not in the mood to guess."

"All right. You wanna know my big fault? If you can't figure it out, then you must be pretty stupid. I guess I'll just have to tell you. It's so obvious. I'm really surprised you haven't figured it out."

"Well, what *is it*?"

"I—I fall in love easily. Too easily. With the wrong kind of guys."

Karl broke into a relieved laughter. "Is that all?"

"This time I've fallen in love with a very, *very* sick man. Someone who's good at putting on an act, and who likes to hurt people—like me. Someone who—"

"Come on."

"He's *you*, Karl! I've fallen in love with you. I even wrote a poem."

"Oh, that's just great."

"You're the one this time. Of course, *now* you change colors like a chameleon—like all men do—and you hurt me. It's happened to me too much already. I know how it works—dammit!"

"I see I taught you how to swear—fair trade for meditation lessons. Look here, Althea, I *am* sorry. I don't want to hurt you. But right now escape's more important to me than having a girlfriend. If we met somewhere other than Eastwood...."

"That's okay. Not your fault. It's mine. I'm the dummy...for not noticing you had no real interest in me. I shoulda seen it sooner, that you were just putting on an act."

He threw up his hands in surrender.

"Jesus H. Christ! Are we talking about the same thing? I'm talking about my life, what I have to do to survive as a human being. I don't know *what* the hell you're talking about, some lovey-dovey shit. I think it's all about how I've rejected you and hurt you and now you're all teary-eyed and pouting."

"Stop it."

"Stop what?"

"Teasing me."

"Hell, you can't be pleased. You think I've turned away from your *affection*. That's not true. You're confusing my dedication to staying alive with ignoring your dumb come-ons. I'm not ignoring you. I just can't do anything until I've taken care of a couple matters."

She turned in her seat to face him. "And I helped you escape. I was gonna be fired, so I quit. Now you escape. It won't take them long to put two and two together. They knew we were close. That's why I was fired."

Karl sat up, facing her across the gear shift.

"Then what the *hell* do you want?"

"I want you. Dammit, you haven't been listening to me. I'm in love with you. I did it because I'm in love with you!"

Gazing at her, Karl felt embarrassed. He suddenly felt a tugging at his heart. He gave a nod. "Okay."

She raised her eyes, regarding him from beneath her eyebrows.

He gave an exasperated sigh. "You have no idea what you've gotten yourself into, Althea. I can't return your love—not now, not for a while. I can't do *anything* until I take care of business—until I settle my *karma*. You gotta understand that, or we better part right now. I got no time for flowers and candy. I have to move fast."

She sat back as Karl grinned, turning the ignition key.

"Your place?" he asked.

Easing the car onto the road, they sped off as the sky transformed from royal blue to morning amber, illuminating the corn fields. She placed her hand over his as he took hold of the gear shift. It felt pleasant, he decided, uncomfortably so. He soon realized that was why she did it.

Nightfall blankets them in the corner of the temple yard, huddled beside the wall and the bushes. The tigress offers a lowly purr from her weary lips. The cubs are restless, nipping at each other's tail.

Roundpaw sits back on his haunches, silent, eyes narrowed in the dark. Far off, echoed on the wind from the village, he hears the cries of Man.

They have learned of the attack, knows they will come to hunt him. He understands the tigress—to protect her wayward cub.

He is also knows Man's lack of forgiveness. It would be different if the female man-creature was attacked as though she were a sambar. She was merely ushered out of the forest as an intruder.

In the hours between the attack and the arrival of dusk, he described to the tigress the gruesome attack on his mate. He told her of the vicious murder by the red-furred hunters, and his vow to hunt them. She understood how that brought him far from his home, to be a rogue cat, drifting from the territory of one tigress to another.

No, she was wrong: he was not drifting like so many aged or crippled warriors. He knew where his path led him. He knew what lay at its end, and he told her so.

She growled disbelief yet confessed he was different than the other tigers she encountered in her territory, including the sire of her cubs, one of the drifters.

The tigress moans, understanding his tragic thoughts. She discerns his request for her to depart with her cubs before the man creatures can return to kill them.

He asks this for their own safety. They remind him so much, so painfully much, of his lost mate and the two cubs they had. This much he has decided to do.

He will save the lives of his kindred, for the memory and sake of his own family.

Roundpaw leans forward on his haunches and brushes his whiskers
   against hers. Surprised at first, she purrs softly in the grass. The cubs
   yelp and bark playfully beside her in the shadows.
A peacock shrieks far up the trail.
Roundpaw freezes. The tigress snorts at her cubs to be silent, waits.
Again the bird cries. The breeze blows stronger as they wait in the
   blackness, listening.

SNAP

Roundpaw's ears flick to the direction of the sound. The tigress watches
   her cubs; their wide-eyed, stubby faces suddenly showing fear.
The rustle of bushes against a passing animal.
The odor of Man stings his nostrils and he snorts. What manner of man
   walks the trails of the night? What manner of man creature indeed,
   when he knows fully of the tiger's presence?
Roundpaw raises his head, tries to see the man through the dark curtain.

SNAP

Another twig is broken underfoot.
He turns to the tigress, squinting his eyes and rumbling, deep in his
   throat. She understands and springs to her feet. The cubs follow her
   with their sorrowful eyes; they do not understand her.
With a nudge and a nip, she draws them close to her flanks and starts
   away from the temple.
Crossing the dirt trail, she and her cubs vanish into the thicket.
Roundpaw's eyes follow their departure.
Long after he can detect their scent no more does he turn his head away,
   knowing he will never see them again. The realization worries him.
He sniffs the air again; they are gone.

SNAP

Another twig falls.
He turns his attention to the approaching sounds, remembering his early
   days of hunting. The man who comes in the night is no ordinary man.
   He is a man who sees in the dark, who feels the night, who senses the
   shape and color of things, who is like all the forest beings.

He is a man who is like a tiger. Such a man is no ordinary hunter—

He hunts in the night because he knows that is when the tiger goes in search of prey. He is a human worthy of respect. He is also to be feared, for he is a creature of wisdom, a creature with cunning equal to his own. It was the night hunter who, when he was a cub, killed his father.

Roundpaw pads lightly down the trail, his eyes searching the shadows for the man creature. He is ready to face him, ready for the confrontation.

Perhaps it is the red-furred man coming, the one who murdered his mate. His anger swells, his fury is roused. The wind brings the nasty scent to his attention. His teeth are licked clean, poised for the first bite as he pads down the trail of nightmares.

A white, luminous spot appears ahead, dancing and bobbing in the night. He cannot see the rest of the man creature's body and he is puzzled. He sniffs for the scent of the fire stick and finds none. His muscles shake nervously as he stops in the middle of the trail, ready to destroy his opponent. He waits, standing straight but tense, watching the glowing disk coming ever closer, sliding along the forest path.

Step by step, pace by slow pace, it moves toward him. As he can now see, the spot is actually moonlight glowing from a short stick held by the Man in his right forepaw. And as he draws near, the light dances across the dirt and dried leaves, always pointing downward.

Allowing his head to droop as he waits for the light to reach him, he positions himself once again, leg muscles coiling for the lunge.

The man approaches. Another step.

Roundpaw moistens his lips, flicks his tail coolly in the night air.

Another step.

The circle of light moves across the ground, soon strikes his right forepaw pressed against the dirt, ready to spring. The light halts, focused on his paw.

Roundpaw steps back, removing himself from the lighted circle. The spot of light moves suddenly, an upward jerk, flashes into his golden eyes, illuminating his face, startling him, blinding him.

His first reaction is to throw a huge, deafening roar at the light source.

The Man screams, drops the light stick in the dirt where the beam of light rolls and dances off the surrounding trees.

Roundpaw roars louder, and the sounds of frantic running and random, confused tripping and stumbling, the slapping of bushes, the growling of the creature sweep rapidly away from him, marking the trail.

He bounds down the trail after the playful creature. In a dozen leaps, he catches the beast, bowling it over.

The man barks loudly, fiercely. Roundpaw steps away. The man scrambles to its feet, throws itself down the trail.

Roundpaw follows, seeing the beast is crippled and limping. Again he catches the beast, nipping at his hindpaws. He gives the upright beast a slap with his paw, knocks him face down in the dirt.

The Man jumps up on its hindlegs, prances away, screaming.

Roundpaw is left standing in the path, listening to the Man fleeing randomly through the midnight forest. He has satisfied his curiosity, turns up the trail to the temple.

Along the way, he regards the light stick, abandoned in the dirt, still burning bright. Roundpaw bends low to sniff it, gives it a nudge with his nose. It is warm. By dawn, however, it has faded to nothing.

12

IAN MCDONNELL SHOOK HIS HEAD madly, gray hair flapping.

"Yer a bloody fool!" he cursed the photographer. "Wha' th' bloody hell yew thinkin ye doin' up a-there? Tha' ol' temple's nae place tae be goin'. Dinna yew think ye was gonna get another photeegraph o' ye birdies? Tha's tiger country up there, don' yew know? Yew have nae bloody business in tha' woods in th' middle o' th' bloody night!"

The photographer held his frown as Hansen treated the long, tender grooves down his back, all from a single swipe of the tiger's paw as he tried to run away.

"I know, but—"

"Yew looky tae be alive—yew bloody fool!"

"Easy now, Ian," said Dr. Hansen. He grabbed another alcohol-dabbed cotton ball, applying it to the next red crease. The photographer jerked at the sting. "We don't want to add to the man's shock."

"I've been trying to tell you gentlemen," the photographer spoke through clenched teeth, "I only went there to find my camera. It's a two-thousand dollar camera and I couldn't leave it out there in the forest all night. It was supposed to rain."

Ian slapped his thigh, glanced at Hansen.

"Is yew life worth a bloody thousand pounds?"

"My camera is my work. It *is* my life. But it was dark: how could they see me? I was very quiet, too."

Ian laughed, shaking his head.

"I need my camera. Without it, I cannot finish my assignment."

"Assignment, eh?" the doctor sighed.

"For my magazine."

"But o' course," Ian snapped, "I shoulda known he was from a bloody magazine. An' might tha' be tha' *National Geographic*? Don' they give yew guns? Don' they know yew goin' tae tiger country? They's bloody fools, too!"

The photographer tried to stiffened his upper lip. "My magazine is the prestigious *International Ornithologists Journal*. Heard of it? I have had assignments also for the *Geographic*."

"Wha's th' bloody 'Inteenashnal Horny-tholly-Jesus Journal'? Some boob rag, eh? Page three gals? I'll wager 'tis a bonny one."

The photographer winced as Dr. Hansen started on a fresh scratch.

"It's 'ornithologists'—a magazine for bird watchers. It's not a *boob* rag, as you call it. It's a scientific journal."

"Yew take photeegraphs o' birds, don' ye?"

Dr. Hansen cleared his throat. "Not those kind, Ian. He means real birds—like peacocks, probably."

"Right," the photographer nodded. "We were about to photograph a gorgeous pair of budgies."

"Damn fool!" Ian paced around the office. "Th' man's a bloody fool, doc. Yew shoulda confined him tae his bloody room. Tha' way he's no bloody harm tae no one er tae his own bloody self. Too bloody curious, too bloody stupid fer his own bloody good!"

"Ian! Enough of your bloodies."

"Aaa, he's a bloody American. Don' know wha' our bloody means. Would yew have me sayin' *fook* this an' *fook* tha', an' *sheet* this an' *sheet* tha'? Like all them bloody Americans? Then I truly be swearin' up a bloody storm, eh?"

"Then I would have to ask you to leave, Captain McDonnell."

"There's nae need tae pull ye rank on me, Major."

Ian grinned, embarrassed.

Dr. Hansen motioned for his patient to stand.

"Looks like it'll heal soon enough, but you keep an eye on it. Don't want any infection to show. Stay off those nipped legs of yours, too. You've had a shock so you'd do well to keep at rest a few days—"

"At least," Ian added, perturbed.

"Quiet," the doctor instructed as he helped the photographer on with his shirt.

"Yew wan' me tae question him aboot th' tigers, fer chrissake, doc. Tha's wha' yew wanted, wa'n't it? I'm jus' doin' me job."

"Your job, Captain McDonnell, is as our *shikari*. You haven't been up to the temple yet, have you?"

Ian looked away.

"Just as I thought," Dr. Hansen snorted.

"Now yew wait a bloody minute!"

The doctor turned to the photographer, escorting him to the front of the office. They shook hands and the photographer thanked him.

"Oh, and Doctor...."

"Yes, I'll have Ian give a look for your camera while he's up there."

Ian heard the conversation from the back office. "I ain't gonna bloody look fer nae bloody camera nae matter how bloody much it costs!"

Dr. Hansen nodded. "Don't you worry."

They parted. As the doctor returned to the examining room where his colleague waited, he wondered about what the photographer had told him.

"Tha' was certainly nice o' yew, 'specially tae th' bloody 'Merican."

"Ian, do you believe what he said about the tiger that attacked him?"

"I dinna know. Tha' man's a bloody fool goin' up a-there after dark."

"I mean, what he said about the tiger being male—throat fur and all. And what about the size?"

"Aye, if he's as big as tha' fool says, he's a big one, fer certain."

"What was it he said?"

"He said its paw was as big as his chest," Ian recited without any amazement, lighting his clay pipe.

"And you've seen the claw marks."

"Aye, bloody claws stretch from one side tae th' other. They be four claws—dividin' his back into quarters. Aye, he's a big one."

They paused, contemplating.

"I wonder what's become of our old tigress."

Ian smirked, drew on his pipe. "Seems she's been a-scared off by this new tiger, I guess. Prob'ly th' rough sort, I says."

"We may have a problem, Ian."

He laughed, took a longer draw on his pipe.

"An' yew wanna me tae go pokin' me fool nose 'round up there, a-knowin' all this infeemation? An' where's tha' broon lad tae help me yew promised, eh?"

"Perhaps you shouldn't go up there by yourself. It's beginning to sound too dangerous."

"Aye, but I'll be goin' anyways."

"But why?"

"'Cause tha's me job...as yew said."

Althea waited impatiently on her futon, her starched white uniform badly mussed. Listening to the splatter of Karl's shower, she began to feel out of place in this new adult world she had recently created for herself. It was her apartment, but it now had a man in it, somehow making it unclean. She was startled by the unexpected silence of the shower ending.

Karl appeared, towel wrapped around his hips, drops of water running down his chest, dripping off his tangled hair. He threw another towel over his head, began drying his hair as he entered the room.

Though she tried not to stare, Althea's eyes followed him. She cleared her throat as he opened the store sacks and fumbled through the clothing charged on Althea's card. He laid out the packages on her futon and carefully removed the labels from the shirts and trousers.

"I don't know about this, Karl...."

"Don't worry, I'll pay you back when I get to my bank."

"I mean—what are we doing?"

He straightened up, faced her, water still coursing down his body which caught her eye. Stepping to her, he placed his hands gently on her shoulders. "Althea...?"

She looked away, recognizing the phrase.

"Yes...?"

"I got something I have to do. It's important, more important than you. But I can't tell you what it is. If I told you, then you'd know I was crazy."

"No, I wouldn't." She sniffled back tears. "I love you—no matter what."

He started to speak, stopped. He summoned courage, cleared his throat, and held his head up straight.

"I have to go hunting."

She blinked, even though she faced away from him, listening to the words echo in her head. Suddenly, she pulled away, holding herself as far apart as she could and looked him straight in the eye.

"*Hunting?*" She screwed her face into a horrible scowl. "Hunting? Of all the self-centered things to do—and at a time like this! It's so *ridiculous*—so—so *stupid*! You might as well have said—"

With a twist of his shoulder, he tore free from her grasp and the towel fell to the floor. He bent over and took his new clothes off the futon, pulled on a pair of boxers.

"You don't get it, do you?"

"I understand I did all this, risked all that I've risked, forfeited my love and my self-respect on this stranger, all so you can go...*hunting*? You *are* crazy, Karl—and I don't care if I said the word. Crazy, crazy, *crazy*! There! I said it!"

"Calm down."

He dropped onto the futon, stretching out and pressing his head against the pillow.

"I'm not crazy. At least I don't think so. I'm as sane as you—or Doctor Lyons—or any of ten million other people who faced trauma. But I have a particular...uh, 'disease' might be the best word." He saw her eyes widen. "Don't worry, it's not any biological disease. It's kind of a mental thing, but it's not insanity."

She slid to the edge, stood, ready to walk away.

"Actually, it was with your help—and Doc Lyons'—that I came to this conclusion. Neither of you intended to give me any assistance. It just happened. It's like the concept of *satori* you taught me: how we suddenly see the big picture all at once. That's what happened. The light bulb blinked on and I knew exactly what I had to do. And it wasn't from sitting around for weeks. No, this was clear, rational, logical thinking. What I came to was a clear, rational, logical conclusion."

Patting the mattress, he invited her to sit. She sank onto the futon, never taking her eyes off his.

"You can't understand, Althea. Not unless you could see through my eyes, see in my dreams what I've been experiencing, and know that what I say is true. I lost my job, my wife, my pride, my self-respect, and maybe my sanity. All because of these dreams—these nightmares—I've had, and still have. Usually they're violent, especially since April. I felt the horror as though it was me doing the killing. And I'll have another and another and another, unless I—"

He paused, staring beyond the eyes of his companion to a place far, far away.

"Do what?" she asked after a while.

He had exhausted himself and threw his head back on the pillow.

"I have to try."

Althea didn't know what to think, sitting beside him on the futon. He turned to her, caressed her shoulder. She took his hand, laid it against her cheek.

"You can believe me or not but...I'm going to India."

Althea nodded slowly, staring at the carpet.

"I have to. There's no other choice for me. I must go. The hunting I mentioned before? That's what I have to do there. My cure is to face my fear—or whatever it is—and overcome it. That's the method used in psychiatry, isn't it? Well, I can do that myself—I'm *that* sane. I must face my nemesis and conquer it. I simply must hunt a tiger—*this* tiger— the one in my dreams." He took a breath. "And kill it."

Althea remained silent but pursed her lips. What did he say? Her hand went to his arm, felt the muscle flex as she tried to contemplate the insanity of her new boyfriend. After a while she stopped and gazed at him.

"Come're," he called to her, motioning with his arm.

Hesitating, she crawled up the futon, rolled onto her back.

She repositioned the hem of her uniform, filled with tension. When he took her hand in his and scooched against her, she became more tense. He stretched further, his lips pressing against hers, withdrawing before she could react. She expelled a breath of frustration.

"I promise to come back to you. Really. And it's not just something I'm telling you to get rid of you. I want you, Althea—I *want* you." His grimace had to be sincere. "I've got nothing now. I need you. Help me start a new life. And to do that, first I have to cure myself. It's a small sacrifice for you—and you'll be rewarded with my undying love."

Her silence aggravated him.

"I can't figure it all out, of course. But I'm getting close. Maybe something in my past—before my wife, before my adulthood. There's something there. That's what I don't know. But I feel it's true. It's like...if I had a disease and felt pain, I would know I had a disease and I would know I was in pain but I wouldn't necessarily know where I got the disease. But this—I know is true."

"Stop it!" she cried, grabbing him. "You're scaring me. Please *stop*. I should've never taught you about meditation and everything. I think you misused it. I think you found something evil in it, something you weren't suppose to find."

He waited for the room to fall silent. "There's nothing evil about this. It's perfectly natural. It has to do with the nature of things. You've got to understand. I'm not asking you to believe everything I say. I'm only asking you to understand what I'm telling you and accept the fact that *for me* it's real."

She felt the urgency in his voice, pulled him close and whimpered into his neck words he could not make out.

"Please—at least pretend to humor me," he whispered.

"I understand what you told me."

"Leona—that's my wife—my ex-wife—she didn't believe me. You expected that, right? She didn't believe, much less understand, what I just told you. I told her I'd prove it...someday, somehow I would. I didn't know how to back then. Hell, I didn't even know for sure it was real. Now, the situation's different. Now, I know what to do."

He pulled himself up, leaning on his elbow, gazing into her eyes.

"Now, I have only you to prove it to, Althea."

"And that's your hunting?"

"Yes. I hope you see it's more than just some strange hobby. I used to go hunting for deer with my dad. And I was in the army for a while, so I know how to shoot. This is a one-time operation, like cutting out a cancer."

She nodded her understanding. "Okay."

"You're all I have now, Althea."

He wrapped his arms around her, pulling her on top of him and rocked her gently. She rested her head on his shoulder and he felt an obscure feeling of joy wash over him. He stretched forward to kiss her, to kiss a woman who really loved him. This time she was prepared and returned the kiss. Her lips parted, their breaths became one.

When they parted, Althea gazed at her lover. "Do you want to sleep now?"

"I think so. We've been up all night."

He regarded her one last time. "You trust me, Althea?"

She tried to smile. "No."

Most uncomfortable indeed, thought Ian, wiping his furrowed brow, straightening his pith helmet. His khaki shirt and shorts were long sweated out. The air was unusually cool, humid from the evening's shower, but with daybreak the clouds hoarded the moisture, the forest was transformed into a vast sauna. He knew there were many signs he would miss in a fog-shrouded forest.

He stalked with measured steps, advancing slowly, scanning the trail ahead and the wood in every direction. Despite holding his ever faithful Evans .470 Nitro Express at the ready, he was more nervous than in times past. And as all good professional hunters did when using the double barreled rifles with one shot in each barrel—he carried his third and fourth cartridges tightly between the fingers of his right hand as it firmly grasped the small of the stock, trigger finger poised.

His scout, to whom he had given the more easily pronounced name 'Jon', brought up the rear. The farmer was a good aide, as Ian had told Dr. Hansen. Not only did he speak the best English of any villager, but he had proudly served a stint in the Queen's 132nd Royal Rifles and was familiar with firearms.

The past night's rainfall should have made the tracking easier. With the great cat's weight, not a single pug mark would fail to be set in the soil. But he didn't count on the ground fog. Thus, he searched diligently with his eyes and ears, and felt the uneven earth with trained, booted feet.

He had a tenseness about him which he had never experienced before, though he would never admit to it. In his career he had killed nine tigers. The first was in self-defense, but the other eight he had hunted as true man-eaters or potential ones. Now, tracking this latest beast, he had the nagging worry of a Classical composer starting on his tenth symphony when the musical law of nature seemed to allow only nine.

It was different this time. Not only had it been four years since his last true tiger hunt, but he was broaching the very heart of the beast. All of the reported attacks by these two cats occurred along the trail he now traversed. He was in their home, with every natural advantage in their favor. He prayed the cloud cover would break soon and the sun would burn away the fog.

Ah, he sighed, pondering the long, sordid history of man-eaters in India. He knew a great many reported man-eating episodes were just as likely the work of leopards. Others were natural events, accidents by people on the road. Still others were outright lies, strangely enough— such as the man over in the next village, he recalled, who wished to be rid of his wife and thus killed her in a nearby wood, blaming the death on a tiger. The reports were full of such episodes. There were also incidents like the attack on the woman photographer, where the victim had been savaged by a surprised cat, or by a mother defending cubs. All were legitimate reasons, he knew, but out of the hundreds of reported man-eaters down through the years, there were always a percentage of true man-eaters—ones that quite simply hated Man and for whatever reason vowed death upon him. And any such tiger that a man hunted could possibly be of that small fraternity.

That was what raised the hairs on the back of his neck.

He slid his back foot forward to balance himself as the trail turned downward slightly, knowing it was not far ahead where the ruins of the temple stood. He was well into the beast's realm.

Glancing back over his shoulder at Jon, he saw his partner too far behind, almost lost in the mist.

As he waited for his aide to catch up, he observed the trail ahead. It bent downward through the trees in such a way that the point where it leveled out was hidden in the overhanging growth. Beyond, it was impossible to see. Once at the bottom of the long incline, he would be able to see the temple ruins about a hundred yards up the trail.

"Cap'n Mookadonna," Jon called ahead to him in as low a voice as he could muster and yet be heard.

Ian took no time correcting his poor pronunciation of his name. He hurried back up the trail to where his aide waited.

Arriving with a pant, he stared at Jon's discovery. Ian motioned for him to stand guard while he knelt down to examine the huge pug mark left by some tiger, most likely his. Through the fog and partially covered by wet, rotting leaves, his aide had found the first fresh pug mark on the trail. He felt its surface, measured its length and breadth visually and with a six-inch ruler from his shirt pocket.

"Tha' be our puss, Jon," whispered Ian.

He stood, placing his size nine army boot inside the boundaries of the paw print, sliding his heel against the heel of the pug mark.

"Aye, he's a fair one," Ian remarked, noting the span remaining between the toe of his boot and the tips of the tiger's toes. "Possibly go tae four-hundred pounds easily, maybe four-fifty."

Jon looked down at the pug mark.

"Donna yew turn yer head 'way from yer task, laddy," Ian snapped in a low voice. "Yew donna wan' yer ol' *sahib* tae be cut doon from behind, do yew?"

Jon immediately struck a firm stance with rifle poised between his boss and the trail. His eyes took in the whole forest at once, cemented together by the gray fog. The place was silent. His heart beat loudly, anticipating the delivery of the beast.

"D'ye wan' tae go further, Jon?" Ian asked, still gazing down at the huge pug mark. "Er have yew seen enough tae know we gotta monster amongst us?"

He did not immediately reply.

"Er yew goin' tae answer, Jon?"

Ian glanced at his aide and his eyes landed on a distant pair of golden orbs settled among the foggy trunks of the tree line, several meters back from a bramble of cut logs and brush. There was a wide open area, part of an attempt at clearing the forest years ago which only served to provide more nests for vermin.

Over the scrambled, forehead-high thicket, beneath the yellow eyes, he could faintly make out the striped pattern, subdued in the white of the fog.

Jon had seen the beast only a moment sooner.

"Cap'n Mookadonna, see what be there?"

"Aye, Jon, I do."

Carefully, Ian stepped sideways from behind his aide, moving several steps down the trail until twenty paces lay between them, not removing his eyes from the tiger.

Positioning his double barreled Nitro Express, he wondered only if the cat was the male or the tigress. The chief difference would be two-hundred pounds of meaty death. They had their rifles—his never-failing Evans .470 and Jon with his Ruger Number One tropical rifle, a single shot military piece—and could likely kill the beast with the three shots between them. However, they weren't situated in the best of locations from which to take a charge. By removing himself from the same space as his aide, Ian made it possible for him to fire at the cat broadside if it charged Jon—and hopefully vice-versa if the tiger charged him.

"'Tis nae quite wha' we expected, eh?" the old hunter said, a bit embarrassed. "If he charges ye, I'll take him from here. If he charges a' me, then ye bloody well better get off a fair shot, laddy, er I'll ne'er speak tae ye 'gain."

"Yes, *sahib*, but...I see tiger be female," Jon insisted, glancing sideways at Ian.

As he focused his eyes on the hidden face of the tiger, she shifted, pushing her head forward out of the patch of fog.

Panicking, Jon raised his rifle to his shoulder, just as the tigress settled down into the fog again, amber eyes watching them.

"Steady, lad, steady."

"Tigress, she be."

"Aye, she's got nae scruff. Sharp eyes, laddy. But where be th' mister?"

At that very instant, with only a vague whim pecking at him, Ian carefully twisted his head to his left, gazing down the trail in the direction they had been heading. At the point where the trail was lost in the overhanging foliage, at the leveling of the incline, posed in the middle of the trail with no shame or fear stood the huge male tiger. So still was the forest that were it not for Ian's keenly honed instincts, he might have been overlooked.

Ian dared not flinch. The cat was just over thirty yards away, but that only amounted to three to five seconds in a full charge, even uphill through the mud.

"Aye, Jon, we indeed have a tiger problem."

The scout started to look at Ian's tiger.

"Don' ye take ye eyes off tha' bloody tigress, lad. I'll be watchin' the mister fer ye. We be in quite a nasty fix here, eh, Jon?"

"Yes, indeed, Cap'n."

"Aye, we be."

"How fix it, Cap'n?"

"How tae fix, eh?"

As heartbeats ticked by, Ian's brain seemed to thaw and began to calculate. With a good, strong shot, he could knock out the male to his left down the slope while Jon took out the tigress. He had one shot, and although he was the best Indian rifleman he had ever seen, one shot was far more risky than he would have wished. There would be no problem if each of them hit the mark with the first shot. However....

Ian glanced left, realizing his attention had drifted. A dangerous habit, but he had no time to slap himself. It was time to act.

In the few second's lapse, the male tiger had padded silently halfway up the trail toward them, never wavering from the center, never pausing. At the same moment Ian recovered his attention, the cat continued to approach at a steady, measured pace.

What is he doing? Ian wondered, eyes narrowed at the beast.

"Jon, yew be on yer own now. I've got tae take out th' mister...right *now*!"

His rifle flew to his shoulder, hands instantly fine-tuned the fit.

At the sudden motion, the tiger's padding cranked into a charge and even uphill, with the trail becoming a muddy slide, the big cat cut the distance almost instantly.

"Cap'n Mookadonna, the tigress, she be gone!"

Ignoring the scout, Ian dropped the post and bead into alignment, centered on the fluffy, white chest of the charging beast.

His finger shaking like his body, Ian leaned into the butt and squeezed the trigger.

Click.

No bullet fired. Having no time to puzzle over it, his finger slid onto the trigger for the second barrel, squeezed.

Click.

Twelve feet lay between him and death.

Six.

The tiger landed on Ian, slamming him against the muddy ground as he wondered why his rifle had misfired. He had zeroed his sights and threw a few rounds at some tin cans the day before. Now, though, the useless rifle was flung over his head, landing front sight first in the mud. The great cat stood upon him, its four paws matching the hunter's outstretched hands and feet, its claws like nails in the corners of his coffin as they met face to face. The great cat's hot, stale breath seared his face as he tried to crawl out from under the beast.

Crack-ack-ack!

He heard Jon's rifle fire, the unmistakable retort of the bolt-action military rifle, but he did not know at which target his aide had aimed. He hoped it was at the tiger he was wrestling.

The cat did not budge, seemed to sit there on top of him, gloating.

"Jon!" the old hunter screamed.

Startled, the tiger opened his huge mouth, large enough to swallow a man's whole head, and offered a tremendous bellowing roar of his own, deafening Ian and blasting him into unconsciousness.

13

KARL STARED OUT between the drawn curtains at a new day, attention on the mussed seam where the azure sky melted into gold, anticipating the sun's entrance. His ears picked up a girl's soft-spoken words. Deep in his mind, he recognized her and listened, not taking his eyes away from the dawn.

Althea's gentle voice continued, as it had for several hours.

"And when my parents were killed in that car accident, I went to live with my aunt. Daddy drank a lot then. They said he was drunk that night, and they were arguing in the car as they drove home. They had been talking—shouting, I guess—about divorce. He used to beat her—and me. A few times. But I was at home with the sitter that night. It's funny, but I remember it so clearly, like it happened yesterday."

Her sweet voice soothed his tortured spirit so well he couldn't bring himself to tell her that he'd already heard enough.

"Those are the only places I've ever been—except for a short trip down south to visit relations. That was really my only vacation trip—overnight, I mean, and not counting Girl Scout camp, too. But I got a passport! I was planning to go see Japan after nursing school. But I never went. I found a *great* job at the Eastwood Institute. *That* sure wasn't a good trade."

He glanced at her, relaxed on the futon, focusing on how silky her wavy hair appeared.

"I guess India would be fascinating, too." She pursed her lips. "But it's such a long way from here."

He listened to her plaintive sigh, her regrets coming together in one breath, turning to the window again.

"Well, I've got nowhere else to go," she conceded with a chuckle. "I just want to *help* people—ya know? That's why I *became* a nurse. Funny how *that* worked out. Now I got that *bitch* to thank for leaving. You think she'll be fired because of your escape?"

The sun unleashed its first rays over the top of the buildings opposite Althea's studio. The brilliance forced him to turn away.

"Well, *I* hope so," he answered, turning to her.

He had slept for three hours, until he awoke from another dream.

"Karl?"

Images of his dream returned to fog his eyes.

She smiled, the almost embarrassed, slightly pouting, virgin/vixen grin she used.

"Are you sure you want to go all the way?"

"All the way?"

"To India."

He didn't know how to answer. He sat beside her and kissed her.

"We better pack."

She kissed him quickly. "This is my first time."

He glared at her.

"Not *that*," she laughed. "I mean taking a big trip. I don't have any luggage."

He threw his head back, laughed, breaking through the plate glass window of his emotions. Sharp splinters flew everywhere but what remained was a murky heart.

She sat comfortably on the edge of the futon. Rubbing warmth back into her arms and legs from the air conditioner's chill, she studied him: a man of action, or determination—like her father whenever he wasn't drunk.

Karl left the futon, stood staring out between the curtains again.

"Careful, someone may see you," she giggled.

He ignored her, scratched his ribs, stretched. "You said you got how much on your card?"

"I always pay my bills," said Althea. "I never carry a balance, and they just keep raising it. I'm never going to buy anything *that* expensive, silly banks!"

"So how much?"

"You mean my credit limit?" she asked, innocently. "Well, the Mastercard's got about ten thousand, I think, and my Visa's got...oh, seven thousand? I don't know. I never pay attention to them. Why?"

"Just wondering. For emergencies."

He faced her. His eyes absorbed her nudity in a single glance, the first time he'd seen her that way in the full light of day, thinking back to the dark embraces, the passion of the night. She had no idea just how sexy she was. Had she been that good or was he so tired?

He smiled politely. "Anyway, today we have to go to my bank, get my passport out of the safe box, then go see a travel agent."

Dr. Hansen trudged back to his bungalow after meeting with the village elders of Tashi.

"How'd it go, doc?" his patient in the back room called.

The doctor stepped inside, lighted the oil lamp.

"Wha'd they say aboot tha' tiger up a-there?"

The light showed a quickly aged face, wrinkles seemingly carved overnight. Hansen leaned against the doorjamb.

"You and your bloody safety," he said with a grunt. "Every hunter knows to flip off the damn safety if he wants to shoot his bloody gun."

Ian's face went white. It had been a long time since his friend had addressed him in such tone. The past week the good doctor had been kept busy. With the death from infection of the woman photographer, the mood of the village had turned fearful. He had the opportunity to end the reign of the *shaitan*, but he failed.

"You're bloody lucky not to be hauled out of here and put to death, they're so crazed," the doctor went on. "You know they blame you for Jon's death. His widow has paid a charlatan to put a curse on you. Did you know that?"

"Aye, b' yew donna 'spect me tae put much faith in tha' cursing, do ye?"

"No, I'm only telling you. A lot of villagers want you dead. They wanted *you* to be the one killed by the tiger. Rather have you as the victim than one of their own. I'm sure you can understand."

"Yew know I did all wha' I canna do."

"Yes, yes, but the result was the same."

"An' I got a bit o' th' beast meself, ye know."

"They don't see it that way. You may've had the cat on top of you, scratch up your face with his sandpapery tongue, but it was Jon who paid the price."

"Aye, 'tis a truly sad thin', I mus' admit, but I canna understand why th' beasts chose Jon tae dine on rather'n me—when they already had me doon. Tha' ol' tigress must've snuck 'round him. I heard him fire. I thought he was shootin' me tiger, not tha' bloody tigress."

"As I said, the result was the same. They brought his skeleton home for the pyre. At least they left his face uneaten. Strange behavior. Perhaps the cat is a *shaitan*. Everyone says so. They say that's why you were left alone—some damn thing about *shaitan*s loving white men, and all that bloody rot. Damn peculiar."

"Aye, 'tis peculiar."

"Well, you needn't worry about it now."

Ian gazed at the doctor. "Wha' yew be meanin' by tha', doc?"

"They voted to call the Government House to have a hunter sent to finish your job. If not a *shikari* from there, then they'll hire a free-lance hunter."

Ian started to sit up, felt the pain of his ribs, cracked where the beast had stood on him. He quickly faltered, sank back to his pillow.

"You'd better not try that again, Ian."

"Jus' as soon as I'm on me feet, I'm a-gonna get back tae tha' wood an' kill tha' bloody tiger."

"Don't worry. The bloody thing's taken care of for you."

Dr. Hansen exited the room just as Ian thought of a worthy rebuttal.

Left alone, Ian massaged his chest, fighting the pain, wondering why the expedition had gone so wrong. Had it just been too long since his last hunt? No, he decided. He had simply been spooked by the vicious attacks on the two photographers.

Then an idea came to him.

"Doctor Hansen," he called from his bed.

"Yes?"

"Listen, I gotta bloody good idea, I'ave. Wha' aboot th' Colonel?"

The doctor rushed, stumbling, into Ian's room.

"What did you say?" he asked, out of breath.

"He'd like a chance to bag a bonny fine cat like tha' one up a-there. He's a' least five-hundred pounds, maybe five-fifty. Maybe *six*."

"Don't be an ass. The Colonel's long retired. Hasn't hunted in nearly as long as you. Can't really expect him to come all the way here from New York City, do you?"

"Why bloody not? An' he'd probably do it fer free, I'd wager."

A smile played on the doctor's lips. He rubbed his chin.

"It won't be like tha' farce in Orissa. Those two young fools hunting doon tha' tiger with spears an' Land Rovers. With th' Colonel, we canna have a proper hunt. Maybe we could get an old-fashioned beat together. Wha' eh?"

"It does smack of the outrageous. However...."

"It's a bloody fair idea, if yew ask me."

The doctor continued rubbing his chin.

"Yew know, doc, th' idea jus' cross me mind. Th' two young lads, why, they wore th' ol' red coats, like good British soldiers. Then, jus' a month or so ago, closer tae here, I hear o' 'nother bloody hunter killed by bloody tiger. Newspaper says he was wearin' a red jacket. We find us a new tiger in our wood, tha' kills one o' our villagers. D'ye think there's a connection?"

Dr. Hansen broke from his thoughts. "Tigers don't think like that."

"Aye, but jus' supposin'...."

"What was Jon wearing?"

Ian frowned, lay back on his pillow.

"Aye, doc. Jon was wearin' a new shirt he'd bought on his last trip up to Bhopal. Bonny fine shirt, alas. London made. Harper and Sons."

The doctor glared sternly at Ian.

"What color was it?"

"'Twas red, doc. Blood red."

Ron Priestley moved stiffly around the foot of the bed, shaking his head desperately, arms waving. Becky, stretching out on the bed, sobbed. She couldn't keep tears from running down her cheeks.

He spun on his heel to face her, anger in his eyes, fist clenched and upraised more a sign of power than ready to strike.

"You got to understand," he growled. "I *have* to go—to go after him. My whole life now is hung up on that crazy bastard. I can't live any kind of free, open life until he's out of it. That means dead."

"You're hung up on him, all right!"

"It's more than that! He tore my career right out from under me. How long do you think before he goes to the police and tells them the whole damn story—"

"Just what *is* the whole damn story, Ronnie? You never explained *that*! Not to me."

"That bastard jumped into my life and ripped out my career. Can't you understand that? He's completely *destroyed* my career—my service to humanity. I can't let that go. He's got to pay for what he did."

"Then kill him," she muttered, "but do it here."

"We already tried that, or don't you remember?"

"Yes, I remember, Ronnie. You fucked up."

He charged the bed, swung his arm down at her, striking the pillow beside her. "I did *not* fail!"

"He's still alive."

"Yes, but—but now he's on the run."

"But you wanted him dead."

"Don't quibble with me, dammit."

"You shot at him and he escaped. That's the bottom line. The cops are looking for you, the 'someone' who *tried* to kill him. Either way, you're scared. Even I can see it. And you always fooled me before. That's why you're running away. Not to get him, no, but to get away from here. That's why you wanna leave me—leave the country."

"No, it isn't!"

"But why the hell'd you choose a god-forsaken shithole like India? I just can't figure it out. What the hell's there for you anyway? Stay here, Ronnie. Haven't I always done everything you ask me?"

"You are *so* damn dense! That's why I had *you* go to the hospital to find where that nurse lives. That dumb nurse's helping him."

"Dammit, Ronnie, you used me. I shouldn't've followed them yesterday. If I knew you were gonna run after them—shit, Ronnie—I never woulda told you what they said in that travel agency. They're gonna put me behind bars, too—being your accomplice. I *hate* you! I should've *never* let you back in my life. You can go stay with that Missus Edwards!"

"He's hiding out with her now. I've seen him there."

"Go back to your Missus Edwards."

"You can't possibly understand," shouted Ron. "I can't go back to Missus Edwards. I like *you*, Becky. Didn't I tell you that? Besides—"

"What? What happened? Didn't she go back to her loony husband?"

"*He*'s her husband!"

"Then what's the big fuckin' deal? So what if she goes back to the jerk from the funny farm. But he's with the nurse now. Kinda funny. Serves her right. What's it to you—or us?"

"She's *dead*!" shouted Ron, slapping the bed.

Becky swung up to the edge. "What the hell did you say?"

"You heard me! She's dead."

"Missus Edwards is dead? That's what you're all worked up about? I see…. So that's why you're running away. You killed her…and he knows you did, so…you're trying to kill *him*, right? Okay, I get it. But why go all the fuckin' way to India?"

"*He* is going to India! The *bastard* is going to India. That's why *I'm* going."

"Can't you just kill him here…*before* he leaves?"

He sighed, shaking his head. "Look, I can't just go to his apartment and blow him away in broad daylight. I have to make it look like, you know, an accident."

"That's why you shot into his window at the psycho ward, huh? So it would look like an accident? That's brilliant, Ronnie, just brilliant! Now you got me in trouble, too. But I'm not gonna go down with you."

"What a bitch, what a bitch," he mumbled, stomping from the room.

"Where're you going?" called Becky.

"To pack."

"The *hell* you are!" she screamed, springing up from the bed and scrambling after him. "You're not leaving me alone this time. You're not deserting me. If you leave me, I'll tell *everything* to the police."

He glared back at her and she was frightened.

"If I leave, then it won't matter," he sneered.

"*Flight two-eleven, now departing for New York's J.F.K. airport is now ready for pre-boarding at gate twenty. Any passengers requiring special assistance or those with children, you may board now….*"

Althea glanced at Karl, the announcement fading in her ears. She listened to the ticking of her heart. Never before had she taken time to wonder what she was doing. She had always relied on her gut instincts, and she relied on them now. But since her state of activity was about to ease into a slower gear—flying was a passive activity—her mind became free to analyze her thoughts.

"Time to go," Althea said, taking his arm.

They stood in line at the metal detector, hands clasped like lovers. She felt very conspicuous. Here she was standing with her man, going on a trip to the other side of the world. Much better than a honeymoon in the Ozarks. She tried to convince herself to rely on Karl's judgment. He seemed to know what he was doing, had a solid plan. Easy enough to believe if she could hold back the nagging question of his sanity.

"Next," the attendant said, and she found herself holding up the line, daydreaming.

"Sorry," she said, smiling embarrassment, and stepped through.

Cutting through the crowd, the tall man in the tan corduroy suit and collarless blue shirt arrived out of breath at the ticket counter. He dropped his bag heavily at his feet and it tumbled over on its side. The long, metal case he sat down beside it looked heavy, but did not hide its contents.

"May I help you?" the uniformed woman behind the counter asked.

He glanced at the line of people at the metal detector, then back at the ticket lady.

"Where's that flight going?"

"That's flight two-eleven to New York."

"Great! Give me a ticket on that flight."

"I'm sorry, sir, but that flight is full. If you'd like to wait and see if there are any no-shows, we could—"

"Shit!"

Ron, turning, caught the last view of Karl Edwards rounding the corner of the twin doors, heading down the ramp to the airplane.

"Would you like to purchase a space available ticket, sir?"

"Huh?" he replied, turning back to the counter.

"Never mind. When's your next flight?"

"To New York?"

"Yes, dammit!"

"All right, you don't have to shout."

He checked his watch. The plane was already ten minutes late departing. If it had been on time, he would have already missed it.

"We have a flight this afternoon at...it's at three-thirty. Will that be all right?"

"When does that arrive?"

"Flight two-thirteen arrives at—"

"Last call for flight two-eleven to New York...."

"Never mind. I'll take it."

The two vacationers settled into their coach seats as the engines outside their window roared to life. Nervously, Althea took Karl's hand, held it in both of hers.

"It's my first time, you know," she whispered.

He smiled. "Are you scared?"

"A little."

"Don't be," and he kissed her cheek. "We're together. We'll be all right. I'll protect you."

"Hope so."

"Besides, Althea, you being a student of the occult, this should be a fabulous opportunity to explore all the old museums and ruins. They got a lot of temples over there, I hear."

"Occult? What do you mean by that?"

"I mean your Buddhism stuff. All that B.S. you taught me."

"It's not B.S., Karl."

"Maybe not all of it. I did learn a few things. I learned how to turn my sanity on and off, like a light switch. And how to tap the ol' inner-self for gossip on my past lives."

She expelled a disappointed sigh.

"Althea, I'm sorry about the bank, really. They must've closed my accounts when I went to Eastwood. Or my *wife* took everything already. I swear I'll pay you back when this is over. I promise."

"That's okay," she said, but switched on her internal tabulator.

The flight attendants marched down the aisle checking the seats and the seatbelts.

He stared at his partner, feeling her fingers on his thigh as the engines hummed louder.

Grinning with delight, a sudden motion outside the airplane caught his eye as the heavy fuselage rolled back, away from the terminal. Running his eyes down the long, silver wing, across the widening gray pavement, he could see through the glare on the terminal windows that someone was waving frantically at the airplane. It was a man, alone at the window wearing a suit.

Strange, thought Karl. Who was he waving at? The man could not see through the airplane's small portholes.

Then reality slapped him across both cheeks. He thrust his head across Althea's lap and pressed his face toward the window, staring hard at the figure waving from the terminal. He recognized him as the doctor his wife fell in love with. There was no mistaking his swarthy complexion and bushy mustache.

"Son of a bitch," he muttered.

"What?" Althea startled. "What's going on?"

"He's here! The bastard's actually here."

"What are you talking about?"

"The *bastard*, the *asshole*, the *fucker!* Who *else* does that describe? He's there—in the window! He followed us here. *Shit*, I can't believe it! What the hell's *he* doing here? What the hell's he want from me?"

"Calm down, Karl."

He threw himself back in his seat as the plane rolled out of sight of the window.

"I can't calm down now."

"Don't worry, we're leaving. He's staying. You'll be away from him."

He sat up straight. "Damn right, damn right." He made a fist. "He can go to hell. *Shit*, I can't believe it. He followed us all the way to the goddamn airport!"

"Calm down."

"What if there's a bomb on the plane or something?"

"Quiet! You'll upset the other passengers."

He folded his arms across his chest, shaking his head.

"I can't believe he followed us here."

"Karl, we're together—you and me. Everything's gonna be all right."

She leaned over, hugged his tense shoulders as the jet raced down the runway and launched into the sky, twisting and turning, heading northeast to New York where their connecting flight would be waiting to whisk them off to another world.

14

*THE END IS NEAR—he knows. It is easy to see because more and more man
creatures follow him into the forest. The last of these bore the fire
sticks used in hunting beasts. He wonders if he did the right thing—
not a moral decision, but a practical one—for he knows next come the
herds of Man barking, slapping stones and sticks, mounted on the
great elephant beasts, chasing him out of the forest into the open
where a Man with the fire stick will strike him dead. That is how it is
done. That was how his mother was killed.*

*The words ignite his mind like a hot flash of lightning from a monsoon
thunderhead.*

—No!

—Do not come here.

*Roundpaw, arching his striped head over the bushes, gazes down the long
hillside at a herd of female man creatures digging in a square of earth.
Nearby, framing the corners of the pasture, the males stand with their
fire sticks, wary of his existence.*

*They know of him now, for none have ventured into the forest since the
day the tigress met the two hunters and made meal of the brown man
with the red-furred torso. It was his hatred which drove him on, but
the tigress made the first strike.*

Once the beast was dead, they could not let fresh meat waste.

He continues to watch the guarded man creatures, but his eyes turn inwardly, glaring at his soul.

He—followed us—here—

Who?   He ponders the words in his head, the feelings in his heart.

His nerves tingle with anticipation. He does not wish to run, to leap, to kill. His muscular form is calm, but his mind is filling like the downstream basin of a burst dike with thoughts of hate, of violence, of action.

Is it his fate that is calling him?

Ever since that terrible afternoon long, long ago when the red-furred hunters ripped his heart from him with the murder of his mate, he has called out to Fate. He has delivered his vow to the winds. No replies have been heard, save an occasional echo, the chattering of monkeys, or the shrillness of bird calls.

Sometimes, there are explosions from the man creatures' fire sticks.

But Fate does not answer.

What lies ahead? He roars at the dawn. When shall I meet thee?

He roars into the looming storm.

A man creature will come. In the cold, unheard, unhearing depths of the darkest corner of his mind, a black pit where even he, its owner, has seldom ventured, a languid pool of blood whose glassy surface seems to extend to the far horizons cruelly mirrors his expression.

In the reflection of that blood-filled sea, he can see himself. It is not the orange and black striped, furred face he wears for the sake of the world, but the face he wears when he wears no body. It is not a sensation that he suddenly knows all, rather he has discovered the door, beyond which lies other doors perhaps, but which none the less hold the answers. All answers. Behind one, he decides, contemplating the outward flowing rings on that red pool's shiny surface, must be his destiny.

He has marched incessantly, physically across the bloody, brutal landscape, emotionally through a bestial hell, mentally to a far away land and back again, forever passing dark series upon dark series of doorways, pathways. If he chose any one of them, he might not be here, or he might be further along the road.

Until now, the tether of his vow of revenge has always jerked him back into alignment.

Until now.

—He comes. In the belly of a great silver bird with a beak that does not feed, wings which do not flap, and clawed feet which do not clench—

Roundpaw twists his head, craning his neck to his left, scanning the azure sky. A crow there. A hawk here. No great silver bird. Is it a cruel jest? He wonders. He cannot lie to himself, so it must be true.

His fate awaits, and his killer shall be a Man from the belly of a bird.

—No!

—Do not come here.

He feels a tug in his heart. It is time to move on, time enough spent in this menagerie of Man. There must be a place, he wonders, where not even the musky man creatures have corrupted, a paradise where the sambar run in thick herds, where the streams run cool and sweet, where—

He will leave at dawn.

—A Man comes: searching for the heart of the beast.

Sailing over cottony clouds, hours out from J.F.K., the golden sheen of afternoon sun reflects off the great bird's silver wings. Drinks, snacks, a line at the lavatories. Calmness settles over drowsy passengers. The rushed, heartless world below left behind, their vapid thoughts turn to future desires, as the cool air in the warm, cradling fuselage brings out the blankets. It is the end of an era for some, beginning for others.

England lay hours ahead, India further. The emerald plate of Ireland waiting on the horizon, the plains of Salisbury, the bustle of Heathrow airport, still far ahead. Now comes the limbo, a pause for meditation, above the agony, terrors, misery, the corrupt institutions of mankind, the pollution, the waste, so close to Heaven, almost god-like. The world below seems strangely devoid of life—

Perhaps it really is, Althea thinks, resting against the vibrating hull of the airplane, becoming bored by the endless flow of cloud patterns.

"Anything wrong?" the man beside her asks.

Turning away from the window, she wipes a tear off her cheek.

"What isn't wrong?" she says, sniffling back tears.

Karl tries to grin. He takes her hand.

"Everything will be all right," he says.

She lays her head against his shoulder. "I'm all right. Just a little sad, I guess."

He thinks her words over. "What's the matter? Not used to flying?"

She shakes her head. "Don't know for sure. I'm getting homesick already, I guess. I know it's silly."

He gives her hand a squeeze. "Home is where your heart is."

She manages a meek smile. "Where is my heart?"

The man creatures are few, and they remain hidden in their nests. The wells, the streams, the paths—all free for him now. With his recognition, his mere presence is enough to appoint himself king. He roams as he wishes and takes no pride in stealth.

As the evening draws close, his empty, rumbling belly sends him in search of food. The woods are devoid of large game, but the man creatures hold herds of small, horned animals in fenced yards.

The animals bleat, scurrying about the pen as he lumbers out of the forest down the steep hillside.

He has no concern for the sharp stares of the fearful upright beasts. Let them wrest his meal away from the grip of his fangs.

The wire fence is no barrier for him, and he slaps down the stick holding it up. The wire tears from its hook and an opening is formed. The black and white goats race to the opposite side of the pen, pushing themselves into tight formation, a few billies daring to face the intruder.

Roundpaw lunges at the nearest goat, knocking it over with his huge paw. It struggles to return to its feet, hips crushed. The others divide, rush away in either direction. He spins on his hindpaws, swatting another goat to the ground. The herd runs for the opening in the fence, and he bounds after them. He catches one more with his outstretched claws before they escape—

"Lord, will you look at that!" a man exclaims to his servants.

The commotion has drawn the attention of the farm's owner, a former British official known in the valley as Nawab of Hoshangabad. His servants and field hands have hidden themselves in the master's large bungalow, fearfully watching the cat ravage the goat herd.

"Bring me my Winchester!" the tall *nawab* shouts, squinting his eyes to better see the impressive dimensions of the beast in the twilight.

He raises his hand to his forehead to shield his eyes from the bright lamp strung high on a utility pole near the pens.

"Christ, he's enormous!"

With the *nawab*'s usual boldness, a few of the servants come out of the house and gather around him, watching the huge tiger.

"He looks about ten-two at least, maybe five hundred pounds—a lean, muscular bastard, all right."

The Nawab chuckles, but his servants do not share his humor.

"They've got a new tiger across the ridge at Tashi, I heard. I thought they were merely boasting. I'd hoped he'd stay there."

He spun around, glaring into the house.

"Prasad! Where's that Winchester?"

The wiry man returns, presenting the rifle lain across a cushioning towel. Another servant follows, two handfuls of cartridges held out for inspection, bowing his head along with Prasad.

The Englishman takes the rifle, loads a cartridge in each barrel, never taking his eyes off the tiger. Its image was smearing in the fading light, beginning to blend with the shadows—

Roundpaw grips the largest goat in his jaw, tries to drag the next largest with a forepaw. With his keen, light-sensitive eyes, he easily spots the tall, khaki-shirted Man raising his fire stick to his shoulder, pointing it in his direction.

He drops the goat he was dragging and leaps through the tear in the fence, his left hindpaw scraping a barb on the wire. Bounding up the hill with the one remaining goat dangling from his mouth, a single shot slices across the yard, pricking his tail as he disappears into the bush.

In the shadows of the forest, he darts and dodges the foliage, tearing the goat carcass through the brush, pursued by barking dogs and the trumpeting of an elephant. A dozen spotlights dance among the trees, searching for him. He has never been chased by so many in the dark of the night. And yet, with the flickering lights, the forest is almost as bright as morning.

Roundpaw reaches the temple where the tigress waits, the cubs whining

their hunger. He throws the goat at her feet, growls for her to take her
cubs into the temple. They will hide in the silent upper floor of the
temple. He will run farther down the trail, lead the hunters away.
She snatches up the carcass and motions for her cubs to follow.
Roundpaw pads onto the dirt path, glaring down the trail at the
approaching lights and noise.
How arrogant they are! Can they not spare one small goat? Will these
man creatures eat his flesh when they kill him? They hunt him when
he steals their food, but when they kill his food—his sambar, his
chital—does he stalk them in retribution?
He turns and pads along the trail, away from it, away from the
approaching storm of man, dog, and elephant. Further up the path he
finds a thicket in which to hide. He sits, waiting.

"Is this the way, Georgy? Did you see him?" the Nawab asks his guide as the weight of the elephant they ride shakes the earth.

"No, *sahib*. The temple is near ahead, to where I have heard the tigers lay up."

"Here?"

"Yes, *sahib*."

"Arjan say to me Doctor Hansen in Tashi village tell him tiger has mate live in this woods. He say they lay up at old temple. He say male is new here, but tigress is old and always live in this woods."

"Balderdash! I don't care who's who in this damn tanglewood. Show me that tiger and I'll plug his brain. I'll not let a damn tiger steal away my goats, that's for damn sure."

The Nawab tapped his *mahout* and the elephant driver directed the beast forward.

"I need more lights here. I'm losing the trail."

"But, *sahib*, the temple is only few more steps along this road."

"Fine, let's headquarter there."

"But—but, *sahib*, that is where the tiger lives!"

"Right, Georgy! If you want to catch some bastard, you wait for him in his home."

The guide led his boss to the old temple. The opening in the forest cover allowed a full moon to fill the monsoon-moistened yard. Silvery droplets of moonlight sparkled on the grass like diamonds. The night was much more quiet as the baying dogs veered away along another trail. The hunter and his party of two dismounted.

Morning light breaches the thick forest cover, warming the earth, drying the dewy grasses. There is only the song of jungle birds, though none cry out in the clearing where stand the temple ruins. None dare disturb the silence. There was a time when he, noble beast, would have stood and taken on three men himself. The days of his youth, a life of innocence, of simple pleasures.

Now, as he grows in age—with his mission laying uncompleted before him—there is hesitancy in his actions.

He does not wish to be pulled from his path.

Escaping from the elephant-borne hunter, hoping to lead the band of men away from the temple, he waited hidden along the trail. Perhaps to ambush them, or to assure their passage. Moments passed, beyond the time when they should have crossed him—

He left his hiding place, padding up the trail to a slope where he could survey ahead. He sniffed the air, could no longer smell the elephant, could no longer feel its weight shake the ground. Circling back through the jungle growth, he returned to the temple, observing it while he could remain hidden.

There in the morning's cool mist, four dark figures recline spaciously in the yard, their backs covered with droplets of dew. He can see two small figures lying together off to the side, almost as a pile, and two large ones strewn about casually, their hindlimbs outstretched.

Waiting for any danger to show itself, Roundpaw breaks from the undergrowth, out onto the dirt path, facing the stone gate.

His ears perks; he expects a shot to sail past him, exposed. He pads through the opening in the wall and the figures horribly identify themselves.

As he sees them prostrated before him, the two smaller forms are the still bodies of the tiger cubs, heaped against each other. The larger forms are man beasts—a thin beast of brown skin with white fur around his head and falling from his waist, and another, dark in color, who sported white fur. Both rest on their chests, their hindlegs spread, and both their forelegs tucked beneath their bodies.

Roundpaw approaches them, rolls them onto their backs with a nudge of his nose. The forelegs seemed bent to contain their liquid essences within their chest cavities, now neatly carved out and lined with beetles. Strips of meat run from their bodies, sliced open with a quick, powerful swipe of a sharpened sheath of claws.

One swipe to each man creature, in the same location, with the same effect. Wide maroon circles mark their graves, staining the grass where they fell wondering why they had penetrated the forest in the dark of the night.

He takes a glance at the crumpled bodies of the cubs, felled by stones flung from the fire sticks. He feels a tightening of his heart at the scene, then he turns away.

Bounding toward the entrance of the temple, he pauses, heeding his senses. Then, slowly he extends his right forepaw, claws poised, and tosses it inside, feeling nothing. He presses forward, pulls his body inside. There are blood stains on the stone floor, and strings of dried flesh shed by fleeing man creatures. The trail continues up the stone steps. He follows it, slowly, cautiously.

As he peers over the top step, he sees two more figures lying across the floor.

He climbs up the last few steps onto the upper floor: backed into a shadowy corner, hidden from the golden sunlight stabbing through countless holes in the wall, lays the tigress, her belly pressed to the floor, her bloody forelegs outstretched, her striped head resting heavily on her paws. Her chest heaves, exhausted—

Roundpaw's eyes flicker.

She opens her tired eyes, regards him across the fallen man's body.

The white-skinned creature, with smooth fur of lightest tan, clenches his fire stick in his two pale fists, knuckles still red.

Roundpaw pads around the body, noting the intactness of the beast's torso. Instead, the man is missing the throat, down to the bare whiteness of the fang-scraped spine, sparsely covered with patches of dark red flesh.

The face of the beast is a mask of astonishment. His eyes wide open, his

mouth agape, tongue protruding through the gap under the chin.
Day warms the temple, blood splatters turning black as they dry, and
Roundpaw gazes at the tigress, her eyes yellow like the sun, dulled like
the face of the moon. Her breathing is low.
Without a second thought, Roundpaw goes to her, lowers his head,
nuzzles her cheek, their whiskers touching, hearts and minds meeting.
He presses his striped cheek against hers and she purrs, sadly.

15

MAHARASHTRA, WESTERN INDIA

THE AUTOMATIC DOORS PARTED and the heat rushed inside, sucking the sweat from arriving passengers. With three suitcases between them, Karl and Althea looked to the left and to the right, sorting the throng of poor, ragged people from the tourists and business-suited figures, and anyone who might seem helpful—or dangerous.

Althea dabbed a handkerchief on her forehead, then wiped her throat. On went her sunglasses. Karl flicked his moist shirt collar, applied his own shades. They stepped from the airport terminal like movie stars into the oven that was India.

The monsoon season had ended, they'd heard. Now the land was laid bare beneath the baked-enamel sky and the searing, brassy sun. Not a white cloud floated above them now. Dust clouds, like chocolate fog, seemed to constantly blanket the dry, cracked pavement, hovering around their ankles.

A small brown man asked, with a polite little bow and an extended hand, to carry their bags. Karl shook his head and the man disappeared.

A taxi pulled up alongside the curb, screeching to a halt, the driver almost diving out the door. As Karl was about to ask the fare, Althea shouted at him and he turned in time to stare down the child about to pick his pocket.

He waved off the taxi, its driver cursing loudly, and they went to board the Airlink coach leaving the Santa Cruz airport, heading south into the city.

Forty-five minutes later they had traversed the 22 km route and found themselves in downtown Mumbai, a city of modern skyscrapers and museum-piece architecture, surrounded by businessmen in suits, women in brightly colored *saris*, ragged beggars, and some skinny children throwing a flattened ball.

They got off the coach, two blocks from their hotel. It was not in a tourist area but a less affluent neighborhood. Karl gave a long look to the businessman's hotel—Indian businessmen, that is, those not having expense accounts. The flop house—that was really all it was, thought Karl—was at least well-lighted. Some kind of doorman greeted them and two bellhops came down the warped steps for the suitcases.

In their room, the manager personally saw to their check-in and to their comfort, not often having guests all the way from America. He had one bellhop pat the dust from the bedcover, and the other flush the rusty toilet twice. On the way out, the manager crushed a cockroach beneath his shoe, smiled, and closed the door, leaving them to stare wide-eyed at each other.

Across the great Deccan—the high plateau that mounts the sub-continent like horseman on steed—down through the valleys, through fields and forests, along rivers, over hills and into city streets, he has come from afar.

Like a cancer that in commencement is too small to be felt, his presence grows as his distance decreases.

On the edge of a world, hidden in the safety of the huge, littered Man nest, he has come.

His is the mind that speaks to him.

His is the heart that cries for him.

His is the hand that threatens him.

Deep in the center of the wood, green foliage sprayed a chalky brown, he waits. Nearby the tigress snorts, scratching her whiskers against a tree trunk.

There has always been Man, they understand, and there likely always will be Man. Like a disease, he waits, clawing, infecting.

Roundpaw drills his eyes deep into her soul, sees it is barren like the
Orissan plain he crossed near his mate's grave.

Though he comes to kill, he comes as a child, not understanding the path
he forges. He is only an unknowing pawn in a game he has invented.

They must flee now. They have killed the man-creatures. Though he did
not teach her, she has learned well their irrational ways. Her tally now
ranks beside his own.

The man-creatures may fear to come immediately, he knows, but they will
come. Perhaps tomorrow, perhaps the next day. And so they must flee.
It is time, long past time, his mind shouts at his consciousness, for
him to once more take up the trail.

The hunt continues, the red-furred Men be damned.

He turns to go and the tigress steps after him.

He growls his disapproval, starts to pad away. But the tigress follows
unabashedly, leaving behind only the sprawled figures of the two man-
creatures, carved for their dinner.

And the cairn of stones that is her cubs' grave.

She never questioned his activity, his strange behavior.

He understands: she has nothing now, like him.

Then they were away, bounding down the trail. The village is quiet as they
skirt the fields, passing through lines of trees and scrub piles, ever
vigilant of their notoriety. Man now fears them. And with fear comes
destruction. Closed within their caves, the man-creatures are safe.

Soon a man will come who will free them from their fears. And they,
demons in the night, the shaitans of the forest, will be long vanished.

Karl awoke violently. He shot straight up in bed, froze there. Around him, visible through the dusty haze, corpses lay stacked everywhere. Most were naked and all of their bodies showed the marks of their deaths quite plainly. Tooth punctures here, long claw scratches there. A throat ripped away, an abdomen torn open. Arm missing, leg mangled. Crisp, white bodies. Deep red marks. The scratches along the bodies resembled the workings of a hot knife on supple wood, the work of an artist. Then he noticed the stench.

Almost an afterthought, he turned and sought Althea through the haze of the room. She was not beside him. Nowhere in the room. Then he realized he heard no sound, not even the beating of his heart.

He panicked, sweat coursing down his bare chest—and the fog melted, the sounds of the living returning to him. And then a voice whispered deep inside his brain just as the last of his nightmare slipped away. It called to him, whispering: *Join us*.... He cried out and a new voice responded, mumbling to him—*Come for me, my brother; my friend, come and kill me.*

The noise of their rusty toilet flushing sent the final echoes in his head to flight.

Althea entered the room, towel wrapped around her slender figure like a *sari*.

"What's the matter?" she asked, seeing him distraught.

He did not reply, staring ahead to his next life.

She sat beside him on the bed, balanced herself as the mattress slumped. She brushed off some settled dust, regarding him.

"I'm doomed," he muttered, eyes wide.

"What...?"

"We should've never come here, Althea."

"What do you mean by that? We haven't even been here a day, and now you're homesick?"

"Not homesick. Home*scared*."

She got up, moved across the room to the dresser.

"You're just homesick." She sifted the varnish peelings around the dresser leg with her foot. "We gotta embrace what's new and different." She glanced around the room. "Even if it's not what we want...exactly."

Carefully she selected clothes from her suitcase, then uncoiled the towel and dressed.

"I *am* home. Don't you understand?" He shook his head. "I've tripped over my threshold—somehow. It's beyond *déjà vu*. It's more than the feeling of having been here before."

She closed the suitcase to keep bugs out. "What is it, then?"

"It's the feeling that I've come home—to a place I long ago escaped from. It's something horrible. I can't explain it. I'm home—I *am* home. I've been seeking my own trap, searching for my own death, and now I've found it."

She fastened the snap on her jeans and turned to him.

"I'm doomed," he said.

Seeing him genuinely upset, she went to him, sat beside him and hugged him.

"Don't worry, dear. You probably just had another bad dream. That's your thing, right? Was it bad?"

He shook his head, afraid of just how close to Leona she sounded.

"Yes, yes, I did. And it was bad. Very bad. I was surrounded by corpses. Stacks of them. They were all marked."

"Marked?"

"Yes, marked—by the tooth and claw of the tiger. The beast—"

"What're you talking about, Karl?" Althea was becoming upset. She wiped an eye. "Don't go talking about all that evil stuff. Please."

"The tiger isn't evil—not in that way. No, he is purity personified. He is the surgeon who cuts the cancers from the land—neatly, cleanly. He rids the herd of the weak, the sick, the lame. He is—"

"All right, Karl! Enough!"

He still looked terrified to her. Althea sniffled, put on a smile.

"I'm sure a day of sightseeing will calm you down," she announced, jumping up. "There's lots we have to see today. Everything is so exotic here. So let's get a move on, okay? The morning's leaving us behind."

She pulled him off the bed and helped him into the shower. With the broom, she swept out the beetles that had accumulated since she took her shower, and he stepped in.

"Will you accept charges from a Mister Ronald Priestley?"

"Yes, I'll take the call."

"Thank you, go ahead," the operator intoned.

"How are you?" Becky asked.

"I'm okay."

"You're there already?"

"Of course. A little trouble at customs. About the rifle. Told them I was a dealer and it was a special order item—high price and all—had to deliver it in person—private sale. They believed me, anyway."

"Have you found him yet?"

"He's shacked up in some seedy joint down the street from here."

"What about the girl?"

"He's got the girl with him."

"What about you?"

"Me? I'm at the Taj Mahal Hotel. Near the waterfront, by some landmark called the Gateway to India. Great view of the harbor."

"When are you—I mean, do you think you'll be able to, uh, *do it* soon? Is it safe?"

"Don't know. Have to wait and see what he does."

"And what does he do?"

"They're just being regular tourists. Acting like sightseers. Strange place to go when you're on the lam, but we know he's insane. He'll leave himself open for the kill shot sooner or later."

"I hope it's soon, darling."

He did not respond.

"Are you okay?" she asked. "You seem a little angry."

"Not angry, tired. Long flight."

"Where are you now?"

"I'm in the lobby, near a coffee shop. Lots of tourists. They bring'em here in the evenings for the disco."

"Oh, that explains the noise."

"It *is* noisy. I should go."

"No, wait, Ronnie."

"What is it?"

"I love you. Be careful, sweetheart."

"Yeah. Bye."

Althea pushed and pulled Karl around the city through the morning. From their neighborhood, they caught a bus to Fort, the downtown district named after the walled city that used to stand there. They saw the Castle, seat of the Mumbai government during the British era. After an escorted tour of the Jehangir Art Gallery and the Prince of Wales Museum, they passed the Hutatma Chauk—the so-called Martyr's Square. They walked down to the Gateway of India and stood under the magnificent arch commemorating the visit to India of King George V and Queen Mary in 1911. Althea took a lot of photographs, changed rolls of film. She gently solicited poses from several passing Mumbaikar. Karl refused to be photographed but was happy to snap shots of Althea.

As the afternoon sun burned down on them, they took shade under the arch and bought lunch from a vendor.

"Need to find a paper," Karl spoke up. "In English."

"That hotel over there maybe," she pointed, chewing a bite of her 'sandwich'—some strips of reddish meat rolled in a flour pancake with spicy sauce. "It probably has a gift shop or bookstand that would have one. If you like, we can go check it out when we finish eating."

"I'm finished," he muttered, tossing the remnants of his lunch.

"You don't like it?"

"I don't like anything right now."

She smiled politely, wrapping up the remainder of her lunch and tossing it into a trash basket.

"Don't be so mad, Karl. It was your idea to come."

They walked away from the arch.

"We're not tourists. We're here on business. Remember?"

It was a touchy subject for her. She still could not decide if she was humoring him, or if she really believed the line she was being fed about the magical tiger. She felt uncomfortable whenever their life together turned away from the normal happy-couple things and bent down the path of insanity. Half the time, she told herself, she was in love and everything was fine. The rest of the time, she could only stand back and watch her lover continue his self-destruction.

Was it wrong to love a condemned man? He was him and she was her, and though she never had any realistic expectations of changing him, there was still a small hope that his eccentricities would pass once he was away from Eastwood and away from his cold, bloody life, away from that horrible city, and off to an old and vibrant land. He said he felt like he'd come home, didn't he? But then he said he was frightened of home.

"I've never ever felt so alive!" she sang, dancing around him. "Thank you so much for bringing me here."

She took his hand as they crossed the boulevard to the Taj Mahal Hotel.

"Here it is," Karl called to her as he plucked an English language paper, *The Indian Express*, from the stand in the gift shop.

He took it to the cashier, counted out the *rupees*.

"We should've had lunch here," Althea remarked, studying the restaurant menu posted on the wall outside its doorway.

"Too expensive."

"Well, what do you want?"

"Let's go," he called to her, starting off toward the twin doors.

"Wait a minute, Karl!" she exclaimed, loud enough to draw the attention of passers by. She caught him, pulled him back from the doors as he opened his newspaper.

"Please, Karl, be more easy-going, okay? Let's eat here. I'll buy."

"It's too expensive."

"I said I'm buying. I bought your clothes. I bought the air tickets. I bought the hotel. Let me buy the damn lunch! Besides, you'll have a table to spread out your paper. How about that?"

"All right, then."

How convenient, thought Ron, leaning at the front desk, waiting for his room key. He calmly witnessed the entire scene between the bastard and the slutty nurse he'd brought with him. Smiling with delight, he felt hungry but decided it would be pushing his luck to dine at the table next to them. Some other time.

Althea ate her curry dish, drank her bottled soda and watched Karl scan the pages of the newspaper, ignoring his food.

"What are you looking for?" she asked.

"News."

"I know, but news of what?"

"Killings."

"You're so morbid, Karl. Like this morning—"

"Tiger killings. They should report killings by tigers, I'd think. It's rare enough."

"Oh?" She wanted so much to be a normal, ordinary couple.

"He's killed...umm, several...people."

"*He*?"

"Yes—and some tigress he's paired with. They've been ravaging a village. I have to find which village."

"What are you talking about? You're looking for one little village in all of India? Are you serious?"

He looked over the top of the newspaper at her, his eyes cold. She felt the stare of a great jungle cat about to pounce, felt the touch of his claws against her breast. She froze. Her shoulders shivered.

"Christ!" she burst, then shook the sensation away.

"I've sent me letter tae th' Colonel," said Ian as he hobbled around the doctor's office on a cane, one hand holding his ribs.

"You shouldn't have," the doctor replied from his desk. "There's no need for him."

"Nae need? Wha' madness yew thinkin' now, doctor? Wha' with th' Nawab—an' his guide—an' his *mahout* all slain in one evenin'. And yew say there's nae need for th' Colonel? Yew mus' be mad!"

Dr. Hansen turned in his chair, removed his reading glasses.

"That's not what I meant. I sent my report to the magistrate. He assures me they'll have a *shikari* to us within the week."

"In a week? There be nae village here ba then."

"Be calm, Ian. It's not good for your recovery having you hopping up and down like that. They've got a shortage of *shikari*, that's the rub. Too many tigers afoot in the land, I suppose."

"So we shut doon th' whole village a bloody week? Nae, more'n a week, 'cause I doubt he'd plug our cats on th' first day. Tha' be disaster fer th' village, wha' with all th' fields goin' bad. Yew know they posted armed lookouts 'round th' fields? They got tae keep on wit' their farmin', but they canna bloody do it wit' them cats ready tae snatch 'em away. Nae, we got tae get a *shikari* sooner'n a week."

"A week is it. There's no one available till then. Unless...."

"'Less wha'? Yew thinkin' I should try 'gain, ain't ye?"

"Not at all."

"Then wha' yew thinkin'?"

"We could hire our own *shikari*. Doesn't have to be a government hunter, does it?"

"But wha' tha' cost? This be a poor village here."

"Whatever the village can't make up for in funds, we'll simply have to play on the sentiment of the poor hunter. Doing a good deed, as it were. That sort of thing."

"I dunno, doc. Looks like we'd be a-handin' th' poor fool a bloody death sentence, a-sendin' him up a-there like a-tha'."

"Nonsense, Ian. A hunter's a hunter. A tiger's a tiger. These aren't phantom cats, you know—"

"Aye, th' villagers think so."

"They're flesh and blood, nothing supernatural." The doctor rubbed his chin a moment. "Bad luck, I suppose."

Ian snorted. "Bad luck, hell!"

"It's not as though they laid in ambush. They are not thinking creatures, not like in comics and films. Only Man received intelligence from God. They're animals—doing things in an animal's good time. Take tha' tigress, for example. 'Twould be easy to attribute all the kills as the defense of her cubs. These tigresses—quite fickle when it comes to their cubs—"

"Wha' aboot tha' mister? He's th' man-eater. He taught'er tae kill men. He taught'er tae enjoy th' taste o' *human* flesh."

"Nonsense. That can't be proven."

"Aye, it can."

"Look here, Ian. Those two photographers saw a cub before they were attacked. You were near their lair when you were attacked. The Nawab even went into the temple—the bloody temple itself!—like he's expected hot tea and biscuits—when the tigress was surely making use of it. All perfectly natural. If one doesn't go stepping between the jaws of death, one will not be bitten. It's that simple."

"Th' Nawab went aft' th' mister 'cause he's raidin' goats from his farm. Tha' proves he's a bloody menace."

"Because he was hungry? Because there's no natural prey in the forest? No sambar, no chital, no large game of any kind?"

"They're a bloody menace!"

"Perhaps they wouldn't have become such if we had treated the situation properly from the start. Now, though, unfortunate as it may be, it would seem the only solution is to hire a *shikari* to shoot them."

"Now yew makin' sense, doc."

"I suppose the villagers would agree to a beat?"

"I believe so. Anythin' tha' be riddin' them o' these two marauders."

"Good. Then I'll start asking around, try to find a good *shikari*."

"If news o' this gotten too far, maybe we canna find us one."

"No, Ian. There's always some fool out there who fancies himself a great hunter."

Malabar Hill sits prominently at the southern end of the fourteen mile-long peninsula of Mumbai. There, amidst the hanging gardens, stands the Tower of Silence. Seventeenth-century Zoroastrians, fleeing their persecution in Persia, settled in Mumbai. Here, they built their fire temples and a tower on Malabar Hill.

Karl and Althea overlooked the expanse, holding their noses, ocean breezes bringing the scents to them.

The followers of Zoroaster, believing both earth and fire sacred, did not allow their dead to be buried or cremated. Instead, isolated tracts were chosen and towers erected for the disposal of the dead by exposure to the elements, and to vultures.

Althea turned and pressed her face into Karl's chest, hiding from the sights and odors, not understanding why he brought her here. His arms wrapped tightly around her as he scanned the horizons.

"I've been here before," he mumbled, his voice almost consumed by the whistling winds. He saw beyond the invisible line dividing sea and sky, looking out from the city that was port to both Sinbad and Gandhi.

She nudged him, begged to leave, and finally they did, returning via several dusty, crowded buses to their hotel's rustic neighborhood.

Darkness had descended over the city by the time they disembarked at the closest intersection to their hotel. The distant silhouettes of the Western Ghats shown starkly against the bright orange evening sky, as though Heaven itself were aflame and the earth below its burnt ashes.

The sounds of *tablas* and *sitar* came from somewhere, down an alley or back street. There was faint laughter, and singing, echoing through the narrow streets. A vendor pushed his cart home, his bare feet kicking up dust as he went. Children tossed a ball to each other in the street. A mongrel dog ran passed them, followed quickly by two boys waving sticks.

They break from the trees, padding across the dusty escarpment to where
    the stream trickles down the jagged rocks to form a small pool.
Roundpaw growls relief; the tigress is silent. Dusty coats are shaken,
    tongues lap at the water, thirsts are quenched.
A day's trek from the temple in the forest, they have risen into the hills.
    The path is wild, strewn with scrub trees and brittle yellow grasses.
    The earth is barren, ragged, void of life.
Somewhere to the far northwest, where the blistering sun sets, in the
    horizon where the hills are cleaved—is their destination. It is a land
    of plentiful game, of dark, expansive shade, of cool waters—a
    paradise.
In that direction lies the den of the many red-furred men. The red-furred
    ones lay placid in his mind, drenched by their own pools of blood,

calm smiles across their white faces.

The men with red fur once sat high atop his mind, their hateful eyes glaring down at him, taunting him.

He is their victim, too. And they, his. One man, the gaur hunter, is avenged. The red-furred man-creature with the deep brown, naked forelegs and face, is avenged, though he had not the white face of the murderers of his mate.

    And what would Brighteyes dare think of him now?

His is a wasted life. His coat is ragged and dirty, his muscles tired, sore, his teeth corrupted by man-flesh. The gleam in his golden eyes is dulled by the reflection of himself in the sun's searing fire.

    What would she think of him now?

And he runs with an old, ragged tigress, her cubs ripped from her in the same manner as his dear Brighteyes was torn from him.

    What would she think of him now?

He has marched across the continent, confronting man and beast alike, always vigilant, always vengeful, always in the name of his beloved mate.

    What would she think of him now?

Would she wish him to forget his vows of revenge, disown his memories, live a new life somewhere?

He raises his head from his drinking, regards the tigress, feels anguish tug at his heart. He is nothing but sacrificial fodder. He is falling, downward, slowly, to Death, holding out its arms to embrace him, to welcome him home like a long-lost pet.

16

THE HAMPTONS, LONG ISLAND, NEW YORK

THE COLONEL COUGHED as though trying to hide it from the staff, then cleared his morning throat with a bass rumble. Ensconced in his red and black satin smoking jacket and burgundy pajamas, his feet tucked into a pair of fleece-lined kangaroo-leather slippers, he sat back in his richly upholstered lounger to ease into the day.

Retirement had not limited his active regimen; rather, it provided more time for rest between his activities. After sleeping until 8:35, a brisk morning swim in his marble pool was followed by a full brunch on the terrace. He spent afternoons on the golf course or at the shooting range. Once in a while he would stop in unexpectedly at the zoological gardens. He was one of the directors. Or he would visit the natural history museum, of which he was not only on the board, but a generous donator of exhibits. He had more than a million dollars in research grants roaming the fields of Africa and Asia. It was money well-spent, he would lecture dissenters. Wildlife was a vanishing luxury, and having enjoyed many species during his sixty years, he would hate to have any disappear.

The east den, his favorite, was unusually crowded compared with other rooms he could have chosen about the sprawling mansion. Its walls papered in baroque red paisley print, contrasting with the white and gray streaked Italian marble floor and the mahogany beams vaulting the ceiling. Two slowly spinning fans, perched high at either end, swirled the air sufficiently to keep it from being stale. One corner was occupied by a huge antique globe, obese in its polished oak frame. Tall, wooden bookshelves stood in the corners, reaching to the beams, packed with leather-bound books, the classics, with a few well-worn paperbacks tucked among them.

The walls of the east den held a collection of trophies: a moose head on the far wall and other trophy heads: the white-tailed deer of Virginia, the Dall sheep of Alaska, the Greater Kudu of Africa, and the Oryx of Asia. The opposite wall held a leopard-skin Zulu shield over crossed spears. Spread on the floor before his chair, forever grinning, was the giant Kodiak bear he shot in '62. One corner of the room, across from the standing globe, bore a full mounted jaguar.

An older gentleman entered the room, dressed in a dark suit and wearing white gloves, carrying the Colonel's breakfast tray. Stiffly, the gentleman set the tray on the cart next to his employer's lounger.

"Your newspaper and prune juice, *sah*," he spoke.

The Colonel took the neatly folded paper off the tray, shook it open.

"Thank you, James."

His man servant straightened, stood stiffly at hand.

"Will that be all, *sah*?"

"That'll be all," the Colonel responded.

James exited.

Sifting through his morning paper, listening to the thunder which had squelched his morning swim and threatening his golf game, the Colonel reached for his glass of prune juice. One minor concession he had made to his doctor, a man who ever so gently tried to look after his robust health. At six-foot-three, broad shoulders and a barrel chest, he was well-muscled from his lifelong pursuit of sports and his routine of weightlifting and swimming. His arms were tanned like leather, his veins like steel pipes beneath the sinewy flex of his limbs. Though he was balding, he paid it no mind. Most of his life, he had worn an extravagant mustache which spread across his cheeks, almost meeting his bushy sideburns.

Despite the Colonel's dashing figure, he had married only once. She was a dear child, a niece by marriage and ten years his junior, and while she lived there was no one but her who could talk back to the Colonel and not get a cross word in reply. He loved her so much that he could not bear to leave her behind and thus brought her with him when his assignment as a game preserve officer in India began. She was pregnant when they arrived and bore a daughter the next year. His young wife quickly endeared herself to the villagers as a nurse and teacher to the children. Then, when their daughter was not a year old, his young wife contracted cholera and died soon after. He did his best to try and raise his infant daughter and never remarried.

Then, when his daughter—nicknamed Candy—was seven, he took her out one day to survey a simple brush clearing operation. While she waited in the open-topped jeep, her father talking with farmers, her life had been stolen from her by an old tigress crippled from the festering porcupine quills in her forepaw. A typical man-eater scenario, he knew; in most cases it was forgivable, but he had been forced to watch his daughter carried away screaming in the big cat's mouth, off into the forest. It took him two months to finally corner the tigress and plant a pair of slugs between her eyes, yet he did not feel adequately avenged. Though he had killed many, the Colonel kept no tiger trophy in the house. But he was not one to mourn all his life.

He sat back in his chair, sipping prune juice, scanning the pages of the *Times*, hunting for any article worthy of his attention. Setting the glass on the cart beside him, a small article, filler between the obituaries and the comics, caught his eye.

DANGEROUS MENTAL PATIENT ESCAPES
CLAIMS ALLIANCE WITH TIGER, VOWS TO KILL

The Colonel noted the location.

"Everything's up to date in Kansas City," he chuckled, reaching for his glass. He sipped the ugly liquid, squinting his eyes as if in pain.

The *Times* did not often have articles related to hunting. This one was indeed a rarity, and he wished to relax and enjoy it. He glanced at the picture toward the bottom, a police sketch of the dangerous escapee.

He chuckled again, reset his juice on the cart. *Karl Edwards*, the caption read.

"What's this?" he inquired aloud, reading down the column.

He took another sip of juice, his attention roused.

"Hell, that's certainly a world-class cat," he mumbled. "What? 'Vows to kill'—hmm."

He tossed down the last of the juice, settled back, continuing.

"Hmm...'under psychiatric evaluation...for attempted murder...his wife...suicide attempt...escaped during the night of August thirty-first ...aid of nurse.' Hmm, that's a good one. 'Stated he knows location of tiger'—Hmm? I'll bet. Poor lunatic. 'Vows to kill if given chance'—Naturally. 'Thought heading to India...authorities notified'—hmm."

He glanced up suddenly.

"James, did you see this in the paper?" Waiting for a response, he returned to where he'd left off. "'Location...a Hindu temple...forest ...claims mental connection'—hmm. 'Sees through the tiger's eyes'—Oh, come now!"

James appeared in the doorway, stiff as a corpse, chin held high.

"Yes, *sah*?"

"Did you see this article?" demanded the Colonel, holding up the crumpled pages.

"I've not touched your paper, *sah*."

The Colonel jumped up and James fell back.

"Some nut-case has found me a world-class tiger." He held up the newspaper for inspection. "Claims it's seven-feet long. That would weigh in at six-hundred pounds—at least that much." He glanced at his man servant, wide-eyed with excitement. "That's as big as the Siberian I bagged back in 'seventy-five! But this one's a Bengal."

Gesturing wildly, the Colonel tossed the paper into his chair, and stormed about the salon.

"I've got to get that cat, James. Oh, a beast like that—my collection can't be complete without it. Yes, yes—one last expedition. My license is good for six more months—yes, that's it. I can see it now. This old colonel puts away his hot water bottle and once again picks up his rifle to squelch a man-eater epidemic. I can see the headlines: 'Colonel comes out of retirement for one last hunt.' One last hunt! Call the press! Get my staff together. I'll bet they're itching for another *shikar* by now, poor bastards. Make the travel connections, James. And bring me my Betsy; I've got to get her oiled for the hunt. We've got to hurry. Can't let that fool get to the cat first. This is it, James. One last hunt for Colonel John J. Barrington!"

"Yes, *sah*," James answered. He had seen his boss get excited many times before. "Will you require brunch?"

"We must hurry, James! No, I can't let this—" he snatched the paper, found the article and glanced at the picture, "this *Karl Edwards* beat me to such a prize. That would be foolhardy! James, why aren't you snapping to?"

Instantly the man servant sprang to attention, slapping an open palmed salute.

"Snapping to, *sah!*"

Elephanta Island, named for the huge, ancient sculptures of sacred elephants discovered there by early Portuguese explorers, lay across the harbor from Mumbai, separated from the Arabian Sea by the city's long peninsula. The island was a honeycomb of caves, each with intricately carved sculptures and rock-hewn temples of the ancient Hindus who lived in Maharashtra before it became a state. The centerpiece of the principal cavern temple was a massive eighteen-foot high, three-headed statue of the Trimurti. Shiva, one of the chief Hindu deities, turned his three heads to view the always-decadent visitors, showing his portrait as the Creator, the Preserver, and venerable Destroyer. Elsewhere, the walls reached high into the shadows of the endless ceilings, towering statues and manifestations of Hindu gods and their subjects, the heroes of antiquity, both the famous and the nameless. Sculptured frescoes of couples in a catalogue of mating positions rose twice as tall as the tallest man, grappling with the digits and curves of their partners.

Althea stood before a rock-hewn couple, observing the modestly chiseled smiles on their faces, their carefully placed hands, their acrobatically stationed figures, and fondly recalled the previous night on their sagging bed. She could do that position—she *had* done that position. Her lover was insatiable. The memories shown pleasantly on her face as she passed among the other tourists.

She studied the figures like an artist trying to decide how to improve the artwork, though she came to no conclusions. Thinking about her teachings through the years, of meditation, of the Hindu pantheon, of Nirvana, she wondered how it all fit together, wondering how such an impossibly complex system of beliefs and rituals could have remained intact for countless centuries to arrive in the modern world without so much as a hair out of place. She wondered how these new impressions she was forming would affect what she'd taught herself the past few years. What was different about sitting down and meditating in the cool, damp chambers of the caves, in the midst the gods themselves, and meditating in her quaint little air-conditioned apartment back in Missouri?

She felt guilt despite no attempt to rationalize it. She had not really suffered, she knew, not any true kind of suffering—not like the people she saw here suffering in their daily existence. And they took it so calmly, she thought. A flood of images returned to her of the poor and distraught people on the streets in the hotel's run-down neighborhood. None of the hardships she thought she'd endured—the deaths of her parents, living with her aunt in a strange new city, living on a tight budget as a nursing student, losing to his mistress the man she was going to marry, being the scapegoat of Mrs. Wolfe and losing her job— there was nothing she could compare with the sights she saw at every turn now. And yet, despite its poverty, India was such an exciting, vibrant land. It was the land which gave birth to civilization.

Her thoughts were interrupted by the inquiry of a boy selling box lunches. She politely declined, remembering the advice of their travel agent not to eat any suspicious foods. However, she was thirsty and so made her way back to the entrance of the caves where tour groups were gathered for a lecture prior to being let loose upon the unsuspecting deities. She felt sorry for them—the statues.

Karl walked through the bazaars in the old quarter of the city, rubbing shoulders with the merchants and shoppers, no longer feeling out of place among them. The shops opened into the streets, canopies shading the customers from the hot September sun, eager merchants calling out to hesitant customers while others asked, argued, bartered over prices, colors, sizes, the poor quality and stingy quantity of the products. Weaving through the stream of humanity was the ever present mix of scents—of spices, waxes, fruits, bolts of freshly-dyed cloth, musty animals, people, perfumes, waste of various kinds sharing space with various kinds of food venders.

After stopping at several stalls, asking questions of the merchants and a few of the customers, he was directed to a particular shop at the end of the main thoroughfare. He was glad to be free of the crowded, foul-smelling lane. He had in mind some special merchandise when he parted with Althea. He knew she wouldn't approve so he sent her on a tour to Elephanta Island.

"Good day to you, sir," the shopkeeper called out as Karl stepped through the twin doors, their dust-coated windows displaying the name of the store and the name of its proprietor. "How be thee this day, kind sir? Well?"

Karl smirked at the greeting, regarded the squat, paunch-bellied, dark-skinned man with rolled-up sleeves, open collar, and knit trousers, smiling wide, showing off his yellowed teeth.

"How may I be of service to such as yourself, on this fine day?"

Karl didn't reply, began looking around the shop, his eyes roving from the ceiling to the floor, from one wall to the opposite wall, finally strolling to the back of the shop where the counter stretched across the room, a cash register on one end.

"What may you be purchasing from our very fine store, today, sir?"

Karl turned at that moment, leaning casually back against the counter. "A rifle."

They were an older couple, dressed like tourists. The man wore a pair of checkered golf pants with an emerald knit shirt, an alligator on his pocket. The woman wore a plain, flower-patterned dress. They had four cameras between them and a shopping bag that could bring home the Taj Mahal.

"Going back?" the woman asked Althea.

"Huh?" she responded, daydreaming.

"Are you going back?"

"I'd sure like to," sighed Althea. Then she looked up. "Oh, I'm sorry. You mean the ferry. Yes, I am."

"Good, then it hasn't left yet."

Sitting on the bench beside Althea, she motioned to her husband. "Sit down, Henry, for goodness sake."

He sat.

"Henry and I spent nearly two hours in there. We almost got lost, but we found a guide who took us back to the entrance. Lucky thing, too. My bag was getting heavy. You done any shopping here? They've got some fantastic bargains."

"Oh...?" Althea remained unconcerned, breathing in the hot, dry air.

"We're just taking a little break from my husband's work. See, Henry's with the airline here. His company sent him here to help their airline with the accounting system. And we just decided to see a little of the country before we head back home."

"Where's that?"

"Independence, Missouri," she responded. "You know it? Harry Truman's hometown. Where're you from? Most of the people here seem to be British. Or Japanese."

"I'm from...Raytown."

"Raytown? We're neighbors! I thought so! Henry never believes me, but I can tell where someone's from just by looking at them. Really. You a tourist, too?"

"Sort of," she began. "My husband is...uh, taking care of some business."

"Oh, really? What kind of business is he in?"

"He's...." She chewed her lip. Not likely to see this couple again, there was no particular reason to care what they might think of her. "He's a hunter, actually."

"My goodness! Really? Henry, did you hear that? Her husband's one of them safari hunters. That's really very interesting."

Althea, spotting the shuttle boat docking, stood.

"Henry, the ferry's here."

Althea walked down to the dock, followed closely by Mr. and Mrs. Henry.

Standing at the rail, gazing out at the scenery as they crossed the harbor, the woman continued talking.

"It's funny you should mention your husband being a hunter. We were—Henry, why don't you tell her? We took the train here from Kolkata, and on the way—Henry will tell you what happened. Go ahead, dear, tell her."

He reluctantly cleared his throat.

"Well, see, we were on the train, and the second night we stopped at a little country station—"

"We left late at night," the woman gaily interrupted. "It was one of those dear old locomotives, like the olden days, so it was rather slow, and it made lots of stops."

"Anyhow," Henry continued, "we stopped at this little town and they were all a-stir, so we asked the conductor what was up. Hmm, he could understand what the people outside were saying, so he said they're all buzzing because they've got a man-eating tiger roaming about—"

"A man-eating tiger!" she exclaimed, clapping her hands.

Althea spun around to face them, suddenly attentive.

"Go on," she encouraged Henry.

"The conductor explained that the stationmaster'd said they've got two tigers in the woods nearby, and they had killed almost a dozen people, and a lot of goats and cattle. They warned us not to get off the train. Their mayor, or some rich guy—I couldn't catch which—"

"It was that Nay-bob fella," Mrs. Henry corrected.

"That's right. He was hunting them and was killed by the tigers—hmm, by one of them—only the night before. They found two cubs, but one of the hunters had killed them—"

"Isn't that so sad?" the woman cried out. "Two cute little darlings—killed."

"What town was it?" Althea asked, squinting in the bright sunlight.

"Hell, some dingy little hamlet. They all look the same. I don't know the name."

"Oh, Henry, you know the name. You bought a paper there. At the station. Henry's very forgetful nowadays."

The woman dug in her shopping bag, found a folded newspaper and presented it to Althea.

She took the wrinkled paper, three sheets doubled over, and studied the headlines.

"It's this one," the woman directed, pointing to one column. "And there's a picture on the other page."

Althea turned the page, saw the small black and white photograph of the bodies laid out in the yard in front of a Hindu temple. She saw two lumps that clearly resembled cubs. And stretched-out bodies that were obviously the dead hunters.

"Oh, it must've been terrible for those boys," the woman cringed against Henry.

"It'll likely be the highlight of our trip," he added. "How often do you get to go to India and come this close to a man-eating tiger? Close enough, I'm sure. Hell, beats turkey hunting in the Ozarks, I tell ya."

Althea flipped the page back, began reading. The name of the town was Barkhera, 70 kilometers south of the city of Bhopal, up in the hills. That was where the train station was. In a forested tract near a village called Tashi was where the man-eaters had been operating. The local *Nawab*—an Englishman named Montague—was killed along with his chief foreman and *mahout*—the elephant driver.

The shuttle boat was docking at the Mumbai side of the harbor as she finished reading the article.

"May I have this?" she asked, regarding them.

They were startled.

"We thought we'd take it home as a souvenir."

"I know—yes, I understand. But, you see, my husband—he's been looking for this exact news. That's why he's here. To hunt these tigers. Please...."

"It's one of a kind," the woman started.

"I just want to borrow it...so my husband can read the article. Give me your address and I'll send it to you."

"We'd better leave, Henry," the woman stated, curtly, snatching the paper out of Althea's hands and pulling him down the ramp.

The room was sweltering, curtains limp and dusty when Althea rushed in, anxious to tell Karl her news. He sat cross-legged on the bed, stripped to his shorts, his skin glistening.

She stood by the doorway, stunned, sweat gushing.

"What is *that*?" she finally exclaimed.

He didn't answer, didn't look up, didn't move as he balanced the rifle across his knees. Though he seemed to be meditating, his eyes were open.

She began to feel frightened.

"Karl?" she called, stepping into the room and closing the door behind her. "I have some news to tell you, dear. I found your tiger. And he's a man-eater, just like you've been saying. It's really uncanny how you knew that."

She moved to the foot of the bed.

"I met a couple from Independence when I was at Elephanta. Yeah, neighbors. They came to Mumbai on a train, and they said they passed through a town that was shut up tight because of two tigers in the area. The woman even had a newspaper with an article about it, with pictures of the victims. It was really awful, even in black and white. I tried to get them to give me the paper but they wanted it for a souvenir."

She dug in her purse, retrieved a crinkled paper.

"But I went to the *Indian Express* office and I got a copy made for you. Aren't you happy?"

She held up the paper, straightening the corners, then lowered it before Karl's eyes: the picture of the two men's crumpled bodies and the bundles of the two cubs in the temple yard.

"Karl, do you see? The picture? Look. I found out the name of the town—actually, it's a village near there. The town is Barkhera, and the village is Tashi. The article says the latest victim was a *nawab*—which is like a plantation owner, or something like that. He and his partners were killed by the tigers after they killed the tigers' two cubs. See them in the picture, Karl? The little striped bumps? They went after the tigers because they killed some goats at the *nawab* guy's farm."

She shook the paper, made it rustle, but he remained still.

"You okay?" She lowered the paper. "Hey, I went to a lot of trouble to get this for you. And, for that matter, I came all the way over here with you—'cause I thought it'd be fun. And because I want you to get over your bad dreams—but now you're acting so creepy."

She began to feel nervous.

"Karl, I found your damn tigers for you. Now will you straighten up and fly right?"

She took him by his shoulders and shook him.

"I found your damn tigers! They're near the damn village of Tashi, in some damn forest, hiding out in some damn Hindu *temple*—"

The spell shattered, Karl's consciousness surged back into him—spinning off the bed, rifle in his hands, shoving Althea to the floor, taking a firing stance at the door to their room, rifle butt to shoulder, cheek to stock, eye to sight, finger to trigger. Then he turned to face the bed, holding the rifle at port arms.

His face was calm, as though contemplating the information.

"I still got it," he mused smugly. "I should never've quit the army. I'd be a frigging Master Sergeant by now."

"Don't *do* that!" Althea cursed, face beet red. "You scared me." Climbing to her feet, she dusted herself off. "I hate it here. I hate it! Being here's changed you, Karl, and I don't like it. I'm ready to go—to go home. Haven't you had enough of this playing soldier? Pretending to be a hunter? Can't we go back home and have a normal life already?"

He cocked his head, regarding her with a sideways glance, his grimy face stern but devoid of anger. "We have business to take care of, my dear. We have another trip to take."

Althea sniffled back a tear. "I'll bet it's to Tashi, isn't it?"

Sitting on the seat in the hotel's phone booth, Ron cleared his throat as he waited for the call to go through.

"Hello?"

"It's me."

"Oh, baby, I miss you so much," Becky exclaimed. "You doing okay? When are you coming home?"

"I'm okay."

"I got your letter. And the postcard."

"They're moving on tomorrow."

"Who...? What?"

"The bastard and his whore. I bribed the bellboy at their hotel. He said they're checking out in the morning. Something about taking a train to Bhopal."

"Where's that?"

"Somewhere east of here."

"What're they gonna do there?"

"How the hell should I know?"

"Be careful, dear."

"This bellboy—he said this afternoon the bastard brought a long, narrow case back to the hotel. Sounds like rifle case."

"Geez—Ronnie."

"Don't worry. He probably doesn't know which end to point. Listen, I'm not sure there'll be a phone where they're going, so I might not be able to call you for a while."

"I understand."

"I gotta go now."

"*Please* be careful. I love you, Ronnie."

"Sure."

John F. Kennedy International Airport was not quite large enough for Colonel Barrington, his entourage, and the media. Busting through the crowded corridors, they rushed for their plane even though it would wait for an important passenger like the Colonel. His P.R. man knew rushing through airports always looked good on his boss, especially when pursued by a mob of reporters.

As calculated, they allowed themselves to be cornered at the gate. Cameras clicked, flashbulbs flashing, the din of questions coagulating into a confused cacophony. The Colonel, veteran of many world-wide publicity blitzes, knew how to deal with the media. Just as quickly as they shot questions at him, he shot back rapid-fire answers.

"Mister Barrington, why—"

"That's *Colonel* Barrington!"

"Why're you coming out of retirement after such a long absence?"

"Got the itch!"

"How long has it been, Colonel?"

"Too long, my friend!"

"What're you hunting this time, or doesn't it matter, Colonel?"

"It doesn't matter," he laughed with them.

"What *are* you hunting, Colonel?"

"Tiger—big, bloody tiger! Tell your readers that!"

"What makes this hunt so special?"

"Yes, Colonel," a young reporter cut in, "what's so special about this hunt it brings you out of five years of retirement?"

"This cat may be a new world's record. I never miss a world-class beast—"

"Colonel, does the world really need another great cat stuffed in a museum?"

"It's also a man-eater! Didn't I say? A *man-eating* tiger! That's why I've been called in to plug that pussy. You reporters oughta know that if you did your homework."

"Colonel," another reporter interrupted, "any truth to the rumor you know Karl Edwards, the escaped mental patient who's claimed to be possessed by the spirit of a tiger?"

Colonel Barrington, caught off-guard with the sudden, unrehearsed question, glared at his P.R. man, who shrugged his shoulders.

"The plane's waiting, Colonel," one of his staff declared instantly, starting to usher him quickly away.

"Never heard of the man," the angry Colonel called back to the reporters, cameras clicking.

"But Colonel," the young reporter again called out, "one of your staff told my colleague you got the idea to go hunting after reading a *Times* article about Mister Edwards. Is that true?"

The Colonel snorted as his staff quickly formed a protective wall around him, turning him away.

"But is it true, Colonel?" a veteran reporter called out.

"Go to hell!" he shouted back, turning away.

The reporters rushed after him.

"Colonel, how big is this tiger?"

"Is this going to be your last hunt, Colonel?"

"Colonel, how long will your safari be?"

"What about the girlfriend in Delhi? Gonna see her?"

The Colonel's staff melded together, pushing their robust charge through the doors and down the ramp onto the plane, a rush of media chatter spilling after them.

"Damn cub reporters!" the Colonel cursed to his worried P.R. man. "I thought you cleared all the damn reporters."

"Sorry, Colonel. He must be new. Not on our pay list."

"No more slip-ups or you're off the tour! We've got a damn show to put on."

17

THE TRAIN SHOOK FROM SIDE TO SIDE as it crossed the arid landscape, dust blowing in through the open windows. The hot season had already turned most of the monsoon-green fields to amber and brown.

"You just going to sit there like that?" said Althea, sitting opposite Karl in the coach.

Karl sat stiffly on the bench, his back hunched, his chin propped on his fist, bent elbow resting on his knee. He stared beyond the cabin, off to a place that did not exist, piercing transparent Althea.

He'd said little more than was necessary since she'd told him about the tigers—enough to buy the tickets and tip the porter. The only person closed out of his world seemed to be her. He seemed to be withdrawing more now, retreating deep within himself. Back at Eastwood they knew what to call it. It was a survival mechanism—a way to preserve strength for the upcoming battle.

"Karl, *say* something," she demanded.

She began to wonder what he was going to do when they arrived at their destination. Was he really going into the forest with his rifle and hope to kill two man-eating tigers? The seriousness of his plan and the strength of his determination hadn't struck her as hard before. She could do nothing but watch him burning with hate. Or was it anger? Or fear? Too calm for any of those, she thought, examining him. Perhaps his true consciousness was hibernating.

The train jolted her back to reality as it began crossing a long trestle bridge spanning a wide valley with a shallow, sand bar littered river below.

She sighed, laid her head back. The bridge seemed to go on forever.

"You're trying to drive me crazy, aren't you? That's it, isn't it? Well, I'll tell you, it's beginning to work."

The train left the bridge; the rumbling of the train against the rails dropped in pitch. Glancing at her watch, she saw they had more than two hours until they reached Indore, the city where they changed trains. Maybe his mood would improve by then.

"Doctor!" Ian shouted, shuffling up the stone path to the bungalow, holding his tender ribs.

Hansen appeared on the veranda.

"Good God, man! What's this hollering about?"

The old *shikari* was waving a newspaper at him as he clambered up the steps.

"Here—read this," he ordered, out of breath, shoving the paper into the doctor's hands.

"You'd better sit and have a drink, man," the doctor insisted, motioning him to a chair in the shade. "You're not twenty years old anymore. You'll kill yourself running around in the hot sun like that."

"Aye, aye—read th' bloody paper!"

The doctor regarded the featured article. Ian dropped into the chair beside the umbrella-bedecked table.

"Th' Colonel's a-comin'," Ian declared.

"So, you've finally gone and done it, Ian. Blast you!"

"Aye, aye—read th' bloody paper! Tell yew everythin' aboot him. He's a-comin' tae kill our cats. But it says tha' he's a-come 'cause o' some loon tellin' him tae comin' o'er tae India. But *I* dinna do tha' thing—nae, he's come aboot th' article in th' paper. Don' ye see it?"

Doctor Hansen set the paper down on the table.

"It'll be a long trip for nothing."

"Wha' ye mean ba tha'?"

"Ian, I do believe our tigers have left our woods. There's been no sighting, no sound, and no killings, nothing to indicate their presence for more than a week—nothing since the Nawab was killed."

"Oh, they be comin' back, doc. Jus' them newspaper men squawkin' an' takin' all their damn photeegraphs up a-there. Why, I've nae doubt they shooed 'em away. But they'll be back. I'm sure o' tha'."

The doctor shook his head.

"Why? 'Tis such an unfriendly wood they left. No peace and quiet. Neighbors too nosy. A limited food supply. Why would they come back *here*? No, Ian, they're away for good, I'm afraid."

Ian chuckled. "Y'afraid? Ye makin' like yew miss 'em."

He shook his head as the houseboy brought a tray of iced tea.

"No, it's that I know the Colonel will be plenty damn perturbed to arrive and find no tigers."

Ian nodded as the houseboy poured the tea.

In silence they contemplated the Colonel's likely response. The doctor took a sip of tea. Ian took his, sipped twice, leaned back in his chair and sighed.

"So...who yew thin' should tell him?"

Stepping out of the main station in Indore, Althea leaned heavily against her man, holding his arm. Her face was painted with a curious smile. Karl lumbered down the sidewalk, bearing her weight. He remained quiet but his hands showed her he was awake.

Taking a taxi to a restaurant frequented by the tourists, thinking it safe, they dined on a large plate of spicy *rogan josh*. It seemed as though they hadn't eaten in days. They quickly went to work, stuffing down *roomali roti*—thin sheets of unleavened bread—with the *shami* kabobs. They dunked the wheat cake *bafla* into the bowls of thick *ghee*, as their waiter suggested. The tongue-tingling sharpness of the *dal*, a rather pungent lentil soup, was balanced by the soft accompanying *laddoos*—sweetmeats. For dessert, they split a mango, and Karl also devoured a guava. With a final toss of *sulfi*, a local brew distilled from the flowers of the *mahua* tree, they left enough money for bill and tip and exited, belching happily down the street.

Althea leaned against her lover as they wandered hand in hand through the neighborhood. They stopped at a corner grocery to buy a sack of dates, then returned to the main boulevard. The third taxi they hailed stopped and took them back to the station in time to catch their connecting train. They were not in time to get a private cabin, though. Instead, they got two seats in coach, along with the other tired, dusty passengers.

Bhopal did not stay up for them, as they quietly disembarked. The station lights glared, platforms empty. The taxi line had dwindled to two—one driver asleep on the hood of his car. They hired the other one. Finding a vacancy in the pre-dawn hours was no easy task. Their driver, in surprisingly good English, suggested they have breakfast while waiting for the night's guests to leave. Catching some sleep on the train, Karl elected to get out at a rental car office.

The 'hire' car was expensive, the insurance more so. The agency clerk wanted Karl and Althea to wait an hour for someone to drive them around, but Karl insisted on driving themselves. The clerk reminded him several times about the talent of the local drivers. He signed for the car—a small, British-made jeep—for seven days plus a higher insurance rate. Althea offered up her MasterCard.

After testing the vehicle going through several streets, Karl asked directions and finally took the right highway out of town, heading south to Barkhera. There was little morning traffic once he left the city, the smokestacks and metal-framed structures of the Union-Carbide plant stabbing the rosy sunrise beside him. Althea curled up in the back seat, the tepid breeze tying her hair in knots as they sped along the road in their jeep.

Thirty-odd miles down the road, they entered the town of Barkhera. Down-shifting through the dirty, narrow streets, slowing but not stopping at intersections, waiting for a wayward goat herd once and an overflowing cotton wagon another time, they found their way through the town. They stopped for gas at the last service station, where Althea's Visa card was the sacrifice. Before continuing south out of the town, Karl got directions to the village of Tashi, somewhere up in the hills.

"Watch for tiger, *sahib*," the station attendant warned, waving.

Althea laid her hand on his leg, enjoying the refreshing morning breeze blowing through her hair. Karl smiled; she seemed to believe his act. Inside, he was growing tense, his heartbeat pounding. His palms sweated against the steering wheel, beads of perspiration formed on his brow long before the copper sun had yet to reach its noontime zenith.

They were in tiger country now.

He had studied for this moment, practiced what he would feel. It fit the reality he saw. On either side of the road grew scrub forest—sparse stalks of wiry branches, yet thick enough to adequately hide a striped, camouflaged beast. At any moment, a mad tiger could burst from the brush, leap into their jeep, and drag one of them away.

His foot grew heavier and the jeep roared faster.

A weathered sign pointing northeast from the highway marked the turn-off. The road was hard-pack dirt, strewn with sharp rocks which threw the jeep from side to side. The road wound upward, passing beneath low-hanging trees, cutting through rough hillsides which offered good ambush sites. Forced by the terrain to slow down, they eventually broke from the last grove and rose up to a knoll which offered a view of the highway along which they had come.

Shacks dotted the barren yellow slopes, surrounded by uncultivated fields. One white, plaster-walled house they passed had a stern-faced man standing guard, his rifle poised for marauders. Was he guarding his farm from bandits—the *dacoits*—or from bestial criminals? Either way, Karl decided, villagers would be jumpy. He slowed more, not wanting to be seen running from anything.

No, he corrected himself, he was running *toward* something. Like the fool he knew himself to be, he was hurtling as fast as he could toward the happy-go-lucky bastard named Death. He knew it. It was impossible for him to step out of his consciousness and look back at the man who was acting in his place, thinking his thoughts, speaking his words, performing his actions. He knew what he was doing; he just couldn't believe it—or stop himself.

"Watch out!" Althea exclaimed, as the road narrowed suddenly, one side of it crumbling away into a ravine.

The road widened again, leveling, and a small village emerged from a clump of trees, framed by the forested ridge behind it and the golden crop fields spreading before it. It was a dusty, dirty village he saw and Althea couldn't hold back a quiet gasp.

They had arrived at the village of Tashi.

Colonel Barrington and company spilled through the gates, legions of spectators and reporters milling around the army of staff members.

"Good evening," an Indian woman, smartly dressed in blue Western blazer and skirt, spoke into a microphone as cameras rolled. "We are here to greet retired Colonel John Barrington, internationally famous big game hunter, on his return to India. It is said by American newspapers that Colonel Barrington has been called to dispatch the two Tashi man-eaters which have been terrorizing the hill country south of Bhopal for these past few weeks."

The Colonel, looking as fit and robust as the moment he first boarded the fifteen hour flight, burst through his exhausted, confused staff and took on the crowd, single-handedly parting them with his leather tote bag.

"We are informed by the American reporters who are accompanying Colonel Barrington that he has been away from his hunting sport— including in America—for a total of five years. Once considered retired to live the life of the country gentleman, this American *nawab* has returned to us for one last, perhaps greatest, hunt of his respectable career, a service to our countrymen who live in fear of the Tashi man-eaters."

The crowd drifted down the white-tiled terminal lobby, following the Colonel and his band, cameras snapping and lights flashing.

"We will bring you regular reports on Colonel Barrington's great hunt. The Tashi man-eaters are surely doomed. This is your reporter, Geeti Punja."

One of her cameramen was already hurrying down the length of the Delhi airport terminal, photographing the Colonel's entourage, and the big man himself.

Karl was angry, and pounded his fist hard on the doctor's table. "So what're you telling me? That you don't have any damn tigers?"

"Easy, dear," said Althea.

"Please be calm," said the *tahsildar*, the village leader, an elderly man of dark skin and white hair.

"Mister Edwards," Dr. Hansen spoke in a restrained voice, "we've no doubt you're a capable *shikari*, but the fact of the matter is there hasn't been hide nor hair of the tigers in a fortnight."

"More than," Ian added from his perch on the bar stool by the liquor cabinet.

"Look, I was—ah, *gentlemen*," Karl began, trying to play the role of a big game hunter, "I was sent here to take care of your problem. So here I come, at my own expense, at no little trouble to myself—or my *wife* here. And now you say you haven't got a problem. What about the newspapers? I saw the reports, the pictures. It certainly looks like it's a problem."

"Mister Edwards," Dr. Hansen tried again, "the papers were quite correct. For a time we did have a very grave problem—"

"Nae pun intend, laddy!" Ian cut in, chuckling.

"It was very serious. It got to the point where the villagers were locking themselves indoors and not tending fields, fearing for their lives."

"You can see how our fields become ragged plots of dried crops," the *tahsildar* said, gesturing from the doctor's bungalow to the hillsides. "We will starve this season because of this."

"They're only now beginning to get over their fear of the cats. But it's probably too late to reverse the damage done—leaving fields untended during the crucial month. They've all withered, as I'm sure you saw as you entered our village."

"Yes, Doctor, we saw them," Althea spoke up, "and it's really bad. But at least—"

"At least let me put them away for good so all your villagers won't ever have to worry," Karl finished.

"We will always worry about the tigers," the *tahsildar* declared, glancing quickly at Ian. "As long as our land breeds the beasts, they will wander among us. As long as they walk the land, we will have worry. But do not fear, good American, for we can live in peace with these gods of the forest. It is a rare instance when we do indeed clash with them."

"I'll drink tae tha'," Ian sang out, raising a urine cup filled with Scotch.

"And so it seems," the *tahsildar* continued in his soft voice, "the striped ones who have blessed our forest, then ventured down to our village to spy upon us—they now have changed their hearts and decided to journey away to bless another district."

"Tigers do tha'," Ian remarked.

Karl let out a long sigh. Althea laid her hand on his arm.

"I'm sorry," the doctor smiled. "But we're simply fresh out of tigers this week."

Karl grinned, looked at Ian sitting behind the doctor.

"Have you got another glass of...of whatever *he's* drinking?"

Dr. Hansen frowned, called his houseboy.

"I tried some of that stuff—*sulfi*, I think it's called—the other night,"

Karl continued. "Damn stuff about burned a hole in my stomach."

"Donna yew touch th' local brew. Tha' stuff kin kill yew," Ian cried out, hopping down from the stool.

"I know I'll never try it again," Karl replied, making faces.

The houseboy returned with a tray decorated with glasses and a bottle of Scotch.

"Now's th' good stuff," said Ian. "Since we donna have nae tigers fer yew tae shoot, s'pose I take yew tae tha' temple an' show ye everythin'? Wouldn't be nae harm in tha'."

"No," the *tahsildar* answered. "If the forest is free for our tigers, then it is free for our people."

"Bonny fair show, eh!"

"Yes, umm...I'd *like* to see this famous temple," Karl said. "And, aaa...my wife is something of an amateur, uh...archaeologist. Isn't that right?"

Althea, caught off-guard, pursed her lips. "Sorta."

They raised their glasses, held them together a beat.

"To tigers," Karl announced.

"An' their hunters," Ian added, clinking his cup to the others' glasses and tossing down his fill.

"I'd like to see where this *nawab* guy was killed by the tigers. We saw the picture in the paper, but I'd like to see it myself. I understand that was their base of operations, so to speak, during their visit here."

"Indeed," Ian replied.

"In fact," Dr. Hansen spoke up, "Ian here even tried his luck with them. Would've been rather amusing were it not for the tragedy of it all. See, he took one of the farmers with him, a man who'd had experience with firearms in the army, and they marched right up there—"

"Yew gettin' it all wrong, doc," Ian smirked. "We was steppin' lightly along th' trail—were nae near th' temple, but we was headin' for it."

"The two tigers charged Ian and his partner, and—well, the male tiger leaped onto Ian, knocked him down and kissed him—literally. 'Twould've been amusing—"

"'Tweren't amusin', doc."

"Jon was hauled away by the tigers, though. Still can't understand why they took him—being up and shooting, instead of Ian, who was down already. A fluke, I suppose. Anyway, he had a couple cracked ribs, bruises, and a big ugly scrape where the cat licked his face with that sandpaper tongue. Ian's lucky to be alive, certainly."

"I should say so!" Althea exclaimed, grabbing Karl's hand.

"Hmm...that's interesting," said Karl. He turned to Ian, chuckling. "You weren't wearing red, were you, Mister McDonnell?"

Ian's mouth dropped open. He nearly spilled his drink.

"How yew know aboot th' red shirt?"

Karl glanced around the table, realizing he had spoken one sentence too many. "Ah—it was in the paper, of course."

"No, 'tweren't," Ian stated.

"It wasn't because," the doctor began to explain, "when the tigers were through with him, there wasn't much of the shirt left. And what was left was burned in the funeral pyre. No reporter saw the red shirt."

"A red shirt?" asked Althea.

"Aye, 'twere," Ian replied.

"Your friend was wearing a red shirt?" Karl asked, dumbfounded, his eyes widening to match Ian's.

"How yew be knowin' o' tha', now?"

Karl glanced around at each of the others, shrugged his shoulders.

"I used to know a tiger that hated red."

After zeroing and firing their rifles, Karl and Ian headed into the forest, marching up to the temple ruins, confident the tigers had fled.

"You okay?" Karl asked Ian.

The old hunter was sweating profusely, and starting to shake as they headed up the trail, approaching the bend where his partner Jon had been killed.

He nodded affirmatively.

Karl backed him up, holding his rifle level, walking backwards every third step, checking his six. His army training came back to him as he searched for the enemy in the brush around them.

"Tha' temple's up 'head a wee bit," Ian muttered. He paused to catch his breath.

Karl jumped at the sudden cry of a forest bird.

"Peacock," said Ian.

They continued.

The dried dirt still showed some of the pug marks from that horrible morning as they stood where Ian took the charge of the male tiger and almost died. He could not control his shaking any longer.

"You sure you're all right?"

Ian nodded. He pointed up the trail and they started off again.

"Aye, s'pose even th' ol' soldier like me gets a-shook when he faces death like tha'." Ian gave a chilly chuckle of embarrassment.

The trail flattened, the forest growth falling away from the dirt path, forming a grassy clearing. The temple stood on their left: cold, silent, haunting. Not even birds cried there. They stepped through the break in the stone wall, moved into the center of the yard. Karl regarded the tall, central temple building, following its sensuously curved tower spiraling upward to the lush canopy of the forest.

"Tha's aboot a thousand years ol'."

Recognition oozed over him as he studied the ancient structure, moss covered and vine entangled.

"Looks like it," Karl remarked.

He recalled the black and white photograph of this same temple yard. The picture had shown the bodies of two men, curled like fetuses in the yard. The limp bodies of the two cubs were piled together like bags of flour. He looked for indications of their positions. The yard was bare, but the grass remained stained where each body had lain.

"Yew reco'nize it?" Ian asked, voice shaking.

Karl stepped back, taking in all three towers with a single gaze.

"Yes, I recognize it. Uh—from the newspaper."

He paused to judge Ian's mindset. Something about this eccentric Scotsman that he couldn't identify gave him confidence. Ian was someone who would understand, maybe believe him. He watched for Ian's reaction.

"And I recognize it...from...*here*." Karl raised his hand, touching his fingers to his forehead.

Ian squinted his eyes. "Enough seen?"

Karl turned left and right, gazing at the entire temple complex, taking in every detail, comparing it with the portrait in his mind. Hadn't he already seen the same temple in his dreams, in his nightmares?

"No."

"Wha' ye bloody wanna see, then?"

"Can we go inside?"

Ian laughed.

"Yew read th' report aboot th' Nawab? He wanted tae see wha's inside."

"You said they're gone now."

"I said we've nae sightin' fer a wee spell."

Karl sighed, discouraged. "Where do you think they've gone?"

Ian suddenly raised a finger to his lips.

Karl tightened his grip on the rifle, pulling it into his shoulder.

A mongoose dashed across the yard, scurrying in front of them as it passed out of sight among the temple ruins. Karl instinctively aligned his rifle at the small creature, caught himself.

"Tiger's bigger'n tha'," Ian laughed.

Karl lowered his rifle as Ian started back.

18

THROUGH THE MOSAIC OF BRANCHES and leaves, Roundpaw sees his future. The tigress hides with him among the bushes marking the border of the man-cleared field. Brown stalks sprout there, rising half way up a man-creature's body. The brown pods burst full with fluffy white fibers, swelling under the late September sun.

Through more than a week of journeying, they have crossed through forested hills, scrub woodlands, and tall grasslands. They have skirted man nests, passed the noisy, rolling boxes of men, and their stone trails. They have seen man-creatures, moving secretly, unnoticed by them. Stealth is their great attribute.

A steady, grueling pace it is, powered by exhausting, unswerving determination. Constantly driven by Roundpaw's passionate vow, they have traveled far from their old temple enclave, far from the man-creatures of Tashi.

Guardians of the forest now exiled as criminals for protecting their territory, defending their own, living in peaceful coexistence with the stench-reeking man beasts.

They have reached the limit of the contiguous forests which have shielded them. Beyond lie barren lands, shelterless reaches which leave them exposed to both the sun's searing heat and the hateful eye of Man. The first step lies defiantly before them.

Roundpaw knows that each step—or the next step, or the next—each brings him closer to that for which he longs yet fears.

Each step draws him closer to his dear, sweet death, and the rest he craves.

The field is wide. Their cover is sparse. Man-creatures are digging at the ground with their sticks. One third of the field has been stripped of its brown-stalked vegetation with the fluffy white flowers, collected in a rolling box stopped at the edge of the field, on a raised trail to the side. Opposite the line of bushes, the field is bordered by another row of tall bushes and a few trees. To the far corner, a skinny horse grazes, tethered to a wooden post.

The tigress returns his gaze. They must cross the field. There is no cover to conceal their movements from the eyes of the man-creatures.

As the afternoon sun blazes down upon the man beasts, they are compelled to halt their labor and traverse the rows of plants to the wagon on the road, to partake of their mid-day meal. With the men away, Roundpaw decides it is safe for them to break from their cover.

They part the brown stalks, the fluffy white tops bouncing against their high, striped shoulders as they pass among them.

A bird cries out—

Another sings.

One man jumps down from the wagon, surveys the field with his forepaw shielding his eyes from the sun's glare. The others regard the field. One of them secures the ancient fire stick strapped to the wagon. He wipes dust from the stock's ornate etching, admires the artwork, inserts a bullet into the cracked chamber, hands the weapon to the first man, still examining the field.

The stalks come to an end, only the naked furrows of dirt ahead, Roundpaw sees. The tigress halts behind him. He lifts his large head, his stripes crisscross the stalks. His coat's orange tint contrasts with the white of the cotton bulbs.

The farmer, rushing to the edge of the field, pulls the ancient firearm to his shoulder, locates the spot of orange among the pale cotton, fixes his sights, weighs his finger on the old trigger, squeezes it as his comrades roar hateful words. The barrel explodes and a shot rings across the field.

The shot clips off the cotton bulb from a stalk in front of Roundpaw.

Alarmed, the tigress bolts past him, out onto the plowed field, her tense muscles tingling, her eyes burning with fire. Perking her ears, she aims her vicious body toward the doomed target.

The farmer hurries to reload his single-shot rifle, crying to the others to grab their farming tools.

She hurls herself down the bare furrows toward the road where the man-creature frantically stuffs the next bullet into his old rifle, thankful that it held together once again.

Roundpaw roars after her, trying to call her to his side. He breaks from the cover, stands exposed on the black soil, roaring his anguish.

The farmer again raises the rifle, tries to calm his fluttering heart enough to hold it steady. His misty eyes try to align the sights but it is difficult, seeing the tigress charging at him.

His shot is rushed and sails high as the tigress bounds up the low embankment and slaps her huge forepaws on the farmer's shoulders, slamming him back against the side of the wagon.

The other farmers are swinging their spades at her.

Roundpaw runs after her, reaches the wagon. There, one man swings his spade desperately at him, missing his nose. Roundpaw throws his unsheathed claws at the man's head, tearing off one side of his jaw. As it swings from one hinge, the man struggles to hold it in place.

Face to face, the tigress kisses the farmer. His rifle falls harmlessly to the dirt at his feet. As they part, the man's face comes away with her teeth, only the blood-bubbling skull remaining. During the brief struggle, the rifle is kicked under the wagon as the last farmer, screaming at the top of his lungs, flees down the road.

Ian spread the tattered map across the table, waving Karl over.

"Brandy?"

"Uh...sure," answered Karl, leaning over the table in Ian's small bungalow.

"Kin yew find Tashi on tha' map? Hah!—I bet ye canna find it. It's a wee spot. Look for Bhopal."

"Found it."

"Find Barkhera?"

"Yes, found it."

He set down two glasses, a small bottle of brandy, with a grin.

"I've me own idea on this," Ian began, pouring. "First, we've tae work backwards a wee bit."

"What is it you're trying to figure out?"

"I got me own theory aboot them cats."

"What is it?"

"Drink up first."

Karl took a sip, felt the poison's age.

"I've had tha' bottle here fer nearly seven years, I wan' yew tae know. But I thin' this be a special occasion fer me. An' fer yew. Aye, I'm a wee bit in years, as yew nae doubt noticed. I done me share o' huntin' an' I've nae regrets. Except poor Jon. I ne'er had—ah, lad, I ne'er had wha' yew call a 'prentice. I be takin' a likin' tae yew, laddy. I'd like tae teach yew some o' th' tricks o' th' trade, so tae speak. I wan' tae think o' yew as me 'prentice. So drink up, lad!"

Karl smiled, raised his glass. "Thanks."

"Wha' I'm a-sayin' is tha' I wan' us tae hunt them tigers tagether. Like we's partnah's. Like we's a bloody team. Th' tigers—there be *two* o' them. Why not two o' us, then, eh? Er yew game fer a hunt, laddy?"

Karl downed a long swallow.

"Yes, I'm ready."

"Bonny! Drink up."

Swallows dropped, glasses refilled. Somewhere among the drinking a partnership was sealed with a handshake. Ever more outlandish toasts finalized the deal. Master hunter, apprentice hunter. Master *shikari*, apprentice *shikari*.

"Looky here, lad," Ian announced, slapping his hand on the map, finger extended to mark a location. "Last spring—'twere aboot April, I think—bein' o'er in Orissa, south o' Sambalpur, tha's where't happen. I heard aboot it later, from th' fool newspaper an' from a colleague er two. Aye, 'twas two lads out o' Kolkata went a-huntin'. I gotta lad who knew them. They 'as bloody aristocrats—sons o' them—lovers o' th' bloody colonial era, vanguards o' th' viceroyalty—nae matter they were nae born 'til long after even Gandhi. Seems th' old man 'as a colonel er such—dinna matter.

"Anyways, lad, they decide tae go huntin' south a wee bit. Have another drink, lad. They 'as wantin' tae bag themselves a tiger. Lord knows why. Er course, yew know tiger's nae legal tae hunt now, eh? Lessin' it be a *man-eater*, an' then only we *shikari* hunt. They bought themselves a band o' villagers tae beat for them—tha's walkin' in a wide arc makin' lots o' noise tae drive th' cat where th' hunter's a-waiting. But they decide tae be some sort o' heroes—they bloody think!

"They get all the Rovers an' the guides, the beaters an' skinners, a whole bloody lot, an' they head out'n th' plain. Someone says they seen a cat nearby, so they turn tha' way. An'—bloody luck!—they spot one in the grassland. Th' cat's breakin' for th' wood. They park th' Rovers'n give chase on foot—on bloody foot, mind ye! They corner th' tigress deep in th' wood—an' o' course she lashes out a' them, takes a few men doon. These lads decide tae be queer, somethin' fer havin' more guts'n their pappy. This bein' as it 'as told tae me, mind ye! They hold back their rifles an' order th' Hindus tae shoot arrows at th' tigress—an' they prick her with spears, too, lad!

"The cat's doon an' dying, an' they're beatin' on her with rifle butts when all o' sudden a grand male cat arrives, king o' th' forest, a-jumpin' amongst 'em, a-slashin' an' bitin' his way tae his mate. He takes doon more men, an' th' guide's shoutin' fer them tae shoot th' bloody tiger, but they decide tae walk away from it—run away, th' fools! Th' Hindu lads, they be full mad fer not keepin' their friends from dyin'—nae shootin' th' cats when they had 'em cornered—tho' they was foolish enough fer cornerin 'em in th' first instance. Even though it's illegal, them villagers went tae th' authorities aboot bein' jilted.

"They bring th' lads tae court, but o' course they got their too bloody high attachments an' go free with a wee fine. Drink up, lad—finish th' bottle. I got more. Now th' bloody villagers've lost their friends an' neighbors. Aye, they got their ol' bloody fee, but they had tae turn it o'er tae th' magistrate—since it's illegal gain. Th' least they kin do's tae recover th' bloody carcass o' th' tigress tha's killed, they thinkin'. But when they return tae th' wood where they left her, she's gone. Queer turn! A farmer saw a tiger nearby diggin' in th' dirt, swearin' he saw another tiger—maybe dead—laying next tae him, an' this first tiger buried th' other tiger.

"I know it's sound queer, but tha's wha' th' report said. After th' tiger went on, some villagers go up a-there an' dug out th' body o' tha' lassie, still showin' all th' broken arrows an' spear punctures. Th' fact o' th' matter was tha' tiger truly dug a grave an' buried his mate! Now, isn't tha' the most queer thin' yew ever did hear, lad?"

Karl swirled the dark liquid around in his glass, calmly watching it form waves which crashed against the edges. Then he tossed it down, let it burn his throat.

"Oh, I don't know, Ian. I've heard some pretty weird stories."

"Aye. I'm sure yew have."

"I've heard that story before, I must admit."

"Is tha' so? An' might I ask yew where, an' from who?"

Karl paused, staring at the empty bottle on the table. After a long silence, he looked up and met Ian's cold, gray eyes.

"If I told you...you'd call me crazy."

Ian took his last swallow of brandy. "Hah! I'd call yew crazy now, jus' fer wantin' tae hunt them tigers."

Karl chuckled to himself, "I saw it in a dream."

Ian pondered his apprentice, then stood up and swaggered over to his liquor cabinet.

"Aye, we be a-needin' another taste, if we're tae get through th' tellin'."

Ian could barely stand, but even as he continued emptying bottles of Scotch, bourbon, and wine they found in the cabinets, his mind remained unquestionably clear.

"Natur'ly, I dinna believe a thin' yew says."

Karl was woozy, his mind swirling like the liquor in his glass and in his stomach. If his tiger was rampaging, he could not feel anything. He had found a tranquilizer. He had also found a kindred spirit in Ian.

"Of course you don't," Karl responded. "You'd be fucking crazy if you did. But I wouldn't lie to you. And I wouldn't call you crazy, neither."

"Tha's good tae know, laddy."

In their drunkenness, neither man quite heard exactly everything the other spoke. They were conversing with themselves but in the same room. They each thought they answered the other, and in their slurred speech and bobbing heads, maybe they did.

"I do dream of tigers. Like I told you," said Karl, gesturing.

"Aye, we all dream o' tigers here in India. He's part o' our lives. He's our bloody conscience. Whene'er we let up our guard e'en an instant, there he is tae punish us. After all, we's th' lads tha' stole his land. Aye, he takes a dozen lives in his man-eating career, an' we take only th' one o' his. 'Tis hardly fair."

"Maybe that's what those two hunters in Orissa had in mind. The report said their father was killed by a tiger. Do you think they wanted to avenge his death by killing one for themselves?"

"Aye, but killin's nae th' answer."

"What about revenge? Do you think maybe this tiger's hunting them? The aristocratic fools? He's traveled over five-hundred miles—if your reports are correct."

"Tiger dinna hunt men. Nae like tha', anyways. Yew got tae be bloody-well crazy tae think tha', lad. It's not as tho' they kin think like yew er me."

"I still believe the killing of that hunter at Kanha was because he was wearing a red hunting vest."

"Aye, there's nae other motive."

"And the killings here were, as you've said, easily explained away by territorialism."

"Aye, tha' too."

"As I see it—through my blurry eyes, thanks to you—that's a straight line running from the Sambalpur hunt to the Kanha preserve killing—"

"Tae our Tashi killins," Ian finished, sipping his potion. "Tha' photeegrapher an' his missus. An' me partner, Jon. An' th' Nawab, his guide an' *mahout*. Tha's enough tae classify him as one genuine, certified bloody man-eater. A cat with a taste fer man flesh. Aye, wha' an awful taste!"

"The two hunters in Orissa...."

"Aye, lad. All dressed up like a pair o' dandies in their grandpappy's colonial garb. Decked out in red from collar tae hip, with th' red stripe on black trousers an' the damn khaki helmets. Th' spittle-flingin' image o' their dear grandpappy."

"Is that so?"

"Aye, lad. This being th' year o' th' tiger in th' Oriental calendar—if yew follow tha' malarkey. This be th' year o' th' tiger. This be th' year when every bonny lad bags his tiger fer posterity. This be th' year every good *tiger* bags his young fool o' a hunter."

Karl raised his freshly refilled glass. "To sporting tigers and young hunters!"

Ian clinked his glass with Karl's. "Aye, tae tigers—but nae tae th' foolish hunters."

They emptied their glasses.

"Tell me, Ian. You're saying that our tigers headed in a generally northwestern direction, following the line we've already drawn on the map, right?"

He nodded, belched loudly.

"Yer tiger's journey from Orissa, as yew say, due north-northwest. When he arrived here, he met up with our ol' tigress—th' lassie tha's been here fer many years. They've taken off together. I'm guessin' tae be th' same bloody direction."

Karl watched the cherry-faced Ian from under a furrowed brow.

"Yes, he seems to have a plan."

"Why does he go tae th' north-northwest?"

"He's got a great sense of direction."

"Aye, lad—like they kin see th' color red! 'Tis but a myth, lad. Tigers canna see colors. Color-blind."

"Where will he kill next? That's the question."

Ian sat up, reached for the nearest bottle to refill his glass, saw a figure coming up the path to the bungalow. Behind the figure the sun was already lighting the distant hills.

"Looks like we've company."

Karl tried to stand, fell back into his chair. "I would think we could predict where he would settle next. I mean, each killing he's stayed in the area for a while."

Ian, grabbing onto furniture to keep himself balanced, opened the door for Dr. Hansen.

"Then he moves on for about the same distance before he settles down again," said Karl, unaware of the doctor's arrival.

"Wha' brings yew tae me humble abode, doc?" asked Ian, stepping aside and motioning the doctor in.

"You're drunk, Ian," Hansen snapped.

Ian clapped his arm around the doctor's shoulder.

"Yew noticed! Lord, I be thinkin it's jus' th' bloody heat, doc."

"Mister Edwards—you're here, too? Your wife's looking for you. She's half out of her wits worried about the two of you when you didn't return when you said you would. I've been worried, too. That is, until Rajneesh told me you were here. You went to the temple yesterday, didn't you?"

"Aye, doc. We've nae tigers up a-there. Wha' kin we do yew fer?"

The doctor let out a sigh.

"I know it's morbid news, but it's news you've been waiting for."

He regarded the two drunkards, wondering if they were too far gone to understand what he was about to say, decided it couldn't wait until later.

"Yes, the news. The postman said they've had a tiger killing up in Aklera."

"You mean, a tiger being killed?" Ian questioned.

"No, tiger killing a man. Yesterday afternoon."

"Where? Aklera?" Ian cried, stumbling to the table and pouncing on the map, soaking up the spilled liquor. "Aye, tha's it! A bloody straight line!" He turned to his partner. "Yew hear, laddy? They struck again—at th' northwest, jus' like yew said."

Hansen cleared his throat, studying the map over Ian's shoulder. "Three cotton farmers were attacked by two tigers in the field. One was killed, one badly injured. Seems one of the tigers tore off his jaw. The villagers think it's our tigers. They've agreed to have a beat...if they can find a good *shikari*."

Deep in his chair, Karl belched.

"There's our man, doc," Ian sang out, thumbing at his guest.

The doctor regarded the drunk American. "Him?"

"Dinna yew worry, doc. He's fit fer th' job. I watched him while we's up a' th' temple. He knows his business. We's partners now, besides. He's ready."

"Yes, well...." The doctor frowned. "Anyway, I'd better help him back to his wife."

Karl's head wavered, fell against the tabletop with a loud thud.

"They've got tae be our cats," said Ian. "Where else in this bloody land do two tigers travel together? Much less be man-eatin' together? Aye, tha' be them."

They lifted Karl, swung his arm around the doctor's shoulders. As Hansen half-carried, half-dragged Karl out the door and down the path, Ian yawned off sleep and set to work cleaning his rifle.

A jeep with one headlight out nearly ran them over as it rushed down the dirt road, heading into the village. Dr. Hansen cursed back over his shoulder at the mustached man driving, noticing the rifle case in the back seat.

Dr. Hansen found Althea sleepy in a white camisole and silk shorts, awaiting her man's return.

After dropping Karl down on the dusty bed, she thanked him for finding him. When the doctor left, she turned to regard Karl. No matter how she tried to hold them back, tears welled up and rolled down her cheeks. Wordlessly, she lay beside him and held him as he rested half in sleep, half in drunken stupor.

The night was hot, humid. The dawn no less warm. Sitting beside him on the bed, she stroked his hair, letting her thoughts fill her head with terror, feeling her sorrow growing. She listened to the hum of insects, the random *baa baa* of goats, the cry of peacock, the weeping of a fading yellow moon left to dry under a shelf of clouds.

Leaning back, she breathed deeply, remembering the yoga exercises and her meditation routine she had left behind.

"The dream is over—if there ever was one," she sighed. "You were right. You're doing everything you can to cast me away. I want you, but you've forgotten me. I think—tomorrow—I should go back to Mumbai, and then fly home—where I can have a simple life. Just me, myself, and I. All alone. With nobody to care for...."

She threw herself across his chest, trying not to cry. Karl's arm swung up and cradled her. His eyes opened. She turned her head and their eyes met, painfully.

"I'm sorry," he whispered.

"What *are* we doing here? Oh, I'm so confused! I feel so sad. I feel like I'm living with a terminally ill patient, just waiting for the day he finally dies, waiting for the end to come."

A smile flashed across his face.

"But I *am* terminally ill," he muttered. "And to save my life, I have only one recourse. If I attempt it and succeed, then I can live a full and free life. If I don't, then I'm...doomed."

She turned her face away from his alcohol breath.

"And if you try it and don't succeed?"

He coughed. "Then I'll die—quickly. With less pain than if I died the kind of slow death I'm suffering now."

She wanted to laugh. He really was insane. Struggling so long to keep the thought from entering her consciousness, she could no longer fight it. She had to face it. Whatever good qualities he might have, they were all a clever front for his foundation of insanity.

Hah!—to go kill a tiger to relieve one's nightmares.

"You're insane!" she laughed aloud, wiping her eyes.

His eyes burned bright, nearly blinding her, as he rolled over her, pinning her down.

"I am *not* insane," he grumbled. "I have *never* been insane, nor will I ever *be* insane. Do you understand? I'm not crazy! I am *not* crazy!"

19

THE DAWN DREW UP BLOOD-RED, like the spilled essence of a great carcass lain across the canopy of the world.

Teary-eyed and exhausted, Althea hobbled down the dirt path from their cottage to the jeep, her arms wrapped around Karl.

With a long regard for the ominous dawn's painting, he helped her into the passenger seat, she in her khaki bush clothes and calf-high snake boots they bought in Mumbai. His outfit nearly matched hers. They had to look the part if they hoped to convince the old Aklera *tahsildar* they were really hunters.

"Why does Mister McDonnell have to ride with us?" Althea asked. "I want more time with you, Karl."

"He's got to come with us. He's our ticket. He knows the *tahsildar*, and he's the one who will be managing the beat."

"But can't he go in his own jeep?"

"Althea, be patient."

At that moment, he saw her wave at someone.

"Good morning, Mister Edwards," Dr. Hansen called, approaching the jeep. He tipped his hat. "Missus Edwards."

Karl nodded.

"Hi," said Althea.

"Thought you could use a little help," the doctor offered, taking the bag Karl was carrying off his shoulder and setting it on the back seat. "I'll be after you tomorrow morning. Also—sorry to mention it—it's best to take this."

They regarded the small box labeled FIRST AID and Karl nodded.

"You're still too woozy," said Althea, tapping his chest.

Dr. Hansen studied Karl. "How's that head of yours?"

Karl brought his finger to his lips.

"Sorry," the doctor said with a wink. "Are you going to be well enough for the beat?"

Karl nodded, already contemplating the day.

"He was fine after sleeping all night," Althea said with a wink. "Too much activity during the night." She gave him a kiss.

They walked up the path to the cottage, leaving Althea in the jeep.

"One thing," Dr. Hansen began once they were inside, keeping an eye on Althea. "I met a man last night...after I brought you back here from Ian's place. Said he knew you."

"Oh?"

"Yes—said he was your, aaa...yes. The girl." He jerked his thumb outside. "He said she was his...*wife*. Said the two of you've run away together?"

"What?"

"It's none of my business, I know. I thought I should let you two know this gentleman's on to you."

"What are you talking about?"

"Don't you know?"

"There isn't anyone in all of India I know other than the people I met here in this village. That's only a handful. Okay, we aren't exactly married, but—"

"That's fine. I understand that's the way it's done in the States."

"No, that's not what I mean at all. I really don't know who the guy is. Are you sure? It sounds like somebody just wanting to make trouble. Maybe some local guy who got a look at her and thought he'd try—"

Dr. Hansen stopped him with a wave of his hand.

"I'm sure you'll believe me when I tell you we don't have many tourists in our end of the woods. I'm positive the man is not a local. Dark skin, dark hair, yes, but he had an American accent. Strange fellow—said he was a doctor, in fact. He had a rifle, too."

They stopped for lunch in Bhopal and hired boys to guard their open-topped jeep.

A long afternoon on the narrow highway took them through the sparse woodlands that covered central India like patches of corduroy cloth. By the time the sun began sinking to the horizon, the highway had become a bumpy, barely paved road, straight yet washboarded. Soon they entered the state of Rajasthan, the western-most state of India.

Ian, acting as their guide, remarked that they were heading out of tiger territory.

"I be damned if'n I knew a reason tha' bloody cat's headin' fer th' desert," he exclaimed, scratching his head as hot breezes blew his white hair in tangles.

The *tahsildar* of Aklera was expecting them when they arrived at dusk. They were welcomed by the cheering of several families gathered around the *tahsildar* and the village elders.

"*Aiye*," they were greeted by the crowd.

"*Bahut dhanyavaad*," Ian called, dismounting.

The *tahsildar* greeted Ian, telling him it was a pleasure to see him again. He extended his hand to shake following British custom. Ian shook hands, then responded Hindu style with his palms pressed together in front of his face and a little dip of his head.

The village was like Tashi though larger. The land was noticeably drier, evidenced by the multitude of cotton fields they passed. There was no cover here for tigers, it was explained by the *tahsildar*, although once in a rare while a tiger would wander down from the hills to harass their livestock. It seemed so this time.

"He says th' tigers've likely laid up in th' wood south o' Jhalawar," Ian translated for Karl. "Tha's aboot twenty clicks from here. Th' field where th' men was attacked aboot seven clicks north. It's th' only wood they got here. There's also some natural caves there—in th' hillsides. Other tigers've been shot there, so he feels confident they be there too."

"Sounds about right," Karl remarked with a tip of his sweat-stained Panama hat to the elderly man whose head was wrapped in white cotton bandana.

Ian talked further with the village council in Hindi, translating bits for Karl where important.

"He says they be glad a *shikari*'s come...but he's sad tha' it's me. Says I muffed it at Tashi. But don' yew worry, lad. Told'em yer me 'prentice. Said yer a good *shikari*, lots o' kills doon south. I think they're buyin' it."

Karl's face was smug. "I don't want to lie to these people."

"Aye, laddy! Don' yew wan' th' job er don' yew? Let me handle it. I know how tae talk tae these folks."

And talk they did, late into the night.

When they finished, the two of them trudged back to the bungalow where their baggage had been taken, along with Althea.

"Says there's nae problem gettin' th' beat up. They've e'en got a elephant. This used tae be prime tiger territory. Many rajahs hunted here, an' th' Brits later. Then th' cotton crop spread east, swallowed this region. Th' forests come doon, an' th' fences went up, and th' tigers moved further east up in th' hills."

"So when do we go after them?"

"What's yer hurry, lad? They're twenty clicks up th' road now."

"Then why do we stop here? Why not go up to the other village?"

"This be th' closest village. No running water at tha' other one, eh?"

"What's the plan then?"

"I know th' place they speak aboot. A small valley, cut by a stream. Lots of *nullahs*, digging back inta th' hills. Thick woods back a-there too—too rough tae be cut doon fer cotton. It'll be a tough clime tae *shikar* in, tha's fer sure."

"What about the beat?"

"Laddy, with a big hole like tha' tae hide in, nae beat's gonna be able tae dig back in there. Best we kin hope is tae corner 'em in tha' gorge, then we go in after'em."

"What? On foot?"

"Tha's right, lad. There's nae other way tae go...'cept tae leave'em lone an' hope they go away on their own. We'll have us a looky in th' mornin'."

Karl held his hands up, his face tight, then slapped his hands on the table between them.

"Now wait, Ian. You mean to tell me these two tigers are holed up in some gorge area with a mess of thick vegetation, and all the beaters are going to do is stand around while you and me just walk in there and say 'peeky-boo, tigers, you're dead' and then play *bang bang* until one, two, or all four of us is dead?"

"Nae quite tha' way, laddy. It's nae likely all *four* o' us would be killt.

One o' th' four'll probably walk out alive—er pad out, heh heh, if'n it be th' tiger."

"You're mad, Ian! You know we can't go in there like that. Just about anything could happen."

"Do yew wanna tiger, er don' yew?"

"I was hoping to go on living after this adventure if I had my preference."

Ian paused, clapped his hand on Karl's shoulder.

"Laddy, 'tain't an adventure if there ain't a wee bit o' personal risk. See yew in th' mornin'."

The tossing and turning did not end until dawn, when Karl was awakened after a few brief minutes of sleep by the noisy villagers preparing for the beat.

Solemnly, he dressed in the khaki bush outfit he had worn the day before, only then bothering to splash water on his face from a basin on the dresser. It did not help revive him. While Althea slept, he sat in the adjoining room, cleaning his rifle. He checked his ammunition. He would take plenty of it with him; no need to play the hero and take the cats with one shot each. Even if he could.

The din outside increased as did the daylight. They gathered their sticks and farm tools. Others wound up the white cloth that would serve as a fence to hold one flank—tigers never dared try and tear through the mysterious white fences. The villagers chattered like a monkey troop, excited by the day's event. The great *shikari* had come to save them.

He—one Karl J. Edwards, mild-mannered former Army corporal, unemployed autoworker from Kansas City, recently discharged from a mental hospital, fleeing for his life. No, literally fleeing *from* life into the jaws of death.

His thoughts bothered him. He kept them imprisoned securely in the back of his mind for the past few weeks since they left the States. As the moment drew closer, however, those thoughts rattled around in his head crying to be let out. Finally, they escaped.

His nerves shook as reality set in.

Rechecking the chamber of the rifle, he wondered if he'd gotten out all the carbon from yesterday's practice shooting. As he listened to the shouted instructions in Hindi outside, he tried to recall the times he had gone hunting before. He had hunted pheasant and quail as a boy with his father, and he went deer hunting with his uncle. One time a buck had charged them. He had never been in combat despite three years in the army. He had read about shooting, gone to ranges occasionally but that was hardly adequate training. He laughed, amused by his stupidity. Shaking his head, he couldn't think of any way out of this situation—

The heavy approach of the elephant Ian said they had available for the beat shook the cabin. The great beast trumpeted and Althea awoke in the next room. The time was getting close.

The door was knocked upon repeatedly.

Karl opened it, greeting the old *tahsildar* and his assistants. Behind them, nearly overpowering them, the gluttonous, crimson ball of sun rolled on the distant horizon like an overripe melon, bleeding into the clouds that dared tease it. He watched it beating like a giant heart in the cool dawn air.

"*Sahib, shikar* ready," the *tahsildar* announced.

"*Dhanyavaad*," Karl replied, thanking him, hands in prayer.

He grabbed his rifle, ammunition belt, and his sweat-stained hat, and followed them down the path to where Baghwan, their elephant, knelt as he was outfitted with a riding basket.

"G'mornin', partna'," Ian called out, then threw a wide gesture at the elephant. "Mite fair lookin' pachyderm, eh? Fair day fer a beat, eh? It be sunny taday, but it'll be cool, thankfully. Nae heat stroke taday, lad. I be predictin' two dead tigers ba noon."

Karl nodded, turned away.

Ian understood. A *shikari*'s thoughts were his own the day of the hunt. Like any sport, the utmost concentration was required. It could not be disturbed by mere small talk or idle prattle.

As Karl walked up the path, absently inspecting the villagers lined up with their farm implement weapons, a ragtag army, they smiled brightly, many greeting him, bowing their heads with their hands joined at the palms. He was a god to them, it seemed. Actually, he thought nervously, he was their *sacrifice* to the gods.

When he came to the end of the line and turned to head back, he saw that Althea had joined Ian beside the crouching elephant, dressed in her matching khaki outfit, camera in hand.

"How are you feeling this morning, dear?" she asked him, holding up her camera. "You seemed to have trouble getting to sleep last night."

Ian grinned, took Althea aside.

"Don' let'm worry yew now, lassie. *Shikari*'s gotta have time tae prepare himself. Yew know, in his head." He tapped his temple.

She frowned. "Oh—of course."

Karl regarded the elephant. Baghwan regarded the man, with a sideways glance of annoyance.

"Picture," called Althea, the camera to her face as Karl stood before the elephant. *Snap.*

"What time will we start?" he asked Ian.

"If we're leavin' soon, we kin be in our startin' places by mid-morning."

He glanced at the sun, feeling the early morning high-country chill.

More photographs. He waved her off.

"Then let's begin."

"'Attaboy!"

"Ian said I could ride the elephant with him," Althea declared. "Is that okay with you, sweetheart? I mean, if you don't want me to be there, then...I'll understand."

"It's okay," he muttered, then stalked away.

"I told yew, don' yew worry aboot him. He'll do jus' fine, I tell yew—jus' fine."

"I'm still worried," she confessed. "He's never h—" and she stopped herself. What could she say now?

Ian took her hand, led her to Baghwan the elephant.

"Up we go, lassie," said Ian, motioning for her to use the elephant's raised foreleg as a step. "Come on, now. Upsy-daisy, now."

Althea set her boot hesitantly on the elephant's foot, found herself lifted higher on the foreleg to where she could climb into the basket. Ian followed by the same route. Their *mahout* stood at the ready and directed Baghwan to slowly stand. The villagers gave a cheer. Althea laughed with pure delight.

Karl climbed into the Land Rover provided by one of the villagers. The *shikari* shouldn't be troubled having to do the driving, too, Ian had translated the man's words. And so he thought about what he was going to do today as they drove off.

The *tahsildar*'s right hand man, a bone-thin *sadhu*—an ascetic—named Singh, gave a signal and the long line of villagers gave another cheer and started to move down the road. They knew it would be a lucky day for a beat. A lucky day for the village!

The village of Tashi was awake at dawn like other villages, ready to go to the fields for another day tending their crops. Instead they stood outside their shacks, gazing fearfully to the northwest. Besides sending their prayers to the young American *shikari* for success in the hunt, they were curious about the phenomena in the west.

Over the trees, above the forested hillsides, a great cloud of brown dust soared, billowing into a long column. They knew the season of heat and dust was now past. The ominous cloud grew continuously larger. Or was it closer? Soon they heard the roar of the earth and felt the ground shaking beneath their feet. They feared some wonderful thing was about to happen.

Colonel Barrington's Land Rover appeared, leading the way as his entourage of a dozen trucks and jeeps wound along the bumpy dirt road into the village. He called out immediately for someone to fetch his old friend, Albert Hansen. Then the big man dismounted and stood tall before his staff. The team of reporters who accompanied the Colonel quickly leaped from their truck, snapping pictures. No questions were allowed until the formal news conference in the evening, enough time for him to talk with his old friend and determine the situation.

"Welcome, Colonel," Dr. Hansen greeted him as he ran down the path, hand extended.

They embraced when they met and parted slapping each other's back.

"Good to see you, Johnny."

"The pleasure's all mine."

"I'm sorry to have you go to so much trouble...making a trip like this."

"Oh, it's no trouble, not for an old friend like you, Albert—especially to help out in the manner I'm best suited for—" he paused, turning to catch the flash of the cameras, grinning from ear to ear, "—killing *man-eaters*."

Dr. Hansen was immediately uncomfortable.

"Where's that old trouble-maker, Ian McDonnell?" the Colonel snorted. "How is that ol' fart these days?"

"Ian? He's his usual pertinacious self—"

"Feisty ol' bastard!"

"Ian's gone hunting, I'm afraid."

"Yes, I hear you have a little problem..." He faced the cameras once more. "...with *tigers*! That's why I'm here, my good man."

"Then you received Ian's letter?"

"Letter...? What letter?"

The Colonel turned to one of his assistants.

"No, seems we left before getting any letter."

Dr. Hansen grinned sheepishly. "Ian sent you a letter asking if you'd help us with this 'tiger problem'—as you so elegantly put it, Johnny, but it seems—"

"Glad to be of assistance anyway I can."

He held the pose as cameras clicked.

"We all do appreciate your generosity, Johnny, but the truth of the matter is—"

"Not a problem, Albert! I'm ready to bag me another world-class cat. Can't wait to get started."

The villagers had formed a ring around the Colonel, his staff, and the doctor, excited by the parade of visitors. The Colonel's entourage were certainly the most interesting. They listened intently to every word, though most could not understand what was being said.

"But, John—Colonel Barrington—there's been a slight mistake."

"How about we talk this hunt through over dinner? Good, good! Don't worry, we've brought some specialty items from Bhopal, and a few from New Delhi. We'll have a feast in the village tonight!"

He signaled to the crowd of villagers and they took what he said to be something good and let out a loud cheer for the cameras.

"We'll all have a great feast tonight, courtesy of Colonel John J. Barrington!"

Ian clapped his arm around Karl's shoulders.

"I dinna wanna yew tae do anythin' foolish, laddy. Yew understan' tha', don' yew? This ain't nae time fer heroics. If yew canna get th' pussies taday, then there's always gonna be tamorrow. Don' yew do anythin' crazy."

Karl nodded. "I'm not crazy," he mumbled. Yet Ian's instructions seemed like a judge's final decree. His eyes shifted to Althea.

"Tha's it, lad," Ian chuckled. "Go kiss th' lassie, fer chrissake."

He went to her, their eyes melting in mist. He laid his rifle against the side of the jeep and took her in his arms, held her tightly. His kiss was deep, passionate, the kind that was meant as a final kiss.

The villagers applauded.

He took the rifle in hand, drew the cartridge belt over his shoulder, set his hat to shield his eyes from the bright morning sun, and turned away from the jeep.

Behind him, villagers had formed a large semi-circle which spread across the huge field of tall, yellowish grass. They faced the line of trees marking the rim of the gorge below, choked with thick vegetation, the haven of tigers.

He walked steadily away from the line of beaters and the elephant carrying Ian and Althea, recalling his teacher's instructions.

He had an hour to get into position before they would start the beat. That meant he was to be inside the tiger's territory, at a certain spot Ian had pointed out on the map. There was a *machan*—a tree platform from which to shoot—in a tree commanding the only large break in the forest cover. As they planned, the cats would be laying up, resting, until the first noise of the beat. Then they would be chased away from the beaters and the natural terrain would funnel them along a path which would bring them directly to the *machan*. That was where Karl would shoot them—safely from the platform. The route for him to take had been well drilled, and he knew that stealth was the most important thing. He did not want to meet the great cats on this side of the *machan*.

With one last look at the distant line of beaters, and at Althea atop the elephant, he split the trees and descended into the gorge.

He had to concentrate, to focus all his thoughts and energy into the one and only task at hand. There was no longer time to contemplate the wisdom of his actions, or their possible consequences. Kill or be killed. And he meant to kill, to rid himself of the tormenting tiger of his nightmares.

The slope was steep. He half-climbed, half-slid down it, grabbing onto tree trunks, bushes, and vines until he landed in a patch of grass alongside the stream. The wide stream was low, long *nullahs*—sand bars—spreading across its breadth. Seeing the distinct impressions in the soft sand of tiger paws, he regained his footing, shifted his rifle in his hands, continued.

He held the rifle ready, up to his shoulder, even as his ears became super-sensitive and played tricks on him. His heavy .458 Winchester Magnum that he bought in Mumbai held one cartridge up the gut, and three more in the magazine. He flipped off the safety at the first rustle of brush, which turned out to be a peahen. Remembering Ian's advice, he gathered two additional cartridges between the second and third fingers of his right hand, ready to shove them into the chamber once his first four shots were expended.

His steps were measured for sound as he avoided dried leaves and brittle twigs. Following the stream along the *khud*—the steep, undercut side of the ravine—he saw more pug marks. He pulled himself down the trail, denying the temptation to pause and measure them. There were two sets, different sizes, a male and a female.

The path turned away from the stream, rose to higher ground which became tunnel-like with tree branches and vines curling overhead to form a canopy. Beneath, the path was nearly bare, free of ground clutter. Again, the pug marks stood prominently in the moist soil. They pointed ahead, in the same direction Karl stalked.

He realized he was sweating, even in the cool of the shade, and he wondered why he had not noticed it earlier. His grip on the rifle was dangerously tight. He could lose control if something like a swinging branch were to hit his arm. Stopping to catch his breath, he calmed his racing heart, wiped his dripping brow. He checked his watch; only thirty minutes had passed.

The forest was unnervingly silent. It seemed as though every creature had shut itself away in anticipation of the day's scheduled battle. He heard only an occasional bird cry, always distant, nothing else. Ian told him it was inhabited by sambar, monkeys, and a few horse-sized *nilgai* antelope. Now, though, he heard only the pounding of his heart.

No, it was not his heart that was pounding. It was the drone of the beater's drums! They had started already. He rechecked his watch, held it to his ear. He was twenty minutes late. Had the beat been going for that long without him hearing it?

He gazed ahead down the path. It grew darker as the vegetation thickened. The hillside to his right grew higher, cliffs with overhanging ledges appeared on the steep hillsides, cliffs from which a tiger might leap down upon him. From his memory of the map and the directions

Ian had given him, he decided he was half way to the *machan*. There was the big stone that split the stream, he saw, looking down through the vegetation. If their plan worked, the tigers would be driven to the *machan*—but he would not be there to receive them. They would race on down the path directly toward him.

Holding the rifle securely again, he hurried down the trail, more than a walk, less than a run, shuffling through the wet, fallen leaves, tripping over downed branches. He had to reach the *machan* before the tigers did. His life depended on that.

To hell with stealth, his frantic mind screamed!

He broke into as fast a run as he dared along the dark, winding trail and the dangerously strewn vegetation. He held the rifle aimed forward, waist-high. Every twenty yards he would stop to catch his breath and listen for any sounds that may tip him off.

The beaters seemed louder. Or maybe it was just the pounding of his heart. He was surprised how loud a noise they could raise, especially from their distance.

He took up jogging, ducking the hanging vines, dodging slapping bushes, jumping over fallen tree trunks, skirting cliff faces with one eye always poised upward.

The patch of sunlight ahead encouraged him. It had to be the clearing where the *machan* was.

The trail turned upward suddenly, and he slowed, breathing hard. He mounted the slope, moist dirt giving way beneath his boots. His breathing was raspy and his heart pumped hard.

He heard the rustle of leaves ahead and paused. The thumping of the beaters was louder than ever, as though they were just over the next rise. He was compelled to listen to the steady banging of drums, the clanging of bells, the shouting of voices. It was enough to drive *him* away through the forest, much less the tigers.

Lifting his head to try to see over the trail's rise, he recalled how Ian had been sweating and shaking the morning they hiked to the temple. Now it was Karl shaking. And he had never met a tiger face to face in the way Ian had.

The trail ahead was clear. The hillsides to his right seemed to grin. Large, dark undercuts formed shallow caves which only looked black against the reddish soil dripping from the wilted brown grass clinging above. Were they empty? He couldn't see into any of them as he moved forward.

The trail leveled out.

Snap! He whirled around to face the twig behind him. Nothing. At least nothing close. He turned forward again, rifle poised. What if one tiger was behind him, he thought, and the other ahead of him?

He wiped his sweaty palms on his pant legs. Wiping his brow with the back of his left hand, he kept his right hand's finger on the trigger. His inner-self was fleeing for its life. *Get out of there*, it was screaming. This was not a good day to be caught gambling.

Another snap of a twig down the trail behind him caused him to spin on his heel. Nothing there.

He could see the trail ahead for about forty yards, so he shuffled forward. He arrived at the bend in the trail. It turned to follow the curve of the cliffs, down toward another clearing about fifty yards ahead. It must be the *machan* clearing, he decided.

A few more snapped twigs behind him drew worry over his brow. He saw the trail was clear ahead and rushed forward, turning the bend in the trail and finally coming upon the clearing.

There, up in a tall, white-barked *saja* tree to the left side of the clearing, sat the *machan*. A crudely constructed treehouse of press board panels, it had viewing windows and gun ports, sitting in the cradle of two huge branches the size of elephant thighs. Running up the side of the trunk were nailed wooden rungs, easily scaled by a man with opposable thumbs. He admired it from where he stood, almost laughing in relief, giddy that he had found it, a shelter safely twenty feet above the ground—

Aaaaargh!

There was no mistaking the sound, the roar of an adult Bengal tiger.

Karl's eyes shifted instantly from the *machan* to the striped beast standing in the trail ahead of him, on the opposite side of the clearing, the tree with the *machan* between them. The beast was framed by ghostly light, illuminated by golden, dappled rays of sun softly filtered through the canopy. The beast was poised on a slight rise, silhouetted against the light, regal like a larger than life, concrete statue.

The cat roared again, louder, announcing its warning, as Karl raised his rifle automatically, more as a shield to hide himself than a weapon to protect himself. His wits flew from him and he started to back away slowly.

The *machan*!

Maybe he could make it before the tiger could reach him. No! Was he crazy? The tiger would surely run him down before he could get to the tree.

He held the rifle against his shoulder. As his eyes fell across the sights, the shadowy, silhouetted image of the tiger split like quicksilver, becoming two beasts, framed in holy light, posed like gods, staring him down in his boots across the twenty-five yards between them.

20

HE WAS EIGHT YEARS OLD when his parents took him on a vacation trip to Seattle. While visiting the zoo, he ventured into the Great Cat House. There in adjacent rooms were many varieties of wild cats, from the bobcat and lynx, to the lion and tiger. The tiger was particularly fascinating, more so considering the special accommodations provided. On the other side of a thin, wooden railing, a clear glass window fifteen feet high and fifteen feet wide separated the human visitors from the magnificence of the giant female Bengal tiger and her two cubs. He stood transfixed before the huge plate of glass, wondering why there were not any iron bars. He saw the sign on the railing advising visitors not to tap on the glass. Were they kidding? No way was he going to tap on that glass. He wondered if the glass was thick enough to hold back the huge beast if she were to be roused to violence.

Thinking back, she had to have been fifteen feet long. But, then, he was a small boy. He wished the other zoo visitors would be more quiet, so they wouldn't disturb this tigress. And where would he run or climb if she were to suddenly break through the glass pane? Standing there before the window, he was absolutely terrified.

Where would he run now? Karl thought desperately. They had finally broken through the glass, and there were two of them.

He held his rifle firmly against his shoulder, steadying the barrel as best he could with his arms shaking. One bullet up the gut, three in the magazine, and two between the fingers of his right hand ready to be loaded. Wrong: he had apparently lost the two bullets in his hand somewhere along the trail as he ran. Four bullets, then. Two tigers. He didn't need any more bullets. They would be charging, he would be shooting. If he didn't stop them in their tracks with the first two shots, he knew, he wouldn't have time to get the third off before he would be struck down and torn apart by their savage scimitars of death.

The smaller cat, forward of the other, was the female, her jawline lacking the white fringe. She stirred in the trail, silhouetted against the sunlit foliage. The other was the male, stocky in the shoulders, large head held regally, surveying the bold human who blocked their escape. The female flicked her tail, pacing back and forth across the path, studying him. The male stood his ground, defiant.

The noise of the beaters was almost deafening now, thundering drums rumbling through the woods, loud bells clanking like empty garbage cans, the fanatic shouts of excited villagers smelling a kill. He knew they were close, probably right above him on the steep hillside, above the canopy of trees in the gorge. They couldn't help him from there, he knew.

Shoot th' bloody cats! Ian's voice roared in his head.

He raised the rifle, having let it slip as it grew heavy. Pressing his cheek against the stock, his eye fell behind the rear sight. The front sight slid to the left and upward slightly, moving gracefully to the center of the target.

He took a deep breath and the world slipped into a slow-motion nightmare.

"I canna hear nae shot," Ian exclaimed over the shouting of the beaters and the pounding of their drums, keeping his balance in the basket atop the elephant. He checked his watch. "He ought tae be bloody well in tae tha' *machan* by now, I swear."

Althea gazed over the rim of the basket, felt her stomach dancing. The swaying, bouncing ride didn't agree with her breakfast. She felt dizzy, watching Ian.

"I need bit o' silence fer a moment," he called to gaunt-faced Singh, head of the beaters. He repeated his call, and it was passed down the line before their racket tapered off.

"What go wrong?" the *sudhu* asked Ian, running to the elephant.

"I canna hear nae shots o'er th' beaters. It's been long enough. He's got tae be in tha' *machan*. Th' tigers've gotta be run past him by now. He has tae've shot 'em by now. 'Tis too long."

"Oh dear, Mister McDonnell," Althea cried, sitting up, "do you think something's gone wrong?"

"There's nae way tae tell from here."

He climbed over the side of the basket and dropped to the ground between the elephant's front and rear legs.

Althea gasped. "Mister McDonnell, what are you doing?"

He stalked away from the elephant with Singh, waving back at her not to worry.

"Wait a wee spell," he instructed Singh when they were out of ear-shot of the beaters and Althea. "We'll wait fer a shot. Th' cats should o' passed th' *machan* long by now. There should've been a bloody shot. Two shots. I canna hear them o'er th' beaters, so' I dinna know if he shot'em."

"Perhaps, *sahib*, the tiger reach him before he reach the *machan*."

Ian made a nasty face, spit in the grass.

"I rather nae consider tha' possibility a' this time."

He has come, the good one, the man-creature from the far land, from the place of dreams. He has come at last.

His eyes burn with hate but he feels a dark wall holding him back. He cannot move, he cannot advance. His heart races as he feels his anger increasing his strength. He has churned himself into his most violent avatar, and yet it is as though he has crashed into an invisible mountain.

Roundpaw's nerves sizzle, muscles aching for release, blood boiling for vengeance.

He roars.

The tigress turns, pacing two steps each direction before turning. She flicks her tongue, bares her great teeth, flings her tail in large circles. She is ready to spring, to wield death in her special way. Man has destroyed her life and she no longer fears them.

She awaits the order of her mate, but he hesitates.

She cannot hold the hot, tense spring coiled any longer—

215

Karl releases half his breath, holds the rest, squeezes the trigger. It seems to take an hour for the rifle to jerk, but it does—finally—throwing him off balance.

> *The female cat charges, eyes aflame, fangs loosed for battle, wearing her stripes like war paint.*

Karl falls back, instinctively throwing out his free arm to brace himself.

> *Paws digging into the moist earth, the tigress propels herself across the clearing like lightning.*
> *Who is this man-creature?*
> *Roundpaw lurches forward, the wall suddenly gone.*

Karl braces himself with his elbow as he hits the leaf-strewn ground, realizing he's pulled the trigger again as he fell, sending his second shot harmlessly into the trees.

> *The tigress is upon him, stretching her livid, taut figure in a horrible grace the man-creature cannot help but admire.*
> *Roundpaw races after her, bounding across the cool earth. He must catch her. He must intercept her.*
> *He must save this man-creature.*
> *Something inside of him has wrapped its icy fingers around his heart and has clenched it like the fist of Death itself, crushing, squeezing from him his very soul.*
> *He must save this man-creature—*
> *He knows who he is. What his life truly is, he now understands in a moment of pain, and what his future will be if he fails.*

Karl scrambles to his feet, contemplating every twitch of muscle and mental command. He rises, twisting on crumpled legs, straightening his back, throwing his weight forward and catching his balance, drawing his rifle to his shoulder.

> *The tigress roars, leaps, claws unsheathed.*

Wake up, Karl! Wake up, he screams to himself, with a spin on his heel just as the tigress is airborne, flying past where once he lay. It is not a dream, he realizes. Feeling a sharp, searing pain shoot up his leg, he swings his arms around, rifle poised, following her motion, striking her underbelly with the butt of his rifle. She lands in a pile of leaves where the clearing begins to sweep up to the cliffs.

He draws his rifle back into his sore shoulder, knowing he has one shot left. He sees two crimson lines where her claws cut his thigh in passing—

Roundpaw is upon him as he aims the barrel at the tigress, righting herself in the pile of leaves.

The man-creature whirls around, fire stick pointing, as his hulk screeches to a halt, his claws digging into the crumbly dirt.

There! The eyes meet his, mounted in an orange and black striped face. Always the eyes, the eyes that mark him, that brand his dreams—calling him—

The tigress bounds from the slope, toward Karl, who swings the barrel around to take the cat. He sees the male tiger to his right, dashing across his front at the very last instant as he squeezes the trigger to his left.

The air explodes as the shot rings through the woods and flesh bursts from the near shoulder of the tigress, burning a cardinal stain on her ruffled white chest and slamming her backwards into the earth.

"A shot!" Ian screams, jumping in the waist-high grass above the gorge beside Singh. "D'ye hear tha', laddy?"

The beaters let out a thunderous cheer.

"Bring me Nitro Ex," Ian calls to the *mahout*, who prods the elephant forward. "I gotta be ready fer them tae reverse direction an' come at th' beaters," he calls to Singh, as he remounts the elephant.

"I heard it, too," Althea exclaims.

"Aye, lassie, I knew he'd find'em."

"Is that good?"

"'Tain't bad," says Ian, waving the beaters forward, their deafening noise resuming.

Karl grabs three cartridges from his belt as he backs up the slope away from the cats. His eyes go for the *machan*, on the far side of the tigers, a thirty yard sprint—if he could make it at all. He throws the bolt, shoves one cartridge into the chamber, the other two down into the magazine. He snaps the bolt back, sets his stance against the angle of the slope.

Embedded in the thick layers of chest muscle, the cruel shot causes no greater damage than a slow leak of blood. Stunned, the tigress scrambles to her feet, blood running from her wound, drawing a map of Ganges tributaries down her white chest. She starts toward the man-creature, slower but with determination.

*Roundpaw leaps at her, roaring. She sidesteps him and charges up
    the slope.*

Karl brings the sights into line on the wound, squeezes the trigger.

The tigress halts in place, half-way up the slope, as though crashing into an invisible wall. Growling her pain and anger, Karl sees that her tail is caught between the teeth of the male tiger, jerking her back. His shot, knocked off-line at the last instant as he swayed, hit the ground where the tigress halted, flinging up a spray of moist, black dirt.

The din from the beaters begins roaring through the woods again, and the cats become unnerved.

*Roundpaw roars at her, tugging on her tail, she complaining with
    her own vicious roars.*

Fascinated by the arguing of the two cats, Karl forgets he came to kill them. The moment to fire is fleeting and his only thought is to take another cartridge from his belt while their attention is diverted.

The tigers tumble down the slope, falling into their own wrestling match, rolling across the ground away from him, clawing each other, biting at each other, growling and snorting.

Two shots sting the air from Karl's left.

*Roundpaw bites at her good shoulder, urging the tigress to surrender
    and escape with him.*
*He growls at her, slaps her head with his huge paw. It brings to him
    the pain of his mate's death.*
*Again, the man-creatures descend to hasten his life, but this one, he
    knows, is different.*
Roundpaw roars a final warning.

Two more shots sail past Karl as he reloads his rifle, kneeling on the slope, watching the tigers fight.

The tigress breaks free from the male cat, rushing past him, down the trail. He bounds after her, both cats heading away from the clearing, returning in the direction they came, the noise of the beaters chasing them from their forest haven.

Karl rested against the muddy slope, unconcerned that his clothes were beyond cleaning. His head pounded in close rhythm with the beaters' drums. He felt the searing pain in his thigh again, longed to examine it. A pair of claw scratches was all it was, though his khaki pant leg sported two wide strokes of stain.

He was afraid to relax, held his rifle ready across his knees, still not understanding why they had suddenly fled. The tigress was about to strike him dead—twice—and the male cat moved to prevent her from attacking each time.

Grabbing the barrel, steadying himself with his rifle, he managed to stand. Gravity threatened to topple him, but he held himself up tall. He stepped down the slope, pausing to examine the blood the tigress had spilled on the ground.

Dropping to his knees with fatigue, he let out a long groan. The reality of the previous five minutes hit him like a hammer, pummeling him into nauseating fear. He was shaking—

"Well, that's about the poorest shooting I've ever seen."

Karl sat up.

"You're about the poorest excuse for a hunter I've ever seen, too."

The man's voice grew distinct as he entered the clearing.

Karl stood, wobbly. He saw a shaded figure moving down the slope from the cover of the cliffs.

"But you managed it anyway. Almost thought they'd do you in, Edwards. Almost wished they had. Oh, well. Lucky at love, lucky at life, huh?"

The man stepped out from the shade, strutting into the light, which dappled his green fatigue clothing.

"The time has come, Edwards."

Karl's eyes widened. "What the hell...?"

The tall, swarthy man came forward until he was fully lit by the sunlight, flicking his mustache, grinning like the madman he was.

"Doctor Priestley...at your service."

The man stood cocky in the camo costume, holding his rifle loosely in his right hand. A big grin hung beneath his black mustache. His dark eyes burned beneath equally black eyebrows. He wore no hat, his curly hair disheveled from the hike through the woods. Around his throat he wore a brown camo scarf. On his feet were tan leather boots, trousers bloused. His belt held a long knife.

"You!" Karl screamed. "You followed me!"

"I know, I know," Ron laughed heartily.

The roar of the beaters forced him to speak louder.

"You were at the airport," Karl exclaimed. "And in Mumbai? And Tashi! Doctor Hansen told me some bastard asked about me in Tashi. Now I see I was right—about it being some *bastard*."

Ron stepped forward, swaggering.

"How kind you are, Edwards. You certainly haven't lost your way with words. The way you greet someone, ah, so delightful—and to me, your special friend."

"You're no friend of mine."

"Ah, but we should be. We have much in common."

"Hold it right there!" shouted Karl, raising his rifle to his hip.

"I would've thought the police caught you and put you away," Karl said. "Or is that why you're here; running away from your guilt?"

Ron sneered. "Would've thought they'd lobotomized you by now, or have they already done it? Anyway, here the fuck you are."

"What the hell do you want?"

"Patience, Edwards. I have a speech prepared."

Karl's rifle clicked. "Don't mess with me, or the next one goes between your eyes."

"Such hostility." He stepped forward again.

Karl raised his rifle to his shoulder, aiming.

"I don't know the laws of this country, Edwards, but I'm fairly certain they do not permit murder."

"Who said anything about murder? Hell, this is just a simple hunting accident."

Immediately Karl slipped the rifle to the right and let go a shot over Priestley's shoulder.

"Careful, man! You might hurt someone."

"I *want* to hurt someone!"

"Me? What did I do?"

"What did *you* do? Have you forgotten my wife so soon?" A thought came to him and he tried to decide how exactly he wanted to remember his wife. She had conspired with their neighbor to get him put away, after all. "How'd you get her to let you come here? A damn, possessive bitch like her would never let you get away so easily. You're lucky—so am I, I guess. Take your freedom and run."

The rifle dropped to his waist, his arms tired.

"Take it easy, Edwards."

Karl smirked, angry, curious, embarrassed all at the same time.

"So what's she doing now? And why the hell're we standing here today?"

Ron turned, started toward the *machan* tree.

"I haven't seen her for weeks. As for you and me," he said, leaning his rifle against the tree trunk, "we are gathered here today to pay our last respects to our dearly departed friend." A nasty grimace appeared. "I'm here to kill you, Edwards. That's why I've come here to this solemn grove on a golden afternoon." He pointed at the ground in front of Karl. "Blood has already been spilled here. This is holy ground now."

"You're crazy!" Karl screamed, dropping his rifle and rushing him.

His eyes were wild, his fists clenched as he pounced. Ron dodged his lunge, and sidestepped his right hook but was knocked back by his left-handed punch.

"You stold my wife," Karl shouted, pummeling Ron in a rain of fists.

"You can't steal what's given away," the man taunted him, launching into his own attack, his fists landing across Karl's chin and cheek.

He fell back under Ron's onslaught, shielding himself with his tired arms. He managed a few jabs at Ron's ribs. Then, as he backed across the clearing, he tripped over a fallen branch and the two of them fell to the ground.

They grasped each other's throats with their hands.

"She wanted me—real bad," Ron cried as they rolled over and over.

Karl's hands came together, cutting off his breath. Ron released his grip on Karl's throat and lay twin karate chops on both sides of his neck. Karl let go his grip on the bastard's throat, boxed his ears, threw him off with a kick of his legs. Climbing to their feet, they rubbed their throats, catching their breaths.

"She loved it, too," Ron spoke, weakly.

Karl ran toward him, sprang feet first at him like he'd seen in the movies, crushing him beneath his heavy boots. Righting themselves on the ground, Ron slapped a spray of dirt into Karl's face. He swung his fist into his jaw and Karl rocked back, swaying on his knees, rubbing his blind eyes.

"Perfect! The position of submission," Ron cried. "Let me get my gun and we'll get this over with quickly."

"Bastard!" screamed Karl, spinning on his knees to knock the legs out from under his opponent.

He pounced on the doctor, hands going for the same strangulation hold. Ron slapped his face, pushed up on Karl's chin, forcing his head back. Karl gouged his eye and Ron responded by kicking his knee against Karl's groin. Falling, Karl caught his balance and punched Ron's face, landing a firm strike against his right eye.

"Christ!" he cried out.

Karl, breathing heavily, was content to hold the bastard down by sitting on him. But Ron was not so easily subdued and tried to throw him off with a lurch of his back.

"Christ! Get off me—I can't breath," Ron cried out, desperately.

Evil filled Karl's eyes, burning hatred like the funeral pyres in Benares—the holy city of Hinduism where thousands came to the *ghats* beside the dirty Ganges, there to die and rise to heaven. His hateful hands shot to their mark, crossing Ron's throat, squeezing. He threw his full weight down, locking his elbows, pushing.

"Christ! I—can't—breath!"

Karl's lips became taut, his face contorted.

Ron grimaced in desperation.

"Now I'll kill *you*," Karl cried, drunk with hate.

His hands continued squeezing, his knees pinning Ron's shoulders to the ground.

A knife flashed from its sheath and slice into Karl's ribs.

He flew back, arching to his feet, arms wildly pulling at the knife, feeling blood flowing down his skin. Stumbling backwards, he held his wound with his hand.

Ron lay on the ground, chest heaving.

Free of the knife, Karl stormed ahead, but Ron intercepted him at the last instant with a kick, striking Karl in the stomach and sending him to the ground.

Ron stumbled to his feet, feeling faint. Rising slowly, Karl rubbed his belly with his hand. His back hurt, too. The leaves where he fell were stained with his blood.

The bastard turned away, starting up the slope to the cliffs, his blurring eyes trying to fix on one or another of the shallow caves that lined the cliffs. The slope swung upward sharply and he swayed back and forth, grasping at saplings.

Karl followed, alternately holding his back and rubbing the pain from his stomach. "I've—got you now—bastard," he growled, wet chest heaving, head swaying.

Ron tried to hurry up the slope.

"I'm—coming—to get you," Karl called, stopping part-way up the slope, breathing labored, struggling to mount the hillside.

"No—you're—not," muttered the exhausted Ron, pushing himself on up.

Karl tried to rush ahead with a short spurt of energy but only gained another two paces—to the next sapling to brace himself.

Reaching the nearest cave, Ron threw himself against the stone, resting against the coolness of the wall, sucking air. He looked about the cave, seeing its end barely six feet deep. He slumped forward. His feet slid out from underneath him and his body rolled against the wall, crashing on the stone floor.

Karl grabbed for the next sapling but fell short. He threw himself ahead and caught his balance. Rocking on his feet, dizziness sweeping over him, the darkness of the cave split into two black disks, merged into one, split again, merged again. He stumbled, dove to the ground, rolling in the fallen leaves, the moist, brown grasses, and the chalky, red dirt. He lay face first, expelling only hoarse wheezes.

The din of the beaters had stopped. They both noticed the silence, but neither knew what it portended.

Ron mumbled something from the shallow cave.

"Why—the hell you—doing this?" Karl asked.

There was no answer but the coarse sucking of air.

"I have to," came the answer finally. "Have to get rid of you. You destroyed my medical career, you and your whore of a wife. You're the only one can identify me. Don't want to spend rest of my life in prison."

"What the hell you talking about?" Karl asked him, too exhausted to move.

"I'm talking about that fuckin' bitch! She was playing games with me. She'd give me some, but then she'd be coy, teasing me. I hated her for that shit."

He disintegrated into unintelligible mutterings, evaporating from reality. He had to take a few deep breaths.

"One day she drags me over to her place, gets me into bed, playing some weird, kinky sex game. Finally get away from her, she chases me into the living room, jumps on me, knocks me down. Hit my head on the damn TV. Then she's over me, seeing if I'm okay, and her dorky old man comes in. She changes into a totally different act, says I'm raping her—shit, that'd be heaven for that slut—and her husband goes berserk. You never saw a dude go so freaking insane before."

Karl pulled himself up, leaning heavily against a bent sapling.

"That was *me*, bastard!"

Ron paused, thinking. "Yeah—you were freaking out, man. I thought you were gonna—kill me. So I—got the lamp—"

"You hit me over my head! Now I remember!"

Karl struggled to rise.

"Then we—we got it on—her and me—"

"Liar!"

"We did it. Yeah, we screwed—right there on the rug—next to you."

"I'm gonna kill you!"

"She wanted the jerk put away, so I signed the forms—said he was always talking shit about tigers. Driving her crazy. Shit, I thought she was driving *him* crazy. So I did it and she screwed me real good."

"It was a set-up?" Karl panted.

"She was so weird, I couldn't take it after that—and the doc's report didn't make it any sweeter, what me getting the clap from that filthy slut. I was so damn fuckin' pissed, I had to. I had to kill her."

"You killed her?" he roared.

Karl tried to launch himself forward up the hill, fell.

"Went back to Becky but they were looking for me—after you told them about me. In a fuckin' mental hospital and they believe you! Christ! What shitty luck I have. You told them about me! That's why I have to stop you—before you tell them more."

Karl grabbed the sapling, struggling to stand. Tears flooded his eyes, rage shooting through his body, but he found no strength within him, and dropped to the dirt.

"But you did! You *did* tell them. They came looking for me—at my apartment, at my hospital. Had to hide out. Had to stay away from the hospital. Then they fuckin' fire me—'cause of you! Third year residency, and they fire me."

Karl was upright, swaying drunkenly. "You're crazy!"

"No, dammit! *You're* crazy!"

He thought the bastard was crying but before he could be certain, the cries of the beaters returned.

"You should've talked to my shrink at Eastwood."

"You did it, bastard!" the doctor shouted. "You and her! Ruined my life! I got her—now I'm here to get you. Then I can have peace."

The cries drew louder, echoing through the trees. Karl recognized Ian's signal; they were coming after him, shouting away the tigers before them.

"Here they come, the fools," Priestley laughed, hearing the noise. "I'll kill you, Edwards. Maybe not today, maybe not tomorrow, but you will not leave India alive. I fuckin' promise that. I'll always be there—watching you, waiting for the perfect opportunity to kill you."

Karl tightened his grip on the sapling, pulling himself up, still dizzy.

"You screwed up your own life—you and nobody else. Why would some asshole like you ever want to be a doctor? I thought doctors are supposed to have compassion. Hell, I don't care anymore."

Ron rolled onto his knees, his back hiding the work of his hands. He heard the shouting and the rustle of leaves, but he ignored them. The words of men and the storm of feet along the trail grew stronger.

Jumping up, Ron managed to launch a fist-sized rock at Karl's face. He tried to dodge it but it struck him on the forehead and blood spurted from the long cut, running down his forehead across his face.

The noise of the beaters was overwhelming as Karl tried to shake off the blow, wiping the blood out of his eyes. The bastard scrambled down the slippery slope, crashing into saplings, sliding on slick patches of mud, tearing through bushes until he was back to where his rifle leaned against the tree bearing the *machan*.

"You think I would let two dumb animals take that pleasure away from me?" Priestley cried out. "You think I was saving your life, like a stupid Samaritan? Hell no. I was just putting off today what can better be done tomorrow. I'll see you later. Then I'll see you in Hell."

Karl watched him lumber away down the trail, the troop of rescuers coming from the opposite direction.

He crawled down the slope, sliding and falling on both knees and one hand, his other hand trying to dam the blood running down his face. His head was spinning, the world turning into a kaleidoscope, not knowing up from down. He toppled forward, skidding down the slope face first, hearing the excited voices of the beaters entering the clearing.

21

WHEN THE POSSE LED BY IAN AND SINGH found him, one of the men was dispatched to bring Doctor Hansen. Ian was busy checking the calm forest, certain the cats had gone. Singh tended to Karl's wounds.

They met the doctor on the road back to the village, rushing to them in his Land Rover. Althea had to be held back as she screamed and cried for Karl.

"You shouldn't move him," the doctor warned.

"He dinna seem tae have nae broke bones," Ian replied coldly, more concerned with removing his partner from the tigers' den.

"Did they get to him?"

"Looks like it," Ian answered him. "Aye, claw scratches on th' leg. Possible swipe 'cross th' brow. Cut on the back. Look more banged up than scratched up, tell th' truth."

"Lost a lot of blood, too, it looks like, mostly from the head wound."

"Aye. He'll be fine, won' he?" asked Ian with a sideways glance. "I hate tae hafta tell th' missus th' bad news."

"Don't worry."

Ian shifted in his chair, surveyed the doctor's make-shift clinic in Aklera.

"The villagers seem happy."

"Aye. They know he did his best. Plugged one o' them—she spillin' blood all th' way up th' gorge."

Hansen shook his head. "Now you've got two cross tigers roaming the land, one wounded. I thought standard procedure was to follow up the wounded beast. Isn't that correct?"

"Aye, 'tis, doc. But 'twas a special situation, being two o' them an' only one man."

"Then why didn't you go with him? I mean, does he really have any experience with tigers? Any experience at all? This could be your fault, Ian. All the way back to when you muffed the hunt with Jon—up to this beat."

He grunted. "Someone had tae manage th' beat."

"And someone had to take the fight to the tigers' lair. Why then not a proven professional hunter?"

"What er ye sayin'?"

The doctor leveled his eyes at Ian, squinted.

"Johnny's at Tashi. Arrived this morning with his staff and a horde of reporters."

Ian spit. "Bloody bad timing."

The Colonel watched her, sitting alone in the shade of a tree, heard her weeping. He wondered if it was right to disturb her. Then again, he told himself, perhaps he might be able to comfort her. So he adjusted his belt, sucked in his gut, and swaggered over to her.

Lifting off his hat, he bent low to speak.

"You're Missus Edwards, I would guess."

Althea looked up, her red, tear-streaked face startled him with a flash of memories.

"I'm sorry to disturb you—I hope I'm not—but, I saw you sitting here, and I thought…maybe you could use some company."

He paused, waiting for her to offer him a seat.

"Let me introduce myself: I'm John James Barrington, Colonel, U.S. Army, retired. I'm a big game hunter, too. Perhaps you've heard of me…?" She shook her head. "Well, no matter."

He lowered himself to the ground, planting his stocky frame on the fallen needles of the cedar tree that shaded them.

"You're Missus Edwards, aren't you?"

She nodded. "Sort of," she added after some silence.

"What's your name?"

"Althea."

"Glad to know you, young lady."

She smiled politely.

"I'm sorry to hear about your husband," the Colonel spoke gently. "That was a truly gallant effort. He's to be commended. I am impressed by his bravery, his courage. The odds were against him."

He smiled warmly, but in his head he held back his amusement at the rank amateur's feeble attempt to do justice to the two great cats. A specialized job like that certainly required an experienced *shikari*. That was him. If only they had waited a couple days, then the whole tragedy could've been avoided. All there was to do now was comfort the future widow.

"Ian and I—we stalked up and down that gorge again this morning. The tiger your husband shot left a mighty big blood spoor. Very easy to follow. If the male's with her, then the two of them've left the area. I'll guarantee that. You've nothing to worry about."

She stared abruptly. "It's not over."

"What did you say?"

She regarded him in his khaki bush clothes. "It's not over."

"What, the hunt? Of course it isn't. Not until the tigers are done in properly."

"No, I mean Karl."

"Karl...? Your husband?"

"Yes."

"What do you mean?"

"He's crazy. Oh, he hates the word, but that's what he is. Crazy."

"All tiger hunters are crazy."

"No, I mean he's insane. Like in a psychiatric way. He doesn't know what he's doing. He's never hunted before. He doesn't know anything."

The Colonel rubbed his chin. "I see."

"No, you don't."

"I apologize. What do you mean exactly?"

"He's not finished with it."

The Colonel flicked at his mustache, wiped beads of sweat from his forehead with the back of his hand.

"You mean he intends to try again?"

She gazed at the far horizon. "Yes."

"But.... Well, frankly, ma'am, he won't be able to find them again until they make another kill. They've moved on up the trail. They're long gone."

"He'll find them, somehow. He knows them."

The Colonel squinted. "Knows them, eh?"

"He knows one tiger, anyway. They are sorta like, mm, *friends*, I guess. I mean, he's hunted him before."

"But why...." He stopped himself, remembering that she had just confessed that her husband had never hunted before. He chuckled. "Why, that's crazy."

She waved her hand at a fly. "Like I said."

"Are you saying your husband's been hunting the same cat all along?"

She nodded. "For months."

The Colonel shifted his position, coughed and spit off to the side, and replaced his hat.

"I've talked with Ian about the hunt. He says you just arrived in Tashi a week ago. Said your husband told him he never hunted a tiger before. Sorry to blow your cover."

"Ian's right. My husband's never hunted in his whole life before now."

The Colonel squinted. "Then why'd he do it, for God's sake?"

Althea leaned back on her elbows. "He's convinced that this tiger—I mean, he has these nightmares—he, uh, thinks he can—oh, I don't know! He says the tiger's been giving him these nightmares, and if he kills it, he thinks his problems will go away."

The Colonel was completely astonished. Never before had he heard such a bizarre ritual. A man did not simply go out and kill a tiger to cure some psychosis. The act was too dangerous, he reflected—and that was an understatement. He knew of people who cured their mental problems by confronting them, even acting out their conquest of them, but in this case it was absolutely preposterous.

"That's certainly an interesting story, Althea. Don't believe I've heard that before."

"Neither have I."

"He *is* crazy if he expects to be able to kill those two. He's lucky he's not cut into several pieces already, with some of them undergoing digestion at this very moment—"

Althea broke into tears.

"Oh—I apologize. I shouldn't have said that."

He heard someone approaching. Looking to his left, he spied three reporters stalking him—one photographing them with a telephoto lens.

"I take it you'd rather have him stop this nonsense and live a long life," he asked Althea, ignoring the clicking camera. "Am I right?"

She paused from her sobbing, nodded her head.

"Then you've got to take him away from here. Let a real professional handle this *shikar*. That's what I'm here for. Did you know? Came all the way from New York to bag these cats."

"Yes, I want to leave here."

"I think that's best."

"I want to go home...with Karl...and him in one piece. I want to live a normal life. I hate it here."

The Colonel nodded, then shot an angry scowl at the photographers.

"How long have you been here?" he asked her.

Tears came to her eyes as the camera clicking grew louder.

Suddenly the Colonel jumped up, swept over to the photographers.

"'Colonel Barrington and friend,'" one of them called out as another took the shot.

"You bastards!" the Colonel cried. "Can't you see the girl's in grief? That was her husband mauled by those cats. Now, back off! I don't want to see any of you around her. Do you understand?"

Two of them nodded, but the third took one last picture—before the ultimatum went into effect.

The Colonel swung his big hand, slapping the camera out of the man's grasp. It fell to the ground, smashing in the dirt, raising a cloud of dust.

"You leave her alone or you're off the tour. That clear?"

He returned to Althea as the reporters left.

"Sorry about that," he said, sitting down beside her. "You know how these goddamn reporters can be—always after a story. They won't be bothering you again, I promise you."

He raised his muscular arm, remembering the time he wrestled the white rhino in Mozambique after it charged him, remembering the time he strangled the jaguar in Brazil, remembering the incident with the grizzly bear in Alaska—and gently wrapped it around Althea's narrow shoulders.

"Now, how long did you say you've been here?"

"We've been in India about six weeks," she spoke in a low, weary

231

voice. "We spent ten days in Mumbai before we took to the road. I really miss home, I really do."

"Well, let me suggest you take your husband with you and scoot off to Jaipur."

He bent low to speak face to face with her, wiping away a streak of tears with his finger.

"It's just up the road a few miles. A beautiful city. I'm sure you'll like it. It's a good place to recover from all this excitement, all this agitation and horror. And it's good for sightseeing. It's the city of 'joy,' you know. *Jai* means 'joy' and *pur* means 'city'. City of Joy. A good place to go."

She nodded. A faint smile began to light her teary face, having already read in her guide book that Jaipur was called the 'Pink City'. Jaipur, she also read, was named after the Mogul prince Jai Singh II, who after ascending to the Amber throne in 1699 first envisioned a city there. If she could find joy there, she would go.

"All right. I'll try."

"Good girl. And if there's anything I can do to help—anything at all—please don't hesitate to ask. I'll have one of my men make a reservation for you. Why, I'll even pick up the tab on your Land Rover. How's that?"

She bleeds.

Roundpaw watches her, feels her pain. It is the same anguish he felt for his mate when he saw the life evaporating from her body.

He knows there is nothing he can do.

The men have come once more. And they will come again.

They will always come.

Her white-furred chest is matted with dark, violet stains. Inside her chest, a bullet lays suspended in layers of muscle, sliding back and forth, grinding her nerves raw. If she lies still, the pain decreases. If she can remain motionless, the blood clots and the hole is sealed.

Yet with each movement, it is ripped open and the bleeding resumes.

They must halt, even though the men are not far behind them. A slow leak, but it will kill her in the end. She knows it may be only days.

Roundpaw is silent. He has witnessed the same scene too often.

The tigress whines, struggles to stand, succeeds. He goes to her, nudges her ruffled collar. She tries to purr, instead whimpers.

He is but one, and she, also one. Yet out of gloom and pain they met, briefly, drawn together as two potions, each to heal the other. Their time has been short. Their remaining time together shorter still.

She takes a step, limps through two others as she feels her flesh burning, tearing. Glancing back, she calls him to continue their journey. The men come, she reminds him. The end is not reached until they can no longer trek.

Roundpaw growls.

And who is the man who comes to him with the azure eyes and the quizzical smile that greets him in his dreams?

The tigress whimpers; she is bleeding again.

He was running, against an endless green mosaic, perhaps a grassy yard. He was three, maybe four. He was laughing, happy. Then the tawny kitten caught him. Together they fell in the grass, wrestling, the kitten licking his face. He hugging the creature. She was yellow with dark brown stripes which gave her the look of a tiger, so that was what he named her.

Karl awoke startled. He was aware of the dust-filtered afternoon sunlight streaming through rips in the window curtains. He heard the gentle rustle of his wife in the other room. He smelled dinner cooking, something spicy, greasy. He felt extremely fatigued, his arms and legs heavy as lead, his head swollen, about to burst.

Wanting to call out, he could not be sure of the name.

The bandage around his head hung against his sweaty forehead. It had stuck to the dried blood. He felt the bandage around his thigh, on his shoulder, and his hand and his arm. Half-dead. He drew in the tepid air. Was he alive? And what had happened to him?

Through his fuzzy vision, shadows from the other room dancing on the walls like evil spirits taunting him.

More rattling of utensils.

A face peered into the room. It was not Leona, not his wife. What had become of her? Puzzled, he tried to sit up, sweeping the blanket to the floor.

"I see you're awake now," the woman spoke. "Good. I fixed you supper. Hope you've got an appetite. You should. You haven't eaten for two days."

Where was he?

"How are you feeling now?" she asked him.

What had happened to him?

"Are you all right? Any pain? Doctor Hansen left some pain pills, if you need it."

Doctor Hansen? The name seemed familiar.

"He also said Ian and Mister Barrington were gonna go after them, so you're not to worry about it."

She left the room, left him in his silence.

Like a stormy dawn, thunderheads swelled and boiled away, parting like two mountains, providing a passage for the rosy sunlight to waft down upon the world. His head split open and his consciousness returned. His memory returned. Then his agony returned.

"Are you all right?" Althea asked. She helped him up off the floor where he had fallen.

"Yes," he muttered, head swimming.

"You sure?"

"I—am—fine."

She laid him down on the bed.

"Are you ready to go home now? Are we finished with this macho-man business? Ian said they would finish it up for you so there's no reason we have to stay. Let's go home. All right, sweetheart? Let's go home and get married like we're going to. We can have a wonderful life together."

He sat up, grimacing. "Then it's true?"

"What?"

"The tigers are still alive? I did hunt them? I did shoot him? But he lives?"

"Karl!"

His eyes took on the dull shine of deep thought.

"Yes.... He lives. I live. I remember it now. The male cat saved me. He stopped the tigress from attacking me."

"What are you talking about?"

He swung his feet to the floor, rocked back before catching his balance and standing.

"It's not over. There is still a lot of work to do. I haven't finished the hunt. I have to continue."

"No, Karl! Ian and Mister Barrington are going after them for you. Didn't you hear me? Please, Karl, let's just leave. It's not good any more."

He took her hands in his, pulling her into his arms. His eyes pierced her heart as they danced stiffly about the room to a silent waltz. Althea cried into his shoulder.

"What're you trying to do, Karl?"

His hands caressed her back, as gently as he'd ever done before.

"My life is over unless I kill him." He felt a stream of tears wetting his shoulder. "While he lives, I'm only half a man, half a person. But—you can't possibly understand. If you could—if you had the nightmares I have, then you'd know. When your life is ruled by the soul of another, there can never peace. That's what I want. That's what I'm here for. That is my dying wish."

He held her out at arm's length, regarding her tear-streaked cheeks, flushed face, pouty lips.

"I need to end it."

She sniffled back tears. "I see a man dear to me dying day by day. Little by little. You're like a terminally ill patient, Karl. Like you know you're gonna die, and you're trying so hard to make it come faster. I can't stand it! Let's just get out of here. Can we?"

"Yes." His voice was low, rough. He shook his head, grasping her firmly. "I have a disease that'll kill me unless I find the cure, unless I take responsibility for finding the antidote. I must cut out my tumor—cut away this cancer—that has made me insane. I must kill that damn beast."

Roundpaw watches the tigress limping along the path. She will die soon. He wonders if he should hasten the ending of her misery. Is not once in a lifetime enough?

The earth is dry, crumbly. The breezes sift it into a brown haze. There are few trees to cover them, to hide them, to protect them from the man-creatures. And water is scarce. He has seen a cool wood ahead, from the heights of a past ridge.

The tigress calls, her raspy voice scratching like a jagged-edged stone.

He goes at her pace.

It trickles, her blood, every few steps as she works her shoulder and chest muscles, opening, closing her wound. Her white chest fur is darkened with dirty, caked blood.

Roundpaw sighs. She is noble, but she is dying.

"They've gone by now, I tell yew!" Ian shouted at Colonel Barrington. "Th' bloody cats're long gone. Yew know tha' fer yew self, Colonel. Yew's th' one tha' said tha'."

The Colonel slapped the table between them.

"Yes, yes, yes. But it's still up to us to go after them before they can take another life. It's that simple, Ian. The rules of the hunt state no *shikari* will allow any wounded animal to go free."

"They're already man-eaters. They're nae gonna turn more man-eater."

"You're missing the point. If that tigress is wounded, she's only going to be able to kill cattle and people. Maybe before, she was just taking after that male brute, but now that she's hurting, she'll be lying in wait for some innocent person to come waltzing down the path."

"Tha' cat's gonna be dead an' stiff by th' time we kin get there."

"It doesn't matter. It's our duty as *shikari*."

Ian tossed off another whiskey, wiped his lips with the back of his nervous hand.

"Yew think I'm cowardly, don' yew?"

The Colonel laughed. "No, Ian. Where'd you get that idea?"

"Hah! Dinna th' good doctor tip yew off?"

"About the Nawab and the photographers?"

"Aye, them."

The Colonel wore his serious face. "Yes, he told me."

Ian frowned.

"But I know you—Christ, how long've I known you? We go way back to that boarding school in Oxford. Let's not get so angry about the minor details. I do believe anyone under the circumstance would've done the same."

"I be an ol' man, now. I dinna wanna go out as dinner fer—fer a—a bloody cat!"

"Oh, for crying out loud, Ian! You don't want to die in a bed with a hot water bottle, do you?"

"Seems a rather peaceful way tae go."

"Then, I understand."

"Do yew? Look at yew. Yew have ten years on me—physically, tha' is. I seen yew with tha' Althea lassie. Yew oughta be 'shamed o' yew self."

"Nonsense, Ian. She reminded me of my daughter, is all. She'd be about the same age now if—"

Ian sneered. "An' have we forgotten wha' happened tae yew wee lassie? Kin yew e'er forget aboot tha'?"

The Colonel stared hard at him, then looked away.

"Of course I haven't forgotten. Dammit, do I have to think about it every blessed minute of every blessed day? It's time to forget. It's long over now."

Ian laughed coldly. "Aye. Wee seven year ol' daughter dragged from th' jeep an' eaten by th' Dongagarh man-eater. No-one's forgot. I'm surprised yew don' recall tha' every time yew pick up th' bloody gun."

"It's finished, I told you! Christ, what a time to bring that up again. That was twenty years ago. It's finished. Time to forget."

"Aye. 'Tis finished indeed."

Ian got up with a loud, impatient grunt, stalking away toward the next room.

"Where are *you* going?"

"'Nother bottle."

"Ian, you really should cut down on your drinking."

He returned with a freshly opened bottle of Scotch.

"Colonel, if I'm gonna have tae look in tae those golden eyes again, I better be a-swaggered. I would nae do it sober, yew know."

The Colonel grinned, raised his glass with a sympathetic nod.

22

JAIPUR, RAJASTHAN, WESTERN INDIA

THE GREAT HEAT THAT SCORCHED THE LAND between the last drop of monsoon rain and the slide into warm, dry winter lingers on the edge of the Thar Desert of western India. The hot wind blows, dust swept up in swirling columns, the land painted in shades of brown. Althea felt it when they entered the city.

In the avenues, legions of bouncy Maruti and Ambassador cars darted among herds of haughty, splay-legged camels. A shoe trader in Johari Bazaar was doing brisk business with a gaggle of girls out on a pre-wedding spree, all of them drenched in silver jewelry and paint-box bright *saris*. Above tiny, plaster store-fronts, agile monkeys frolicked in the trees, some dancing on the city's pink facades. Deep within the jeweler's caravan, the latest European designs twinkled next to the traditional Jaipur baubles. And down a narrow bazaar, an assistant to some top Western designer was seeking out new ideas for next year's shows, jostling with jewel-bedecked ladies swathed in yards of dazzling mango-orange, tomato-red, lipstick-pink, and lagoon-blue cotton cloth.

During the 250 mile trip from Aklera, Karl hadn't uttered a word as they drove along the hot, dusty highways. He would moan whenever she hit a bump, feeling his wounds, and grimace when she made a sharp turn.

She drove past the *Hawa Mahal*, or Palace of Winds, with its exotic facade of 953 windows, designed so ladies of the harem could watch the world outside without being observed by commoners.

Karl paused to stare at it. He craned his neck as they hurried past the most famous landmark in Jaipur. A block beyond it, he looked forward again. Something was wrong, he knew.

Althea noticed his attention on the pinkish palace and circled the jeep around a few blocks, returning in front of the multi-windowed wall where she coasted to a halt.

"I suppose you're gonna tell me you were here before, too, huh?"

He was silent.

"That's it, dammit." She started up the jeep and drove on. "You're driving me crazy!"

He grabbed her arm as she took the gear shift. "Don't."

"What?"

"Don't ever say that word."

She shook off his grip and drove.

"I should've left you behind with Ian," Althea cried. "But then you only would've gone hunting again. You would've been killed this time for sure. No more of this hunting for you. We're through."

He studied the scowl on her face.

"Then why have we come here?" he asked, finally.

"Mister Barrington suggested it might be a good place for you to recuperate."

"Recuperate for what?"

"Not recuperate for what, recuperate *from*."

"I'm fine—really."

"You're crazy, Karl."

"You're right. I am crazy. That's why we're here. You are correct. This *is* a good place. Here is where my sanity lies. Somewhere nearby. *He* is here...somewhere."

Karl stared at himself in the mirror. His ten-day beard had to go, he decided. His eyes looked sunken, dark circles beneath. His lips were dry and chapped.

Taking the razor, he began to shave meticulously, like a man preparing his death mask. The man he saw when the last strip of foam had been flushed down the drain in a stream of bronze water was a man he no longer recognized. He knew the person, but the persona was different. Somewhere between his first silent session with Dr. Lyons at Eastwood and his recent battle royale with the cats, he had lost his facade, his sheen of humanity. What he saw in the mirror frightened him. He saw his soul stripped bare, cut to the core. It was the face he wore when he did not wear a body.

Quickly, before Althea awoke from her toss-and-turn sleep, he dressed and slipped out of the room.

The hot morning sun beat down on him like a giant iron pressing him into the earth. He shifted his sweat-stained hat to shield himself, trudging away, a wrinkle on the fabric of the world.

In the bazaars he found the same items for sale as in Mumbai. The scents were the same, the sights, the colors, the sounds, all the same to him. Familiar, comforting. He was not interested in any of them today. Hawkers solicited his attention and money. He ignored them like they were only the whistling desert wind.

Strolling far from the modern business district, Karl counted the office buildings rising over the old market. A camel brayed, struggled against its bonds, backed into Karl as he pushed his way through the tame crowds. The caretaker apologized—

Was a man insane who asked himself if he was insane? If he knew the difference within himself between sanity and insanity, did that prove he was sane? Karl pondered the question, proceeding through the bazaar. Or was it possible a man could be insane, know he was insane, and still not be able to do anything about it?

Shaking his foot, he knocked off some camel dung which had stuck to his boot.

He thought of Althea. She had to be the crazy one. After all, who was more of a lunatic, a locked up mental patient or the girl stupid enough to throw away everything to be with him?

He kicked at a scraggly dog, missed.

Why debate it? He turned up an alley darkened by the overhanging eaves. He felt he was on the threshold of a great secret, one that with a little more patience would reveal to him a sea of forbidden knowledge. It was everything to him now. It was not so much the killing of the tiger that he sought as the one final, nagging, pestering mystery he was desperate to solve. *Why this? Why me?*

A woman appeared at her doorstep, caressing her breasts through her bright purple *sari*, smiling at him. He thought of Althea. She had looked good that night in Mumbai when she wore her own *sari*, dancing for him, seducing him into bed.

They'd had a good talk the previous night. By good, he meant thorough. It ended with nothing resolved, however. Althea expressed concern for his health, of course. He verbalized his desire to finish what he had begun. Then they argued. But somehow they both ran out of steam about midnight and went to their own twin bed.

Another prostitute appeared in a bright orange *sari*, calling him.

Didn't Althea understand that once he survived the debacle she would be rewarded with the grand life of wife to an unemployed blue-collar worker in job-poor America? If he wasn't arrested upon arriving back there. What more could she want? Maybe he should marry her here, in Jaipur, just to shut her up. That would also cut his last ties to Leona, the bastard doctor, and everything in his former, miserable life. Nothing remained there. Only a ransacked apartment with yellow police tape across the door.

He paused as the alley broke into another bright marketplace. Feeling the presence of the women he had drawn out to their doorsteps, he spun around. They were startled, all eight of them. Some were even beautiful. He punched his fists to his hips, pulled a scowl across his face and stared them down.

"Where can I find a good *shikari*?" he called out.

Their faces went blank, not understanding English.

Tired and angry, he started to leave but the last girl caught his attention. Her lithe body was wrapped in a golden *sari* so thin the dark circles around her nipples showed through as she waved at him.

Karl regarded her.

"I know...a man...you for look," she spoke gently.

"Do you? Do you really?" He cocked his head.

She nodded quickly.

"It wouldn't just be some ploy to get me inside there to fuck you, would it?"

Her head swung back and forth confidently. "Oh, for not, kind sir."

In the shadows of the grove, she waits for Roundpaw, waits for her dinner. He has gone, left her to track down game in this dry, unwooded land. He has promised to return to her, but her belly is empty, aches.

Her right foreleg is paralyzed with pain, her shoulder festered, infected. She dares not move it. Laying still no longer eases her pain. On her side she rests in the grass beneath the low hanging branches, hidden, lurking.

She is only a child, but a man-creature none the less. With others of her kind. They are all young.

They do not see the tigress, nor do they smell her.

She is the shadows to them.

They toss a small, round object among themselves, a game man-creatures enjoy regularly, especially the young ones. She can imagine how her cubs would have enjoyed playing with the bouncing sphere.

The girls call to each other, laughing, hurrying along the path through the grove.

The tigress does not dare breathe as they approach. Her eyes are steady, her huge paw poised as she suppresses the pain in her shoulder and chest.

The ball is tossed to Usha, the thin girl with the long, braided hair. She leaps but cannot reach the ball which falls uncaught in the dirt and rolls toward the grassy plot among the trees.

Her friends tell her to go get it. How clumsy of her, they cry. Pouting, Usha skips to the edge of the grass, looking for the ball. Can you not find even a simple ball? No, she cannot locate it—

Will they come and help her?

The other girls start toward her, stop suddenly, eyes wide with horror.

As Usha reaches for the roundness she believes to be the ball, the shadows shift to reveal a pair of evil, golden eyes among the branches. Before she can react, a heavy striped paw whisks her into the darkness. There is no scream, no struggle, no pain.

Beneath the low boughs, deep among the shadows, within the soft grass the moist sound of chewing permeates the grove.

Ian snapped his double barreled rifle, checking the fit, examined a scratch in the hand-carved stock. He wiped it but it did not go away.

Going to his knapsack hanging from the roll bar of their land rover, he retrieved a handful of fresh cartridges.

"Fine day for a hunt," the Colonel offered, stepping around the front of the vehicle, slinging his rifle over his shoulder.

"Aye," Ian snorted.

"Take it easy," the Colonel laughed, clapping a hand on his shoulder and almost knocking him over.

"Yew should be th' one tae be sad. Tha' wee lassie they says 'tweren't e'en ten. How kin yew have such a fine an' dandy mornin' with tha' on yer head?"

Ian pulled on his hunting vest, emptied pockets of non-essentials that would only rattle.

"You don't have to go," the Colonel spoke.

"We drank on it, din we?"

The Colonel's face was cold.

"Besides, I be goin' after any cat tha' takes a wee lassie like tha'. Let's get on."

He stalked off.

The yellow grass was almost hip high, a whole field of it stretching to a tree line nearly a kilometer away. They went single file, the Colonel following step by step where Ian cut the path. This was a private hunt; they had to sneak away from the reporters. This hunt was to kill a man-eater, not for the media.

"Really, you don't have to do this, Ian," the Colonel insisted.

Ian stopped in his tracks, turned angrily.

"I be here 'cause I dinna back out'n me word, Johnny. Now tha's th' end of it!"

In the old days, Roundpaw lounged as a jewel on the crown of his hillock. He would survey his domain, proud and content, at peace with his world.

He would watch the herds of sambar and chital grazing endlessly on the grassy plains, listen to the chattering of langurs in the forest, the caw-caw of peafowl. He would sit with his mate, refusing to abandon her to solitude outside the mating season, and he received the flicks of her tawny tail with patient silence. The sun would rise in bronze glory, and set plump and juicy like an overripe melon on the dark horizon. And it would rise again. It would always rise again, he discovered.

How far he had come from that eastern hill, from the dusty grave of Brighteyes, shaded from the cruel sun by the gnarled branches of that ancient tree.

And how far had he yet to go? The men were so many. Even the red-furred men, whom he had vowed to hunt down in the fashion of the man-creatures, seemed to vanish. Had he veered in the wrong direction?

He had always followed the crimson evening sun, setting new courses whenever necessary to re-align his path with the path of the red-furred men. He had forever followed their blood-spotted trail.

And the tigress, what should he do about her?

She would be dead soon, probably in days. He had returned in time to see the remains of the young man-creature she had consumed, and the small, round object it had chased into the shadows.

He knew the act would hasten their downward spiral into madness. With each killed Man, ten more would spring up to take its place. It was endless. The cut forests, the scattered herds of deer, the lines of rock upon which rolled boxes of man-creatures, they with their hungry fire-shooting sticks, the noise of beaters, the huge nests of Man, tall and ugly, sprawling as though they owned the entire land from horizon to long horizon—can it go on forever?

Through the mosaic of leaves and branches of wilting bushes, he looks out over the endless sea of yellow stalks, waving in the hot air—

There—two heads.

No place can he venture in this wide land where Man does not reside. There is no place that will hide him from the relentless pursuit of the shikar. Even now they come for him, across the sea of grass, their heads bobbing like ducks on a smooth lake.

He knows by the way their trail bends through the grass that they are following the bloody drips of the tigress.

Shall he wait for her to die, or end it quickly as he did for his mate?

Or, with hunters approaching, shall he simply abandon her to her fate, escaping to fight another day?

It would be another day to stalk the red-furred men, another day to face the burning sun, another day of uncertainty, of hatred and anger, of pain.

The tigress is doomed, by days or the hunter's fire-stick. There is nothing
*   he can do. It is best that he not surrender here for his time is yet to*
*   come, he knows, and he will choose it.*
There is a place for him to make his stand, and he will know it when he
*   finds it. It will call him.*
He springs to his feet, brows pinched, eyes squinting to focus on the heads
*   of the two hunters.*
It will be quicker this way for the tigress, he sighs, flicks his tail—rather
*   than his lingering agony.*
He pounces down from the rocks and turns away from the autumnal
*   forest, continuing west.*

The morning sun was blazing. Ian wiped a stream of sweat from his brow, pushed his old pith helmet back on his head.

"Awfully hot for this late in the year," the Colonel remarked in a hushed voice.

Ian was silent.

When they came to the edge of the grass, where the forest began, the Colonel, bringing up the rear, turned to check for any creatures following them. He thought he heard the guttural snarl of a leopard, maybe a young tiger. As they paused, however, he heard nothing, not even the birds, surrounding them.

He caught Ian's eyes with his own. They were serious, set sternly in his head.

Breaking into the forest, the Colonel leading the way now, they stepped slowly, carefully avoiding dried leaves that had blanketed the forest floor. Ian followed several paces behind, turning every few steps to check their rear.

Descending a knoll, they reached a dirt path, partially strewn with leaves. He looked up at the break in the canopy, then at the dirt.

They both saw them at once. Pug marks—large ones. There was definitely a tiger in the forest. The Colonel squatted, his rifle held at the ready in his right hand, his left examining the deep indentations of the big cat's paws. He laid his palm flat at the bottom of the depression, heel to heel. The pug mark was twice as long as his own large hand.

Ian startled, halted as a peahen scurried through the brush. He had been holding up fine, he thought, until then. It was too much like the morning he took Jon to meet the cats. He was too easily spooked now. He decided at that moment he would give up the *shikar* business after today. He was getting too old.

The Colonel motioned for him to hurry up.

Ian quickly caught up, maintaining the proper interval. He had let his mind wander again, a very dangerous habit for a hunter. Maybe he should have quit before this hunt, but the news of the girl's death hit him harder than he expected. He had no children of his own—not withstanding the possibility of a bastard or two from his early days in India.

And whatever happened to that fair lassie he'd courted in Glasgow before coming out to India as a young officer? Or that brown lassie in Kolkata who told him he had a son? Already so long ago it was like a dream—

The Colonel was frantic, waving his arm. He preferred not to make any motion, but one had to be made. His partner was dragging.

Their eyes met. The Colonel's: 'What's the problem? Why're you dragging your ass? Pay attention and keep close.' Ian's eyes replied: 'I kin understand me mistakes but I be powerless tae stop 'em, 'cause I be an ol' man now. I dinna really wanna be here today.'

They moved on down the trail.

The forest sloped up gently on either side of them, their pathway a temporary trough during the monsoon season. The ground clutter was minimal, the trees half-bare, the earth spread with brown leaves. They had good sight, but the many crisp leaves slowed their progress.

The splotches of dried blood were regular.

A breeze stirred the trees, knocking a few more leaves to the ground. The air was cooler, the forest silent.

The Colonel caught a scent on the wind, motioned to Ian a new direction. Ian's old nose didn't detect anything but his own sweat.

The two started up the slope to their right, mounting it quickly. The Colonel scanned the deeper forest from its crest. The vegetation there was greener, thicker, darker. He pointed ahead.

Ian nodded.

They descended the opposite slope side by side, spaced ten paces apart, slipping on wet leaves stuck to the soil like paper sheets. Catching their breaths, they moved on more slowly, parting the thicker brush cautiously. In dense forest, the lead man broke the trail and thus was open to attack while the rear man's responsibility was to take the attacking beast off the front man—or, hopefully, take it down before it could reach the front man. Ian felt easier when the Colonel was in the lead.

Damn coward, he cursed himself.

A wayward bush snapped back at Ian, slapping his thoughts back to the hunt. Why couldn't he concentrate? Was he really so old, or was it the night of drinking? He had no hangover, he was certain.

The forest rapidly closed in on them, rushing from every direction, crowding them together in a flora-lined coffin. Ian's nerves sizzled and even the Colonel was flustered. He halted, gazing over the high bushes surrounding them, trying to get his bearings. He pointed back the way they had come. Ian turned. It wasn't good being blocked in by tight vegetation in tiger territory.

He stepped forward, now the lead man.

They had gone only twenty yards when the Colonel tapped Ian on the shoulder and had to hold him down from his sudden leap. Once calmed, Ian understood the Colonel's new directions. They turned up the slope and broke free of the bushes.

From the tiny clearing, the forest looked like a russet nightmare. All the trees and bushes were brown or reddish-brown, thickly grown, motionless in the morning silence. Night hunters were asleep now. They started back through the bushes, their only way out, heading for lower ground where a *nullah* offered a clear path through the forest.

Down the slope they went, the Colonel leading again, step by slow step, parting bushes, dodging low hanging branches. Ian was beginning to feel a lack of confidence in the Colonel. Was he too old also? He watched the back of the man's head as he led the way.

They crossed the empty stream bed, leaving boot prints in the soil. The Colonel turned alongside the bank, continued parallel to it. Ian followed, his rifle continuing to feel heavier.

Another breeze brought a faint odor to the Colonel's well-trained nose.

"Rotten meat," he whispered to Ian, only arm's length behind him.

His eyes asked where. The Colonel chinned ahead. In that direction the slope leveled off, spreading into a wide, flora-packed plateau. The Colonel climbed up from the *nullah*, Ian trailing.

After a few more steps, Ian could smell the stench and wondered why he couldn't catch it earlier. Maybe the wind had shifted. And if it had, maybe they were throwing their own scents in the tiger's direction. He began to shake.

The Colonel noticed, paused to calm him before continuing.

They stalked into the level forest, dull-green bushes rising waist-high, covered with leathery leaves, forming a dense sea. Above waist height, the forest was clear, the straight tree trunks standing like great columns in a temple. The ground cover was too thick for them to see where they were setting their feet. The Colonel had worn his calf-high snake boots, Ian noticed. He didn't own any; in India, he knew the most dangerous snakes dropped from the trees.

He glanced upward.

With his eyes diverted, Ian stumbled into the Colonel's back where he had halted.

Untangling themselves, the Colonel pointed ahead to where the trees grew closer together. Two trees were nearly side by side, a vine winding up one trunk and stretching over to the next tree to continue its climb. Just below the tops of the green bushes in front of the two vine-choked trees, there was movement.

Ian's right hand slid around the stock, his index finger automatically positioning itself against the trigger as his other hand stretched forward to balance the barrel.

The Colonel motioned for him to go wide to the right so they could come upon the cat from two angles, allowing enough space for clear fields of fire.

Ian held his ground as his partner stepped away to the left, rifle poised for immediately use. He felt uneasy. He knew that movement and, in these woods, it was most likely a mongoose. But for now he would do as the Colonel directed. After all, these endless green bushes were not tall enough to hide a full-grown tiger.

He caught the Colonel's livid glare before he started right.

It was silly, he thought. The tigress was long gone, or dead already. Of course, he was for safety, but with getting lost in the bushes and all the backtracking, his confidence in the Colonel was waning. The man was just as old, thinking back to the boarding school in England where they first met.

Ah, what wonderful days they was, Ian sighed, fading gently from the present.

The sharp motion of the Colonel's hand caught his wavering attention.

"It's only a bloody mongoose!" Ian exclaimed.

At his outburst, the bushes two paces before him instantly opened as if commanded by Moses and the burnt orange and charcoal striped head of the wounded tigress rose like slow fire, sitting like a tangle of flames atop the bushes.

He knew her in that moment and she seemed to recognize him. But she was wounded, fatally, by the American's bullet. There were none she now counted as friend as she raised herself out of the green sea. Her charge was in slow-motion as her right foreleg and shoulder were crippled, yet she was already close enough for her weight to throw her big body forward and topple the old *shikari* from Tashi.

Ian was slammed into the earth, the green of the leaves around him like the flowers of his funeral parlor. The body of the tigress hovered over him, and he lay face up staring deep into her glassy, amber eyes, seeing the pain reflected there. And there was hatred in her eyes, cool, determined, vile hatred. He shivered. They had lived together in Tashi district for years, respecting each other. Then she had met the male tiger, and Ian had been joined by the Colonel. Each of them thrust into their roles, pushed out of their harmonic balance, they meet again in this emerald theater, the final curtain drawing closed on them.

She growled, a raspy, chalky sound.

"So, tha's th' way it's tae be, eh?" Ian sneered defiantly, following with a string of obscenities.

Lord, where was that rifle shot?

The tigress opened her jaws, lowered her head, and thrust her fangs around Ian's throat. With a savage jerk, she ripped away the obstinate windpipe, scattering his purple blood in every direction.

Make it quick, lassie, the echo seeped from the tube.

His eyes fell shut, wishing for the end to arrive quickly, but his nervous right hand quivered along his side, felt the sheath of his 12-inch hunting knife. In a heartbeat, which sloshed fresh blood like an open fire hydrant, the knife was retrieved. He felt the weight of the cat on top of him, the scoring of his flesh with her dull claws as he drew back his knife-clenching fist and rammed the long silver blade into her white-furred chest, piercing the left lung, slicing into the heart of the beast.

The tigress gasped, her eyes rolling upward in their sockets.

Boom!

The blast of the Colonel's rifle thundered in Ian's ears and a satisfied smile spilled across his cheeks. The cat's body toppled off him, falling in the crushed green bushes beside him. He glanced over at her, saw her bloody yaw still holding the strips of flesh torn from his throat.

Karl exploded awake screaming, screams that echoed down the corridor of the hotel and through the narrow alleys outside their window.

It had happened so quickly. The tigress had pounced, the sudden movement catching the Colonel off-guard. He spun on his heel, tripping on the roots of the bushes and fell. Although he scrambled to his feet immediately and planted a solid shot in the tigress' brain, it was just not fast enough.

He sat up trying to calm his breathing, sweating like he was in a sauna of Hell.

It could not have been more than three seconds, he thought, if even that long.

Ian was dead. The pompous Colonel Barrington was not to blame, but his friend and one-time partner, Ian McDonnell, was still dead.

Althea comforted Karl, holding him, wiping the sweat from his face and neck. He jumped as her hand ran over his throat. She knew it was one of his tiger nightmares. She hugged him tight, as if trying to squeeze the horrible dream from his mind.

Staring off into the night, he breathed hard, sweating, listening to the hollow echoes of his screams.

He looked at her, suddenly, with such intensity she cringed.

"Ian is dead."

Althea nodded. They had received the news three days before. Three nights, three nightmares.

"Yes, dear," she replied softly, "I know."

23

HE SQUINTS AT THE COPPER SUN, low on the horizon. Days he has
traveled—hot, blistering days of hunger and thirst.
There is no road for him, no gently shaded jungle path, no forested trail.
He is surrounded by the endless horizon, stretching to the edge of the
world and reaching for more.
Roundpaw coughs, longs for water.
The sun beats down. He is alone again, as he was when first he vowed to
track down the red-furred men. The hatred returns. Could they have
come so far, across such barren terrain?
He gazes about as he pads across the rocky, dusty, flatlands. Where is he?
Too far from his ancestral home to ever return. When would he face
his mate's murderers? Where in all the vast landscape is their lair?
The faint sound of men comes wafting along on a current of tepid air.
He hesitates, scanning the dreariness of his new domain, eyes focusing on
distant images. To the left he spots figures moving in a line.
There are several man-creatures, riding in rolling boxes or walking. One
has a cart drawn by thin, white horses. He hears the noise of one
rolling box, cawing like peacocks, and the men on foot drift to one side
and allow it to pass.
If there is such a collection of upright beasts, surely some of them might
have red fur.

He bounds toward the line of men—one line going to the right and an opposite line to the left—he sees they travel on the stone trail. The man-creatures never travel except along these stone trails.

His presence is noticed—at first suspicious, then startled and curious. When he draws close enough to take down any of them in a charge, he realizes their stupidity and laziness. The road is only a line across the stone-strewn desert, but they act as though they are protected within its borders.

As he reaches the edge of the road, several men bolt in different directions, barking fearful words. He is amused by his power over them. He steps onto the hot black stone trail, feels it sear the pads of his feet. Quickly leaping from it, he looks back at the fleeing men.

Resting beside the man trail, he watches the sky in the distance, rumbling like a storm, billowing clouds of chalky brown dust.

A box of men comes, pausing to observe him. They do not carry the deadly fire sticks so he allows them to share his territory. He shows his teeth with great yawns, but they only shake their heads, frown. When they depart, he continues across the barren landscape.

The land rises. Short, brittle grasses stand as yellow whiskers across the land, covering the rusty slopes. He runs at a steady pace, his attention on the churning storm ahead.

Long before he comes to it, he is forced to rest, exhausted. Still he has not found water. Nor food. He has not seen another animal in days, except for the men. Even the short yellow grasses have grown sparse. The first sprays of dust from the storm begin blotting out the sun. He carries his tongue over the side of his jaw, craving water.

The land is drier, more dusty, and the grass is gone now. He pants, gags, chokes on the swirling dust that settles around him.

The dust blasts against him, tiny grains of sand scratching his flesh, coating his fur. He cannot see his path in the blistering haze. His eyes are drawn to slits, head bent against the fury of the storm. Night is turned to twilight by the whiteness of the swirling storm and its torrid clouds of glass splinters shearing his aura, mincing his soul.

Roundpaw breathes with effort, though he tries not to breath in the chalky air. He stumbles, catches his balance, goes on. His steps are hesitant, shaky. He treads ground he cannot see. He wills himself to press on, knowing the storm cannot last forever.

Wishing he were not alone, that the tigress was still alive to accompany him through this hell, he imagines if she had. He can hear her low whining, calling him through the bellowing wind. With uncertain, hesitant steps, she falls further behind. Without his internal fire of hatred, she cannot keep the pace.

She halts, exhausted, blinded in the dust, watching him move steadily away from her. She is going to be left behind, whining loudly for him to wait. He cannot wait.

She tries to roar but only coughs and gags. He is barely visible through the choking haze. She collapses, her chest heaving. Frightened, she tries to stand, fails. She struggles to pull herself up, to continue after him. The winds blast her and the dust covers her. Sand blows around her fallen body. She tries to call him but she cannot utter a sound. The haze thickens, engulfing her, burying her.

Roundpaw pushes onward, as alone as he would be if the tigress had followed him.

Stuck indoors while the dust storm off the Thar desert billowed around the city, choking it, Karl leaned against the windowsill of their hotel room, brooding. He mulled over his dreams in his head, searching through them like some zoological archive.

The girl's breathing disturbed his thoughts.

Althea felt his gaze, looked up from her reading, finally nearing the end of the fat paperback she bought at the airport kiosk before they departed for India.

He jumped up and she cringed automatically.

"What's the matter?" she asked.

"I have to be ready."

Immediately, he dropped to the floor, slapping two clouds of dust with his palms, and proceeded to do push-ups. Five. Ten.

Althea watched him until he reached twenty.

"Karl, I'm not sure if I want to stay here with you. But I don't want to leave you, either. I think you need help, and I want to help you."

He did ten more.

"You think I'm crazy, don't you? That's it."

"No, I don't."

He paused in the raised position, catching his breath, then dropped for three slow repetitions.

She sighed, crossing her arms. "Yes, I do."

His arms were shaking with fatigue, struggling to raise himself from the floor.

"I'm sorry, Karl, but I guess I do."

Satisfied, he rolled onto his back, bending his knees up, hooking his feet beneath the bed frame.

"Karl, I'm serious."

In the months with him, as his nurse and his lover, she had always been on his side. She had defended him, supported him, comforted him. She had waited for him to shed his skin of insanity. In most daily matters, he was perfectly normal, but that one sad aspect of his life couldn't be stripped from him. And it seemed to have grown tougher. Whatever had attracted her to him, she no longer knew.

Sitting back in her chair, she watched him progress through a regimen of stretching and flexing, bending and stooping, twisting and turning, working his muscles. He didn't seem to feel any pain from his injuries. Sweat ran thick down his back and his scent permeated the room. She saw the tautness of his muscles, the renewed vigor of his body, his wounds obviously healed.

Finally, he collapsed. He dropped on his back, gazing up, meeting Althea's passionate eyes.

"I don't want to lose you," she cried, sliding down and over him. She held him tightly as they made mud from their sweat and the floor dust. "I see a man who is drowning. Or dangling from a rope—or perched on a steep precipice. I want to help you. I've come this far with you, dammit. I'll see it through. Do what you have to do. I'll be waiting for you. But I cry every day I think about it. I remember last time and...I'm so frightened, Karl—for me and for you."

He smiled, embarrassed at her sentimentality.

She took his face in her hands. "When I look in your eyes, I see a man who's afraid of death. Afraid of living, too. I think you want to die. That's why you've come here, taken up this dangerous sport. You're too afraid of taking your own life. You want some innocent animal to take care of that for you. I don't know, Karl, but that's what I feel."

"I feel it, too," he sighed, and she saw a tear floating in the corner of his eye. "Maybe you're right."

How peculiar, thought Colonel Barrington, scanning his copy of the latest *Indian Express* from Bhopal, amused by an article reporting the antics of some wayward tiger on the Ajmer-Jaipur highway.

"Did you read this, Albert?" he called out from the sitting room of the doctor's bungalow.

Returning, Dr. Hansen sat in the wicker chair opposite the Colonel.

"What's that you say?"

"It's about some tiger wandering the highway between Jaipur and Ajmer, right out in the damn desert. He's more than lost, I'd say. That's far from tiger country."

"Could be a worm in the brain, like some of the deer get from time to time. Throws off their sense of direction."

"But this tiger, it says, lounged on the pavement for a good hour, right on the highway, yawning and posing as people took pictures of him, and—"

"Him?"

"What do you mean?"

"How do they know it was a him?"

"Just presumed." The Colonel sat up, glancing out the window. A couple reporters from his weary entourage passed by. "What are you thinking?"

The doctor also checked for spies. "Could it be...*him?*"

The Colonel frowned. "Who? What *him?*"

"You know.... *Him,*" Dr. Hansen insisted with a sly grin.

"Who?"

The doctor leaned across the aisle between them. "Our tiger."

"What the blazes you bringing that up for?" roared the Colonel. "That cat's long dead. Lord, what a ghastly sense of humor you have."

"I'm sorry to bring the subject up again, but...it's been questioned by the media. Your reporters, in fact. They reported you killed both cats, but only one carcass was shown."

"That's because the villagers wanted to see the corpse of the tigress—the killer of the little girl."

"But that male cat you yourself said was world record size. Why wouldn't you want everyone to see it properly measured, Johnny? I thought you'd want the new world record marked in the books."

"All right!" the Colonel exploded.

"Then it's not true, is it?"

"Apparently, you've known me too long, Albert, for me to fool *you*."

Again he looked around for spies. "I had to see to Ian. I couldn't keep on after the other cat. Actually, we didn't see a sign of him, only the tigress."

"Then it's possible...?"

"What's possible?"

"That your cat's been showing off on the Ajmer-Jaipur road."

The Colonel shook his head. "That's crazy. No cat could travel that far. Besides, what would a tiger be doing in the desert?"

"I don't know, but you're the one reading about it in the paper. He's there, no doubt. But is that your tiger?"

The Colonel was frantic.

"What's with this 'your tiger' shit?"

"Isn't he?"

"Oh, you'd love that to get out, wouldn't you?"

"I'm not about to tell tales on you, Johnny, but all the villagers between Ranthambhor and Tashi sleep safe in their beds believing you shot and killed *both* those man-eaters."

Jumping to his feet, the Colonel threw down the paper, storming about the room.

"There's no tigers in the Thar! It can't be him. He couldn't have gone that far in two weeks. You're trying to goad me into another hunt. But—by God, you might have an idea there, Hansen! My reporters've been sitting on their collective duff long enough."

"Also." Dr. Hansen went to his desk, retrieved a sheaf of papers from the Bhopal police. "I received some reports in the past week—in my capacity as *patwari*—you know, the official village registrar, births and deaths, that sort of thing. You shouldn't tell anyone I showed them to you. You'll want to peruse them, I'm certain. It seems the American— The one who visited? That Mister Edwards?—was no ordinary hunter. Seems he isn't a hunter at all, in fact. Not even a regular tourist. This report confirms what I was told by the Barkhera constable."

"Oh...?"

"Indeed. Our Mister Edwards is an escapee from a mental hospital in the States. Not a very good one, I surmise—"

At that moment, the Colonel's memory was flooded with the stark words of that small newspaper article stuck down on page 18 next to the obituaries. Yes, the man mentioned had been in a mental hospital, he recalled. He claimed his intention to kill a tiger. Then he escaped. What was his name?

"Fancy that, eh?" Hansen went on. "And the young woman, whom he was passing off as his lawful wife? That's Miss Althea McCartney, the nurse who helped him escape."

The Colonel's eyes widened. "Helluva time for truth to rear its ugly head."

"Where are they now?" Hansen regarded the Colonel. "I'd think some authorities would be looking for them. What do you think?"

The Colonel grunted. "And I sent them to Jaipur!"

Moonlight glistens across the wind-polished surface of the salt plain.

With wavering steps, Roundpaw tracks his way over the sharp salt crystals. He has survived the heat and the thirst. He has survived the laughter and fear of the man-creatures. He has survived the power of the storm, held his breath against the choking clouds of dust, willed his fatigued body to carry him further.

Now the land has turned to salt and splinters of crystal cut into the pads of his feet with every begrudging step. His rounded forepaw gives way with his next step and he crashes to the ground, his chest heaving, his flesh stung by the salt.

Wounded by the elements, he ponders his cruel existence, his wavering will to continue. It cannot be true that men also live here. They could not have crossed this land. Perhaps he has lost their trail in the storm. It does not matter, for he has strayed too far from them.

Has he hated enough? Has he vowed enough? Has he avenged enough?

He breathes with effort, smelling the acrid scent of the salt covering the caked ground, stretching as far as he can see in every direction. He is lost. His journey is ended.

Man-creatures or not, his trek has reached its conclusion. If he lies as he is, he will soon sleep and never awaken. There is a paradise to soothe his agony, there beyond the painful threshold of death.

To sleep the peace of death. It is so easy—
No!
He must avenge his mate. Sweet, gentle, peaceful death. His head is
  spinning. He must avenge his mate but peaceful sleep calls him.
Brighteyes, he roars in his mind, we are finished on this world!
Ours is a past existence, an unwelcomed present, a vanquished future.
  I will join you—now—
The wind sings, whistling in his ears as it sails across the salt plain.
Brighteyes, I am coming to you....
In the deep recesses of his mind, he seeks his soul and conjures tears as
  melancholy saturates his body and death grows in his heart.
Brighteyes....
The wind calls him again, from the north, singing in his ears, tugging at
  his ragged coat. In its melodious breezes he hears her reply—

Avenge me....

His chest heaves. Feeling weakness, he cannot will his legs to lift him.

Avenge me....

He senses strength seeping into his muscles, feels energy surging once
  again through his body.

Avenge me....

He pushes his paws beneath himself and rises, slowly, shakily. A step
  leaves him fighting for balance and feigning dizziness.
He rests, up on his legs, face into the wind, ears capturing the essence of
  his fears and the love of his mate. Stepping gingerly ahead, he pauses.
He glances back over his shoulder, yellow eyes glowing against the blue-
  tinted moonlight, shiny on the salt plain, reflected in its myriad
  mirrors. He can no longer see the horizon whence he came, but his
  direction is clear. He will turn into the wind, pushing his weary body
  northward, willing himself away from the course he has followed all
  the seasons of his hatred, away from the setting sun.
In the graying dawn, he sees a ridge stretching from horizon to horizon
  and he knows it is the end of the salt plain. He can see stalks of grass
  as he approaches, waving in the cool breeze.

Mounting the ridge, he climbs out of hell. Beyond lie fields of tall, yellow grass. And a grove of trees. Several groves. And reeds.

And a pond with lilies floating on its clear surface.

He takes a long, long drink as the morning's slow fire rises over the white-washed walls of a man nest, still lost in deep shadows. Then, finding soft grass among the trees, he rests, sinking into sleep and dreaming of Brighteyes.

At mid-day he is awakened by the chatter of man cubs playing near the pool. He hears older females splashing in the water. He peers through the grass and reeds. They are washing their fur in the pond.

He presses his striped face through the reeds for a better look.

The air is pierced by the screams of the adults, pointing their fearful forepaws at him, grabbing their cubs, rushing away from the pool. He does not understand why they fear him. Can they not see how weak he is? Do they not see he does not hunt them?

With the pond evacuated, he pads down to its shore and drinks again, knowing he has found the peaceful paradise that lies beyond the cruel frontier of hell.

24

WEARING FRESH KHAKI CLOTHES, KARL stepped cautiously into the souvenir shop through the squeaky double doors. A few steps behind, Althea, dressed fashionably in a flower-patterned skirt and crisp white blouse, followed timidly, reverently. The baptism was about to begin.

Inside, the empty shop smelled of sun-warmed dust, waxy wood polish, and wicker straw. To either side of the two aisles long counters and shelves overflowed with dirty trinkets, ugly hand-woven baskets, hammered brass trays and coffee pots, and rolls of frayed oriental rugs. It looked as though no customer had been in the shop for the past few years. On the walls were more elaborately patterned rugs, several faded pictures of politicians and the Hindu pantheon, and a few dusty trophy heads—four antelopes, a water buffalo, one small tiger whose fur was dulled by the constant sunshine through the windows.

Taking in the shop, Karl strolled up one aisle while Althea took the other, arriving at the back counter where an ancient cash register stood like a sentinel. Behind the long counter, a bead curtain hid the back room from the shop. Karl rapped his fingers impatiently on the top of the glass case.

They heard muffled talking behind the beads and soon a short, swarthy salesman appeared, hurrying through the strings of beads, knocking off his white skullcap.

"*Salam!*" he greeted the customers.

The chubby salesman offered them a toothy grin, bowed his head, apologized for not being immediately available. He tugged his black beard with his greasy fingers, brushing crumbs from his shirt.

Karl responded with a nod.

"Ah, you...you, umm, English, yes?" the salesman asked, smiling enthusiastically.

"American," Karl replied, turning and resting his back against the glass case as he surveyed the shop.

The salesman, in white caftan, trotted around the end of the case and appeared before Karl, awaiting his order, almost daring to take a glance over at the svelte woman examining the merchandise nearby.

"Keen I helpee you, good *sahib?*"

Karl straightened, expelled a sigh. "Yes," he answered finally.

"Very good, *sahib,*" the salesman sang, nervously watching the woman wandering casually back through the shop, touching everything. "We hab many, many good theens for you today, *sahib.* We hab dee famous baskets, an' we hab most all dee good brass coffee, umm...er, to pour dee coffee for you, an' we hab—"

Karl stopped him with a wave of his hand.

"Actually, I'm looking for...."

The salesman leaned in. "Yes...?"

"I'm looking for a guide."

The salesman frowned suddenly.

Karl narrowed his eyebrows. "I was told I could find one here."

The salesman seemed offended.

"By who do tell you dees?" the man asked with a long, sideways glare. He seemed to have been asked previously.

Karl stepped toward him. "A woman told me to ask for a guide here. Was she wrong?"

"An' what be hees name, dees guide?"

"The guide?" Leaning toward him, Karl whispered the magic words he had been told to say: "*Haira Shere Khan.*"

The salesman's eyes widened, stark white against his dark face.

"Pleezah you say again, *sahib.*"

"I said '*Haira Shere Khan.*'"

"I theenk dat what you say." He frowned, made a face like his lunch was bad. The salesman moved behind the glass case, safe from the American. He knew the name—nickname—the code for his employer: Tiger King.

"What guide for?"

Karl gave a smirk. Wasn't it obvious? He extended his index finger and drew the letter 'T' in the dust on the counter. Before he could dot the 'i', the salesman wiped the word away with his thick brown hand.

"*Yahan*, American," he spoke. "I take you see Daorum. He know dees Shere Khan."

Through the beaded curtain, past stacks of dusty boxes and broken crates, down narrow wooden steps leading to a cool basement. The small, dingy room was lit by a single bulb dangling on a frazzled cord, highlighting a warped table in the center of the floor, strewn with playing cards and mostly empty liquor bottles. Around the table deep shadows hid piles of poached hides and illegal trophy heads. The salesman stepped aside, nervous, started to speak but stopped.

"Gin," the larger man at the table growled, throwing his cards down.

Across the table, the smaller man, wearing a turban, slowly laid out his own cards. Leaning back in his chair, one foot propped up on the corner of the table, he glanced up, noticed the salesman and the other two standing in the shadows.

Daorum, the swarthy, bearded man with the maroon *pugrees* wrapped around his head was a Rajasthani James Dean, at once both traditional and rebellious, draped as much in old as new. He wore ragged, faded Levi 501 jeans and a New York Mets t-shirt. Staring up at the uninvited guests, his eyes closed to slits, his ragged scowl bespoke years of rough living and countless shady deals. Tough and muscular but not so tall, he was the opposite of his business associate, Vic, the rotund Australian with the handlebar mustache.

Seeing Daorum's expression, Vic whirled around, faced the guests.

"What? Ya bringin' th' bloody tourists down here now?"

Vic jumped up from his chair.

The salesman dipped his head. "Daorum, dees American...he...he want *shikari*...for...tiger."

Sweeping the cards to the side, Daorum leaned back, teetering to one side, a twisted grin between mustache and trimmed beard.

"We don't do that," Daorum said. "He must mistake us for some others. Plenty down the street. Go on." He flicked his hand at Karl.

But Karl remained undeterred. Althea held her pose behind him, trying to appear bored.

Then the Rajasthani laughed, his dark eyes glimmering as he lit a cigarette and pinched out the match. Vic took his seat again as Daorum collected the cards, began shuffling them. As he dealt, he glanced at Karl, standing smugly beside the table. Just some dumb tourist down on his luck. Then, looking quickly at his cards, he noticed Althea in the corner of his eye and turned to her.

"*Kitna khubsurat!*" Daorum exclaimed, remarking on her beauty. Her clean, white skin impressed him the most, and how sophisticated she looked in her skirt and blouse. A real looker, he decided—did she need any assistance?

His eyes swept over to Karl.

"So, you be the one looking for guide?"

Karl nodded, a bit apprehensive. He shot a glance at the salesman for a clue. But the salesman, shaking in his boots, took a carefully timed step toward the beaded doorway, checking with Daorum, who nodded approval, and exited.

Daorum reached for his glass, took a long sip.

"No can do," he said, setting the glass down. "No way José."

"Why not?" Karl asked, desperate. "It's important."

Vic played his hand. Daorum lost again, gathered up all the cards.

"Is it a matter of money?" Karl asked.

They were ignoring him, playing cards.

Karl cleared his throat.

"Lessee some identeefeecation," Vic demanded. Then he reached out for Karl's shirt collar, his long, thick arm somehow extending across the table.

Startled, Karl jumped back, bumping against Althea.

"It's okay, Vic," Daorum spoke, tossing Vic's cards. "I'm sure he can only be who he say he be—just nobody."

Vic laughed like a bull and the basement shook.

"Don't mind him," Daorum said with a flick of his hand. "He's harmless. Yes, after you get to know him. We have to be careful, understand. You might be some government agent—"

"'Cept y'ain't, naw by the looks o' ye," added Vic, with a sneer. "Wimpy 'Merican shit! Like yooz own the whole bloody world, eh."

"Take a seat," Daorum instructed, motioning at the other chair at the table.

Karl sat at the table, careful not to disturb the cards.

"You're American, yes? And you want *shikari*, yes?" He chuckled.

Karl nodded his head, warily, keeping an eye on Vic.

Daorum reached for the most full glass on his side of the table and emptied it.

"Cannot do," he sighed with a belch.

Karl glanced at Vic, busy examining his cards. "Why not?"

Vic reached back and grabbed a bottle from a crate against the wall, then refilled Daorum's glass, poured himself a glass. He paused, then hesitantly offered one to Karl.

"No hunt tiger," Daorum replied.

Karl waited patiently as he took a drink.

"You know *shikar* law? Cannot hunt in India—not elephant, not rhino, not leopard, not tiger."

Karl nodded, cleared his throat. "That's why I came to you."

The two guides chuckled between themselves.

"And who sent you?" Daorum asked.

Karl glanced at Althea sitting on a crate in the corner, knees bent up, knowing she wouldn't approve of his dubious source of information.

"I was told about you...by a girl."

Daorum gave him a sideways glance. "Yes...?"

"A girl...in a yellow *sari*...named Jaya."

Vic jumped up, stood with mouth agape in disbelief. "Bloody!"

"Sit down," Daorum ordered. He turned to Karl. "He gets mad like that when anyone talks about his...girl friend."

"She's...? Sorry—I didn't know," said Karl.

Vic sat. "S'aw right."

"I wasn't her customer, if that sets your mind at ease" said Karl. "But she told me I could find a *shikari* here. At this address. Someone who would be discreet and...not ask personal questions."

Daorum shook his head playfully. "Jaya say this to you?"

"Yes, she did." Karl paused. "For some cash. So I come to you. I know hunting tigers is illegal—endangered species and all—"

"'Cept man-eaters," Vic cut in.

Daorum nodded, took another drink.

"Jaya said—she said you're the best guide," Karl spoke, "on the black market."

"Go on now," said Vic, "flatter th' bastard."

Daorum sat up suddenly, almost spilling his drink over the table. Regaining his composure, he stared at Vic with an angry scowl.

"Your girl friend, she has a big mouth."

"Aye, she's gotta big mouth, awright. Has to," said Vic with a snort, patting his lap and demonstrating a crude gesture for Althea's benefit.

Sitting comfortably, Daorum raised his glass, admiring the color of the drink while he drew on his long-ashed cigarette.

"It'll cost you," he spoke up at last.

"I can pay," Karl matched him.

"No, I mean, it *will* cost you." He poured another glass. "Yes, few years past it cost you...oh, supplies, beaters, porters, discreet taxidermy, the *guide's fee*, all of it...about twenty-thousand."

"Twenty-thousand *Rupees*?"

"*Dollars!* You think I'm fool? Now it's thirty-thousand." Daorum took a quick drink, emptied the glass, slammed it on the table. "But now...now you cannot kill tiger. No price."

"Not even a man-eater?" Karl pointed at Vic. "Like he said?"

Daorum leaned against the table, grinning, suddenly amused on this slow weekday afternoon. "You know this tiger?"

Karl glared at him seriously. "Yes."

The room went silent. Daorum poured and finished his drink, sat back and belched. "You know a man-eater I not hear about?"

Karl straightened his face. "You hear about Aklera?"

"Aklera? Where the hell's that?" asked Vic.

"Heard of Tashi?"

"Same."

"A pair of them," Karl continued in a low but steady voice.

Daorum drew on his cigarette, blew a long stream of smoke in Karl's direction. Vic got up and paced around the table, glancing alternately between Karl and Althea.

"Two?" Vic growled.

"He's killed a couple people," said Karl, even-toned.

"A *couple?*" Vic laughed. "Th'ain't man-eaters 'til they top a dozen, mate!"

He glanced at Daorum, Vic chuckling.

"But I know where he is," Karl continued. "Exactly where he is."

Daorum sat up straight. He expelled a sigh. "You come here to tell us where to find tiger? Why then you need guide? Seem one very foolish joke you play on us, American."

"Because," Karl started, felt cold sweat settling on his back, "because I'm not actually a hunter. I've never hunted tigers. Not really."

Sweat burst upon his forehead.

The two men stared at him for a moment before erupting into laughter. Daorum stood slowly, stretching his arms and shoulders—he was bigger than Karl had suspected upon first seeing him—and paced the room like he was looking for a way out.

"Can you pay for beaters?"

"No, I—" Karl cleared his throat. "I had in mind a kind of surgical strike. You and me. Nobody else. In and out, like a scalpel. No publicity, no G-men looking over our shoulders. Just us, you see?"

"You know what you do, American?" exclaimed Daorum, throwing his arms up.

Karl's face tensed. "I need this tiger. It's important. To me."

Daorum swirled his drink, standing beside the table.

"Yes, yes, we all need tigers. Their skins bring a great price."

"No, you don't understand," Karl exploded. "I need this tiger. I have no choice in the matter. I need *this* tiger."

Daorum slammed his drink down and leaned against the table with his outstretched arms, displaying his tattoos of bare-breasted Hindu goddesses.

Vic laughed at his partner's consternation.

"Shut your hyena mouth!" Daorum shouted, swinging at Vic. As he did so, his *pugrees* came slightly askew but his cigarette remained glued to his lower lip. He stared intensely into the American fool's civilized eyes. Pushing his *pugrees* back in place, he pinched his thick eyebrows and gave a smirk.

"Why this tiger so special? Will not any tiger do to hang on your wall, lay across your dirty American floor, impress your fat American friends with your big feat of daring? Why this special tiger, American?"

Daorum jerked his sinewy fist behind him at the piles of animal hides in the shadows behind Althea.

"Take one of *those* skins and tell them you shot it. We do that every day for tourists. You tell them big story about bravery in the jungle and we give you tiger skin to show off. It's done deal."

"But I need this one particular tiger. I want him dead. *You* can shoot him, for all I care." Karl sighed. "It's a little hard to explain. But you'll be paid well enough; you won't need to know why."

"I *want* to know why."

Daorum's face lit up as he moved back to his chair.

"Ahhh, yes. I see it in your face: revenge. That's it, isn't it? The men he has killed they were your, umm...comrades, yes?"

Karl smiled. "That'll do as a reason."

Dust flew off the crumpled map as they flung it down on the table. Hands quickly spread it out, placed glasses on the corners to hold it open. Vic found a cigar to puff on, Daorum drawing another cigarette, Karl sipping their warm beer. Althea stepped close enough to catch glimpses of the map between them, her arms crossed over her chest, silently observing the bonding ritual, pinching her nose at the smoke.

"This tiger," said Karl, "started on a plain. A plain that still had some sparse woodland."

Daorum pointed to a few places, his hand sweeping over the map.

"That would be here...or here. Or here."

"No, it was in the east," said Karl.

"How you know this?"

"I've followed him from there."

"For how long then?"

"Months."

"You said months?" asked Vic. "Bloody hell."

"Then he moved across a drier area...like a savanna, I guess it's called."

Again, Daorum pointed. "Here...or here."

"No," Karl objected. "He was always heading west...always going toward the setting sun. Always."

"Always...?"

"Always." His eyes beamed. "Then he entered some jungle area. It was wet, maybe because of the monsoons. Up in the hills somewhere. And he found a temple—ruins of one, anyway—in that jungle."

"There ain't much true jungle left here'n India," Vic announced, scanning the map through a thick cloud of smoke.

Daorum pointed to a few patches of forest, releasing an impatient sigh when Karl shook his head.

"I think your tiger crazy. He cannot walk across entire continent."

Karl grinned slyly. "Trust me."

Vic chuckled, stepping away from the table, amused as he listened to Daorum growl in frustration.

"How you know where this tiger?" Daorum asked.

Vic approached Althea who was leaning against a post. He regarded her, puffing his cigar, deciding. After a long draw, he offered it to her. She refused with a wave of her hand.

"You his wife?" Vic spit out a fleck of tobacco. "Or just a traveling companion?"

"He's my...I don't know." She wanted to leave. After a moment, "Boyfriend. I guess. Every day he's something different. Tomorrow he'll be the great white hunter. After that, who knows?"

Vic grinned at her, winked knowingly.

"...near a village," Karl explained, "white, clay walls. It sits among a sea of tall, yellow grass—maybe wheat, I'm not sure. There's a pool, too—with reeds."

Daorum watched Karl. The American's eyes had closed.

"There's a dirt road that...cuts through the field...between the village and the pond. And there's a forest—a small grove of trees—to the side of the village.... *There* it is. That is where he sleeps."

Daorum was puzzled.

"Yes, he's there," Karl continued, seeing within. "And there's a salt plain near it—big enough you can't walk across it in a single day. And it has large, *damn* sharp, salt crystals—"

The silence was shattered by Daorum's hand slamming down on the map, index finger extended pointing at the tiny dot which marked a village.

"Here," he cried. "We try here. At *Dhow*."

Karl regarded the guide across the table. "Yes. That seems right."

"Near Khetri...on the edge of the Thar."

"What?" cried Vic. "In the desert?"

Karl exhaled loudly as though he had just completed a session of calisthenics.

"What will be the cost?" he asked, catching his breath.

Althea eased over to the table, followed by Vic, both gazing at the map. Karl stood, leaned against the table, examining the places he'd already been as Daorum measured the road mileage with his thumb.

"You are crazy fool, American," Daorum snickered. "Crazy enough to die killing tiger. No beaters, no elephant, no legal *shikari*. Hah! I don't know how old are you—I'm thirty-seven and I got twenty-nine tigers to my credit, and sixteen leopards, four rhinos, and a bull elephant—but you crazy like young man! I don't know why you going out of your way to kill yourself. You should let me and Vic ping your cat for you. But I understand your feelings—wanting to prove yourself, it is said. So, we got deal, yes?"

He glanced at Karl, then slapped his shoulder.

"You have tough belly, American."

"The cost?" Karl asked.

Daorum frowned, eyeing Vic who leaned over the table.

"Five-thousand now," said Vic after the silence went on too long, looking up, "five-thousand after."

Karl straightened, knowing Althea disapproved. In a few heartbeats, he tallied her credit card limits and the cash they withdrew before leaving the States. He would have his cat, but they would be tapped out. Maybe not enough to get home. But he did not care, looking away as Althea came up to him and wrapped her arms around his shoulder.

"I need half now," said Daorum, "in case you are killed. It's...how you say? Par for course, yes? No, mm, it's...." He snapped his fingers. "It's standard procedure."

Karl nodded. "Can we get started tomorrow?"

"Let me make some arrangements." Daorum extended his hand. "You are crazy, American. But I like that. If you so ready, mmm, we can leave in the morning, if you wish to be so anxious."

"I do."

They shook hands.

The dark girl writhed on the thin mattress as Ron Priestley returned to the bed. Their eyes met. Hers spoke fear, desperation above her gag. His searched for the end of the night. Her shoulders shook with fright, wrists tied to the bedposts like her ankles, tattered *sari* strewn across the floor. Too weak to struggle, she mumbled curses through the gag. With a grin, he bent low over her, kissed her.

"You *are* beautiful," his hushed voice spoke.

She lay in pain, shocked by the American's mercurial violence.

"Why couldn't I meet you first? You're so beautiful, I want to cry. I can't stand it anymore." His hands slid over her bruised, bare body, then fell against her, crying as he'd promised.

He'd seen the girl talking to the bastard in the street, wearing a yellow *sari*, looking so innocent. He couldn't stand the thought of the bastard laying with her, but fortunately he moved on up the alley.

When Ron arrived, she was ready, eager, for a customer. Once their private business was concluded, he asked about her conversation with the bastard. In practiced purr, she told about his inquiry of hunting guides. And then? She had told him of the one she knew. She told the address after he threatened to beat her. When shecollected her fee and insisted he leave, he slapped her and dragged her back to the bed.

In her eyes he saw Becky there before him. He saw her tear-streaked face as he cradled her head. Her calm countenance relaxed him and he untied the gag but held his hand over her mouth. Her breathing was shallow, her eyes dull. The time had come, he told himself, and it did not matter that the flesh of the girl before him was dark, that her hair was long, black, that her body was curvaceous—none of that mattered. The girl, representative of all women, lay silent, as peaceful as a corpse. She awaited liberation from her earthly pain. They all did.

Ron watched the girl's dark eyes, waiting for a twitch, for any sign of life as she gazed at the ceiling and Nirvana beyond.

"I'm sorry," he spoke to her lifeless body, "but I must be right. I know it was bad. But bad people *must* be right. Why else do they have the power to take the innocent down?"

He lay his hand over her face, closed her eyes.

The taxi wound through the crowded market streets of Jaipur, eventually taking him to the dusty street where the souvenir shop was located. Inside, he found a salesman who knew nothing about the American or his girlfriend, so he left.

Dawn caught him napping on a bench outside their hotel, hidden among the other street people, dreaming in black and white of the brown girl in the yellow *sari*.

The roaring of the helicopter drowned their final instructions, but they already knew the plan. Karl helped Althea, dressed in olive drab shorts and a sleeveless beige top, step up into the vibrating aircraft. Daorum followed, regarding her with a lustful leer. With their gear packed and the pilot briefed, Vic signaled it was clear for them to take off.

As the chopper lifted into the air, wheeling around the helipad, Vic held tight to his hat. He held tighter to the envelope of cash. He began chuckling to himself, tempted to count it right there, as the chopper turned away.

He noticed a stranger approaching at a trot, a well-tanned man with a mustache looking almost like one of the local Rajasthanis. Waving goodbye to the chopper, he turned to confront the stranger.

"Was that Mister Edwards?" Ron shouted, jogging up to Vic.

"Whassit ta yooz?" Vic snarled.

"I needed to give him this bag," Ron panted, holding up a small satchel. "I'm his doctor. He's a very sick. This bag's got his medicine. The man's sick."

"Whadya take muh for, mate?"

"Look, I know he's going hunting. He's been trying it for months now—against my advice. He's insane—mentally unbalanced. I'm his doctor and I'm telling you that man is insane!"

"Ya don' say?"

"I've got to get this to him. Please! He *must* take his medication."

Vic cursed as he stalked away from the helipad.

"Look, I've got to meet him wherever it is he's going. Can't you understand? His life depends on it. Dammit, how can I make you understand?"

Vic stopped suddenly, raised his handful of money into a more obvious pose.

The helicopter whirred away into the western sky, its thunder fading with every breath of dust he inhaled.

With a nod, Ron reached for his wallet.

25

THE VILLAGE OF DHOW, RAJASTHAN, WESTERN INDIA

HE AWAKENS.

After a long moment listening, his eyes open, tired and angry. Resting in a thick clump of grass beneath shade, Roundpaw's peace is disturbed by a faint noise. A whirring sound, like a monsoon thunderhead, but regular like a thumping heartbeat.

To his feet he springs, gazing out through the trees at the white clay wall of the village. Overhead, in the clear blue sky, he sees a strange bird with wings that move in a circular motion.

Villagers pour from the gate, fill the clearing among the fields of grain. They wave forepaws excitedly, holding onto their head fur. A bent old man-creature is ushered to the center. The young man cubs jump up and down.

What is this thing that causes his heart to stir?

The flying beast circles the village, hovers over the crowd. The men fall back from the clearing as it descends among them, throwing up great clouds of dust. Touching the soil, its side opens and man-creatures emerge.

The swarthy man with the head fur is familiar to him: one of the native beasts in the guise of a killer of beasts. Next is a female, in khaki fur, her long mane tied back, held down with some type of covering. The first man-creature helps her down from the opening and they pause beside the flying thing to empty other objects—hard-edged boxes; soft, rounded bundles; and long, narrow things. The herd of men gather their belongings and pull them out from under the whirling wings.

A third creature emerges from its belly and his heart skips. He is tall but not too tall, fair of hair and face, sheathed in smooth fur.

Standing tall once he is away from the whirling wings, his eyes scan the crowd and survey the horizons. He is searching for the striped beast, Roundpaw knows.

He is not any hunter, but his hunter.

Roundpaw knows his mission; the man has come to kill.

He remembers the shot this man threw into the tigress that marked her for death agonizing days later. He recalls that day, how he felt something strange stir in him, how he drove the tigress back from the man—just before he pointed the fire stick at her and loosed its deadly magic.

He is the shikari, the hunter, the killer—his killer, his god.

Hot wind blew shifting streams of dust across the road in front of the jeep. Ron Priestley wiped his brow, perspiration running down the back of his sweat-soaked tanktop. He studied the wrinkled, torn map, trying to locate the proper back roads. That was all that was available. Being written in Hindustani characters did not help.

He scanned a hundred-eighty degrees, noting endless barren fields of caked dirt and lines of windbreak trees. He compared the map with his surroundings, tried to make sense of the Australian's directions. Two-hundred dollars wasted if he didn't find him.

The noontide sun beat down on him.

With a shake of his head, he stuffed the map down beside the passenger seat and drove on, turning left at the fork a kilometer ahead, almost knocking over the DHOW 50 KM sign in his hurry.

Karl set their bags on the foot of the bed and ancient dust floated up from the mattress and slowly settled back. Althea hung her suit bag on a wall hook, examining the room with a frown. The window facing into the tiny village had a broken pane, the bed was only a low cot, the floor covered by a ragged straw mat, and the bathroom was in a separate shack behind the main building. She stood in the middle of the floor holding back her temper.

Daorum arrived in the open doorway, interrupting the dusting off of the bed.

"I don't know how you do it, American," he said, "but you pick good place for *shikar*. *Tahsildar* say tiger come to Dhow three day ago. Scare everyone to death because no tigers live here—too dry, no cover. No one go out at night. No one tend fields. No one sleep in peace. *Tahsildar* is happy we come. He say they called for government *shikari* only yesterday."

Karl thought for a moment. "Called...?"

"How could it not be? The only tiger, I'm certain, in all the Thar." Daorum chuckled. "You settle yourself here. We'll talk to the *tahsildar* again at evening meal. You are invited." Daorum caught sight of Althea. "Except her. Take no offense, please, ma'am. It would only bore you."

Althea looked up. "It wouldn't bore me."

Daorum grimaced. He leaned to Karl. "Please—they are traditional Muslims. Only the men." He regarded her, an embarrassed grin on his swarthy face. "It's men talking we do. You can join the village women, if you like. Old Indian custom. And don't wear short clothes here."

She was about to speak her mind but held back at Karl's gesture.

Daorum turned to leave. "We scout the area at dawn, American."

Karl closed the door behind him.

Althea slapped the mattress, raised a huge cloud. "Old Indian custom—shit!"

"Oh, come on, Althea. New country, new customs."

She made a face. "Old country, old customs."

"We are the foreigners here."

She grit her teeth and moaned. "Look at that," she cursed, pointing to the thin, torn mattress. "What a mess."

She pouted, kicked the cot's leg. "Home sweet home."

He went to her, swung an arm around her. "It's not bad. A step down from Holiday Inn. We'll only be here a few days. Then...home."

"I don't know if I can stand it." She sighed. "It's so—dirty, so—so primitive."

She opened her suitcase, began unpacking. With a stack of folded clothing in her hands, she returned them to the suitcase, deeming it cleaner than the dresser drawers.

"I'm sure they have a stream around here," Karl joked. "You can beat the clothes on some rocks."

"Women's work, huh?" She made a face. "And how about the bathroom? Do we dare use it?"

"You go out back, follow your nose."

Althea glared at him.

"Well, that's how the people live over here. What, no McDonald's in town? Oh, how shocking!"

"No air-conditioning, no running water, no plumbing, no john, no lights, no bed." She paused and regarded the dust settling back onto the cot. "I can't sleep here. There's no way I can be comfortable."

"Three days," he said in a soft voice, "then you'll get everything you want. I promise."

Her face reddened and tears came to her eyes. "I hate it here."

He embraced her.

She wiped her dusty face. "Why are we here?"

He stared out the back window at the *bajra* fields and the grove of trees, feeling a presence there.

"To regain my sanity," he replied.

Colonel Barrington, lighting a fat Bangalore cigar, sat up in his wicker chair at the arrival of one of his aides.

"Good God, man, calm yourself," he exclaimed. "Tell me, what's all the huff about?"

"On the wireless...." He paused to catch his breath. "I picked up the news, sir...from Jaipur, sir. Something...about a tiger—"

"Good God!" the Colonel exploded, jumping up.

Hansen hurried into the room. "What's the problem?"

"Tell him."

"I heard on wireless just now—someone in Jaipur—they say a tiger's shown up at a village south of Sikar."

"There're no tigers that far west, that far into the desert," the doctor stated.

"That's what they said," the aide insisted.

"You see?" Colonel Barrington cursed, pointing out the glass doors. "That's got to be him. Get me the map, son. We'll check the position."

A map was pulled from a nearby bookshelf and spread open over the coffee table.

"Ah, hah! You see?" the Colonel sang. "Look at the line. Each time he's been reported, I've marked it. Here's Kanha. And Tashi. Barkhera. Then Aklera. And on up to Indargarh and Ranthambhor. And over here, he continues. The sighting on the Ajmer-Jaipur road. You can draw a straight line from southeast to northwest as he goes."

The doctor scanned the map, rubbing his chin. "Yes...yes, I think you're right."

"Damn right! Now he's at this place west of Jaipur, south of Sikar. Lord! It's a goddamn straight line."

"A bloody straight line," Dr. Hansen muttered. "Ian was going on about something like this before. What does it all mean, I wonder?"

The Colonel looked up suddenly.

"It means that fool is going to have another chance at the cat!"

The Colonel turned to his excited aide. "We're leaving right away. Spread the word. Get'em packing. I want to be out of here before dawn."

"You're going after him?" asked Dr. Hansen.

"Damn right! I won't let him get away this time, by God! I'll not be made a fool of! And I'll not let some dumb brute take the life of my bud without any suitable vengeance."

Dr. Hansen clapped his shoulder.

"Excuse me, sir," the aide interrupted.

"Yes, what is it?"

"They said, on the wireless, *shikari*'s already arrived. Three—arrived by chopper...a Rajasthani, and a white couple, they said—"

"Oh, good God!" his boss screamed.

Dr. Hansen's eyes widened. "Edwards, his girl, and some guide probably. It fits. Could be them."

The Colonel punched the bookcase. "As sure as that's our cat."

He gestured wildly and the aide turned to go.

"Then you must hurry, Colonel."

"Yes, before that poor fool kills himself."

"And the reporters?" the aide called from the veranda.

"Oh, hell, yes," the Colonel cursed. "Tell the whole damn lot of them—if they can rise that early."

Karl got up to answer the knock.

"Maybe Daorum's returned to invite you to dinner," he chuckled to Althea's pout.

Then he swung the door open.

"Edwards! Nice to see you!" proclaimed Ron Priestley, sweeping inside along with the steamy night air. "How goes it with you?"

Karl jumped back, expecting a gunshot.

"What the *hell* are you doing here?"

"And this must be the girlfriend," Ron went on. "I've heard so much about her. Good in bed, they say."

"What are you here for?"

"Edwards, don't play ignorant. I know all about that."

"I'll bet you do."

"Yes, I know everything now. I have the newspaper clippings in my pack, if you're interested. Pretty slick. They say a crazy man couldn't have pulled off such an escape. But then...you had inside help." He glanced at Althea. "Didn't you?" He returned his glare to Karl. "I can't believe you don't know why I'm here. Probably the same reason you fled the U.S.: guilty people always flee."

He stepped forward, away from the door. Karl held his ground, limiting his advance. Satisfied to stand by the door, he grinned with delight, like a child who had gotten for Christmas exactly what he'd asked for.

Althea took a step forward. "Who *is* this guy?"

Karl waved his hand toward the uninvited guest.

"This is the Bastard. This is the man I've been cursing for the past year. You remember, don't you, dear? He's the cause of all my worries, the instigator of my troubles, the devil incarnate."

"Devil incarnate!" He roared with laughter. "I do like that."

"I'm sure I've mentioned him," Karl spoke, keeping his eyes on the man and his anger tightly controlled. "Don't you remember? He tried to shoot your car out from under us the night we left Eastwood. Oh—and he also saw us off at the airport. You remember, don't you, dear? Then, get this: he followed me to, uh—well, I didn't see any reason to bother you with it—but he followed me into the gorge at Aklera, on my hunt, on a *tiger* hunt, believe it or not, trying to trick me. He tried to kill me then. We had a good fight. No, it wasn't the tigers. It was *this* bastard."

Ron grinned, teeth bright in the lamp light.

"I would've thought you'd given it up now," said Karl, then shot a glance at Althea. "He's the doctor I told you about, the one who killed my wife."

"I didn't kill her!" Ron lost his cool. "It was an accident...like I've been saying. It's one of those things that just *happens*. Like shit. It's nobody's fault. It just happens and it's too bad."

"And that's why you followed me here? To tell me this bullshit all over again?"

"I don't know what kind of trick you were trying to pull there," Ron started in, "setting me up like you did, but it didn't work."

"What the hell're you talking about?"

"Or maybe it *did* work." Ron shuffled over to the bed. "*You* know what you did." He glanced into the open suitcase, regarding Althea's underwear. "You set it up to look like I broke into your apartment and hit you on the head so she and I could get it on. But you just couldn't stay unconscious. You had to get up and cause trouble." Scanning the suitcase, he flicked his hand. "You were a lousy husband, anyway, she always told me—always away in that make-believe world of yours, off playing tiger. That's one of the oldest psychoses in the books. It was driving her crazy. She said so."

"You're completely off your rocker," Karl growled, gesturing madly.

Althea grabbed his arm.

"What really gets me," Ron continued, rummaging through the suitcase, "is what you did to my career. You *ended* it, shit-for-brains— like I told you in the forest. You timed it oh-so-very-perfectly. Getting me to come over on that *particular* day, at that *exact* hour—that was the *perfect* touch, the *coup* of *grace*. That way not only did I get trapped in your absurd plan, but in case I *did* escape, I'd have no damn future afterwards worth living for. Yeah, you really did one helluva job in crushing my career as a doctor. You fucked my residency. How am I supposed to serve mankind *now*?"

"I suggest you get the hell out of here," Karl spoke in a firm voice, stepping forward with fists clenched. "And get out of my life, too. I'm too busy to fool with this shit."

Ron gestured toward Althea. "How does she compare with Missus Edwards? Or *is* she Missus Edwards now?"

"Get out!" Karl shouted, and Althea pulled him back.

"Control, Edwards. We must maintain our self-control in a civilized society."

Karl was steaming. "It's not civilized outside the walls of this village, you sonuvabitch."

"So it's not."

Karl glared at him, ready to pounce and pummel him to death.

Ron lost his smile suddenly. "I'm here to kill you, Edwards."

Althea inhaled sharply, her grip on Karl's arm tight.

Ron selected a pair of pink lacy panties and held them up, studying them. He noticed the deathly silence, erupted in maniacal laughter.

"You thought I was serious, didn't you? ...I *am!*"

He demonstrated his notorious grin, all his teeth exposed, like the grimace of a tiger ready to bite.

"I was just gonna keep you from talking to the cops. But you *did* that! You *already* fucking told them!" He drew the panties to his nose, sniffed. "Now all I have is that sweetest of all vices: revenge."

Karl scoffed, hands on hips. "I've got more important things to do than be killed by you. Or see you locked away the rest of your life. Oh, I hate you more than anything—but not enough to kill you. Hah! Maybe you and Leona deserve each other! I prefer to see justice done publicly, to let your humiliation and failure be done on the stage for everyone to see. But now I'm here to hunt. Nothing else."

"Okay, I'll be patient, if you like," said the man, "but I *will* kill you this time. I won't be soft-hearted like in the forest. I've got time now, *you* don't. You go do whatever you have to do. Just don't run away. Then I'll wish you a *bon voyage*."

"Can't you understand? You screwed up your *own* life."

Ron shook his head. "It doesn't matter now."

"What...?"

"You're here. I'm here. Why waste time? Let's have it out. It's show time."

Karl clenched his fists. "Get out! Now!"

"*You* screwed up my life," Ron shouted, retreating.

"You killed my wife!"

"You ended my career!"

"You're insane!"

"You're damned!"

"Can't you just leave us alone?" Althea shrieked above them.

Ron backed toward the door, shaking his head solemnly. "What can I do now? My life, my career, my service to humanity—*everything* is ruined, thanks to you. Thank you very, *very* much—you goddamn turd of a bitch."

Karl, face stern, held his anger in check.

"I'll leave you lovers alone now...for a while." Ron grinned. "When you're finished with your business, I'll be waiting. I'm not particular. It won't take long. And she can watch if she wants to. So enjoy her while you can—a kind of bastard's last meal, if you will. Leave her at least a memory, okay?"

He swung the door shut gently, and they listened to his footsteps fading away.

26

KARL WAS READY WHEN DAORUM KNOCKED in the morning. He had refused to talk more with Althea about the strange incident, the crazy man who came to them, knowing he needed to get some sleep. Instead, he had tossed and turned all night, thinking of what he should've said to the mad doctor. He'd felt her hand on his chest a few times, her calling his name softly, as though wresting him from a bad dream.

With rifles in hands, they marched out of the village gate, into the *bajra* fields surrounding the village. They were only scouting for signs of the cat, not expecting to meet the cat that morning. The farmers remained safe inside the walls, neglecting the crops until the menace could be removed. The white *shikari* had come to save them.

The thought pleased Karl as he removed his Panama hat and wiped his forehead, damp from the hot morning sun. He knew it would get hotter.

Daorum took the lead down the path to the pool where the women washed and children played. He pointed out that as it was the only water for miles around, there was no doubt his tiger would visit it.

His tiger, Karl thought.

The moist sand around the pool was covered with pug marks. The reeds were bent, marking the direction from which he had arrived. And returned, Karl suggested.

Daorum nodded, put a finger to his lips. He bent down to one of the larger pug marks and measured it with his hand. Karl stood behind his guide, glancing around the fields, anticipating the tell-tale spot of orange flickering among the golden waves. Slinging his rifle over his shoulder, Daorum pulled a ruler from his shirt pocket, opened it and laid it inside the foot print.

He shot a glance at Karl, who was scanning the field like an old pro.

Daorum noted that the pug mark was not as deep as it should have been in the soft soil. The cat was probably starved from the trek across the salt plain. They had seen the white expanse from the helicopter as they flew to the village. He used to be a big one, Daorum remarked. The tiger had a large frame, but he was no doubt dehydrated, starving, probably to the tune of a hundred pounds lost.

Didn't matter, Karl insisted. He was not after a trophy.

Daorum grinned politely, wondering what his real motive might be.

It was dangerous stalking in the tall grass, they knew, but no elephant was available at the edge of the desert. Besides, it was a simple matter of closing in on the cat hiding somewhere among the trees.

The forest was not large, barely five-hundred feet at its widest, Daorum estimated from what the *talsildar* had told him. Most of it was sparse, the trees stunted, empty of ground clutter, the marsh spreading from the pond its only water source.

Doubling back down the trail, they turned up a side path cutting through the fields. The *bajra* there came to their waists with the thick crown of seed heads to their chests whenever they stepped off the path to check the soil for pug marks.

The tracks clearly led into the wood. It was not difficult to locate where he was laying up, but the nasty part of the hunt had yet to come: going in after the beast, or trying to flush him out of his cover.

After extensive tracking, they called it a day. As they entered the village, the mad doctor watched them from the balcony of his room. Daorum asked who he was. Karl only shrugged and quickly returned to his room.

"Daorum said it was all right to wear this when I'm in here," Althea explained, her sweat-soaked red halter and blue jean cutoffs catching Karl's attention. "But I better not go outside like this. But it's too hot to wear anything else. I can't put on the whole robe thing like the women here do. I sure don't know how they stand the heat in those. I'm okay covering my hair, though. Too much dust, anyway."

He sat on the edge of the bed, shirtless. Althea knelt behind him, massaged his shoulders with sweat running down his skin.

"I'm sorry you didn't have any luck today."

Karl grunted. "We weren't expecting to meet him today. Just taking a look around."

He pinched his shoulders, grimaced as she massaged.

"That's okay. There's always tomorrow—right?"

"Right."

He lay his head back with a loud groan. Althea stopped massaging, cradled his head as though wondering what he was thinking. Then she resumed her massage as his head fell forward.

"You know," he spoke as she dug her fingers into his neck muscles, "if I concentrated really hard—like that meditation stuff you taught me—I bet I could probably pick up on his thoughts. We're close enough, I think."

"Who are you talking about?"

"There you go again. I mean the tiger."

Althea sighed. Every time she thought life was going smoothly, he would talk tiger and upset the very delicate balance she had achieved. She would have to start over pretending everything was all right. The sooner they could go home, the better.

"Yeah, I could hook up with his half of our mind. Like telepathy, you know? Like talking to my brother."

"Stop it, Karl. You're scaring me."

He lay his head back again. Dropping her hands from his neck and shoulders, she wrapped her arms around him from behind, held him firmly, pressed her cheek against the back of his head.

"When I kill him, I'll own all of my soul."

She tapped his shoulder. "Dammit, Karl. Don't say that. You're scaring me."

"There's nothing to be scared of. It's not like Halloween and the ghouls are after us."

She tightened her embrace. "How about me being scared of you getting hurt? Doesn't that count?"

"Don't worry. Nothing's going to happen."

"What're you talking about? You're going into the woods after a man-eating tiger, and when you're not doing that, there's that stupid maniac looking to murder you."

He reached back and patted her arm. Tears dropped on his arm.

"I don't want you to die, Karl. I wish you'd stop all this nonsense. You're gonna get hurt. I just know it. What would I do if you were killed fooling around?"

He turned within her embrace, pulled her around onto his lap.

"Stop worrying. Nothing's going to happen to me. I feel good about it now—very confident, very relaxed. I'm not a rookie anymore. I learned a lot from Ian. I won't make any mistakes."

Her tears ran faster.

"Hey, you know I wouldn't do anything to hurt you."

She pouted. "I know I'm being selfish. I've been scared of what I would do if you were killed. But *you* would be worse off."

He chuckled. "Yeah, that's true. But don't—"

She kissed him hard on his cheek. "You go right ahead, dear. Go on hunting that dumb ol' brute and I won't say a word. I won't interfere. I won't bother you. Even if you're killed by that tiger, I won't say a word. Don't worry about me. You go ahead—"

"Oh, for crying out loud," he snapped. "Don't be that way." He rocked her against his chest. "We'll probably be heading back home tomorrow night. Or the next night. It *will* be soon, I know. I promise you. We'll find that animal by tomorrow."

"Oh, Karl, do you think so?"

"It's so easy. He's only got a small forest to hide in. He can't go too far away from it, either, because of the desert. He's trapped there. And I know exactly where he is. All I have to do is go there and shoot him. One shot, Althea. *Pow!* Right between the eyes. That's all it'll take."

The world awakens, somber black night melting into a sleek red crest,
   arching high above the horizon.
He blinks his golden eyes, watching, waiting. Another dawn greets him.
   He acknowledges it, feeling a dreary sense of relief. How many more
   will there be? How many more days must he endure?
Cowering in the reeds, he searches for man-creatures.
He breaks from his hiding place and moves up the moist bank of the pond,
   showing his path with deep pug marks. Drinking his morning draft, he
   regards the sky: looming gray like the decaying carcass of a giant
   beast, its blood running downward like rain over the silhouetted

palace ruins high on the distant hillside, far across the fields.

With a snort, he seems to recall this place. There are images which prance through his memory. His flesh prickles with strange and perverse sensations, as though the pattern of nerves within him remember an earlier time. He knows that up on that rocky hillside beyond the village lie the ruins of a once formidable castle—a center of learning and culture in its era, set amidst the now arid land.

Once it flourished under an amber sky, the land flowing green with life.

Today it sits dark and abandoned, haunted by violent memories.

A lone bird cries out as the sun's eye winks on the horizon.

Today will be his day, he senses, catching a scent on a sudden breeze. The village is calm but he knows the hunters are awake, preparing for the hunt. They are coming for him, hidden as he is. He cannot escape them. How much longer can he evade them? And how much further is the lair of the red-furred men? It is clear now he has come to the end of his long trek.

Perhaps it is enough that he managed to do what he did, even without the ultimate act of vengeance. Now, there is only one course of action left for him.

He pads off to the grove to rest, awaiting the inevitable.

"I managed to borrow plow horses," Daorum announced over cakes and tea, meeting Karl at the *tahsildar*'s house for breakfast. "Can you ride? The fields are too high, not safe for tracking by foot. Horses not much better, but they a little better. The farmer is happy give them to us to help with killing the tiger. Anything we need."

Karl nodded, agreeable. "That's good."

"We can track the same paths as yesterday, then we can go to look for the tiger in the wood."

Karl drank his tea. "Sounds like a winner."

Daorum smiled, bit into another flat, unleavened bun lifted from the communal plate.

"I still don't understand how you see tiger here at this village, American. *Tahsildar* say you must be divine angel sent by Allah to protect them. Anything you need or want shall be yours, he say."

Karl nodded at the grinning old man with the storm of white hair and beard. "Tell him I'm grateful."

Daorum translated.

"He say village cannot pay you for killing tiger. But I already explain you hunt for vengeance. Of course, it's not Muslim thinking to be vengeful, but for a tiger...they make the exception."

Karl chuckled, took another cake.

"He thank you for whole village," his guide continued, translating as the *tahsildar* spoke. "They will lay many offerings and say many prayers to Allah for your health."

"Thanks," Karl replied, his mind focused elsewhere. Then he stared at his guide, tired of the adoration. "Let's get going."

His guide belched and Karl politely followed suit.

"Very good, American."

They rose from their cushions.

Chattering children distracted Althea from her daydream of home. Going to the window, she saw the children gathered around the man who had burst into their room the night before. Karl had called him a doctor, but she didn't know his name. She was still confused.

She leaned against the window sill, staring at him, staring at the crowd of children. What was he doing?

Sitting on the veranda of the *tahsildar*'s house, the man seemed to be mending one child's injured arm. A few mothers stood at the edge of the group. He was speaking to the children as he examined each of them. The children were laughing, and the mothers were smiling. He grinned at them and gave them candy, the happy children calling to the others what kind theirs was.

She watched carefully, pondering. The thought hit her that in the time she had spent wandering through India, she hadn't once offered her medical training to any of the poor people she had encountered. Wasn't that why she became a nurse, to help people? But then, she was on vacation, wasn't she? Just a tourist.

She was embarrassed. Now this crazy man, who was terrorizing her boyfriend, who had acted so disgusting the previous evening when he barged into their room—was tending to the children's medical needs. There had to be a catch, she thought.

Feeling ashamed, she dressed in suitably conservative clothing, and pulled a cloth over her head, tied it. Then she stepped out of the room and went over to the crowd.

"May I help?" she asked the man.

The villagers smiled at her, welcoming her, rejoicing in her charity.

"Just a moment," he mumbled, finishing the gauze dressing over an infected sore on a young girl's arm.

When he looked up at her, the sunlight broke around her head like a halo, her shirt collar moving in the breeze like angel wings.

"I would be glad to have you assist me."

By mid-morning, the hunters had retraced the previous trail to the pool, checked for fresh pug marks. Doubling back to the west through the fields, the tracks veered off toward the nearest edge of the grove. Daorum muttered how he expected that. The forest was small, but he hesitated to just charge straight into it.

They urged the horses on toward the village, directed them around the eastern side of the wood. Coming to the north side, they halted.

Daorum pulled out his binoculars, scanning the grass, mumbling a few Hindi sentences.

Before them spread an idle field, barren soil chopped in preparation for planting. The opposite side of the field bordered the forest. Daorum remarked on the wide knoll to their right, at the northeast corner of the field. Karl studied it.

Daorum dismounted at the edge of the dry furrows, checking for pug marks.

"This will be good place to hang bait, American," he explained. "We can sit on that hill over there, have a clear vision of this field. He will cross here."

Karl glanced up at the bright noontide sun, wiped his brow beneath his floppy hat.

"We get goat from the village," his guide continued, feeling the soil dry under the sunshine. "Anything we want for killing tiger, they told me."

Karl nodded.

Mounting, Daorum turned his horse toward the knoll, coaxing it into the barren field. The horse shied.

Karl's did also when he tried to maneuver the animal forward.

Daorum motioned toward the tree line, a hundred yards across the dark red soil. Half way along it, toward the middle, the ground dipped, lowering into undergrowth. He could not decide if the flicker he thought he saw was the breeze or not.

Karl pulled his horse left, out of the field, pressing ahead through the stirrup-high grass to the knoll.

The horse halted, whinnied.

Daorum followed until his horse refused to go further.

"Something's out there," he said.

Karl nodded and his eyes searched the tree line for a fleck of orange.

"Probably he is watching us at this moment."

Karl turned in the saddle to check the fields behind them and his horse began backing away.

An orange blur streaked out from behind the knoll, leaping across the ragged rows of overturned soil, aiming for the cover of the thicket.

"There's your tiger," Daorum shouted, pointing. "Shoot him!"

Karl jerked his rifle up into his shoulder in one sharp motion, fighting the jostling of his horse, and located the tiger through his scope. His eye followed the striped beast across the field, his finger weighing on the trigger.

The cat slowed, then halted one leap short of the thicket, glancing back at the hunters.

Karl hesitated as the crosshairs fell across the tiger's broad, snow white chest.

"Shoot it!"

The words lunged through his ears, striking his brain like a bullet, but the ringing of the explosion numbed his nerves. His finger grew heavy on the trigger and his hand began to shake. The horse jerked sideways beneath him. A bead of sweat ran down his tense face, burning his eye.

Perfectly framed in the scope, the big cat waited, padding in wide circles, pausing at each turn to pose.

Karl's finger ached against the trigger, his mind forcing it to pull back at the same time his finger, having its own will, pushed off the trigger, locked in a desperate struggle. His sweat-burned eyes closed and a spasm rippled down his back.

"Forget it, he's gone," Daorum announced, cursing.

Karl looked up, eyes gazing over the scope at the thicket, catching the final splash of orange in the leafy shadows.

He lowered his rifle and met Daorum's cold stare.

"Why you not shoot? It was perfect, American."

Karl dropped his gaze, shaking his head.

Between patients, Althea wanted to scan the fields, looking for her boyfriend. Ears trained on the wind, she listened for a gunshot. But her work took her mind from her worries and gave her satisfaction.

"Thank you for your help," the doctor said.

"You're welcome. You're a good doctor."

She offered her hand and he shook it.

"And you're a good nurse."

He continued to regard her.

Looking down at him, seated at the examination table they had set up in the *tahsildar*'s house, she felt the hot breeze blowing against her, reminding her where she was.

"Please don't kill him," she spoke in a hushed voice, caught on the edge of her emotions.

His smile dissolved.

"I know I am going to hell. Some kind of hell."

He regarded her, tried to smile, couldn't.

"This is something that might help balance my fate. Karma is a bitch, you know. That's what they say. It's too late for me. I am falling and cannot stop falling. No one can catch me."

The Colonel's jeep rolled to a halt on the side of the road, his entourage coming to a stop lined up behind him.

"Blast it," Colonel Barrington shouted. "Can't you find the right road?"

"It's an old map, sir," his aide explained.

The Colonel dismounted, stalked back to the truck bearing the band of reporters.

"What's the problem, Colonel?" one called to him.

"Nothing," he lied. "Got a man sick. That's all it is. A few minutes bent over the grass oughta fix the malady."

He knew a tale of compassion for his staff would make a good story.

"When do you think we'll arrive at...?"

"Where are we...?"

"Colonel, where is it exactly we're going?"

He waved the reporters to silence. "You'll find out when we get there."

"Why the big secret?"

"We're after tiger, I told you. You don't need to know more."

"But, sir," the young reporter called, sticking his head out of the window, "I heard before we left Tashi that the American, with the girl, who hunted with you the first time, was already there—where we're going."

The others quickly asked him if it were true.

"That was my old friend, Ian McDonnell, I hunted with. Not that lunatic." The Colonel gave a sheepish grin. Damn reporters, he cursed, returning to his jeep. "Found the road, yet?"

His driver shook his head.

"Lord, what an embarrassment."

"Colonel, it's rather difficult to find a road to a village no one has heard of."

"Just so." He leaned against the bumper, expelling a heavy sigh.

"I'm sorry, sir."

"Sorry, hell. We've got to hurry. A man's life is at stake."

"What? You never told us that."

"There was no need. Might be dead by the time we get there."

His aide pointed out a local man walking down the road toward them, Gandhi-like with a long cane pole.

The Colonel grunted. "Why not ask that gentleman for directions?"

27

AS THE SUN BURNED LOWER ON THE HORIZON, rusting into evening, she heard the expected knock on the door and rose from the bed. Releasing the catch, she fell back as Karl pushed the door open and the blackness of the late hour spilled in around him. His eyes fell upon her, clad in a pair of panties, sweat glistened over her skin.

She stretched up to kiss him but he was too tired to respond.

Moving across the room, he dropped onto the foot of the bed as though he was setting down a great weight he had carried on his back the whole day. He rubbed his eyes, sighing. The day had been too long and too intense. And too much of a failure.

Althea went to him, sat beside him. "How'd the hunt go, dear?"

"You don't see me packing for home, do you?"

He threw himself back on the bed with another sigh.

She regarded him. "What happened?"

He shook his head, bent his arms up beneath his head. How could he tell her about his failure? There he was, tiger in his sights, his finger itchy on the trigger, and—nothing. He froze. The cat even stood there grinning at him a moment before bounding happily away into the trees. He couldn't figure out what had happened.

Giving her a stare, she didn't press.

Sliding around the side of the cot, she gazed at him but his eyes were fighting his heavy eyelids. She ran her fingers through his matted hair. Lacking response, she returned to the end of the bed and grabbed one of his feet, proceeded to pull off his boots. She grabbed the second boot, wrestling it off as she held it in her lap, the day's dirt staining her panties.

"I thought maybe...maybe we could, you know...make love tonight," she spoke, throwing the boot on the floor and crawling up the bed. "If you want to. Make you feel better?"

"You gotta be kidding," Karl sighed.

"Figured by now you might be needing some, you know, relief."

"You're the one that needs relief. Me? I'm too damn tired."

She unbuttoned his shirt, slipped it off him.

"Honey?" She massaged his shoulder. "Sweetheart, I got something to tell you."

Karl summoned his last energy, sat up, supported on his elbows.

"Can't you get it through your head I'm too tired to fool around? Give me a break, will ya? Geez, I'm out under the hot sun all day, out hunting this cat that would just as soon bite me in half as look at me, and all you want to do is make me exercise some more."

"Sorry, Karl." The pout emerged.

"Dammit, can't you knock it off for just one night?"

"I said I'm sorry. What more do you want?"

"I want some rest. I just wanna lie here and not move for a while. I wanna not be bothered."

She watched him a few minutes, stretched out on the bed. His breathing swayed the flimsy bed.

"Did you see him?" she asked in a gentle voice. "Your...tiger."

His eyes popped open. "Goddammit! He's not *my* fuckin' tiger!"

"I didn't mean anything."

He closed his eyes again. "Yes, I saw him."

"Are we still gonna be going home in a couple days? Like you said?"

He gritted his teeth, as though in pain.

"I hope so," she answered for him. "I'm so sick of this place. I want to go home."

He expelled a sigh. "Got a dawn tracking tomorrow. I need to sleep."

She waited, then snuggled up against him.

"Karl...? I have something to tell you."

He was asleep. He was dreaming.

Beneath the pale glow of the oil lamp, Ron Priestley inspected the rifle he'd taken from Becky's father's house, lifted right out of the closet. He wiped excess lubricant from the bolt, refitted the firing pin. His summer medic training was coming in handy. Beside him stood a row of bullets, neatly polished.

The night closed in on him like a hangman's noose.

What had she said? He was a good doctor? Yes, that was what she'd said. Of course, he knew that all along, but it was a moot point since Edwards took a sledgehammer to his career. He could never be a doctor again, he knew. Not in America, at least.

Shaking his head to fling sweaty hair off his forehead, he wondered if he'd become obsessed with Edwards. No, his feelings were genuine, reasonable. If he didn't eliminate Edwards, he would be stuck obsessing over Edwards the rest of his life.

He snapped the breech closed. He stared through the sights, wiped off dust which collected. If only those ROTC assholes could see him in action now.

Was it too late? He had traveled ten-thousand paces in the maze of his mind. Now the last square lay before him. How could he refuse to go ahead and step on it and complete the journey?

The jeep nearly slid off the road as it rounded the bend.

"Good God, will you watch it?" The Colonel grabbed his seat.

"You said to hurry," his driver snapped.

"We want to get there alive, by God!"

The headlights flashed on the rocks in the road, the vehicle dancing over the sand and gravel.

"The men are tired, Colonel. We should stop for the night. These roads are too dangerous."

"Nonsense!"

The driver cursed, swerved around a large hole.

"Sir, what's the rush?" his aide asked after riding out a stretch of washboard.

"We've got to get to the village of Dhow as soon as we can. That American in Tashi—the one with the girl—he's passing himself off as a professional *shikari*. Hansen said the police report on him said he's never hunted before. The man's a psycho. Without a real hunter beside him, he's going to get himself killed."

"Killed? By whom?"

"Killed by that Tashi man-eater. Damn cat's wandered across the whole country, found its way to this village. The lunatic's found him. Now I'm trying to find the lunatic. If he goes hunting for that cat, mark my words, he'll be eaten alive."

"But sir," his aide exclaimed, suddenly alarmed, "you called him a psycho. Is this the man the papers wrote about a couple months ago?"

The jeep hit a rock, tossed them off their seats.

"I don't know about that."

"Your gentleman, James, told Smitty."

"Nonsense!"

"Some of the reporters mentioned it at the start of the trip. They said he was talking about tigers in the mental hospital. They said he boasted about knowing where the tiger was, and vowed to kill it."

"That's ludicrous! Why would a man say anything like that? Most ridiculous thing I ever heard. Why would a man make such a boast, or such a vow? He wouldn't, that's why! Only a lunatic! He's obviously raving."

They hit a string of bumps, the jeep twisting along the shoulder.

"Then why are we rushing down dangerous roads like these in the dark, headed to a no-name little village in the middle of nowhere?"

"Part of the adventure, eh? What're you talking about?"

"I mean, sir, are we really eager to save this lunatic from himself, or are we merely trying to beat him to the prize?"

The Colonel stared at his chief aide through the moonlight.

"You're mad! My only concern is to save the poor fool from his gruesome fate. We'll drive through the night to reach him if we have to, by God!"

Pale moonlight casts a bluish, fluorescent tint on the world. Evening airy,
    light, peaceful. Sky of deep purple, almost black, starless, calm.
    Ancient tree gnarled down through the years, sweeps low to greet him,
    welcomes him in the embrace of its muscular boughs. Serene and
    silent at its crest, the hill's neatly padded patch of dirt is as it was.
His golden eyes strike the kindling of the night, sparking a storm in his

heart, as he mounts the hill and sits regally upon his haunches,
scanning his plain, surveying his domain.
At the base of the hill, parting the tall, amber grasses, comes a man.
He wears the smooth khaki fur of the hunter yet he bears no fire stick.
Seeing the mighty tree and its guardian beast from the edge of the
grass, he hesitates, remembering.
Clouds transform the moon into obsidian, the Man bathed from head
to hindpaw in fluorescent blue.
He studies the upright beast, recognition growing in his mind, as he
stalks up the hillside, carefully stepping across the rocky terrain,
treading gingerly in reverence.
He has no urge to attack, or flee.
This Man is different. He is no enemy.
He stands before him, marking the hill like a totem, presenting himself
as a sacrifice. He waits—listens, regards, senses. It is to this end
that he has come, to meet at last, to meld their auras. His journey
has ended. He is home.

Karl draws his hand from his trouser pocket, retrieving a slice of goat meat, freshly cut but bloodless. Stepping back, lower down the slope, his outstretched hand becomes level with his brother's striped head. He presses his arm toward the beast and his hand does not shake with fear.

Roundpaw leans forward, sitting on his haunches, taking the meat
between his incisors, avoiding the man's open forepaw. With
animated motion, he tosses his head back, gulps down the meat.
They regard each other in the cold, eerie blue moonlight and crisp
night air.
What shall we say to each other when we meet?

Karl steps forward, rising up the hillside, again reaches out his hand, palm down, drawing it above the cat's head.

Roundpaw puzzles over the action, feels the gentle touch of his hand as
the man pats his striped forehead.
His golden eyes reflect the moonlight, glowing cobalt blue.
The man's hand slides tenderly over Roundpaw's forehead and down
his cheek, scratching the ruff of white mane under his jawline.

The cat offers a deep bass purr before curling his cheek into Karl's open hand.

No birds call, no monkeys chatter, no black storm clouds rumble, as if they are the only inhabitants of their world.

In the silence of the night, they await the dawn, side by side, as brothers on the crest of the hill, overlooking their domain.

As dawn mounts the charred horizon, they begin to burn. Brightly.

With a sweep of his hand, Karl wiped sweat out of his eyes, realizing he had been asleep.

Waking from his nightmares was so common that he remained prone as he shook his head to clear his mind and breathed deeply to calm his heart. The thin mattress was soaked with his sweat but the relative coolness of the pre-dawn air seeped through the open window. The fluorescent blue of his dream darkened into the charcoal dawn outside.

He threw himself up to a sitting position on the edge of the bed, rubbing his face in his hands. In April, that first nightmare sent his world spinning, how he had felt his heart ripped from his chest, absorbing the pain of the tiger within him. He remembered being man-handled out of his apartment by the men from Eastwood, wrapped in a white straitjacket as he watched his wife kissing the bastard.

And he remembered the *gaur* hunter kneeling in the grass, the two photographers in the forest, and Ian and his hunting partner, and the crumpled bodies of the two cubs, climbing the steps inside the temple only to find the tigress in shock after nearly decapitating the Nawab. And the scents of Malabar Hill, with its dead exposed to the elements, not in his dreams but directly, the feeling of frightening familiarity, knowing he was looking at his home among the dead. He could never forget stalking through the cool forest by Aklera, the noise of the beaters echoing in his ears, as he came upon the twin beasts, facing them—

Drenched in a cold blueness yet somehow warm and peaceful, sitting hand-in-paw with his brother, as though all his troubles were resolved. Shit, he was a mess, he cursed.

No, he would not allow it to continue. The whole world called him crazy. Every night a different horror, every day new humiliation, every thought squarely on the heart of the beast. It was enough. *Enough!* The tiger was not his brother, and no dream would ever convince him. Imagine him, petting, hugging the striped beast—it was insane!

His rifle rested in the corner, uncleaned from the previous day's tracking, fresh cartridges in a box on the table next to it.

He didn't need any guide's help, he knew as he slipped hurriedly but quietly into the previous day's dirty clothes. Daorum could sleep in this morning. He didn't need any help hunting his cat. If his estimate was correct, he could locate the beast by closing his eyes and focusing his mind on the beast, his twin. Mind to mind they would lock, like a bee to honey, like a compass and the North Pole—a perfect barometer. If not that ancient knoll far to the east, then a small thicket to the west of the village. The cat would be sleeping. He would gaze down upon the beast, briefly admire its great feline physique, then raise the rifle, pull it to his shoulder, firmly squeeze the trigger and they would be back to Jaipur by sundown, back to America a couple days after that.

He grabbed the rifle and stepped through the door with a lingering glance back at Althea, at the child-like pout on her sleeping face. No need to bother her; he would go it alone and be back before she could awaken.

The village was still asleep, safe in the belief that they would soon be rid of their striped menace. Until that time, no-one ventured outside the walls, taking the solemn opportunity to sleep in. The paths would still be in shadow when dawn melted across the sky.

As Karl hurried along the path, carrying his rifle in one hand, stuffing cartridges into it, dark eyes watched him. He headed toward the west gate, frenetic energy and renewed strength surging through his body. A few early risers waved to him, their *shikari* savior, but he had no words or smiles for them.

Where was the Indian guide? Ron Priestley wondered as his gaze followed Karl's movement to the gate. And why was he in a hurry? From his second floor window, he could see everything. Where was he going so early this morning? Ron cursed. He was trying to run away! *Yes!* His prey was fleeing under cover of darkness. The coward was running away, escaping for his life!

Quickly, he slapped his rifle together which he'd been cleaning all night, unable to sleep. He threw on his red plaid hunting vest, stuffing its pockets with cartridges, and sprang toward the door. The bastard wouldn't get away so easily, Ron Priestley vowed as a crack of light sliced the far horizon.

Behind the somber veil of shadow cast by the village wall, the sun rose fat and lazy, bleeding into the shelf of clouds. Karl saw his shadow and turned to regard the sun. Voluminous and brilliant like the plume of a nuclear explosion, lounging in the crux of two hills, it seemed to engulf the universe, laughing at the vulgarity of the humans below, mocking *him* especially.

He split the wide *bajra* field to the south side of the village, finding the path to the pool.

There he examined the pug marks in the sandy soil. None seemed fresh. He sat on a mound of dirt at the edge of the pond, set down his rifle, leaned his head into his hands, pressed his elbows against his knees, and began to meditate.

Green—a mosaic of twisted green patterns, flexing into focus. Stripes, orange and black, white fringe, two eyes closed. There, amidst the wood, asleep, lost in dreams of youth. None can know his thoughts save one. His conscience has been stripped from his dark essence, his pitiful soul laid bare, showing the world that horrible face he wears when he wears no face.

Karl raised his eyes to the crimson sun, offering an ancient prayer, words that seeped into his memory, and a sacrifice: the heart of the beast.

Bending back the branches to regard the beast before him, he lifted the rifle to his shoulder. There, calm as a kitten, he lies, a full-grown Bengal tiger stretching to a length of ten-feet, paws fifteen inches long, canine teeth protruding five inches from his gum lines. How he sleeps and dreams, this magnificent beast!

Karl hesitates, Beauty overcoming him. Shivering, he hates himself, despises what he has become.

Steeling his soul, he pulls the rifle butt into his shoulder, directs the end of the barrel at the chest of his noble target, aligns his eye with the sights, wraps his finger tightly around the trigger.

He pauses, clouds of remorse fogging him.

His breathing deepens, throwing off his aim. Sweat beads on his weary brow. His back stiffens as he stands, fearful of pulling the deadly switch. The idea explodes in him of beauty causing sadness: the way Man fears that Beauty will outlast him and conspires to destroy it.

His shoulders relax, the rifle stock dropping from his cheek as his heart cries out its hollow anguish. He cannot act.

He cannot kill—

The air exploded around Karl, echoing the retort of a rifle shot from behind him sizzling past his ear.

In that flash, the great tiger awakened and burst from the thicket, bowling him over in its escape.

Karl dove into the warm, matted grass where the tiger had lain to escape a second shot.

Through the bushes, he saw Priestley standing among the *bajra* stalks, rifle poised, big grin stamped on his menacing face. Karl knelt behind the bushes as he checked his rifle.

Enough of this damn bastard!

He drew the gun to his shoulder once more, anger boiling inside him. He set his sights on the bastard's nose. The trigger jerked, sending a shot before he realized he was firing. He was shooting at another human being! That he missed his target left him with mixed emotions.

Backing out of the thicket, he crawled through the brush on hands and knees until he reached denser cover. He circled around the grove and out into tall grass to the southwest. Rushing across a fallow field, he reached a line of bushes near the pond.

He rested there, seeing Priestley running hunched over, moving back toward the village.

The bastard was retreating, Karl thought, then decided not. He spit into the dirt and jumped up, aiming his rifle at the fleeing target, and squeezed the trigger.

Priestley reacted when he heard the shot, tripping and falling into the tall grass, out of sight. He scrambled back to a kneeling position and returned a shot into the bushes where his opponent was.

Karl was gone. Using his army training, he had slipped around the bushes when the bastard fell. Now he was kneeling in the grass near the pool, watching Priestley crane his neck to survey the field.

As the doctor's head rose above the grass, Karl brought his rifle up. He tried to release the bolt after checking his ammo and it slipped, the *click-ping* echoing across the field.

Alerted, Priestley whirled around and fired from the hip, laying down three blasts which knocked Karl prone in the dirt. He cursed, rolling away from the bushes. Another shot in his direction persuaded him to try and make a run for the opposite side of the pond.

Karl dove behind the wide dirt mound he'd earlier sat on, hearing the bastard swearing as he fumbled with reloading.

Recovering, Karl peeked over the mound.

Priestley, his rifle poised, immediately squeezed off a string of shots, the spray of bullets ripping the mound, splattering dirt into the air.

Silence told Karl his enemy was reloading. He peered over the top of the crumbled mound. The doctor was kneeling in the grass again with his curly, black hair visible.

He had to get to better cover, Karl knew. Gazing over the *bajra*, he chose the location where he would make his stand. In the tall amber grass, he could hide. The bastard would have to come to him.

As Priestley reloaded, Karl popped up from behind the mound and charged away from the pond, barreling wildly through the grass, racing the clock in the seconds it would take his adversary to reload, aim, and fire. In that time, he crossed the wide field caught in the shadow of the village's south wall.

When Priestley looked up, rifle reloaded, Karl had dropped down, lost in the waving stalks of *bajra*, the distant baying of goats covering his disappearance.

Priestley stood up in the grass, scanning the fields, listening for the click of a rifle bolt or the crunch of *bajra* stalks beneath boots.

Karl froze in the grass, afraid to move and tip off his location. As he lay against the dry earth, the buzz of the locust returned, setting up a rhythmic din that permeated the air as the sun warmed the *bajra* fields. He listened for the bastard approaching, heard only the insects and the wind. One locust hopped onto his shoulder, walked over his head, and departed.

He rolled onto his back, eyes staring absently at the rooftops inside the village walls. He heard no sound from the bastard. What if the mad doctor had quit the battle, returning to the village for Althea?

Pulling himself up into a crouch, Karl kept his head below the tops of the *bajra*.

A dark figure stained the golden sea in the corner of his eye. The bastard was stalking him.

"Edwards!" the man called out, wading through the waist-high *bajra*, rifle chest high.

Karl remained motionless in the *bajra*.

"Where are you, Edwards?"

He felt a cramp tightening in his calf as he sat curled up among the *bajra* stalks.

"Come on, Edwards."

Other feelings began to grow within him. Where was his courage? Where was his anger? He grit his teeth, cursed himself, realizing that deep inside he preferred the bastard simply leave him alone—

"Stop playing games, Edwards."

Karl checked that his rifle was loaded as the bastard stepped closer.

With a sharp inhale, Karl jumped up and pulled off a shot at the doctor thirty meters in front of him. Both were surprised how close they were to each other, and immediately dropped out of sight.

Crouching again in the *bajra*, Karl listened, rifle tight in his hands.

"Don't give up so easily," the doctor called, hidden in the grass.

A spasm hit Karl, shaking his body, and he felt sick to his stomach. All the running around, as hot as it was, was making him ill, he decided. His body was wracked by another spasm like a blast of frigid air. He shook his head trying to clear his mind, but the more he shook, the foggier his head seemed to become. Dizziness hardened into a pain which wedged between his eyes, forcing him to press them shut. What was wrong with him? How could he fall apart now, with the bastard so close?

He fought it off and pulled himself up to his knees. With another breath, he sprang up and planted a bullet in the *bajra* where he'd last seen the doctor and just as quickly popped back down.

A new wave of dizziness swept over him. He fell over in the grass, the world spinning around him.

"Not very good aim, Edwards."

Karl tried to raise his head but the dizziness pounded him down. He held his eyes closed and tried to mentally squeeze away the pain. Anger was building inside him, along with frustration and confusion. *It had to end!* He had to end it. No time for this...this migraine! He had to finish off this maniac terrorizing him.

"Come on, you son of a bitch," the doctor taunted.

The pain grew intense as Karl lay crippled in the *bajra*. Inside his head, kaleidoscopic images were trying to sort themselves. He rubbed his forehead. Laying down his rifle, he grabbed his head, willing the pain to go away. Of all the times to get a migraine, he cursed.

"Can't you do anything right?" the doctor called.

Karl could not move, engulfed in nausea, paralyzed.

"Come on, shoot me," Priestley laughed. "What're you waiting for?"

The pictures slowed, separated, came into focus in his mind's eye. Or was it in his *mind*? He saw Priestley bent over in the grass, his rifle held ready, his head barely above the top of the *bajra*.

"Come on! Let's get it over with."

A sensation shocked him like the kiss of a lightning bolt, and the universe split open for him like a ripe pear.

His pain fell away and he could see once more—but not with his eyes. He could see the doctor, just as he saw him before: crouching in the *bajra*.

But now the view was from behind him.

Karl dropped his hands from his head and opened his eyes, seeing the dirt and *bajra* beside him with a ghostly, superimposed image of the doctor—the reverse view. His mind raced with calculations before confusion made the final realization hit him.

"No," he whispered, so intensely the doctor heard him and stood up in the grass, looking for him.

Karl closed his eyes again. The front view disappeared. The rear view remained and, as he watched, moved closer to the doctor.

Electrified, Karl squeezed his eyes shut and the world became quite vivid. He saw the bastard's backside. Karl ordered himself to lift his hand in front of his face and he saw the rounded forepaw, striped in orange and black. He set his paw down in the grass.

"No," he spoke, hushed, shaking his head. He sat up. "No!" he cried.

Ron Priestley stood tall in the grass, rifle on his hip, awaiting his prey, turning around.

Karl sprang up from the grass. "Get away from there!"

The doctor was momentarily startled, puzzled by Karl's strange behavior.

Then the tiger was all over him.

Karl watched the carnage from twenty meters with the solemnity of the funeral it was. Blood sprayed up from the *bajra* in violet fountains. Strips of flesh flew into the air like fireworks. The tiger's striped tail whirled among the stalks like a vain ballerina in a dance of death. But it was a quiet ceremony, only an occasional grunt or crunch of bone. The doctor had only screamed once.

In the corner of his eye, Karl saw the villagers gather, watching the scene from the walls and from the main gate. Some of them saw dust clouds boiling in the southeast marking the approach of vehicles—stretched out like a string of pearls below the fat, red sun ripening into a golden morning globe.

Karl thought of nothing but the sight before him. His eyes didn't waver. He gorged himself on the savage spectacle. He felt no fear. Rather, he felt an attraction for the beast. He understood what it was that had drawn him to the other side of the world and cut him to his very soul. Separated at birth, he did indeed have a twin brother.

He didn't know how long he watched, but when the tiger seemed to have ended its attack, he slowly stepped forward. Moving toward the blood-stained grass, unconcerned his rifle rested far away.

The *bajra* fell away for him and he gazed down at the huge beast nibbling on the meaty skeleton.

Roundpaw looked up, a string of flesh hanging from his teeth, blood wetting his jowls and whiskers, and regarded the Man.

Karl's eyes met his, matched them, melded with them.

What shall we say to each other when we meet?

The great cat yawned casually, licked blood from his teeth, gazed serenely up at the man, knowing he stood before a friend. They felt the bond, the pull, their connection, regarding each other silently in the bloody field. It was not love but a very deep respect that drew them close, like awkward participants at a school reunion, the bully and his victim together once more for the sake of a joke. They were oblivious to an ignorant world, and Karl ached with nostalgia.

Behind them, the line of trucks and jeeps roared to a halt a hundred meters from the village gate. All eyes were on the man and the beast posed together in the field—including Colonel Barrington's binoculars, his eyes blood-shot, body and mind weary of the night's hard journey.

Daorum stood with rifle in hand at the gate, asking questions. He had been awakened by the shooting, but it didn't last long. Luckily, his foolish client hadn't been injured or killed. Someone told him the American doctor was also hunting. Another told him the doctor had been shooting at their blessed *shikari*.

He hurried into the field.

"There he is!" The Colonel jumped up from his seat. "Hurry! We must save that man!"

He directed his driver to charge into the field as his aide handed him his rifle.

Jerking to a halt fifty meters from Karl and the tiger, the Colonel leaped from the jeep, ran ten steps ahead and raised the rifle to his shoulder.

"He's in shock," he mumbled, seeing the man standing so close to the tiger, so hypnotized. "I'll have to take him the hard way."

Daorum charged toward Karl. "What you shooting, American?"

The Colonel looked up, saw the guide running.

"Stay back! Back, I say! He's mine!"

Returning his eye to the sights, the Colonel aligned the barrel in the center of the tiger's long flank. He steadied himself, glared down the length of the barrel, across the *bajra*, catching Karl wheeling around in the trampled stalks to face him, shouting:

"*Noooo!* Don't *Shooooooooot!*"

The Colonel had already squeezed the trigger.

A spray of bullets struck the tiger's side, drawing a pock-marked line from his shoulder down his chest, across his ribs to his stomach, each blast popping flesh open, striped fur flung into the air.

"*Noooooooo!*" Karl cried out. He grabbed Roundpaw's head as the cat's legs collapsed beneath him and his great weight crashed to the ground.

Daorum ran to them.

The Colonel lowered his rifle, staring at the downed beast as photographers snapped rolls of film.

"You okay, American?" Daorum arrived beside Karl, grabbing him around the shoulders. "You should not hunt tiger alone."

Karl slumped, fell into his arms, his face wrinkling in pain. He cried out, grabbed the side of his khaki shirt.

Daorum saw the dark, wet stain growing there. He jerked the shirt tail out of Karl's pants, tore the shirt open, exposing his abdomen. The bruise there had broken open and bled freely. As Daorum watched, another spot turned purple, darkening until the skin pulled open, blood trickling out. Another spot darkened, another bruise broke open.

Wild-eyed, he shouted for help from the crowd.

A fourth bruise formed and became a bullet wound, all the tiny rivulets of blood pouring across Karl's belly and collecting against his belt before dripping to the ground. Blood flowed heavier as a fifth spot erupted.

The crisp crack of the rib fracturing echoed in his ears as Karl let out a howl of agony.

"*Shaitan!*" Daorum screamed. He turned to the crowd that had gathered. "Help me here!"

Two men from the village ran to them.

The world blurred as Karl felt his muscles grow numb. His head swirled as he tried to keep conscious, trying to understand what was happening.

Three of the Colonel's staff arrived to help carry Karl into the village, and the Colonel's medic was close behind.

Storming into his room, the men laid Karl down on the cot, head rolling on his shoulders, eyes open.

Althea shrieked in horror.

"Stand aside, I'm a doctor," shouted the Colonel's medic coming through the doorway.

He pushed through the men, knelt beside Karl. His eyes widened at the sight of the wounds, knowing immediately there was nothing that could be done to save the man's life. His entire side was a sea of bloody pulp, skin broken open in five places from his shoulder down to his chest, across his ribs to his stomach. As they watched, his skin seemed to pull back from the openings, each wound widening, blood spilling over the mattress and running thick on the dirty floor.

Althea pried them away, threw herself down beside him.

"Oh, Karl," she whimpered, "why'd you go after him yourself? Why couldn't you wait for the guide?"

She stroked his face and he opened his eyes.

"No, Althea," he spoke weakly. "You don't understand. He was ready to lay at my feet and—let me pet him."

He stared at her tear-streaked face, then his eyes fell shut.

"No, Karl. Oh, *please*, no!"

He reached absently for her. His naked guts slipped against the open edge of his torn flesh as he clasped her hand.

His raspy voice strained to speak: "It was somebody else—shot him. And when his half—of our mind touched—my half, I felt the pain. I felt his wounds. I *made* his wounds. I bleed—just like him."

"Oh, Karl, I'm scared. I'm so scared." She sobbed. "What am I gonna do? How'm I gonna get home?"

He rose up on his elbow, straining against the pain, a blood-soaked finger pressing her lips to silence.

"Just a freak of nature. You know, my—wife didn't believe me. I—promised I'd prove it. Now—I proved it—to you." He jerked with a death-spasm, fought it. "We were born with one soul—split into two bodies. Two of a kind, me and him. We're like doubles. Twins—"

"Karl, no! Stop. Listen, Karl. I—"

"Two of a kind.... A pair...of *doubles*...."

"I—I gotta tell you something, sweetheart."

Althea stopped, staring wide-eyed at him as his eyes rolled up into their sockets. She clasped his hand tighter and leaned over him, the wet warmth of his blood soaking into her shirt, feeling strength draining from his grip. She pressed her mouth to his ear.

"I'm gonna have a baby," she quickly whispered.

28

THE CONFUSED, ANGRY VILLAGERS watched as the Rajasthani police patrol man-handled the big *sahib*, Colonel John Barrington, forcing him flat against the reporters' truck where they jerked his arms behind his back and handcuffed him.

"Why won't you listen to me?" he cried. "I tell you, it's a mistake! I didn't kill that man. It's the tiger I shot!"

"You're being arrested for manslaughter," explained the sergeant. "Perhaps it is a second-degree murder. The court will decide later."

The police pulled him away from the truck and the reporters' cameras clicked ravenously.

"This way, Mister Barrington," the sergeant spoke, taking his arm.

"It's *Colonel* Barrington."

"This way, *Mister* Barrington," the sergeant repeated.

"I had a license for the cat, I tell you. The tiger was facing him. I couldn't have shot *both* of them. You know the man was shot—I *mean* he was *wounded* by the tiger—on the right side. Dammit, the cat was on my left and the man was on my right—*facing* each other. Now, how in blue blazes could I have shot *him* if his wounds are on the side *away* from me. By God, think about it, will you? For God's sake! I—I'm innocent!"

The flash of light bulbs blinded him as the police truck doors were closed, severing the unkind cameras from him but forever preserving him in the next day's headlines.

During the day, villagers claimed the corpse of the tiger, drawing it within the walls of the village like a trophy. Its coat was badly shot up and of no value, but they took great relief in its motionlessness.

In the center of the village, where the American doctor had treated the children only the previous day, the cat's body was laid out for all to examine. Paws were pulled back, tail straightened, wooden pegs were hammered into the ground at its nose and the tip of its tail. Once the body was rolled away by four strong men, the distance between the pegs was officially measured as being eleven feet four inches. The cat's body was decimated by starvation and dehydration, its bulk greatly reduced, yet because of the sheer size of its frame, it still weighed over four hundred pounds.

The American *shikari* had hunted a terrible beast, the villagers knew. He sacrificed his own life to save them. In reverence for his death, his sacrifice, they offered the tiger's teeth and claws to the *shikari*'s young widow. Respectfully, Althea requested that the cat's body be burned along with that of her husband on the funeral pyre, and the ashes buried together in the dry earth that would now grow fertile absorbing their offering of blood, there in the center of the *bajra* field.

Late the next afternoon, as the sun dipped low enough to cut the day's heat, Daorum observed the young woman moving through the *bajra* field to the site of the attack. Head covered, she stood there, almost at the edge of the flattened oasis, where the grass had been pressed down.

As he watched her, even his long-hardened heart softened. He decided he wouldn't insist on the other half of the payment. How could he ask that of her? Vic would just have to live with it.

She stood a long time before she finally knelt in the crumpled *bajra*. Then, from his vantage point, she seemed to be offering a prayer. Hands pressed together before her face, head bowed. Was it for the American doctor who had stayed with them for such a short time and then died so horribly?

No one in the village knew much about him—yet he had come into their lives and healed many of them, then vanished just as quickly. It must be the will of Allah that he came to them. Of course, they knew about the police patrol's search of his room, finding a sizable cache of ammunition along with a telegram to someone in the States named

Becky.

<pre>
MISSION ACCOMPLISHED STOP
HOME ONE WEEK STOP
</pre>

Not realizing what the English said, the Rajasthani telegraph operator sent it anyway. The case was closed on him, a smuggler of firearms, a rapist, a murderer. He had paid for his crimes with his life.

Althea stood. Daorum watched her rubbing her belly so gently. She put her hands to her face and cried. The painful sounds mixed with the loud song of the locusts.

Daorum thought of Althea's passionate declaration of her desire to remain in the village. She told him of her desperate situation, having no money or plane ticket home, and a baby due in seven months. He had to offer her the chopper ride back to Jaipur, but she refused him.

She laughed at his concern, saying that Fate had brought her out into the desert the way Heaven sends an angel to help the needy. Until she could solve her husband's mystery, she wished to stay there in the dusty, dirty village of Dhow. She would be nurse to the villagers who had welcomed her. Someday, she would return home, she confided— when the time was right.

The following day, Daorum accompanied the new widow to the funeral ceremony outside the walls. A tall wooden pyre had been erected, and all the villagers had gathered in their mourning clothes. She regarded the assemblage, felt their sorrow. Gazing into their faces, meeting their eyes, she turned next to the pyre. Together they lay on the wooden shelf, among the straw kindling, the bodies of her husband and his striped twin, his nemesis, the tiger with the rounded forepaw.

The *tahsildar* presented her with the torch and she took it firmly in her hands, but hesitated. One tongue of flame and her journey would be ended. Her lover would be at peace. His tortured soul calm at last.

Then, with a flutter in her heart and a tightening of her throat, she pressed the torch to the straw and watched the flames rise to consume the pyre and its guests. The fire quickly raged high into the air, as the tearful congregation chanted and prayed.

Afterwards, the ashes were buried together as she had wished, there among the *bajra*, there among the blood-stained grasses.

Althea regarded the ancient manuscript open on the table before her, and thought back to her husband's funeral, now four months past. As the warmth of the springtime sun swept over her, she felt the child stirring within and pondered the meaning of the *tahsildar's* translation of the sacred text...

> *ON A NEARBY MOUNTAINSIDE three hundred years or so earlier stood a great city with a fantastic palace of gold, the Amber Palace. There lived a Moghul prince who enjoyed the grand life of richness and excess. He also prided himself on his courage, and since he had quickly conquered his enemies, he hunted to satisfy his desire for blood. He lived but forty years, reigned only ten, hunted in only the last three of those. In the first of those years, he killed twelve tigers. In the second year he killed seventy-two tigers. Within the first eleven months of the third year, the Great Prince killed one-hundred and sixteen tigers. But in his last month, he hunted twenty-eight days for one tiger, the largest and most clever of them all, and on the last of those days, it was he, the Amber Prince, mighty among men, who was pulled from his elephant mount and killed by the tiger. After an elaborate funeral, the Hindu sages read in the stars that their beloved dead prince, and all of his many succeeding generations, would be reincarnated into the body of a tiger, there to run wild across the land, hunted by the legions of men. The tiger, however, in reward for its sacrifice, would someday return to life in the body of a man, there to make sport as does man.*

About the Author

Stephen Swartz grew up in Kansas City where he dreamed of traveling the world. His writing usually includes exotic locations, foreign characters, and smatterings of other languages—strangers in strange lands. However, he chose to study music, including composing a symphony, and planned to be a music teacher before he turned to fiction writing.

Year of the Tiger was born from a dream which led to a science-fiction story about a fearsome beast on a far away planet. That story was later converted into the Earth-based story you now have, then revised into a screenplay, then revised into a novel—his first novel, but now his thirteenth.

Fresh from hunting for just the right word, Swartz teaches English at a university in Oklahoma while writing fiction late at night.

Also by Stephen Swartz

Contemporary Literary Fiction

After Ilium

Aiko

A Beautiful Chill

A Girl Called Wolf

Exchange

Fantasy & Science Fiction

The Stefan Székely Vampire Trilogy

I. A Dry Patch of Skin

II. Sunrise

III. Sunset

Epic Fantasy *With Dragons

The Dream Land Trilogy

I. Long Distance Voyager

II. Dreams of Future's Past

III. Diaspora

www.ingramcontent.com/pod-product-compliance
Lightning Source LLC
Chambersburg PA
CBHW072131250626
47159CB00007B/2651